Robert Fabbri read Drama and Theatre at the University of London and has worked in film and TV for 25 years. As an assistant director, he has worked on productions such as *Hornblower*, *Hellraiser*, *Patriot Games* and *Billy Elliot*. Now, his life-long passion for ancient history – especially for the Roman Empire – has drawn him to write his first novel. He lives in London and Berlin.

VESPASIAN
TRIBUNE OF ROME

ROBERT FABBRI

CORVUS

This paperback edition was first published in
Great Britain in 2011 by Corvus.

First published in hardback and trade paperback in Great Britain
in 2011 by Corvus, an imprint of Atlantic Books Ltd.

A CIP catalogue record for this book is available from
the British Library.

ISBN: 978-1-84887-911-9
Also available as Ebook

Printed and bound by CPI Group (UK) Ltd, Croydon, CR0 4YY

Corvus
An imprint of Atlantic Books Ltd
Ormond House
26-27 Boswell Street
London WC1N 3JZ

www.corvus-books.co.uk

For Leo, Eliza and Lucas with all my love.

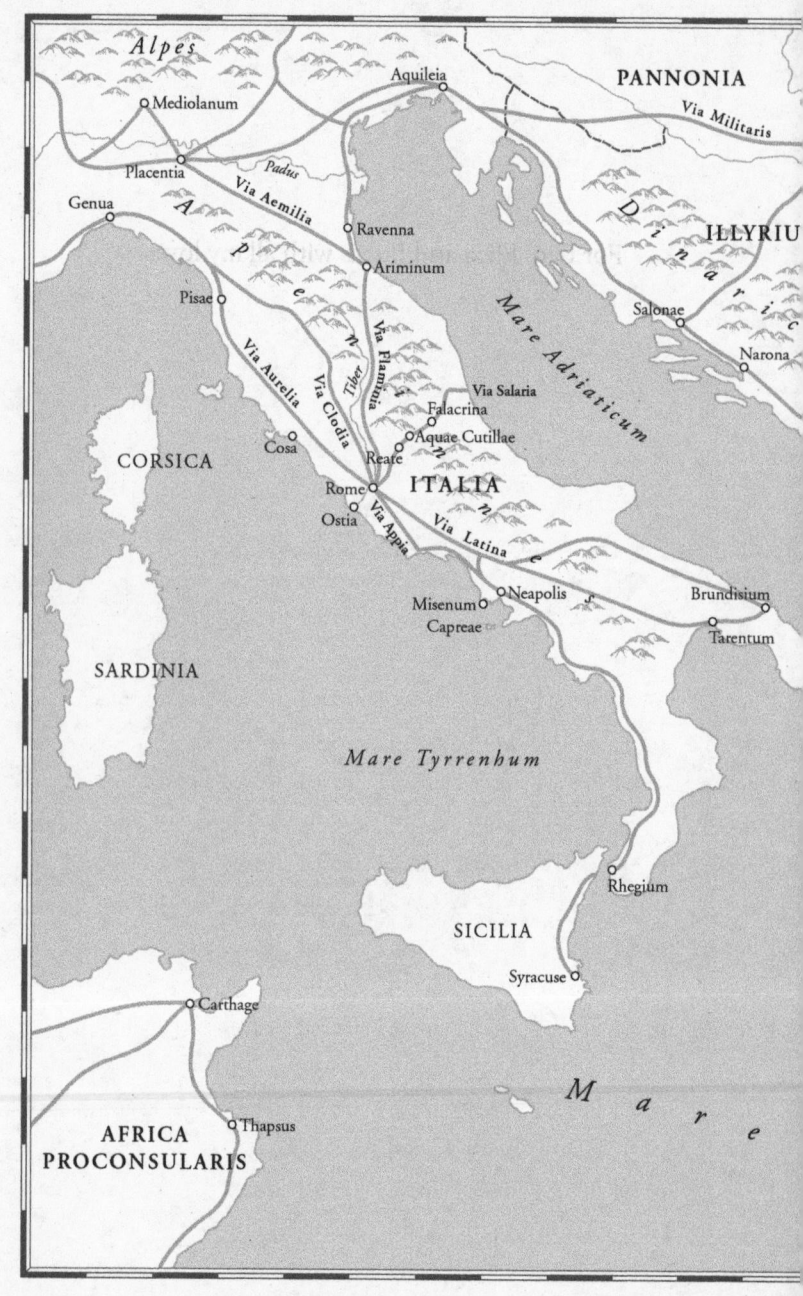

VESPASIAN
TRIBUNE OF ROME

PROLOGUE

FALACRINA, EIGHTY MILES NORTHEAST OF ROME, AD 9

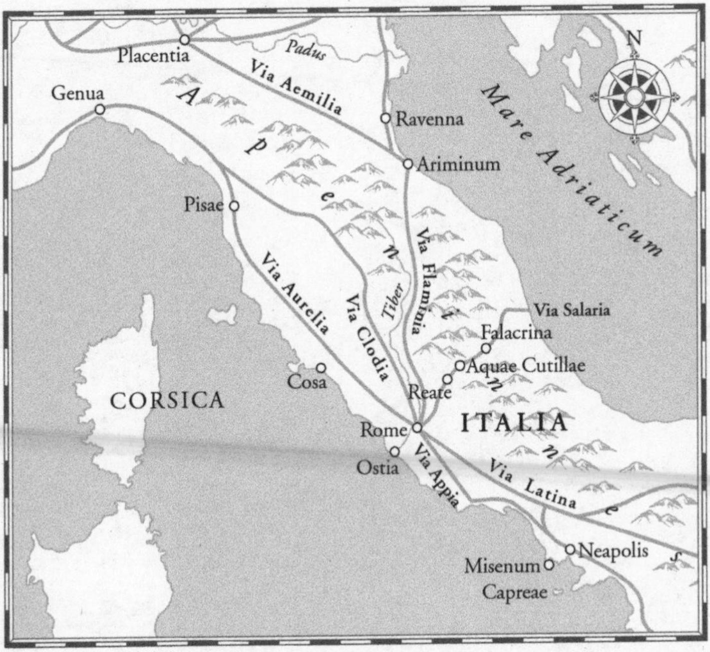

'WITH THE GOOD help of the gods may success crown our work. I bid thee, Father Mars, to take care to purify my farm, my land and my family, in whatever way thou thinkest best.'

Titus Flavius Sabinus held his palms up to the sky in supplication to his family's guardian god whilst reciting this ancient prayer. A fold of his pure white toga was pulled over his head in deference to the deity whose favour he invoked. Around him stood all his dependants: his wife, Vespasia Polla, held their newborn son; next to her was his mother, then his elder son, soon to be five. Behind them were his freedmen and -women, and then finally his slaves. They were gathered around the boundary stone at the most northerly point of his estate in the pine-resin-scented hills of the Apennines.

Titus finished the prayer and lowered his hands. His elder son, also named Titus Flavius Sabinus, stepped up to the stone and beat it four times with an olive branch. This done, the solemn procession around the perimeter of Titus' land was complete and they started back towards the family's homestead.

It had taken over eight hours since dawn to complete the circuit and, as far as the young Sabinus could tell, nothing untoward had happened. His father had said the right prayer at each corner of the estate; there had been no ill-omened flights of birds; no lightning had come from the cold, clear, late-November sky; and the sacrificial ox, pig and ram had all followed placidly.

Sabinus led the ram; its horns were decorated with brightly coloured ribbons and its dull eyes looked around for what would be, unbeknownst to it, its last glimpses of the world.

The ram's imminent death would have caused Sabinus no concern in normal circumstances. He had seen animals sacrificed or butchered many times and had even helped Pallo, the steward's son, to wring the necks of chickens. Death was a natural part of life. Yet he wanted to prevent this death since through it a new life, the life of his infant brother, would be purified. He wished that he could disrupt this ceremony, which was now nearing its climax, but he knew that to do so would bring down upon him the anger of the gods, and he feared them as much as he hated his new sibling. On the day of his brother's birth, just nine days earlier, Sabinus had overheard his grandmother, Tertulla, bring the news to his father that an oak tree sacred to Mars, which grew upon the estate, had sprouted a shoot so thick that it seemed that another tree had appeared, not just a branch. When his sister had been born it had sent out only a short, thin, sickly shoot that had withered and died quickly – as had she. In his case the shoot had been long and healthy, promising a good fortune, but that was nothing compared to what this omen presaged for his brother. He heard Father shout his thanks to Mars for such a child, and promise his best ox, pig and ram for the lustration ceremony of purification where he would officially recognise the boy as his son and give him a name.

'I'll nurture this one with great care, Mother,' Titus said, kissing her on the cheek. 'This boy is destined to go far.'

Tertulla roared with laughter. 'You're going senile before I do, Titus. With the Republic dead and the Empire ruled by one man how far can a child from a family of equestrian farmers from the hills be allowed to go?'

'You can laugh as much as you like, Mother, but if an omen points to greatness it is the will of the gods and not even the Emperor has the power to deny them.'

Since hearing that exchange he had been on the verge of tears every time he had seen his mother holding his brother. For nearly five years he had felt the exclusive love and protection of his family, but now someone who was to share that love would be favoured over him.

He steeled himself as they finally neared the house; he knew that he had to play his part in this ceremony with the dignity befitting the Flavii, the ancient Sabine family into which he had been born. He would not disappoint his father Titus.

The procession entered the stable yard and assembled at the far end before a stone altar dedicated to Mars, upon which lay a pile of oil-soaked wood. To the right of it stood a flaming torch in an iron holder; to the left, on a wooden table, were placed an axe and a knife.

Sabinus made sure that the ram was standing waiting on his right-hand side, in the way that he had been shown, and then looked around at the gathering. Beside his father, holding the swaddled form of his new little brother, stood his mother. She was dressed formally in a black woollen dress or *stola* that fell to her ankles; a long, crimson mantle, her *palla*, which half covered her tightly braided jet-black hair, wound around her body and draped over her left forearm. She felt Sabinus' gaze and looked over at him; her thin lips broke into a smile that lit up her slender face. Her dark eyes filled with love and pride as she saw her young son standing there in his toga, a diminutive image of her husband.

His grandmother stood next to her. She had travelled over from her coastal estate at Cosa, north of Rome, for the birth of the child and the naming ceremony. Now in her seventies, she still wore her hair in the fashion popular in the last years of the Republic, curled at the fringe and pulled tight over her head then fastened into a bun on the nape of her neck, accentuating the roundness of face that she had passed on to both her son and grandsons.

Behind the family were the freedmen and -women from the estate. Salvio the estate steward, who always contrived to have honeyed cake or a dried fig to give to Sabinus each time he saw him, held the ox's halter. His twenty-year-old son Pallo stood next to him holding the pig's lead. Both the animals waited docilely, the light breeze playing with the coloured ribbons that they too had been decorated with. Behind them there were twenty or so other men and women whose existence Sabinus was aware of, but whose names and duties were unclear to him.

Then there were the slaves, almost fifty of them, whom he generally treated as being invisible, but today they were present to witness the naming of the new son of the family and to share in the feast that would follow.

Titus approached the altar, bowed his head and muttered a brief private prayer; he then retrieved the burning torch from its stand and plunged it into the oil-soaked wood. The flames caught instantly, giving off an acrid black smoke that spiralled up into the sky.

'Father Mars, permit my harvests, my grain, my vineyards and my plantations to flourish and to come to good issue, to which intent I have bidden these offerings to be led around my land. Preserve in health my mules, my shepherds and my flocks. Give good health to me, my household and to my newborn son.'

Vespasia gently placed the swaddled bundle into his arms. Sabinus watched in stony silence as his father lifted the baby.

'In thy presence and witnessed by Nundina, goddess of purification, I accept him into my family and I name him Titus Flavius Vespasianus, and I declare him to be a freeborn citizen of Rome. With this *bulla* I place him under thy protection.'

He slipped a silver charm on a leather thong over the

baby's head; this he would wear to ward off the evil eye until he came of age.

Titus handed the infant back to his wife and picked up from beside the altar a jar of wine and three flat, crisp cakes made from flour and salt. He poured a few drops of wine and crumbled a cake on to the head of each victim. Picking up the axe he approached the ox and, touching the blade on the beast's neck, raised it for the killing stroke. The ox lowered its head as if consenting to its fate. Momentarily disconcerted by the animal's seeming willingness to be sacrificed Titus paused and looked around. His wife caught his eye and with a slight widening of hers urged him on. He called out to the clear, blue sky: 'To the intent of purifying my farm, my land and my ground and by way of expiation, I make the offering of this, the finest ox on my estate. Father Mars, to the same intent, deign to accept this gift.'

With a sudden brutal motion the axe sliced through the air. The ox shuddered once as the razor-sharp blade cleaved clean through its neck, half severing its head, sending out jets of crimson that sprayed over Sabinus and those others, both animal and human, close by. All four legs buckled simultaneously and it crumpled to the ground, dead.

Spattered with blood, Titus discarded the axe and picked up the knife. He approached the pig that stood next to Pallo, seemingly unconcerned by the violent death that had just been dealt so close to it. He repeated the prayer over the doomed animal and then placed his left hand under its jaw, pulled its head up and with a quick, vicious tug slit its throat.

It was now the ram's turn. Sabinus wiped some warm, sticky gore from his eyes and then placed a hand on either side of the ram's back and held it firmly as the prayer was repeated once more. The ram lifted its head and bleated once towards the heavens as Titus drew the knife sharply across its throat; blood flowed immediately, coating the ram's forelegs as they juddered and folded beneath it. Sabinus supported the dying creature, which made no attempt to struggle, as it bled to death. Its back legs soon gave out, followed, a few beats later, by its heart.

Salvio and Pallo rolled the sacrifices on to their backs for Titus to make the long incisions down each belly. The assembled household held its collective breath as the two men heaved open the carcasses and strained to pull back the ribcages. The rank stench of viscera filled the air as Titus plunged his hands into the entrails of first the ox, then the pig, then the ram and, with great dexterity, removed the hearts, which he threw on to the fire as offerings to Mars. Now completely drenched in blood he sliced out the livers and placed them on the wooden table. His eyes widened in astonishment as he wiped the organs clean; he gestured to the congregation to come closer and examine the livers that he held up, one by one. On the surface of each were large blemishes. Sabinus' heart leapt; they were not perfect. He had seen enough sacrifices to know that a liver with an unnatural mark on it was the worst omen that could be found; but to find marks on all three was surely a catastrophe. Mars was not going to accept this runt of a sibling.

As he drew nearer Sabinus could clearly make out the shapes of each mark. However, it would be many years before he would truly understand their significance.

PART I

Aquae Cutillae, fifty miles northeast of Rome, AD 25

CHAPTER I

VESPASIAN CAUGHT THE aroma of crisp roasting pork as he drove his horse the last few hundred paces up the hill to the farmhouse on his parents' new estate at Aquae Cutillae. Ahead of him, the westering sun still held some warmth; it caressed the stonework and terracotta tiles of the low buildings, accentuating the different shades of red, amber and copper, causing the complex to glow amidst the dark conifers and fig trees that surrounded it. It was a beautiful place to come home to; situated high in the foothills of the Apennines, overlooked by mountains to the north and east, and overlooking the plain of Reate to the south and west. It had been his home for the last three of his almost sixteen years, since his family had moved there with the money that his father had made from farming taxes for the Empire in the province of Asia.

Vespasian kicked his heels into his mount's sweating flanks, urging the tired beast to greater haste in his desire to be home. He had been away for three exhausting days rounding up and moving over five hundred mules from their summer pastures on the eastern edge of the estate to fields closer to the farm buildings, in preparation for winter. Here they would spend the colder months, with access to shelter and feed, safe from the snows and high winds that would whistle down from the mountains. In the spring they would be sold to the army, by which time a new batch would have been foaled and the whole process would start again. The mules had, of course, not wanted to go and a long struggle had ensued, which Vespasian and his companions had won by sheer bloody-mindedness and judicious use of the whip. The satisfaction he felt upon completing the task had however been tempered by the number of mules that were missing from the final stock-take.

He was accompanied by six freedmen and Pallo, who had taken over as estate steward after his father Salvio's murder two months earlier on the road between Aquae Cutillae and the family's other estate at Falacrina, where Vespasian had been born. Since that incident they had never travelled alone or unarmed, even within the estate. Aquae Cutillae was surrounded by hills and gullies and as such it was perfect country for bandits and runaway slaves to hide out in. They preyed on the livestock from the estate and on the traffic that plied the Via Salaria that ran along its southern edge from Rome to Reate and then on across the Apennines to the Adriatic Sea. Nowadays only a fool would travel without bodyguards, even so close to a major town like Reate, which was just visible on top of a hill nine miles to the west.

The smell of cooking grew stronger as they drew closer to

the farm and the bustle of household slaves became apparent. Thinking that the activity around the house seemed livelier than usual Vespasian turned to Pallo and grinned. 'It looks like my parents are laying on a feast to celebrate the return of the heroic mule-wranglers from their annual struggle with the four-legged enemy.'

'And no doubt we'll be invited to paint our faces red and be given a triumphal parade around the estate,' Pallo replied. His young master's high spirits were infectious. 'If only we'd shown mercy and brought some captives home to sacrifice to Mars Victorious in grateful thanks for our victory.'

'Mercy?' Vespasian cried, warming to the theme. 'Mercy for a foe as ruthless and terrible as we have faced? Never; it would lead to mule uprisings all over the estate and before long they would be leading us in triumph, and you, Pallo, would be the slave riding in the mule-general's chariot tasked with whispering into his long ear, "Remember, you are only a mule!"' Vespasian rode through the heavy wooden gates of the homestead followed by the laughter and mock-braying of his comrades.

The farm buildings were set around a rectangular courtyard, sixty paces by thirty, with the main house on the right forming one side, and the stables, storage rooms, freedmen's lodgings, workshops and the field slaves' barracks the other three. With the exception of the stable block, which had the house slaves' quarters on the first floor, all the buildings were single storey. The courtyard was full of people, either slave, freed or free, all busy but careful to bow their respects to the younger son of their master as Vespasian passed. He dismounted and giving his horse to a waiting stable boy asked him what the commotion was in aid of. The young lad, unused to being directly addressed by a member of the family, flushed and stuttered in thickly accented Latin that he did not know. Realising that probably no one outside the immediate family would be able to tell him what was going on, Vespasian decided to wait and ask his father, who would no doubt call for him after he had received his steward's report on the state of their livestock. He nodded to the boy and headed into the main house by the side door straight into the *peristylium*, the courtyard garden surrounded by a covered colonnaded walkway, off which his room lay. Any hopes that he had of avoiding his mother were dashed as she appeared out of the *tablinum*, the reception room leading to the atrium.

'Vespasian,' she called, stopping him in his tracks.

'Yes, Mother,' he replied warily, meeting her stern gaze.

'A message from your brother arrived whilst you were away playing at being a farmer. He's returning home; we expect him this evening.'

Her dismissive tone immediately soured his excellent mood. 'So the preparations are not in honour of my return from three days in the field?' he asked, unable to resist goading her.

She looked at him quizzically. 'Don't be impertinent; what makes you think that you would be honoured for doing menial tasks around the estate? Sabinus has been serving Rome; the day you decide to do the same rather than skulk up here in the hills fraternising with freedmen and mules is the day that you can expect some honour. Now go and get cleaned up. I expect you to behave civilly to your brother this evening, though I doubt that anything has changed in the way you feel about him in the years that he has been away. However, it would do you no harm to try and get along with him.'

'I would do, Mother,' Vespasian replied, running a hand through his sweaty, short-cropped, dark-brown hair, 'if he liked me, but all he ever did was bully and humiliate me. Well, I'm four years older and stronger now so he had better watch himself, because I won't stand for it like an eleven-year-old boy any more.'

Vespasia Polla peered at her son's round, olive-skinned face and noticed a steely determination in his normally good-humoured, large brown eyes; she had never seen that before.

'Well, I'll speak to Sabinus when he arrives and ask him to do his part in keeping the peace, as I expect you to do yours. Remember, it may be four years since you last saw him, but it is eight for your father and me as we were already in Asia when he joined the legions. I don't want your fighting to ruin our reunion.'

Giving him no chance to reply she disappeared off in the direction of the kitchen. No doubt to terrorise some lowly kitchen slave, Vespasian thought as he went to his room to change, his good humour now completely destroyed by the unwelcome news of his brother's imminent return.

Vespasian had not missed Sabinus at all for the four years he had been serving as a military tribune, the most junior of the officer ranks, with the Legio VIIII Hispana in Pannonia and Africa. They had never got on. Vespasian didn't understand or care why, it was just a fact: Sabinus hated him and he, in return, loathed Sabinus. However, they were brothers and nothing could change that, so they kept their dealings confined to frosty formality in public, and in private – well, Vespasian had learnt at a very young age to avoid being alone with his brother.

A bowl full of warm water had been set for him on the chest in his small bedroom. He pulled the curtain across the entrance, stripped and set about rinsing off the dust accumulated from three long days' mule-wrangling. That achieved, he rubbed himself dry with a linen sheet and then pulled on and belted a clean white tunic with the thin purple stripe down the front that indicated his equestrian rank. Picking up a stylus and a new scroll he sat down at his desk that, apart from the bed, was the only other item of furniture in the small room, and began to record from notes on a wax tablet the number of mules that they had transferred. Strictly speaking this was the farm steward's job, but Vespasian enjoyed record-keeping and stock-taking, and looked upon this task as good practice for the day that he inherited one of the family estates.

He had always thrived on estate work, although manual labour by someone of the equestrian class was frowned upon. His grandmother had encouraged his interest in farming in the five years that he and his brother had lived on her estate at Cosa whilst their parents had been in Asia. Throughout that time he had paid more attention to the doings of the freedmen and slaves working the fields than he had to his *grammaticus* or tutor. Consequently his rhetorical skills and knowledge of literature were sadly lacking, but what he didn't know about mules, sheep or vines wasn't worth knowing. The one area in which the grammaticus had been successful was arithmetic, but this was solely because Vespasian had recognised the importance of the subject for calculating profit and loss on the estate.

He had almost finished when his father came in without knocking. Vespasian stood up, bowed his head in greeting and waited to be spoken to.

'Pallo tells me that we have lost sixteen of our stock in the last month, is this right?'

'Yes, Father. I'm just finishing the numbers now but sixteen looks to be about right. The herdsmen say that they can't stop the brigands from pinching the odd one now and again; there's so much space to cover.'

'This is going to have to stop. Those bastards will bleed us dry. With Sabinus back we'll set a few traps for the vermin and hopefully nail some up. We'll soon see which they prefer, nails through their feet and wrists or keeping their fucking hands off my fucking property.'

'Yes, Father,' Vespasian ventured to his father's retreating back.

Titus paused in the doorway and looked back at his son.

'You did well, Vespasian,' he said in a calmer tone, 'to move all that livestock with so few men.'

'Thank you, Father. I enjoy it.'

Titus nodded briefly. 'I know you do,' he said with a regretful half-smile, then left.

Feeling buoyed by his father's praise Vespasian finished his calculations, confirming that they had indeed lost sixteen, tidied up the desk and lay on his bed to rest until his brother arrived. When he did so, a half-hour later, it was quietly and Vespasian slept through it.

Vespasian woke with a start; it was dark. Fearful that he was late for dinner he leapt from the bed and stepped out into the torch-lit peristylium. He heard his mother's voice coming from the atrium and headed in its direction.

'We must use my brother Gaius' influence to secure the boy a posting as a military tribune soon,' his mother was saying. Vespasian slowed as he realised that she was talking about him. 'He will be sixteen next month. If he is to go far, as the omens prophesied at his birth, he mustn't be allowed to spend any more time on the estate shying away from his duty to the family and Rome.'

Vespasian edged closer, intrigued by the mention of a prophecy.

'I understand your concern, Vespasia,' his father replied. 'But the boy's spent too much of his youth putting his energies into the estate, not into learning what he needs to survive amid the politics of Rome, let alone in her armies.'

'He will have the goddess Fortuna holding her hands over him to ensure that the prophecy is fulfilled.'

Vespasian struggled to contain himself; why was she being so vague?

'What about Sabinus?' Titus asked. 'Shouldn't we concentrate on him as the elder son?'

'You spoke to him earlier, he's a grown man now; ambitious and ruthless enough to make his own way, maybe even to progress beyond praetor, unlike my brother, which would be a great honour for the family. Of course we'll support him in every way we can, but we only need to support him, not push him. Titus, don't you see that Vespasian is this family's route to renown? Now is our time. We've used the money that you made as a tax-gatherer in Asia well; you bought this land cheaply and you've developed it successfully. With that and what I brought as a dowry to our marriage, we were worth over two million sesterces at the last census. Two million sesterces, Titus. That and my brother's influence is enough to guarantee our family two places in the Senate; but they must be earned, which they can't be up here in the Sabine Hills.'

'You're right, I suppose. Vespasian should start out on his career; and I can see he'll need to be pushed. But not just yet. I have something in mind first, for him and for Sabinus now that he's back. There's nothing to be done until the next year's magistrates take up their positions in January.'

Vespasian was listening so hard that he failed to notice the figure creeping up behind him until a hand jerked back his hair.

'Sneaking around and eavesdropping, little brother? Your behaviour hasn't improved, has it?' the familiar voice of Sabinus drawled as his grip tightened on Vespasian's hair.

Vespasian jammed his elbow back into Sabinus' belly and wrenched himself free; spinning around to face his brother he ducked under a straight jab aimed at his nose and lashed out a return blow. Sabinus caught his fist and, with an iron grip, slowly forced his arm down, cracking his knuckles, twisting his wrist and forcing him on to his knees. Knowing that he was bested he ceased to struggle.

'You've got some fight in you now, have you?' Sabinus said, looking down at him malevolently. 'That almost makes up for your lack of manners; it's very impolite not to greet an elder brother after four years.'

Vespasian raised his eyes. Sabinus had changed; he wasn't the podgy sixteen-year-old who had terrorised him four years ago, he had become a man. He had replaced fat with muscle and had grown a couple of inches. His round face had slimmed to become squarer, but his brown eyes still had a malicious glint in them as they peered at Vespasian over the prominent, wide nose that was a characteristic of all the males in the family. It looked as if military life had suited him. He held himself with a haughty dignity that stifled all the sarcastic remarks that Vespasian could think of in reply.

'I'm sorry, Sabinus,' he muttered, getting to his feet. 'I meant to greet you but I fell asleep.'

Sabinus raised his eyebrows at this contrite admission. 'Well, little brother, sleep is for the night; you'd do well to remember that now you are close to becoming a man. You've still got your country accent – most amusing. Come, our parents are waiting.'

He walked into the house, leaving Vespasian burning with shame. He had shown weakness to his brother and had been corrected and patronised by him; it was intolerable. Resolving never to be so effeminate as to take a daytime nap again he hurried after Sabinus, his mind turning on the intriguing mention of a prophecy. His parents knew of it, but who else? Sabinus? He doubted it; his brother would have been too young at the time and anyway, if he did know of it, he would never let on. So whom to ask? His parents – and admit that he had been eavesdropping? Hardly.

They entered the main house through the tablinum, and passed through into the atrium. Titus and Vespasia were waiting for the brothers, sitting on two colourfully painted wooden chairs, next to the *impluvium*, the pool that collected the rainwater that fell through the oblong opening in the centre of the ceiling. At each corner of the pool was a column that supported the weight of the roof. These were painted deep red in stark contrast to the pale greens, blues and yellows of the detailed stone mosaic on the floor illustrating the way that the family made its living and spent its leisure time.

The October night outside was chilly, but the atrium benefited from both the underfloor heating, provided by the hypocaust, and a large log fire that blazed in the hearth to the right of the tablinum. The flickering light emitted by the fire and a dozen oil lamps illumed the haunting wax death masks of the Flavian ancestors that watched over the family from their recess between the hearth and the *lararium*, the altar dedicated to the household gods. On the walls around the room, just visible in the dull light, were decorative frescos of mythological subjects painted in rich reds and yellows and punctuated by doorways that led to lesser rooms.

'Sit down, boys,' their father said cheerily, evidently enjoying having his close family all together again after eight years. The brothers sat on two stools placed opposite their parents. A young slave girl wiped their hands with a damp cloth; another brought them each a cup of warm, spiced wine. Vespasian noticed Sabinus eyeing the girls appreciatively as they left.

Titus poured a few drops of the wine on to the floor. 'I give thanks to the gods of our household for the safe return of my eldest son,' he said in a solemn voice. He raised his cup. 'We drink to your health, my sons.'

The four of them drank, and then set their cups down on the low table between them.

'Well, Sabinus, the army treated you well, eh? Not cooped up on garrison duty, but a proper war. I bet that you could hardly have believed your luck?' Titus chuckled, proud to have a son who was already a blooded veteran at the age of twenty.

'Yes, Father, you're right,' Sabinus replied, meeting his father's eye with a self-satisfied grin. 'I think we were all disappointed when I was assigned to the Ninth Hispana in Pannonia; with just the occasional cross-border raid to deal with it was going to be hard for me to excel there.'

'But then Tacfarinas' revolt in Numidia came to your rescue,' Vespasia interjected.

'We should thank the gods for rebellious kings with ideas above their station,' Titus said, raising his cup and grinning at his elder son.

Sabinus drank the toast enthusiastically. 'To Tacfarinas, the madman who threatened to cut off Africa's grain supply to Rome and then sent emissaries to negotiate with the Emperor.'

'We heard the story,' Titus said laughing. 'Apparently Tiberius had them summarily executed in front of him declaring: "Not even Spartacus had dared to send envoys."'

Sabinus joined the laughter. 'And then he sent us down to Africa to reinforce the Third Augusta, the only garrison in the province.'

As Sabinus carried on his tale Vespasian, unable think of anyone who he could ask about the omens of his birth, found his mind wandering back to the problem of the mule-thieves. It had far more relevance to his life than martial tales of rebellions and long marches of which he had no experience and very little interest. Although Hieron, his Greek weapons and wrestling master, had left him reasonably proficient with sword – *gladius* – and javelin – *pilum* – and he could also lay most opponents in the ring on their backs, due to his stocky build and broad muscular shoulders, he felt that he was first and foremost a man of the soil; that's where his battles would be fought, in the day-to-day struggle with nature as he strove to wring a profit from his family's lands. Let Sabinus make his way in the world and rise up the *cursus honorum*, the succession of military and civilian offices.

'I remember the feeling of marching to war,' Vespasian heard his father say wistfully; he turned his attention back to the conversation. 'Our spirits were high, confident of victory, because Rome will accept no other outcome; the Empire cannot countenance defeat. Barbarians surround us, and they must never be allowed to think of Rome as weak. They need to be shown that if they take Rome on there is only one outcome – and it will be inevitable: death for the men and enslavement for their families.'

'No matter how many lives it costs?' Vespasian asked.

'A soldier must be willing to lay down his life for the greater good of Rome,' his mother replied tersely, 'in the sure knowledge that its ultimate triumph will keep his family, his land and way of life safe from those who wish to destroy us.'

'Exactly my dear!' Titus exclaimed. 'And that is the principle that binds a legion together.'

'And because of that our morale remained high for the two years we were there,' Sabinus agreed. 'We knew we would all do everything it took to win. It was dirty war; no pitched battles, just raids, reprisals and small actions. But we rooted them out from their hiding places in the hills and group by group we dealt with them. We burned their strongholds, enslaved their women and children and executed all males of fighting age. It was slow, bloody work, but we persevered.'

'Ha, what did I say, Vespasian?' Titus' face lit up in triumph. 'Now Sabinus is back we have someone who knows how to deal with the vermin lurking in hills. We'll have those murdering mule-thieves up on crosses before too long.'

'Mule-thieves, Father? Where?' Sabinus asked.

'In the mountains to the east of the estate,' Titus replied. 'And it's not just mules; they've had sheep and a few horses, as well as murdering Salvio two months ago.'

'Salvio's dead? I'm sorry to hear that.' Sabinus paused, remembering with affection the kindly man and the treats that he had given him as a child. 'That in itself is cause for revenge. I'll take a party of our freedmen over there and show the scum how a Roman deals with their sort.'

'I knew you'd be eager to have a go at them. Well done, my boy. Take your brother along as well, it's time he saw something other than the rear end of a mule.' Titus smiled at Vespasian to show that he was only teasing him, but Vespasian had not taken offence; he was excited by the prospect of dealing out summary justice to the mule-thieves; it would benefit the estate. This was the sort of fighting that he was interested in, something real, close to home, not battling strange tribes in far-off places that he'd only vaguely heard of.

Sabinus, however, looked less than keen at the suggestion, but his father insisted.

'It'll be a chance for you to get to know each other as men

and not squabbling brats, fighting at every possible opportunity.'

'If you say so, Father.'

'I do. You can both go and have your own mini African campaign and nail up a few rebels, eh?' Titus laughed.

'If the boys can catch them with only a few freedmen to help,' Vespasia said, adding a note of caution to her husband's exuberance, 'it will be a far cry from fighting with the resources of a legion behind you.'

'Don't worry, Mother, I learnt enough in my two years in Africa about how to encourage plunder-hungry rebels out into the open. I'll find a way.' Sabinus had an air of confidence that made Vespasian believe him.

'You see, Vespasia,' Titus said, reaching over the table and slapping his eldest son's knee, 'the army has been the making of him, as it was me and will be for Vespasian, very soon.'

Vespasian jumped up, looking at his father in alarm. 'I have no wish to join the army, Father. I'm happy here, helping to run the estate; it's what I'm good at.'

Sabinus scoffed. 'A man has no right to land if he hasn't fought for it, little brother. How will you hold your head up amongst your peers in Rome if you haven't fought by their side?'

'Your brother is right, Vespasian,' his mother argued. 'They will laugh at you as the man who farms land that he has never defended. It would be an intolerable shame to you and our family name.'

'Then I shan't go to Rome. This is where I belong and this

is where I want to die. Let Sabinus make his way in Rome, I'll stay here.'

'And always live in your brother's shadow?' Vespasia snapped. 'We have two sons and both will shine. It would be an insufferable insult to the family gods for a son to waste his life on mere agriculture. Sit down, Vespasian; we shall have no more talk like that.'

His father laughed. 'Absolutely. You can't live your life here in the hills like some provincial country bumpkin. You will go to Rome and you will serve in her army, because it is my will.' He picked up his cup and downed the rest of his wine, and then stood up abruptly. 'As you know, a man is judged first and foremost by the achievements of his forebears.' Titus paused and gestured around the funeral masks of their ancestors in their recess on the wall next to the lararium. 'This being the case, I am a man of little worth, and you two, even less so.

'If we are to improve our family's standing both of you will have to struggle up the cursus honorum as new men. This is difficult but not impossible, as Gaius Marius and Cicero both proved in the old Republic. However, we now live in different times. To progress we need not only the patronage of people of higher standing than ourselves but also the backing of officials in the imperial household, and to get their attention you will have to impress in the two disciplines that Rome holds in highest esteem: military prowess and administrative ability.

'Sabinus, you have already proved yourself a capable soldier. Vespasian, you will soon follow that path. But you have already shown an aptitude for administration, through your knowledge of the running of our family's estates, a subject in which you, Sabinus, have shown very little interest.'

At this Vespasia looked directly at her sons, a faint smile of ambition flickered across her face; she could see where Titus was heading.

'Vespasian's first step will be to serve in the legions as a military tribune. Sabinus, your next step is an administrative position in Rome with the Vigintiviri as one of the twenty junior magistrates. I propose that for the next two months you share your knowledge and teach each other. Vespasian will show you how the estate is administered. In return you will give him the basic military training received by common legionaries to enable him to not only survive, but also to thrive in the legions.'

Vespasian and Sabinus both looked at their father, aghast.

'I will have no argument, this is my will and you will comply, however you may feel about each other. It is for the greater good of the family and, as such, takes precedence over any petty squabbles that you two may have. Perhaps it will teach you both to value each other in a way you have been unable to in the past. You will start once you have dealt with the mule-thieves. The first day Sabinus will be the teacher and the following day Vespasian, and so on until I am satisfied that you are both ready to go to Rome.' Titus looked down at his sons and held their gazes each in turn. 'Do you accept?' he demanded in a voice that would only countenance one answer.

The brothers looked at each other. What choice did they have?

'Yes, Father,' they each replied.

'Good. Let's eat.'

Titus led the family into the *triclinium* where the couches were set for the evening meal and clapped his hands. The room was suddenly filled with bustling house slaves bringing in plates of food. Varo, the house steward, motioned them to wait whilst the family were made comfortable, by deferential slave girls, on the three large couches arranged around a low square table. The girls removed the men's sandals and replaced them with slippers, then they laid napkins out on each couch in front of the diners and again wiped their hands. When all was ready Varo ordered the first course, the *gustatio*, to be laid out on the table.

Sabinus surveyed the plates of olives, grilled pork and almond sausages, lettuce with leeks, and tuna fish pieces with sliced boiled eggs. Selecting a particularly crispy-looking sausage he broke it in half and then looked at his brother.

'How many bandits are up there in the hills?' he asked.

'I'm afraid I don't know,' Vespasian confessed.

Sabinus nodded and placed some sausage into his mouth and started to chew noisily. 'Then we'd better find out first thing tomorrow morning.'

CHAPTER II

'THEY COME FROM over there,' Vespasian said to Sabinus, pointing towards the craggy hills opposite. 'In that direction there is nothing but hills and gullies for miles and miles.'

It was the third hour of the day; they had dismounted before a hill crest and then, keeping low, crawled the last few feet to the top and were now cautiously peering over. Below them was a large area of grassland that fell away, for about half a mile, down to a gully that divided it from the rocky slopes to the east. To their right was a wood that ran down from the crest of the hill halfway to the gully.

Sabinus surveyed the terrain for a while, formulating a plan.

The brothers had left soon after dawn, taking Pallo, half a dozen other freedmen and two dozen mules. Pallo, who had his father to avenge, had selected the men to go with them. They were all freedmen from the estate who worked as overseers of slaves, or foremen, or as skilled artisans. The younger three, Hieron, Lykos and Simeon, had, like Pallo, been born into slavery. The others, Baseos, Ataphanes and

Ludovicus, a huge ginger-haired German, had all been taken prisoner in border skirmishes and had, for one reason or another, been spared execution only to be sold into slavery. They all had one thing in common: Titus had manumitted them all after loyal service to his family and they were now Roman citizens bearing the Flavian name and were ready to die for it if necessary. Each of them carried ten javelins in a bundle across their mounts' backs and, hanging from a belt on their right, a gladius. They all had hunting bows except Baseos, an old, squat, slant-eyed Scythian, and Ataphanes, a tall, fine-boned, middle-aged Parthian; they both carried short, recurved compound bows, the type favoured by the horsemen of the East.

'So, lads, this is where we'll leave our bait,' Sabinus said finally. 'Vespasian, you and Baseos take the mules down the slope and tether them individually between the end of the wood and the gully. Then pitch a tent and build a good fire; use damp stuff, if you can, to make a decent amount of smoke. We want people to know that you are there.

'Pallo, you take Lykos and Simeon and skirt behind this hill and get yourselves into the gully a couple of miles to the north, and then work your way back down it to the far side of the field. Once you're there get as close to the mules as you can, without revealing your position to any watchful eyes on the hills opposite. Me and the rest of the lads will make our way down to the edge of the wood and get as close to the mules as possible.

'Vespasian, give us an hour to get in position, then you

and Baseos ride back up over the hill, as if you're off hunting, and then double back down through the wood and join us. Then we'll wait. If we're lucky and we attract our quarry we'll let them get to the mules, then charge them. Pallo and his lads will cut off their retreat over the gully and we'll have them trapped. Right, lads, let's get to it.' Sabinus, pleased with himself, looked around the men: they nodded their approval. It seemed a very workable plan.

Vespasian and Baseos made their way down through the wood, leading their horses. The mules had been securely tethered on long ropes, the tent pitched and a good smoky fire set. Ahead they could see the edge of the wood where Sabinus and his group were waiting, their horses tied to trees. Vespasian sat down next to his brother.

'I saw Pallo's boys enter the gully about two miles north. I hope they weren't seen by anyone else,' Vespasian whispered.

'Doesn't matter if they were,' Sabinus grunted. 'There's nothing to connect them to the mules, they could be just another group of runaways out hunting.'

They settled down to wait. A hundred paces down the hill the mules were grazing peacefully. The day wore on and the fire began to die down until there was just a small wisp of smoke rising from it.

'What happens when it gets dark?' Vespasian asked, breaking a loaf of bread in two and offering half to Sabinus.

'I'll send a couple of the lads out to build up the fire and check the mules, but I'm hoping that we won't have to wait that long,' Sabinus replied, overcoming his natural antipathy to his brother and taking the proffered bread. 'So, little brother, I shall teach you to be a legionary and you will teach me how to count mules or whatever it is that you do. You had better make it worth my while.'

'It's far more than mere stock-taking, Sabinus. The estates are huge; there's a vast amount to administer. There are the freedmen who work for us: in return for a smallholding of their own they make farming tools in the smithy, shear the sheep, supervise the impregnating of the horse mares by the donkey stallions, look after the weaker new-born mules and lambs, oversee the slaves in the fields and so on.

'Then there are the slaves themselves.' Vespasian was warming to the theme despite the glazed look on his brother's face. 'They need to be put to work at different jobs, depending on the season: ploughing, pruning vines, harvesting wheat or grapes, threshing grain, pressing olive oil, treading grapes, making amphorae. It's pointless having three hundred pints of wine or olive oil if you can't store it; so it's about thinking ahead, making sure that you're using your work force efficiently and get the most out of each man at any time of the year.

'Then everyone has to be fed, clothed and housed, which entails buying in a large variety of goods. They have to be bought in advance at the cheapest time of the year for each item, so you need to know the local market. Conversely our produce needs to be sold at the most advantageous time of year for us. Think ahead, Sabinus, always think ahead. Do you know what we should be selling at the moment?'

'I've no idea, but I assume that you are going to tell me.'

Vespasian looked at his brother with a grin. 'You work it out, and then tell me tomorrow at our first lesson.'

'All right, you smug little shit, I shall, but it won't be tomorrow, tomorrow it's my turn.' Sabinus looked at Vespasian malevolently. 'And we're starting with a route march, twenty miles in five hours, followed by sword drill.'

Vespasian rolled his eyes but didn't retort. As he tore off some bread and popped it in his mouth he realised that, of the two of them, Sabinus was going to have much more scope for causing pain over the next couple of months than he had. He put that unpleasant thought from his mind and looked around, chewing on his bread.

The sun, well past its zenith, was now behind them, front-lighting the rocky slope on the other side of the gully. Vespasian peered towards it; as he did so a momentary sparkle caught his eye. He nudged Sabinus.

'Over there, by that fallen tree,' he whispered, pointing in the direction of the light. 'I saw something glint.'

Sabinus followed the direction that his brother was pointing in; there was another flash. Through the heat-haze shimmer he could just make out a group of a dozen or so men leading their horses down a narrow track that wound through rocks and crags down towards the gully. Once they got to the bottom of the slope they quickly mounted up and started to follow the line of the gully a hundred paces south.

Here it wasn't so sheer and they managed to coax their horses down the bank, through the stream, and up the other side on to the Flavian pasture.

'All right, lads, we've got company. We'll wait until they've untethered most of the mules before we rush them. That way they'll have their retreat impeded by loose animals. I want as much noise as you can make when we charge. Those of you who can shoot a bow from a moving horse do so, the rest wait until we're in javelin range, then let fly, and mind those mules.'

'Don't worry about them, Sabinus,' Pallo said darkly. 'I won't be wasting any javelins on the mules.'

The others grinned and went to retrieve their horses.

'You stay close to either me or Pallo, little brother,' Sabinus growled as they mounted up as quietly as possible. 'Father wants you back in one piece. No heroics. It makes no difference to us whether we get the bastards dead or alive.'

The idea that he personally might have to kill a man came as a shock to Vespasian; dealing out summary justice to brigands had not featured in his life thus far – a life that had been relatively sheltered – but he determined to acquit himself well as he pulled his horse up next to Sabinus; he would not give his brother cause to think worse of him than he already did. He gripped his mount hard with his thighs and calves and reached behind him to slip five of the light javelins from his supply. He kept four in his left hand, which also held the reins, the fifth he held in his right. He slipped his forefinger through the leather loop, halfway down the shaft, which acted as a sling on launch, greatly enhancing range and velocity. He was as ready as he would ever be. He glanced at the others, who were also checking their gear but with an air of studied nonchalance; they had all been through this before and he felt very much the novice. His mouth was dry.

They waited in silence, watching as the runaways advanced up the hill slowly so as not to startle the mules. Two of their number had stayed down at the gully, covering their retreat.

'Pallo and his lads will deal with them,' Sabinus said, relieved that the odds against them had gone down slightly.

Vespasian counted eleven of them. They were mounted on a variety of horses and ponies, all no doubt stolen from their estate or those nearby. They were dressed mainly in shabby clothes; some were wearing the trousers favoured by barbarians from the north and east. A couple had fine cloaks around their shoulders, presumably once the property of wealthy travellers who had fallen victim to their raids. None of the party had shaved in weeks; their ragged beards and long hair gave the group an air of menace that Vespasian imagined would hang over a tribal raiding party on the borders of the Empire.

They reached the mules. Six of the company dismounted and crept up to the tent. At a signal they stabbed their spears through the leather to skewer anyone hiding inside. Finding it empty they returned to the mules and started to untether them. The rest of their comrades circled slowly, keeping the anxious animals in a group, their javelins and bows ready to fell the mules' minders should they return.

Sabinus kicked his horse forward, yelling at the top of his voice as he broke cover. 'Get the bastards, boys, don't let any escape.'

The others followed him at full pelt, in dispersed order, yelling the different war cries of their own people. Within moments they were halfway across the open ground to the confused runaways. Those that had dismounted struggled to find their horses amongst the panicking mules, which dragged their tethers around entangling the legs of men, mules and horses alike.

Baseos and Ataphanes let fly their first arrows. Vespasian forgot to yell as he watched in awe as they drew, released, reloaded and drew their bows again with such speed that they were able to have two arrows in the air at any one time and still maintain perfect control of their mounts with just their legs.

The first shafts thumped into the chaotic crowd, felling two runaways and a mule that went down whinnying shrilly, kicking out at everything around it, causing the rest to start rearing and bucking in panic.

'I said watch out for the fucking mules, you cretins,' Sabinus screamed at Baseos and Ataphanes as they wheeled their horses away to the left to pass around the top of the mêlée.

The mounted runaways had disentangled themselves from the chaos and turned their horses uphill to face the onslaught, releasing their arrows as they did. Vespasian felt the wind of one buzzing past his left ear and felt a wave of panic. He froze as Sabinus, Ludovicus and Hieron hurled their javelins. The momentum of the downhill charge gave added weight to the shots; two slammed into their targets with such force that one passed clean through a horseman's belly and on into the rump of his mount, leaving him skewered to the beast as it tried, in its agony, to buck its screaming rider off. The other exploded through a horse's skull; it dropped stone dead, trapping its rider beneath it, spattering him and his colleagues with hot, sticky blood. This was enough for the remaining three, who turned and fled towards the gully that was now devoid of their two companions who had been left there as a rearguard.

'Leave them to Pallo's lot,' Sabinus shouted as he and Ludovicus wheeled their horses back round towards the mules. Vespasian, burning with shame for having faltered, followed, leaving Hieron to deal with the unhorsed runaway who had now managed to pull himself free from his horse. He struggled to his feet, wiping the horse blood from his eyes, only to see Hieron's blade flashing through the air at neck height. His severed head fell to the ground and was left staring, in disbelief, at his twitching, decapitated body as the last of his blood drained from his brain and with it his life.

Baseos and Ataphanes had been busy. Three more of the runaways lay on the grass, feathered with arrows, and the sixth was making a break for it. Sabinus drew his sword and galloped after him. The slave looked over his shoulder and, although he must have known that he stood no chance of escape, put on another turn of speed – but to no avail. Sabinus was upon him in an instant and, with the flat of his sword, struck him on the back of the head, knocking him cold.

Vespasian looked down the hill towards the gully to see one of the three fleeing horsemen fall backwards off his mount, pierced by an arrow. His companions, seeing their escape blocked and their two erstwhile comrades lying on the ground with their throats ripped open, immediately wheeled their horses left and headed north, along the line of the gully, at full gallop. Vespasian urged his horse into a gallop, realising that they would escape unless he could cut them off. His desire to prevent the two men avoiding justice, heightened by the urgent necessity to redeem himself, produced a strange new sensation within him: blood-lust. The wind pulled at his horse's mane as he raced diagonally down the hill, closing in on the two riders. He was aware of Sabinus and Hieron following behind him, shouting at him to wait, but he knew that there was no time.

The angle between him and his targets quickly narrowed, he raised himself in his saddle and, with all his strength, launched a javelin at the lead rider. It buried itself deep in the horse's belly, sending the creature spinning head over hoofs to land on its rider, snapping his back with a sickening crunch. The second man had to check his speed to negotiate a path around the thrashing animal, giving Vespasian the advantage that he needed to draw level. His adversary slashed wildly with his sword at Vespasian's head. He ducked it and, at the same moment, launched himself at the now off-balanced rider. They came crashing to the ground, rolling over and over each other, trying to find a firm grip on any part of their opponent's body, an arm, throat, hair, anything. Coming to a stop, Vespasian found himself underneath the runaway, winded and disorientated. As he struggled for air, a fist smashed into his face and he felt a searing pain and heard a sharp crack as his nose was flattened; blood sprayed into his eyes. Two rough hands closed around his throat and he realised that he was fighting for his life; the desire to kill was replaced by the instinct to survive. Terrified he twisted violently left then right in an unsuccessful effort to prevent his assailant tightening his grip. His eyes began to bulge. He peered through streaming blood at the man's face; his cracked lips tightened into a broken-toothed leer and his rancid breath flooded Vespasian's senses. Vespasian's flailing arms slammed wild punches into the side of his head, but still the downward pressure on his windpipe increased. On the point of blacking out he heard a dull thud and felt his attacker shudder. Vespasian looked up. The man's eyes were wide open with shock and his mouth had gone slack; a bloody javelin point poked from out of his right nostril.

'What did I say about heroics, you stupid little shit?'

Vespasian focused through the blood and made out Sabinus, on foot, holding a javelin in two hands, supporting the weight of the now limp runaway. Sabinus tossed the body contemptuously aside and held out his hand to help his brother up.

'Well, now.' He grinned maliciously. 'Whatever good

looks you may have thought you possessed have been ruined by that little escapade. Perhaps that'll teach you to listen to your elders and betters in future.'

'Did I kill the other one?' Vespasian managed to ask through a mouthful of blood.

'No, you killed his horse and then his horse killed him. Come on, there's one left alive to nail up.'

Vespasian held a strip of cloth, torn from the dead runaway's tunic, over his bleeding nose as he walked back up the hill; it stank, but that helped him to remain conscious. His head pounded with pain now that the adrenalin had subsided. He breathed in laboured gasps and had to lean on Sabinus. Hieron followed behind with the horses.

They reached the mules, which were calming down after their ordeal. Baseos and Ataphanes had rounded up those that had run off and had captured eight of the runaways' horses. Pallo and Simeon were busy tying the animals together into a column. Only two had been killed; four others had flesh wounds that would heal with time.

'Not a bad day's work, eh boys? Two mules down, eight horses up, Father won't have to take you to court for careless shooting,' Sabinus chuckled at Baseos and Ataphanes.

Baseos laughed. 'We'd have had three horses more to take back if you stick throwers had bothered to aim at the riders and not their mounts.'

Ataphanes clapped him on the back. 'Well said, my squat little friend, the bow is a far more effective tool than the javelin, as my grandfather's generation proved over seventy years ago at Carrhae.'

Sabinus did not like to be reminded of Rome's greatest defeat in the East, when Marcus Crassus and seven legions had been almost annihilated in a day under the continuous rain of Parthian arrows. Seven legions' eagle standards had been lost on that day.

'That'll do, you lanky, hook-nosed horse-botherer; anyway you're here now, having been captured by proper soldiers who stand and fight, not shoot and run away. What happened, ran out of arrows?'

'I may be here but I'm free now, whereas the bones of your lost legions are still lying in the sand of my homeland and they'll never be free.'

Sabinus could not bring himself to rise to the argument; the lads had fought well and deserved to let off a bit of steam. He looked around for their prisoner, who was trussed up on his stomach still unconscious.

'Right, let's get him up on a cross and get home. Lykos, dig a hole to plant it in right here.'

Ludovicus and Hieron appeared out of the wood a short time later carrying two sturdy, freshly cut branches. With the tools that they had brought along especially for the purpose they cut two joints in the timber, then laid the cross out and started to nail it together. The noise brought the prostrate prisoner to; he raised his head to look around and started to scream as he saw the cross. Vespasian saw that he was a little younger than he.

'Sabinus, don't do this to him, he can't be more than fourteen.'

'What do you recommend then, little brother? Smack his wrists, tell him he's a naughty boy and not to steal our mules again and then send him back to his owner – who will crucify him anyway, if he has any sense.'

The terror that he'd just felt at the prospect of losing his life at so young an age made Vespasian sympathise with the young thief's plight. 'Well, we could take him back and keep him as a field slave. He looks strong enough and decent field workers are hard to come by, and very expensive.'

'Bollocks. The little bastard has run away before; who's to say he won't do it again? Anyway we need to nail one up and he had the misfortune to get caught. Would you feel better if he was lying over there, full of arrows, and we had an old, grizzly one to crucify? What difference would it make? They've all got to die. Come on, let's get him up.'

Vespasian looked over at the hysterical boy, who had fixed him with a pleading stare, and, realising that Sabinus was right, turned away.

Pallo and Hieron lifted the screaming captive, fighting for all he was worth – which was not much – on to the cross.

'Please, mercy, please, I beg you, masters. I'll give you anything. I'll do anything, anything. I beg you.'

Pallo slapped him around the face. 'Quit your snivelling, you little shit. What have you got to give anyway, a nice tight arsehole? It's vermin like you that murdered my father, so I wouldn't even give you the pleasure of one last hard fucking.'

Spitting at him he cut his bonds and he and Lykos pulled his arms out and stretched the struggling youth over the cross. Hieron and Baseos held his legs as Ludovicus approached with a mallet and nails. He knelt by his right arm and placed a nail on his wrist, just under the base of the thumb. With a series of crashing blows he drove the half-inch-wide nail through the wrist, home into the wood, splintering bones and tearing sinews. Vespasian had not thought it possible for any creature, let alone a human, to make the noise that the boy emitted in his torment. It was a cry that pierced his very being as it rose from a guttural roar to a shrill scream.

Ludovicus moved on to the other arm and quickly skewered it to the cross. Not even Pallo was enjoying it any more as nails were forced through each of the writhing boy's feet. The cry stopped abruptly; the boy had gone into shock and just stared at the sky, hyperventilating, his mouth frozen in a tortured grimace.

'Thank the gods for that,' Sabinus said. 'Get him up, then haul the two dead mules over here and leave them under the cross; that should leave a clear enough message.'

They lifted the cross into the hole and supported it whilst wedges were hammered in around the base. Soon after they'd finished the cries started again, but this time intermittently as the lad ran out of breath. The only way he could breathe was by pulling himself up by his wrists whilst pushing down on the nails through his feet; however, that soon became too painful to endure and he would let himself slump down again, only to find himself suffocating. This ghastly cycle would carry on until finally he died in one or two days' time.

They rode away up over the hill with the cries echoing around the valley. Vespasian knew that he would never forget the boy's face and the horror that had been written all over it.

'What if his friends come and cut him down, Sabinus?'

'They may well come, but they won't cut him down. Even in the unlikely event that he did survive he would never be able to use his hands again, or walk without a severe limp. No, if they come they'll stick a spear through his heart and go home. But they'll have learnt a lesson.'

The screams followed them for what seemed like an age, and then were suddenly cut short. The boy's friends had come.

CHAPTER III

IT WAS STILL dark when Sabinus' right foot connected with Vespasian's left buttock, sending him rolling out of bed and on to the floor.

'Get up, legionary,' Sabinus shouted in his most centurion-like voice. 'You need to make a fire now if you want any chance of a hot breakfast before we march at sun-up.'

Vespasian sat up and looked around. 'What do you mean?' he asked groggily.

'I mean that if you want breakfast you had better make it now because we start the route march at dawn. Is that any clearer? Now get moving. There's wood, kindling and legionary cooking gear and rations out the back.'

'What about you?' Vespasian asked, getting to his feet.

'Oh, don't you worry about me, little brother, I'm not in training. I've got breakfast waiting for me in the triclinium.' And off he went in search of it, leaving Vespasian struggling with his sandals in the dark and cursing the throbbing of his nose. It had been set on their return by Chloe, an old Greek house slave whose father had been a doctor. She was the only person on the estate with any medical knowledge;

having assisted her father until his death, she had sold herself into slavery as an alternative to destitution. She had clicked the cartilage back into place, a process that had been more painful than the original injury, and then applied a poultice of wet clay mixed with herbs and honey that she secured in place with bandages. The poultice had hardened overnight and was now putting pressure on the swelling.

When he got outside he found his supplies in a heap on the ground. He pulled his cloak close around his shoulders against the chill, pre-dawn air, and started struggling to make a fire as best he could in the gloom.

Once he had a decent flame going he could finally see his rations: a cup of barley, a thick slice of bacon, a hard bit of cheese, a pint of water and a skin of sour wine; next to these stood a single cooking pot. Having never attempted anything more adventurous than roasting a rabbit or a chicken over an open fire, he was at a loss as to what to do. As time was short he decided to put the whole lot, except the wine, together into the pot and boil it up.

A short while later, he had produced a stodgy mess that looked very unappealing but was just about edible. He was halfway through his porridge, made slightly more palatable by the wine, when Sabinus arrived on his horse. The first light of the sun bathed the rugged ochre hills with its soft red glow, and the cicadas, alerted to the arrival of the new day, had started their relentless rattle.

'Get that fire out and bury all the traces,' he shouted. 'And get your cooking gear in this.' He threw down a sturdy pole with a T-bar at one end to which was attached a large pack.

'What's that?' Vespasian asked.

'That, my hardy little brother, is the difference between a pleasant country stroll and a legionary route march. It is about the same weight as a legionary's pack, give or take; I have a hazy recollection of these things, so I've erred on the generous side.' Sabinus smiled innocently.

'I'll bet you have,' Vespasian grumbled as he emptied the remains of his breakfast on to the fire and covered it with soil. He tied his cooking gear to the side of the pack and then shouldered the pole, so that the pack hung behind him. He grimaced at the weight.

Sabinus looked down at his brother. 'Now you know why legionaries are known as "Marius' Mules". Considering your fondness for the creatures you should be very pleased to have the opportunity to be one. Giddy up, little brother!' Laughing at his own joke he rode off, leaving Vespasian to follow.

'Why aren't you marching?' Vespasian called after him.

Sabinus looked round with another wry grin. 'As I said: I'm not in training.'

They had gone about a mile before Sabinus slowed his horse and let his brother catch up with him. He took short reed whistle from his pack and blew it, paused briefly, and then blew it again.

'That's a standard army beat; a steady three paces a beat for five hours with two brief stops for water will take you twenty miles.' Sabinus paused, took a swig from his goatskin of water for added effect, and then carried on the lecture. 'That is the speed a legion, or smaller detachment, travels if it is unencumbered by the siege and baggage trains. If they need to go faster the pace is increased to quick time, which is just over three and a half paces per beat – twenty-four miles in five hours. If, however, the full army, with all its logistical encumbrances, is marching then the most it will achieve in five hours is ten to twelve miles, travelling at the speed of its slowest component, which are the oxen pulling the baggage wagons and siege train.' Sabinus looked down at his brother, who was starting to sweat in the rising heat. 'But for our purposes we'll concentrate on being a detachment. If you can keep up with this pace then marching in a full column will feel like a holiday.' He led off, whistling the beat for his brother to march to.

'Why do they only march for five hours?' Vespasian asked after a few hundred paces. 'Not that I want to do more,' he added hastily.

'Work it out for yourself. Where does a legion wake up in the morning?' Sabinus said, taking the reed from his mouth but not stopping.

'In camp,' Vespasian answered.

'Exactly. And where will it sleep that night?'

'In another camp.'

'Precisely. And who is going to build that camp, or do the gods just magic it out of thin air?' Sabinus was enjoying himself.

'Well, the legionaries, of course,' Vespasian replied testily. The sweating skin beneath the poultice was starting to irritate him.

'You've got it, little brother. Digging a defensive ditch, putting up a stockade, pitching the tents and, most importantly, cooking supper will take up the best part of the remaining hours of daylight. That is the basics of a legionary's day. Wake, eat, strike camp, march, build new camp, eat, sleep.

'Of course there's far more to it than that: guard duty, drill, foraging, latrine fatigue, maintaining equipment and so on. But all this serves only to ensure that the legionary arrives, fit and prepared, in the right place for what he really exists for; and that is fighting and killing, whether it be in a small skirmish or in a big set-piece battle.'

'Were you ever in a big battle?' Vespasian asked, his curiosity overcoming his antipathy to his brother.

'The rebellion in Africa was not like that. Tacfarinas' Numidian army was mainly light cavalry and light infantry. They're devious bastards, always harassing you, picking off stragglers, attacking foraging parties, never letting themselves be drawn into battle. The one time they did, at the start of the rebellion, the Third Augusta trounced them. After that they changed tactics and stayed well away from a full legion and started to pick on smaller fare. They managed to destroy a whole cohort of the Third Augusta a few months before we arrived.'

'How did they do that?' Vespasian asked as he worked his legs harder against what was becoming quite a steep slope.

'They caught them on their way back from a punishment raid out on an open plain. The cohort formed up for a hand-to-hand affair, but the Numidians were having none of it. Their cavalry just rode around them, pelting them with javelins, whilst their infantry fired slingshot and arrows at our boys from a safe distance. Every time the cohort tried to charge them they just fell back and carried on shooting. It was a mini Carrhae. Most were dead within four hours; the unlucky few who were captured were pegged out naked in the desert sun with their eyes gouged out and their cocks cut off.

'The Governor, Lucius Apronius, was so furious when he heard of this humiliation that he punished the rest of the legion by decimation, even though they hadn't been there.'

'That doesn't seem fair,' Vespasian said. His sandals were beginning to rub at his heels.

'Who said it had to be fair? The legion had collectively suffered a deep wound. Losing an entire cohort, four hundred and eighty men, at the hands of rebels sullied the honour of the legion as a whole. The only way to restore it was with blood, so Lucius Apronius had them parade in front of him unarmed, wearing only tunics. Then they were counted off. Every ninth man was given a sword and had to behead the tenth man, his comrade, to his left. He might have been his best mate; someone he'd known for years, someone he'd shared a tent with, meals, battles, women. Or maybe he was a complete stranger, a young lad who had just joined up. It didn't matter; if you hesitated then you were for the chop as well.'

Sabinus paused and reached into a bag that hung from his saddle and pulled out a floppy straw sun hat, the Thessalian type popularised by Augustus during his reign. Placing it on his head he carried on, indifferent to Vespasian's rising discomfort.

'One of the Third's tribunes told me about it soon after I arrived. He said that it was the most terrible thing he had ever seen; a whole legion covered with the blood of their comrades, standing to attention, in front of a pile of more than four hundred severed heads, begging the Governor to forgive them. However, after that they had a deep and lasting hatred of Tacfarinas and his rebels, whom they saw as ultimately responsible for their suffering, and they set about the task of subduing them with a savage vigour. Eventually, a few months after we'd done the hard work and left, they trapped the remnants of rebel army in a fortress called Auzera; after a three-month siege it fell and the Third Augusta spared no one, not even good slave stock. Tacfarinas, unfortunately, fell on his sword before they could get to him, but they found his wives and children, who I'm sure made up for it.'

They had reached the top of the hill and Sabinus pulled up his horse and passed the water skin to Vespasian, who sucked on it gratefully.

'So Lucius Apronius was right to do what he did,' he said, wiping the excess water from his chin.

'Absolutely,' Sabinus replied. 'A legion cannot fight and win unless every one of its men has confidence in his comrades. By showing that they could execute their own mates they proved that they could kill anyone, and so restored their faith in themselves.'

Vespasian looked at his brother and remembered his father's words about the principle that bound a legion together; if he had to stand in its ranks someday then he would want men like Sabinus on either side of him.

The brothers stood still for a moment, looking out over the hills of their estate. In the distance, to the northeast, was the peak of mount Tetrica waiting for the winter snows that would crown its summit within the month. Way below them, to the south, ran the Avens, a tributary of which ran through the gully that they had used to trap the runaways the day before. At a right angle to the river they could make out the line of the Via Salaria, threading its way through the valley east to the Adriatic. Where it crossed the river a substantial stone bridge had been built towards which, from the east, sped a large party of horsemen.

'They look to be in a hurry,' Vespasian remarked, shading his eyes against the glare.

'Which is more than can be said for you. Let's go.' Sabinus kicked his horse into action and headed off down the hill, resuming his whistling. Vespasian followed wearily, all the time keeping an eye on the horsemen on the road below them. He could count about twenty; they seemed to be armed and, one thing was for sure, they were travelling fast. As the riders reached the bridge they slowed and crossed it at a trot. Once over, the lead horseman pulled his horse off the road to the right, and started to follow the line of the river. The others followed.

'Where do you think they're heading?' Vespasian asked.

'What?' Sabinus replied; his mind had been elsewhere.

'The horsemen, they've left the road and are heading along the river, our way.'

Sabinus looked up; although the riders were five or six miles away he could clearly see that they were armed: sunlight glinted off spear tips and helmets.

'Well, they're not military, that's for sure. They're not in uniform and they're riding in a ragged formation.' Sabinus gave his brother a questioning look. 'If they're not military but they're armed and they're heading in our direction at speed, I think that we should start to assume the worst, don't you, little brother?'

'Runaways?'

'Planning a little revenge for yesterday, I'd say. We'd better get back fast; drop your pack and get up here behind me.'

With an increasing sense of foreboding Vespasian did as he was told. Sabinus wheeled his mount round and, going as fast as was possible with his brother riding pillion, started to retrace the seven miles they had travelled. Vespasian clung on tightly as he was bounced this way and that by the swift movement of the horse over the rough ground; his broken nose beneath the poultice was jarred with each step causing him to wince in pain.

'If we can keep up this pace,' Sabinus called back to his

brother, 'we should arrive back at the farm half an hour or so ahead of them. That will be just enough time to arm and position everyone there. The people way out in the fields will just have to trust to Fortuna and look after themselves.'

'What do you plan to do?' Vespasian asked, hoping Sabinus would outline an ingenious plan.

'I don't know yet. I'm thinking.' Not an inspiring reply.

As they raced back Vespasian imagined the fury of the runaways when they found the young lad hanging on a cross and the bodies of their comrades lying rotting in the sun. He wondered why no one had considered the possibility of reprisal and realised that they had all underestimated their opponents. They had been dismissed as a small, ill-equipped bunch of badly led thieves who were capable of nothing more than mule-rustling and highway robbery. Yet here they were attempting an orchestrated attack on the Flavian farm. He realised that it would be a bloody fight; the runaways would neither expect nor give any quarter.

The brothers hurtled through the gate and into the courtyard, scattering chickens and small children in all directions. Pallo came running out of the estate office as they dismounted.

'Pallo, quick,' Sabinus shouted, 'arm all the men and as many slaves you can trust and get the women and children locked safely inside, then get all our people from the nearer fields in here as quickly as possible. It looks like we can expect company in about half an hour, twenty or so runaways bent on exacting revenge. They meant to surprise us, so let's make them think that they have. We'll leave the gates open with a couple of men hidden behind them. If there's no one to attack outside, they'll come charging straight into the courtyard; the two lads behind the gates will shut and block them from the outside, then we'll have them. We'll need all the rest of the lads, armed with bows and javelins, on the roofs and in the rooms above the stables. Hieron, fill as many buckets as you can with water and take them up to the roofs; the bastards may try to torch the buildings. Vespasian, go and tell our parents what's happening.'

Not long later Vespasian returned to the yard with his father. They had left Vespasia and the female slaves barricaded in the main house with Varo, whom Titus had ordered to assist Vespasia in taking her own life should they be overwhelmed. That his mother had acquiesced to this plan brought home the seriousness of the situation to Vespasian.

In the yard the defenders had been busy. A wagon had been placed outside the gate, ready to block it. Swords and daggers had been issued, stacks of javelins, bunches of arrows and buckets of water had been positioned all around the roofs. Access to the roofs was via ladders that could be pulled up after use. Manacled parties of field slaves were being locked into storerooms to prevent them from aiding their attackers, whom they would no doubt wish to join, given half a chance.

Vespasian helped Titus onto the roof of the main house, and then followed him up.

'I'm looking forward to this,' he chuckled to Vespasian. 'I haven't thrown a javelin in anger in I don't know how long, and to have such a worthwhile target will make it doubly pleasurable.'

Vespasian looked around the roofs; he could count fifteen men, and another three looking out of the windows of house slaves' quarters above the stables. Simeon and Ludovicus were hidden behind the gates ready to spring the trap; Lykos and Pallo were stationed above them. Baseos and Ataphanes were heading out of the gate on horses, nonchalantly stringing their bows.

'Where are they going?' Vespasian asked Sabinus, who was a little further along the main house's roof from him; in his hand he had the end of a rope that trailed down across the yard and up through a first-floor window opposite, through which Hieron could be glimpsed.

'We need to have some people outside otherwise it would look suspiciously quiet. As soon as they're spotted they'll race back through the gates, hopefully bringing the raiders with them.' Sabinus raised his voice so that everyone around the yard could hear him. 'Now remember, keep down until they're coming through the gate. We don't want them seeing any heads on the roofs and becoming suspicious. We want them to charge in here in blissful ignorance of what awaits them. There will be freedom for any slave who acquits himself well today.' A small cheer went up. 'Pallo, you keep watch; everyone else get down and stay down now. Don't start shooting until at least ten of them are in the yard – by that time their momentum will be too great to stop. May Fortuna and Mars look down kindly upon us.'

They settled down to wait with the midday sun burning down on them. Time started to drag; the eerie silence around the yard seemed to slow it even more. Vespasian considered the possibility that it was just his and Sabinus' over-active imaginations that had caused the panic, and thought of the humiliation they would face when it became apparent that it was a false alarm. He almost let out a sigh of relief when he heard the first faint screams and shouts from far off in the fields. The raiders had evidently come across a work-party that was too far away to be warned and were warming up by butchering them. The men around the yard tensed as they listened to the cries of their fellow estate-workers. Knowing that their chance for vengeance would soon be with them, they checked their weapons and flexed their muscles. The screaming stopped. Silence descended once again on the yard. Then faintly, in the distance, they could hear the rumble of fast-moving horses. As it grew they knew that the runaways were heading in their direction and would be with them imminently.

'I can see them,' Pallo called. 'They're about half a mile away. They've got burning torches.'

'OK. Steady, lads, keep low,' Sabinus growled.

'They've seen Baseos and Ataphanes; here they come.'

The sound of horses was getting louder and they could now hear the shouts of their riders. Vespasian thought that if they were trying to surprise them, they were going the wrong way about it. This thought was banished from his mind as Baseos and Ataphanes came thundering through the gates, one swerving to the left and one to the right, towards the last two ladders that had been left for them. They leapt from their mounts and quickly clambered on to the roof, pulling the ladders up behind them, just as the lead riders burst into the yard, brandishing flaming torches, followed closely by the main body of the runaways. The lead riders passed over the rope and threw their torches, wildly, at open windows.

'Now!' Sabinus shouted.

A hail of missiles rained down on the attackers, striking rider and mount alike. Four fell immediately. Such was the speed of the others following behind that they were unable to stop. They raced through the gates and on into the yard, trampling the bodies of their fallen comrades. As the last raiders charged through the gates Simeon and Ludovicus leapt from their hiding places and pulled them shut. Incensed by this attack on his home, Vespasian felt the heat of blood-lust rise in him for the second time. This time he would kill. Screams echoed around the courtyard as arrows and javelins found their mark. He hurled a javelin directly at the nearest raider, an older man with a thick beard, a pock-marked face and his dark hair tied in a topknot, German style. The shaft hit him full in the centre of his chest, crunching through the sternum, its point coming to rest in the backbone, severing the spinal cord. Paralysis of the lower body was immediate and the man's legs went limp. He slith-ered from his horse, hit the ground and lay there unable to move, blood rising in his throat, in the hideous realisation that he was breathing his last.

Sabinus pulled with all his strength on the rope. It sprang

up from the ground catching two horses by their throats, sending them up on to their hind legs and throwing their riders under the hooves of the horses behind, who in their turn went careering into the rope. The impact pulled the rope savagely from Sabinus' hands and sent him toppling off the roof. He managed to land on all fours and instantly stood up, drawing his sword as he did so. Two unhorsed raiders sprang at him, armed with spears and vicious-looking curved daggers. They were too close to Sabinus for the defenders to risk a shot. Vespasian and Titus, who both had one javelin left, ran along the roof, closer to Sabinus, to try and get a better angle.

The first man lunged overarm with his spear at Sabinus' face. Ducking to his left, Sabinus brought his sword in a crosswise slash across the man's belly; it burst open, like an overripe fig, spilling its contents on the ground. The man howled, dropping his spear as he tried to halt with his hands the tide of guts that flowed from his gaping abdomen.

The next man, a stocky, muscular Iberian, realising that he was up against a canny fighter, approached Sabinus with more caution. As he did so, two of the few remaining mounted raiders charged towards Sabinus, flinging their javelins. Catching their movement out of the corner of his eye, he managed to duck the first, but the second, aimed much lower, seared straight through his right calf. The Iberian saw his chance and leapt forward, thrusting his spear towards Sabinus' unprotected chest, only to come to a sudden stop, looking down in surprise at Titus' last javelin, which protruded from his ribcage.

The two horsemen came bearing down on the crippled Sabinus, swords drawn, yelling wildly. Without thinking Vespasian flung himself off the roof and, picking up the gutted man's spear as he landed, stood, terrified but determined, at his brother's side. One horseman, seeing a new target, made straight for him, leaning down to his right, his sword pointing at Vespasian's chest, his wild eyes fixed upon his target. The adrenalin pumping through his veins seemed to slow time for Vespasian as he gauged the speed of the charge. His heartbeat pounded in his ears and, despite his fear, he felt a sense of calm flood over him; he had killed and he would now kill again. At the last moment he jumped to his right, jammed the butt of the spear into the ground, and held it at forty-five degrees. Half a ton of horse drove itself straight on to the spear head, burying it far into its heart, which exploded in a spray of deep-red blood over Vespasian and his brother. The creature dropped dead, catapulting its rider over its head and straight on to Vespasian. The second rider slashed at Sabinus as he sped past. Sabinus, with the javelin still piercing his calf, wasn't nimble enough to dodge the blow; he caught the tip in his right shoulder and went down. Vespasian recovered quickly; throwing off the body of the winded rider, he drew his sword, pulled back the prone man's head by his hair and slit his throat. He then stood over the body of his brother as the second rider wheeled his horse round and urged it back towards him. He'd gone no further than five paces when two arrows simultaneously thumped into his back; he fell from his horse with a shriek and rolled along the ground, breaking off the arrow shafts, and came to a stop just short of Vespasian, his dead eyes staring unblinking at the sun.

A cheer went up and Vespasian looked around realising that he was the last man standing. All the raiders were either dead or dying in the dust whilst the surviving horses waited patiently in little groups. He looked down at Sabinus who was clutching at his wounded shoulder; blood oozed through his fingers.

'Well fought, little brother,' he muttered through gritted teeth. 'It seems that I have you to thank for saving my life, not that you ever thanked me for saving yours yesterday.'

Vespasian held out his hand. 'Well, you can consider yourself thanked now,' he said, pulling Sabinus to his feet.

'You can thank me properly by pulling this fucking thing out of my leg.'

Vespasian knelt down to examine the wound. All around them cheering men were coming down from the roofs to put out the few fires that had taken hold and to slit the throats of those runaways still breathing.

'Well done, my boys, that was a fine display,' Titus called as he clambered down the ladder. 'I trust that you are not too badly hurt, Sabinus?'

'I'll be fine, Father, I need a few stitches from Chloe, and—' He let out a huge roar; Vespasian had used the distraction of his father to remove the javelin. Sabinus went pale and almost fainted. 'Gods, that hurt, you little shit. I bet you really enjoyed that. Come on, get me into the house.'

They hobbled towards the door that had been unbolted

by their mother, who had heard the cheering. She stood waiting to help her son into the house.

'Oh, by the way, wool,' Sabinus mumbled.

'What?' Vespasian asked, thinking that his brother was rambling.

'What we should be selling at the moment, wool. It's in demand because winter's approaching.'

'Oh, yes, that. You're quite right, well done for working it out,' Vespasian replied.

'I didn't work it out, I just asked Pallo when we got back yesterday.' Sabinus grinned. 'Oh, and get that poultice seen to, you look ridiculous.'

Vespasian looked with a half-smile at his brother and, shaking his head, thought that it was unlikely that he'd ever change. He left him in the care of the womenfolk.

He turned and surveyed the scene in the yard. The fires were now out; just a few wisps of smoke marked where they had caught. The manacled field slaves were being let out of the storerooms and taken back to work. Pallo was organising the piling up of the dead runaways on a pyre outside the gates. Vespasian watched as his javelin was extracted from the top-knotted German and the body was hauled away, leaving a thick trail of blood. It had been his first kill and the thought didn't shock him. He'd slit the throat of the second man without even thinking; he'd done what he'd had to do to survive and to protect his brother. Anyway, these had just been slaves whose lives were worth only what they would fetch at auction.

Pallo saw him watching the removal of the dead, and walked over. 'You did well today, Titus Flavius Vespasianus,' he said formally, according him the respect of a man. 'Your father must be proud.'

'Thank you, Pallo, we all did our share; it was a well-conceived plan of my brother's. How many of our lads were hurt?'

'One killed and four wounded, none of them too badly.'

'Who died?' Vespasian asked.

'Brennus, a Gallic house slave; he was hit in the eye by a javelin. His son Drest is one of the wounded,' Pallo replied.

'We should free the son, it will send a good message to the other slaves should this happen again. I'll speak to my father.'

As he turned to go a thought occurred to him. 'Pallo?' he asked, lowering his voice. 'Do you know anything about a prophecy to do with me? Something that happened at my birth; you were there, were you not?' Vespasian looked Pallo in the eye but the steward could not hold his gaze and looked down. 'Why won't you answer me?' Vespasian pressed.

'I am forbidden to speak of it,' Pallo whispered uncomfortably.

'Why? Tell me, Pallo, who forbids you?'

'The gods,' Pallo replied, meeting Vespasian's eye again.

'Which gods? Why?' Vespasian was getting more and more agitated and grabbed Pallo by the shoulders.

'All of them. Your mother made the whole household swear an oath in front of all the gods never to speak of it.'

CHAPTER IV

SABINUS' WOUNDS MEANT that Vespasian's training was curtailed for a few days. Route marches were not possible but gymnastics, trench-digging and weapons drill were. Vespasian spent hours attacking a six-foot post with a wooden sword and wicker shield, practising the prescribed cuts, thrusts and parries. The sword and shield were designed to be heavier than the real items. This was, explained Sabinus, to strengthen his arms, so that he would find it that much easier to wield regulation weapons. When he was not attacking the post with his wooden sword he was throwing heavy javelins at it. As the days passed the exercises began to feel easier and, although never enjoyable, became less of a burden.

In return, Vespasian began his estate administration lessons with Sabinus. Once they had started on the subject Vespasian found that he knew so much more than he had previously realised and, in his eagerness to get it across, ended up baffling his prostrate brother with a barrage of facts and figures. At first, because of his wounds, Sabinus was forced to sit in one place and was unable to escape the stream of constant information; but as he mended the lessons were held walking or riding around the estate. In this more relaxed atmosphere Sabinus' eyes were opened to the complex logistical problems faced by an estate manager trying to use his land and manpower to full effect every day of the year. He began to realise that an estate was just a microcosm of an army, or indeed Rome, and to fully understand its workings would greatly improve his chances of success in public life. Vespasian became someone well worth listening to. For his part Vespasian found that sharing his knowledge with his brother helped him to order his thoughts, and strengthened his confidence in what he already knew.

This sense of mutual reliance plus the knowledge that each was indebted to the other for their life precipitated a thawing in their relationship.

The following weeks surprised not only themselves but also their parents; dinner in the early evening stopped being such a confrontational event, becoming instead a review of the subjects mastered or feats achieved during the day.

November passed quickly in this pleasanter atmosphere. The snows arrived on the surrounding peaks and the activity on the estate slowed down for winter, entering a period of make and mend. Walls were repaired, new tools fashioned, a new barn erected and countless other jobs, which had been waiting throughout the summer, were tackled and completed.

Sabinus took advantage of this industry to have a light ballista constructed, so that he could teach his brother the rudiments of artillery fire. He set up an ox head in front of a large sheet of leather and instructed his brother in the science of trajectory, speed and wind variation. Within a week Vespasian could hit the ox between the eyes at a hundred paces with the same ease that Sabinus could write a work roster for fifty slaves and their overseers or tally a profit and loss account.

The season of goodwill, the Saturnalia, came and went with its round of feasting and gift-giving. Three days after its close, on 25 December, Sabinus had just finished celebrating the miraculous birth in a cave, witnessed by shepherds, of Mithras, a new god from the East into whose mysteries he'd been enrolled whilst in the army, when their father called the brothers into his study.

'Well, my boys, January is almost upon us,' he began without inviting them to sit down. 'You have kept your side of the bargain, so I shall keep mine. I have arranged for us to stay, as you did, Sabinus, four years ago, at the house of my brother by marriage, your uncle, Gaius Vespasius Pollo. There we shall have access to the highest social circles in Rome and even to the imperial household itself. Gaius now counts amongst his patrons Antonia, sister by marriage to our illustrious Emperor.

'As you know, Gaius has no children and is therefore eager that you, his sister's offspring, should thrive. He will introduce you to wealthy and influential people and write many letters of recommendation and introduction. He is to be respected and honoured; who knows, he may even decide to adopt one of you.' He paused and looked sternly at his two sons. 'I have been most impressed by the progress you have both made, not least in your abilities to set aside petty personal differences and work together. This is one of the most important attributes for a Roman nobleman. You will be in a society that is ruthless and competitive where everyone is out for themselves and their family. You will be elected to offices or serve in the legions alongside men who for no apparent reason are your enemy and only see you as someone to outdo. Yet for the good of Rome you must work with these men, as they must work with you. Keep your eyes on them, never trust them, but co-operate with them; if you do that you will be serving both Rome and yourselves well.'

'Yes, Father,' the brothers said in unison.

Titus rose and guided both his sons out of the study into the atrium, past the rainwater pool with its spluttering fountain, to the alcove by the household altar where the death masks of the family's ancestors hung on the wall. He stopped in front of the sombre array of lifelike, or deathlike, waxen images.

'Each one of these men had a life with its own successes and failures, and every one of them did his utmost to serve our family and the Sabine tribe. Then, after they had won for us our citizenship, they served Rome. You, my sons, will build on what they have done and raise the family of Flavius from obscurity here in the Sabine Hills to greatness in the greatest city of all. I'll do everything in my power to aid you; provide money and use what contacts I have, but I shan't be around for ever. When I'm gone you will have to support each other. To this end I have brought you here before our ancestors. Here you will swear to be ever faithful to one another, always to look out for each other and, above all, to support each other in whatever enterprises you find yourselves in.'

'But, Father, to be bound by oath as well as blood is unnecessary. Our blood-tie compels us to do all that is being asked in the oath,' Sabinus argued.

'I understand that, but this oath will be made in front of not only all our ancestors, but also all our gods, including your Mithras. It will therefore be the most binding oath you have ever taken and so will supersede any other. If there comes a time when one of you is unable to properly aid the other because of a previous oath this will nullify it. Do you see, Sabinus?'

Sabinus met his father's eye for a few moments, then he nodded and looked at Vespasian, who played dumb. He now felt certain that Sabinus knew of the prophecy since his father was giving him a way to break his mother's oath. At some point in the future, when Sabinus felt the time was right, Titus wanted him, Vespasian, to know its content, and because of this oath Sabinus would be able to tell him.

Titus then looked at Vespasian. 'This is the last time you will be addressed as a boy.' He lifted the leather thong of the bulla over Vespasian's head. 'I decree that from now on, my son, you, Titus Flavius Vespasianus, are a man. Take up a man's duty, dignity and honour and go out into the world and thrive in your own right to your greater glory and to the glory of the house of Flavius.'

Vespasian bowed his head in acknowledgement of his father's wishes.

Titus then turned to the lararium, where the images of the *lares domestici*, the household gods, were kept. He placed the bulla on the altar and arranged around it five small clay statuettes that he took from a cupboard next to it. He pulled a fold of his toga over his head, muttered a short prayer, and then filled a shallow bowl with wine from the altar jug. Standing with the bowl in his right hand he poured a libation over the altar in front of the largest of the figures, the *lar familiaris*, who represented the founder of the family. He then motioned his sons to join him, one on either side of the altar, and gave them each a sip of wine, before draining the rest himself and setting down the bowl.

In the fading light the three men stood in front of the altar whilst Titus, invoking the gods and the spirits of their ancestors, administered the oath to his sons. The words he used to bind them together echoed through the columns of the atrium as the death masks, staring down with unseeing eyes in the half-light, bore witness to the solemn ritual.

Once he had finished the ceremony he removed the toga from his head and embraced each son in turn, wishing upon them Fortuna's blessing and placing the honour of the family in their hands.

'Always remember where you come from, and to what family you belong. Each time you return home do so with greater *dignitas*, so that this house may grow in stature through the glory of its sons.'

They stood together in silence, each making their own requests of the gods in private prayer. The room was now almost completely dark. The household slave whose duty it was to light the lamps and the fire waited at a respectful distance in the corner of the room, not daring to disturb the paterfamilias as he prayed with his two sons. The only sound to be heard was the gentle patter of the fountain.

After a short while Titus clapped his hands, breaking the silence. 'Varo, where are you? Bring wine, and why are we in the dark? What's going on in this house? Have you all fallen asleep?'

Varo came scuttling in, aiming a kick for good measure at the backside of the lamp slave, who leapt into action.

'I'm sorry, master, we were waiting for . . .' Then he trailed off.

'Yes, yes, I know, and you did right. But now I want wine and light.'

A short time later the room was filled with the light of numerous oil lamps scattered around the room and a fire crackled in the hearth. Vespasia arrived to find her menfolk seated near it with cups of wine in hand.

'Ah, my dear,' Titus said, standing up, 'you are just in time. I am going to propose a toast; take a cup.' He handed her one that was already filled with slightly watered best Caecuban wine. Lifting his own he raised it above his head, spilling a few drops in his enthusiasm.

'Tomorrow we leave for Rome and the household of your brother. We shall make a sacrifice to the gods before we depart, so that they will favour our endeavours and to ensure that we may all return here safely. To Rome and the house of Flavius.'

'To Rome and the house of Flavius,' echoed his family as they drank the toast.

PART II

ROME

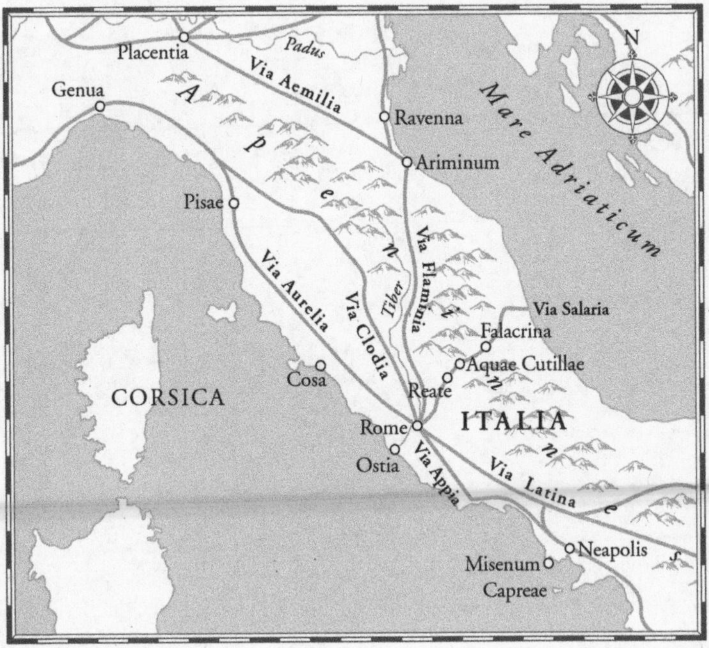

Placentia
Padus
Via Aemilia
Genua
Ravenna
Mare Adriaticum
N
Ariminum
Pisae
A p e n n i n e s
Via Aurelia
Via Clodia
Tiber
Via Flaminia
Via Salaria
Falacrina
Aquae Cutillae
Cosa
Reate
CORSICA
Rome
ITALIA
Ostia
Via Appia
Via Latina
Neapolis
Misenum
Capreae

CHAPTER V

THE BROWN CLOUD on the horizon was growing larger. It was the morning of the third day of their journey and as they neared the greatest city in the world Vespasian could feel its wealth seeping out into the surrounding countryside and beyond. Evidence of it could be seen everywhere. Farmland and farm buildings gave way to extensive market gardens where thousands of field slaves tended the long rows of lettuces, leeks, onions and herbs. Armed gatekeepers eyed passing travellers, as if each one was a potential house-breaker, from behind lavishly gilded gateways that led up to imposing villas with magnificent views on the slopes above. The road itself was busier than he could have imagined; every imaginable form of transport passed them heading back up the Via Salaria, and overturned carts with broken axles, spilt loads and slow-moving columns of shackled captives meant that they found progress was quicker just to the side of it, and easier on the hoofs of their mounts.

Their party was made up of Vespasian, his brother and father all riding horses; next came Vespasia in a four-wheeled, mule-drawn, covered carriage, a *raeda*. She sat on deep cushions under the awning being fussed over by two maidservants as the cumbersome vehicle rattled and jolted its way down from the hills. Behind the raeda came a cart with their luggage, driven by two household slaves. Finally came three more household slaves, the men's body servants, riding mules. As guards, Titus had hired three mounted ex-legionaries, who had so far proved to be forbidding enough to ensure a trouble-free journey.

Progress down the Via Salaria had not been quick, owing mainly to the painfully slow speed of the raeda. This had had its advantages in that they had spent two nights on the road rather than one, staying with families with whom they had ties of hospitality. At dinner the families had traded favours to their mutual advantage. Titus offered promises of his brother-in-law Gaius, the ex-praetor, interceding in a court case or a civic matter in return for a letter of introduction to a magis-trate or a member of the imperial household. Titus had been happy to trade on the name of his brother-in-law as Vespasia had assured him that all reasonable promises would be honoured, at a price – naturally – to himself some day in the future. For Vespasian it had been interesting to see at first hand the heads of two families supporting each other for common benefit one day, knowing that they could become arch-rivals the next.

As the small party drew closer to their destination Vespasian contemplated how he would advance himself in this highly competitive society that he was being forced into, where the only permanent loyalties were to Rome, one's family and one's personal honour and dignity. He looked up at the brown cloud in the distance as his horse pressed on up a hill and wondered whether he would be suited to, or even wanted, such a competitive life. The road ignored the steep incline as it forged ahead and before he had arrived at any firm conclusion it reached the summit.

Vespasian stopped and gasped. Forgetting all else he stared in disbelief at the most magnificent sight that he had ever seen. Five or so miles before him, crowned with a thick brown halo formed from the smoke of half a million cooking fires and the discharge of countless forges and tanneries, its seven hills encircled by huge red-brick walls punctuated by mighty towers, stood the heart of the most powerful empire in the world: Rome.

'I remember stopping and marvelling in this very place forty years ago when my mother brought me here at your age,' Titus said, pulling up next to him. 'When a man sees Rome for the first time and feels her power and his own insignificance in the face of it, he realises that he has but two choices: serve her or perish under her, for there is no ignoring her.'

Vespasian looked at his father. 'In that case there is no choice,' he said in a quiet voice. Titus smiled and stroked the smooth neck of his mount whilst he contemplated the scale of the city below them.

'If that sight overwhelms us so, imagine how some hairy-arsed barbarian from the forests of Germania or Gaul must feel when faced with such might. Is it any wonder that their chieftains are now falling over themselves to become citizens? Like our Latin allies over a hundred years ago, who fought a war against Rome for their right to citizenship, they too want to serve her rather than perish under her. Rome sucks you in, son, just take care that she doesn't spit you out.'

'One taste of that little runt and I'm sure he'll find that in his case mistress Rome is a spitter not a swallower.' Sabinus laughed at his own wit as he drew level with them.

'Very funny, Sabinus,' Vespasian snapped. As much as he enjoyed a coarse joke he was feeling far too unsure of himself to appreciate such flippancy. He kicked his horse forward and headed off down the hill to the sound of Titus admonishing Sabinus for his foul mouth.

As he gazed at the centre of the empire, immovable on the plain below him, bathing in the morning sun and feeding off the roads and aqueducts that pumped life into her, he felt inspired by her magnificence and power. His nerves steadied. Perhaps no longer would he be content to limit his horizons to the hills that surrounded his rural home. Perhaps no longer would he count himself fulfilled by the mundane business of farming and raising mules with nothing to mark the passing of time other than the change in the seasons. He was going to enter a larger and more perilous world, and there he would survive and prosper. With a growing sense of excitement he descended the hill, oblivious to his father's calls to slow down. He weaved his way through the other travellers thinking only of arriving as soon as possible.

After a couple of miles the traffic slowed out of necessity as tombs, large and small, on either side of the road squeezed it in. Vespasian paused and felt the hand of history upon him as he read the names carved into the walls of each one. There were famous families alongside names that he had never heard of. Some tombs were very ancient, others newly erected, but all had one thing in common: they contained the remains of men and women who had in their lifetimes contributed to the rise of Rome from a few mud huts on the Capitoline Hill, almost eight hundred years before, to the metropolis of marble and brick before whose walls they were now interred. All the joys and disappointments of these past Romans, whose souls now resided in the shades, all their achievements and failures were now just part of the sum total of their city's glory. They had all had their time, and he hoped that they had made the most of it because there was no coming back from that dark land once they had been ferried across the Styx. He vowed to himself that before he made that same journey he would do his utmost to leave the city that he was about to enter for the first time greater, in some small way, for him having been there.

Coming out of his reverie he realised that he'd got far ahead of his party and decided to wait for them there, amongst the tombs. He dismounted and tied his horse to a small tree and, pulling his cloak around his shoulders, sat down to wait, idly watching the passing traffic. After a short while a wagon pulled off the road near him and disgorged a family with its house slaves. The slaves immediately started to set up a table and stools in front of a small, new-looking tomb. The paterfamilias poured a libation and said a prayer, and then the family sat down and were served a picnic meal which they seemed to share with the occupant of the tomb by laying food and drink upon it. Vespasian watched this curious ritual as the family ate and drank with their deceased relative, talking to him as if he was still alive, seemingly oblivious to the traffic rumbling by on the road only a few feet away. Even death, it seemed, did not stop honour being shown to a man, if in life he had earned it in the service of his family and Rome.

The meal was coming to an end when he heard his brother's voice bellowing at him. 'What do you think you're doing, you little shit, sitting by the side of the road without a care in the world? Do you think you're a match for the cut-throats and worse that live amongst these tombs?' Sabinus jumped off his horse and kicked his brother hard on the thigh. 'You've had our mother half crazy with worry running off like that.'

Titus pulled up next to them. 'What in Hades are you up to, Vespasian? Don't you realise how dangerous it is travelling alone on these roads, even though they're crowded? Which one of these travellers is going to stop and come to the aid of a young lad being mugged, eh? Only the very stupid, that's who, and what good are they? No one in their right mind is going to risk themselves for the likes of you, if they even noticed you being hauled off behind a tomb.'

'I'm sorry, Father,' Vespasian said, rubbing his bruised leg as he hobbled to his feet. 'I didn't think – Sabinus just told me—'

'Get back on your horse and go and apologise to your mother,' his father snapped.

Vespasian mounted up and did as he was told, but he could not stop thinking about the dead man in the tomb. Would he, Vespasian, ever earn such honour?

The road grew even busier as it approached the junction with the Via Nomentana less than half a mile from the Porta Collina, the gate through which they would enter the city. The tombs that still lined the way had become shantytowns housing the dispossessed dregs of the urban poor who could find no affordable accommodation within the city itself. The stench of their unsanitary dwellings, made of bits of wood covered by strips of sackcloth, permeated an atmosphere already thick with the smoke from their cooking fires to make breathing an unpleasant but necessary chore.

The city walls were now only a few hundred paces away. Their scale was awe-inspiring: solid mountains of brick dominating the skyline. To the north of the city, two miles to his right, he could see the graceful arches of the newly built Aqua Virgo, sixty feet high, as it entered the Campus Martius at the end of its twenty-three-mile journey ferrying sweet water from a spring that, legend had it, was shown to thirsty, victorious Roman soldiers by a young maid after some long-forgotten battle.

The noise of the crowd coupled with the grating of the unsprung iron-shod wheels of countless carts and wagons pulled by baying beasts of burden rose to a crescendo as the two roads, quite literally, collided. Vespasian surveyed the chaos of the free-for-all as vehicles, humans and animals pushed and shoved in all directions trying to get off one road and on to the other. No one was willing to give way, for to do so would mean more delay and, no doubt, a savage push from the vehicle behind.

The family's ex-legionary guards were now leading the way, beating a path through the crowd with sturdy poles as they inched their way on to the Via Nomentana. Once they had negotiated a passage on to the new road progress became easier as to their left and right the trade wagons and carts, which were not allowed into the city during the day, pulled off the road to wait for the sun to set. Once night had fallen they would continue their journeys to their final destinations, ensuring, with the rumble of their wheels and the cries of their drivers, that peace would never come to the streets and lanes of Rome at any time of the day or night.

Titus had just secured the services of a litter for Vespasia to transfer into, close to the Porta Collina, when from behind them came the deep boom of a horn and shouting so loud that it could be heard over the surrounding din. Looking back over his shoulder Vespasian could see the dyed-red horsehair-plumed helmets of a *turma* of cavalry, a troop of thirty men, wading through the crowd.

'We'd better wait for them to pass,' Titus said. 'They look to be Praetorian Guard cavalry and they're not very polite, especially if they're escorting someone important.'

They cleared the road as the turma approached, four abreast. Their white, high-stepping stallions, eyes rolling and mouths frothing at the bits, forced their way through the crowd, stopping for no one. Any fool unlucky enough to come too close was beaten aside by their riders with the flats of their swords or the butts of their spears.

'Make way, make way, imperial business, make way,' their decurion shouted. The trumpeter gave another blast on his horn. The guards' bronze breastplates and helmets inlaid with silver sparkled in the sunlight; red cloaks edged with gold billowed out behind them; everything about them spoke of the wealth and power of the imperial family that it was their duty to guard. They kept their formation with a rigid discipline, their muscular thighs and calves gripping the sweating flanks of their mounts, steering them in a straight line down the centre of the road. In the middle of the troop travelled an ornately carved wood and ivory litter whose occupants were enclosed by lavish maroon curtains decorated with astrological signs embroidered in gold and silver thread. From each corner protruded a pole that was supported at waist height by three massive Negro slaves marching in step, double time, in such a skilful manner that the litter appeared to glide along without so much as a jolt to disturb its precious cargo. The smoothness with which they carried the litter could only have been learnt by years of practice under the watchful eyes of overseers keen to punish any mistake with a liberal use of the whip.

Vespasian watched the imperial cortège scythe its way

down the Via Nomentana. 'Who do you think is in that, Father, the Emperor?'

'No, I doubt it. When he's not in Rome Tiberius spends more and more of his time down south and would never enter the city from this direction. That must be someone in the imperial household with estates up in the hills to the east,' Titus replied as the litter drew level with them.

Just then a rabid dog, foam oozing from its jaws, startled by the booming horn and the loud clatter of the horses, leapt out from under a cart close to Vespasian and launched itself at the lead group of Negroes. It sank its teeth into the left thigh of the man nearest the litter. He went down screaming, desperately trying to tear the maddened beast off him. His comrades stopped abruptly, causing their burden to sway from side to side. Guards immediately encircled the immobile litter, spears pointing out towards the onlooking crowd as their decurion raced back to assess the situation. He took one look at the unfortunate slave wrestling with the mad dog and with two quick thrusts of his spear put both out of their misery. He shouted a swift order and the guards re-formed their marching order and the column prepared to move forward.

Before it did the curtains of the litter opened slightly and a young girl looked out. Vespasian held his breath; he had never seen such beauty. Her thick black hair, which contrasted perfectly with her ivory skin, fell in ringlets that rested on her slender shoulders. Jewels hung from her ears and around her throat. Her lips, full and painted dark pink, sat perfectly between a delicately pointed nose and a firm, proud chin. But it was her eyes, two shining blue stars, that held him transfixed as they rested on his, for a few quickening heartbeats, before she withdrew back inside and the litter began to move forward again.

A loud snort brought him back to reality.

'Look at that, Father, your youngest son sitting there with his mouth flapping open like some carp just landed in a fisherman's net,' Sabinus roared. 'I think the poor little sod has just caught a shot from Cupid. I'd bet he'd give his right hand to know who she is. Not that it would help much, he's way below her league.'

Vespasian reddened as his father joined in the laughter. 'That, my boy, was the most vacant that I've ever seen you look. I don't suppose you liked her, did you?' Still chortling, he turned to order their guards to lead off.

Vespasian was left staring dumbstruck at the dead dog whose jaws were still locked on to the black slave's corpse. He had been hit by two thunderbolts in the space of as many hours: sudden, instant and inexplicable love for a city that he had only seen from afar and for a girl that he had only glimpsed for an instant. Who was she? But he'd probably never see her again. Gathering himself with difficulty, he turned his horse to follow his family, yet as he passed through the Porta Collina and entered Rome, his heart was still pounding.

CHAPTER VI

ONCE THROUGH THE gate the Via Nomentana narrowed so that two carts could just pass each other. The makeshift huts and tombs on either side were replaced by three-, four- or even five-storeyed tenements – *insulae* – that prevented the sun from reaching the street level except for an hour or so around midday. Each building had open-fronted shops on the ground level selling all manner of products. Costermongers squeezed in between pork butchers and leather-goods salesmen; stores selling live poultry next to taverns, barbers, fortune-tellers and purveyors of small statuettes of gods and heroes. Sweating smiths hammered at ironwork on open forges alongside tailors hunched over their stitching and bakers filling shelves with loaves, pastries and sweet buns.

The cries of the shopkeepers advertising their wares resounded in the air, which was already bursting with the aromas, both sweet and foul, given off by such a variety of human activity. Vespasian was overwhelmed by the throng of people, free, freed and slave, going about their everyday business pushing and shoving each other in an effort to remain on the raised pavements so as not to soil their feet in the mud, made up mainly of human and animal excrement, which covered the road.

On the outside of the lower buildings, in order to maximise the rentable living space inside, rickety wooden staircases led up to equally precarious balconies that gave access to the rooms on the first and second floors. Women, mainly, populated these upper levels; they scrubbed garments on wooden boards beneath lines of nearly clean washing that fluttered in the breeze. They prepared the evening meal, which would be cooked in the local baker's oven, whilst gossiping with their neighbours as their children squatted at their feet playing at knucklebones or dice. Brightly painted whores called out their services and fees to the passersby below and made lewd jokes with each other, cackling with unashamed laughter, whilst the elderly and the infirm just sat and stared greedily at the life they could no longer participate in.

An underclass of thieves, confidence tricksters, charlatans and cheats preyed on the unwary or the dull, weaving their way stealthily through the crowds looking for likely targets and picking them off with a finesse born of a lifetime's dishonesty. What profit they could not cream off they left to the lowest of the low: the beggars. Blind, diseased, maimed or malformed, they struggled, with a desperation known only to those who have nothing, to elicit some scraps or a small bronze coin from the few who cared enough to even notice them.

All forms of human existence were here – except the wealthy. They lived up on Rome's hills in the cleaner air, above the heaving masses that they saw only when they had to pass the squalor on their way through the city to or from their more fragrant country estates.

The Flavian party made its way along the street that plunged, downhill, straight as an arrow, towards the heart of Rome.

'We need to keep on this street until it divides in two, then we take the right-hand fork,' Titus called out to their hired guards, who were doing a fine job of easing their passage through the crowds. He turned to look at his younger son. 'Well, my boy, what do you think?' he asked.

'It's a lot bigger than Reate, Father,' Vespasian replied, grinning. 'Though in truth I don't know what to say . . . it is everything that I was expecting, except magnified by ten. I was prepared for a lot of people, but not this many. I knew that the buildings would be tall, but this tall? How do they stay up?'

'Well, sometimes they don't,' Titus replied. 'The landlords build these insulae as quickly and cheaply as possible, and then cram them with as many tenants as they can. They often collapse, and when they do they just put up another and to Hades with the poor buggers who got crushed to death. There'll always be people happy to pay rent to live in the city, even in a death trap; it's that or in the tomb shantytowns outside the walls. At least in the city the poor can take advantage of the free corn dole; the Emperor won't let his people starve, that would be political suicide. Anyone with any money will tell you that we are only ever an empty granary away from revolution.' His father smiled at Vespasian. 'But you don't have to worry about all that, it's no concern of ours; let others take care of their own as we do of ours.'

They came to the fork in the road. At its apex stood a tavern outside of which lounged a group of hard-looking men drinking and playing dice on rough wooden benches. As Titus' party took the right-hand fork one of the group stood up and approached Titus.

'You'll be needing protection, sir, if you're thinking of going down that road,' he said in a quiet, menacing voice. He had the build and cauliflower ears of a boxer; the scars on his face attested to his profession. He stood squarely in front of Titus and made no attempt to move as Titus tried to push his horse past him.

'I said that you'll be needing protection on that road. My name is Marcus Salvius Magnus and my crossroads fraternity here can provide you and your party with that reassurance,' he insisted. 'A denarius apiece for me and two of my lads will see you safe enough on your way.'

'And from whom do we need protecting, Magnus?' Titus asked, his voice filling with suppressed rage. 'You and your murdering bunch of cronies no doubt.'

'There's no need to be uncivil, sir,' the boxer replied. 'I just wouldn't advise you to proceed without an escort who knows the area. Who knows where to go and not to go, if you take my meaning?'

Titus struggled to control himself; the last thing he wanted to do was to lose his dignity to a mere thug. 'Why do we in particular need protection?' he asked and pointed to a passing group of travellers. 'What about them, why don't you offer them your protection?'

'They don't look like they could afford it, sir. Them that can't afford it don't need it, because if you're too poor to afford protection you're too poor to rob. Your party on the other hand looks as if it can afford to buy the protection that it therefore quite obviously needs.' Magnus looked pleased with the logic of the argument.

'Ah, but we have our protection, three armed guards all very capable of looking after themselves and us,' Titus said, gesturing towards the ex-legionaries who had now dismounted and drawn their daggers.

'And very lovely they look too, sir, but there are only three of them and there are a lot of very bad people down that way, I can assure you of that.'

'I'm sure you can,' Titus seethed, 'but what if we decide not to take your very well-meant advice?'

'Then that would be very risky, sir, and somewhat foolish, if I may be so bold.' Magnus gave a smile that did not reach his eyes. Behind him his comrades had started to get up; the whole situation was getting rapidly out of control.

'Just pay the man, Father,' Sabinus whispered, realising that they would come off worst if it came to a fight.

'Over my dead body,' his father replied forcefully.

'Let's hope that it doesn't come to that, sir. It's to prevent that that I'm offering you our services. Tell us where are you heading and we'll see you safely on your way,' Magnus insisted. The Flavian guards had now surrounded him, yet he showed no sign of backing down.

'Just what is going on here, Titus?' Vespasia had got down from her litter and stood next to her husband.

'These thugs wish to—'

'As I said, there is no need to be uncivil,' Magnus cut across him.

'Uncivil! You disgusting, uncultured ape,' Vespasia shouted. 'How dare you delay us? I shall speak to my brother as soon as I see him.'

'Hush, my dear, I'm afraid that won't help us at the moment.' Titus looked at Magnus' cronies, who were now completely blocking both their way forward and their retreat. He realised that fighting was futile and made a mental note to one day extract a painful revenge. 'We are going to the house of Gaius Vespasius Pollo,' he spat out, 'on the Quirinal.'

'What? The ex-praetor? Why didn't you say so before, my friend? That changes everything. I know him well; there'll be no charge. A silly misunderstanding; please accept my apologies, sir, madam, and pass on our greetings to the honourable senator.'

'I shall do no such thing, you impertinent little man,' Vespasia said darkly as she turned and made her way back to her litter.

'Nevertheless it will be our pleasure to escort you and your party to his house, sir. Sextus, Lucio, with me, we shall lead this noble family to their destination.' With that he walked off down the right-hand fork leaving the rest of the group to follow him.

'What was all that about, Father?' Vespasian asked Titus as they moved off.

'That, my boy, was part of the most powerful force in Rome after the Emperor and his Praetorians: the crossroads fraternities,' Titus replied, still bemused by the rapid turn of events. 'They're gangs who base themselves at all the major road junctions in the poorer areas of the city and extort money from the local traders, residents and people passing through by selling their protection. If you buy it they won't rob you, and if you don't they will. It's as simple as that.'

'But surely that's illegal,' Vespasian said appalled. 'Why doesn't the Emperor do something about it?'

'Well, it may sound strange but they are tolerated because they also do a lot of good.'

'What good can a bunch low-life who specialise in demanding money with menaces do?' Vespasian scoffed.

'Well, for a start, rather ironically, they keep the crime rate down in their areas just by being there. Other thieves caught operating on their patch get pretty rough justice from all accounts. If you think about it it's in their interest to keep their areas safe so that business will flourish; the more traders, the more money they rake in. On top of that they also look after the crossroads shrines. Your uncle evidently tolerates them at the very least, if not actively encourages them, judging by their reaction to his name just then.'

'You're making them sound like they're a good thing,

Father, a nice bunch of religious boys with nothing but the community's best interests at heart and supported by the great and the good.'

'Well, in a way yes, they are,' Titus said as they turned off the main road and started to make their way up the Quirinal Hill. 'However, they do have a very nasty habit of pursuing vendettas with rival gangs; and they're also prone to fighting other factions at the circus who support a different colour team to them.'

As they climbed the hill the insulae disappeared and were replaced by single-storey houses with no windows to the front, just a doorway. Narrow alleys separated them from each other, so that the effect was like one long wall with lots of doors in it. There were fewer people on the road up here, and those they did pass wore much finer clothing; even the slaves were well dressed. Already they could detect a difference in the air quality; the light breeze was blowing away the fumes of the city below whose hubbub had now been reduced to a faint murmur.

They had made a few turns left and right when Magnus stopped outside a yellow-painted house. 'This is the house of the senator Gaius Vespasius Pollo, good sirs,' he said, pulling on the bell chain. 'I'll leave you here. If there is ever anything that I can do for you, to make up for that unfortunate misunderstanding, please feel free to ask.'

He made to help a grim-looking Vespasia down from her litter, but she slapped his face. He bowed his apologies to her, wished them all a good day and left with his two companions, leaving his erstwhile charges waiting for the door to open.

'I shall be speaking to my brother about that ghastly man, Titus,' Vespasia said as she joined her husband. 'How dare such a low-life threaten people so far above him?'

'I don't think they care about the social standing of their intended victims, unless it is to judge how much they can extort from them, my dear,' Titus replied. Vespasia scowled at her husband aware he was mocking her, but was prevented from retorting by the door opening, revealing a man so old and frail that he was almost bent double. He peered at them with moist, bloodshot eyes.

'Who may I say is calling?' he asked in a reedy voice.

'Titus Flavius Sabinus and his wife Vespasia Polla and his two sons Sabinus and Vespasian,' Titus replied.

'Ah, yes, I have been told to expect you. Please come in and wait in the atrium. I shall announce you to my master,' the ancient retainer wheezed, bowing even lower as they filed past him. Vespasian was worried that he wouldn't be able to right himself again, but with the aid of a stick he heaved himself up, closed the door and hobbled off to find the senator at a speed that made it inevitable that they would be waiting for some time.

Vespasian looked around the room. It was almost twice the size of their atrium at home and decorated far more lavishly. Brightly coloured frescoes of naked young men hunting and wrestling, amongst other less noble activities, adorned the walls. Statues of well-formed gods, leaving nothing to the imagination, painted to look lifelike, inhabited niches between the frescoes. The floor was covered with the most beautifully executed mosaic showing a superbly muscled Achilles despatching a doe-eyed Hector, both also mysteriously without clothes. Vespasian noticed his mother grimace as she took in the surroundings and realised that she was the only feminine thing in the whole room.

'I am not sure that I approve of my brother's taste in décor,' she whispered to Titus. 'It's very vulgar and most unsuitable for our young lads. Why didn't you tell me, Titus? You have, after all, been here before.'

'So has Sabinus, don't forget, and it didn't seem to affect him adversely,' Titus pointed out, also sotto voce, slapping his eldest son on the shoulder. 'Besides, what would you have done had you known? Changed our plans? You've always been aware of your brother's foibles, so this can't come as too much of a surprise. Anyway, we're here now and cannot leave without causing great offence.'

'Foibles?' Vespasia snorted. 'Is that what you call them?'

Sabinus caught Vespasian's eye. 'Keep your back to the wall when Uncle Gaius is around, little brother.'

'That will do, Sabinus,' Titus hissed. 'Remember your uncle is to be honoured and respected.'

'But not submitted to,' Vespasian mumbled under his breath, unable to resist a smile, which was greeted by a fierce look from his mother.

'Whatever else my brother may be, he's very influential, so do as your father says and keep your thoughts to yourself.'

Vespasian nodded his assent and tried not to stare at the frescoes.

'Vespasia! How lovely to see you again,' boomed a deep voice in an accent that Vespasian recognised as being very close to his own. 'And, Titus, my friend, what a pleasure.'

Vespasian looked up to see a hugely fat man waddle into the room. He was dressed in a white tunic with a thick purple stripe down the front that struggled to cover his bulk; any belt that he may have been wearing had disappeared in the rolls of fat that wobbled as he walked. His round face showed signs of make-up, rouge on the cheeks and kohl around the eyes. It was framed by a series of carefully tonged brown curls that covered his ears and forehead. On his feet, which seemed far too small for his body, he wore a delicate little pair of red leather slippers. Vespasian had never seen anyone so outlandish in his life and had to fight to suppress a gasp.

Gaius came forward and embraced his sister. Despite her distaste for his lifestyle and obvious surprise at his size, she seemed genuinely pleased to see her brother and submitted to his affectionate greeting.

'Gaius, it has been too long,' she said as he released her from the folds of his body. 'I trust that we find you well.'

'Never better, never better,' he replied, taking Titus' arm in a firm grip. 'You're looking well, my friend; the country air must suit you. Is that why you don't come to Rome more often? Well, you're here now and it will be my pleasure to offer you all hospitality. Now, Sabinus, it's been four years since you were here and it must be ten years since I last saw Vespasian.'

The brothers stepped forward and bowed their heads to their uncle, who put a hand on each of their shoulders and looked them up and down. 'Fine boys, Titus, fine boys, you must be very proud. Sabinus, I look forward to hearing about your military service. I'm sure that it was the making of you.'

'Indeed it was, Uncle,' Sabinus replied. 'And now I wish for a junior magistrate's position.'

'Of course you do, and you shall have it, my boy, you shall.' Gaius turned to Vespasian. 'And what does the younger brother want, eh?'

'To try to serve Rome and my family,' he replied.

'Well said, my boy, you'll go far with that attitude.' Gaius squeezed Vespasian's arm. 'But in what capacity first, eh? The army?'

'Yes, Uncle, like Sabinus, as a military tribune.'

'Excellent. I'm sure that can be arranged, I still have connections with the two legions in which I served.' Gaius saw Vespasian's eyes widen in disbelief, and laughed. 'Oh, dear boy, do you think that I was this size all my life?'

Vespasian reddened, mortified that his thoughts had been read.

'No, I was once as fit as you two, as your mother will confirm. I choose to be this way now; or rather I choose the good life that makes me this way. Rome now has an emperor who tolerates lifestyles like mine, unlike his predecessor, the divine Augustus, who was a prude who led an austere life and expected everyone else to do so too. The gods bless Tiberius for allowing me to indulge myself and to be fat and happy.' He smiled at Vespasian. 'Well, let us hope that I can be of service in promoting your careers in this fine city of ours. That is after all what you are here for, eh, boys?' Gaius chuckled.

'Yes, Uncle, thank you,' the brothers said in unison.

'No, no, don't thank me yet, I haven't done anything. Wait until you have just cause, then I trust that you'll find a way to thank me,' Gaius said, turning back to his sister. 'Now, Vespasia, I'll have you shown to your rooms, then I'm sure that you would all appreciate a bath and a change of clothes after your journey; I have a set of very excellent baths here, unless of course you would prefer to go to the public ones?'

'No, Gaius, we would be most happy to use yours,' Vespasia replied.

'As you will. I shall have them brought up to temperature immediately.'

He clapped his hands and four house slaves appeared from the corner of the room. They were all youths in their early teens with long blond hair down to their shoulders. They wore bright red tunics that seemed very short to Vespasian's eye.

'These boys will show you to your accommodation,' Gaius said. He looked apologetically at his sister. 'I'm afraid, Vespasia, that there is a shortage of female slaves in this household. I trust that you have brought your own.'

'Indeed, brother, they are outside with the rest of our belongings.'

'Excellent, I'll have Priscus my steward make arrangements for them all. Now, please, make yourselves comfortable, I'll see you when you are refreshed, and then we shall make plans for these boys of yours.'

The bath had indeed been refreshing, although both Vespasian and Sabinus had felt a little disconcerted at being expertly massaged and then rubbed down by two very pretty youths, who, despite their age, seemed to have no hair on their bodies at all, apart from their long golden locks.

They had joined their parents who were sitting in the shade in the courtyard garden. It was dominated by a statue of an unnecessarily large Apollo placed in the middle of the fishpond at the centre of the garden. Vespasian was sitting at the pond's edge idly trailing his fingers in the water when Gaius arrived.

'Don't do that, dear boy,' he warned. 'That pond contains my lampreys; they'll dig their teeth into your finger in a trice, given the chance. Unfortunately they enjoy eating us as much as we enjoy eating them,' he said cheerily as he sat on a stool proffered by yet another beautiful slave boy. 'One of my slaves fell in last year and was dead before he could be pulled out. Apparently the whole pool just seethed as they rushed to sink their teeth into him. I believe he died of shock. I was furious as I was particularly fond of the lad and had only recently bought him.'

Vespasian quickly moved away from the pond and sat down next to Titus. Two more slave boys appeared, one with a table and the other with a tray of sweet cakes.

'It's my custom at this time of day to take something

sweet,' Gaius said as one of the boys set down the table. 'I do hope you will join me, it will be a little while before dinner is served.'

The boy with the tray bowed to Vespasia and offered a cake, displaying as he did a pair of smooth well-shaped buttocks and a tight, hairless scrotum, which Gaius eyed appreciatively. Vespasian felt his father, next to him, shift uncomfortably in his chair at the sight and wondered how his mother would react when his side of the table was being served. Thankfully Gaius became aware of his guests' discomfort and before Vespasia was subjected to the ordeal he slapped the boy's arse.

'Arminius, how dare you serve my guests in a state of undress? Go and put your loincloth on at once.'

The boy stared uncomprehendingly at his master, having obviously never before been told to put on that particular item of clothing, if indeed he even possessed one.

'Go!' Gaius barked. 'And leave the cakes on the table.'

The poor boy did as he was told and ran off. Gaius smiled at his guests. 'I must apologise, they can be very forgetful, these Germans. Good workers, but a bit sloppy.'

'Please don't mention it, Gaius,' Titus replied. 'No harm done. Are all your slaves Germans? I believe they are very expensive.'

'Oh, they are, but worth every denarius,' Gaius said with a faraway look in his eye. 'I have mainly Germans, but also a couple of Mesopotamians and a Briton.'

'Where are Britons from?' Vespasian asked.

'Britannia, an island to the north of Gaul. Surely you've read Caesar? He went there twice over seventy years ago, but they were a vicious bunch and he never managed to subdue them; that will be someone else's task in the future, no doubt. But come, Titus, haven't you given the boys any education. Surely they must have read the classics?'

'I'm afraid Vespasian was more interested in husbandry than history, and much of his reading was neglected.'

'That is something that must be repaired. Vespasian, I shall lend you my copy of Caesar's *Gallic Wars*; in it you will learn about Britannia and Gaul and Germania as well. You need to know these things as a soldier; who knows where you'll be posted? You boys may have free use of my library whilst you are my guests.'

'That is most kind, dear brother,' Vespasia said. 'I shall make sure the boys use it to their best advantage.'

Gaius gestured to the cakes. 'Please, in the absence of a serving boy help yourselves, these almond and cinnamon cakes are particularly good. Tuck in, my boys, we have a busy day tomorrow so you need to get your strength up.'

'What have you planned for tomorrow, Gaius?' Vespasia asked.

'Your boys need to be seen and introduced,' Gaius replied, stuffing a cake between his plump, moist lips. 'Tomorrow is yet another public holiday, so where better to go to be seen and introduced than at the chariot races in the Circus Maximus?'

CHAPTER VII

AT DAWN THE ancient doorkeeper opened up and admitted the crowd of clients waiting outside to pay their morning respects to their patron. Gaius sat on a stool near the hearth and greeted each of his forty or more clients in order of precedence. Vespasian and Sabinus sat on either side of him and were introduced only to those deemed worthy enough. A young secretary stood behind them taking notes on a wax tablet of any verbal requests, and receiving written petitions from those clients who had problems that they thought could be resolved by their patron.

Those for whom Gaius had some use that day were asked to wait by his study for a private interview. The rest were all given something to eat and drink and then they waited in respectful silence near the door for their patron's departure. Each held a small purse of coins that, as it was a race day, had been given to them to gamble with. Once the greeting was over Gaius disappeared into his study and dealt with the return favours that he needed from those indebted to him. Vespasian was impressed by the quiet dignity with which both clients and patron conducted themselves as they exploited to the full this symbiotic relationship.

Business concluded, Gaius waddled out of his study and caught sight of Vespasian. 'Dear boy, be so good as to fetch your parents. It's time we were leaving; the crowds will be horrendous.'

Once all were assembled in the atrium Gaius made an offering to his household gods, mumbled a prayer, and then made his way outside followed by his family and then his clients. To Vespasian's surprise, waiting to escort the large party through Rome to the circus were Magnus and six of his crossroads brothers, all sporting sturdy staffs.

'What are these men doing here, Gaius?' Vespasia asked. 'They threatened us yesterday and showed no respect to their betters. I meant to have a word with you about them last night.'

'Good morning, madam, please accept my apologies for yesterday—' Magnus began.

'Have some manners whipped into this man, Gaius,' Vespasia demanded.

'Calm my dear,' Gaius soothed, 'Magnus is—'

'Magnus!' Vespasia exclaimed. 'That's a very big name for such a little crook.'

'My grandfather fought for Pompeius Magnus at Pharsalus. He named—'

'I've no interest in your sordid little family's history.'

Gaius stepped between them. 'Vespasia, please. Magnus is a trusted friend of mine and a great source of information.

For my sake, won't you overlook this misjudgement on his part and let us be on our way to the circus? He and his comrades will prove their worth by beating a path through the crowds.'

Vespasia paused and looked down her nose at Magnus and his men who bowed their heads in abject apology.

'Very well, brother, for your sake I shall,' she replied loftily.

Magnus nodded in acknowledgement and then turned to Gaius. 'I assume that you are heading to your normal place, the senators' seats to the left of the imperial box.'

'Indeed we are, my good man; I've had five slaves there reserving seats since before dawn.'

Gaius headed off down the Quirinal Hill surrounded by his family, clients and bodyguards. As they descended Vespasian saw many similar parties of important-looking men escorted by crowds of hangers-on; the more important the man, the bigger the crowd. All were heading in the same direction: to the games.

Nearer the circus the crowds did indeed become horrendous, as Gaius had predicted. Magnus and his brothers sweated as they pushed through the hordes of race-goers all sporting the colours of their favourite team, Red, Green, White or Blue. They cheered passing groups of the same faction and hissed and jeered supporters of the opposition. They chanted songs praising their teams at the tops of their voices whilst waving the coloured flags that proclaimed their allegiance. Here and there scuffles would break out as the press of the crowd forced two rival groups into each other, but in general the mood was good-natured, mainly because it was too early in the morning for anyone yet to have drunk too much.

They passed groups of racing horses and wagonloads of chariots and equipment being transported from the four teams' stables on the Campus Martius outside the northern walls of the city to their race-day bases.

'They'll be bringing horses in and out all day,' Gaius shouted above the din. 'With twelve races of twelve chariots each, most of which will be four-horse, they'll get through a lot of animals.'

'Five hundred and seventy-six,' Vespasian said without thinking.

Sabinus scoffed but dared not criticise his brother's calculation in case it was right.

'And at least another two hundred spares,' Gaius said, raising an eyebrow at the speed of his nephew's arithmetic. 'Plus the mounts of the *hortatores*, the riders who lead each of the chariot teams around.'

Vespasian savoured the atmosphere. His mind filled with the images of the city that they had passed on their mile-long journey: the arches on the Sacred Way; the temple of Jupiter, resplendent in the early-morning sun, perched on the Capitoline Hill above the Forum Romanum; the Senate House and next to it the Rostra, adorned with the rams of Carthaginian ships captured in the battles of Mylae and Cape

Ecnomus in Rome's first struggle with its ancient foe long, long ago. He had seen the new forum of Augustus, the forum of Caesar and other public buildings both religious and civic, buildings he had only heard of, never seen, and had been struck dumb by their size, splendour and beauty.

The outer walls of the circus were now in sight. Four storeys high, they rose majestically above the swarms of people pushing and shoving their way through their arches and into the belly of the building. Once in they would make their way through the colonnaded interior, filled with vendors of hot food, cushions, wine and other necessities, then up one of the many sets of marble steps that led into the huge stadium seating nearly a quarter of a million people.

To his right Vespasian could see the temporary camps of the racing factions set up in the Forum Boarium in front of the narrow, straight end of the circus, through which all the competitors would enter. Thuggish-looking guards, who made Magnus and his friends look like acolytes at a religious ceremony, kept this area secured from the riff-raff keen on getting a sneak preview of the teams being readied for the day.

They passed underneath an arch into the heaving bowels of the circus and Gaius' party started to diminish as his clients paid their respects to their patron and wished him good fortune, before leaving to try their luck gaining access through one of the many public entrances. Magnus' job became increasingly difficult in amongst the colonnaded passageways, beating a path through the tightly packed mass of humanity, occasionally pausing to give way to another party of higher status, then following on in their wake. Slowly they made their way to the entrances reserved for senators and their guests.

Gaius called out greetings to acquaintances as they passed close in the heaving mêlée: 'Good day to you, Lucius, may the gods smile on you and give you good fortune . . . Postumus, I hope your Whites fare better today. I shall be backing them in the second race . . .' all the time giving Vespasian and Sabinus a brief résumé of who they were and how influential they may or may not be.

Close by a fight broke out as one of the entrances was closed, being full to capacity, leaving hundreds of people stranded outside and forced to try to get in through another gate – all of which were already choked with eager race-goers desperate for a seat inside. Screams and shouts filled the air as skulls and bones were cracked by club-wielding marshals, who, intent on pulling shut the gates, fiercely pushed back the disappointed many who had arrived too late to get in.

Eventually Magnus and his brothers forced their way through to the far less congested senators' entrance.

'I shall leave you here, sir,' Magnus said as he and his fellows turned to go. 'May fortune favour you and your companions.'

'And you and yours, Magnus,' Gaius replied, slipping him a weighty purse. 'Use this well, although I have no doubt that you will just bet on your beloved Greens without any thought of who's driving and how their current form is.'

'Well, sir, once a Green always a Green,' Magnus said seriously as he left.

Gaius smiled and pulled out a wooden ticket from within the folds of his toga and showed it to the marshal on the gate, who bowed and let the party through into the long passageway that led up to the stadium.

Nothing could have prepared Vespasian for the sight that greeted him as he came out of the tunnel into the sun-filled circus. Over two hundred thousand people, a quarter of Rome's population, were crammed into the huge seating areas that surrounded the track, a hundred paces wide, a third of a mile long. Down its middle, slightly offset to one side and closer to one end of the arena than the other, ran the *spina*: a long, low barrier eight paces wide with turning posts at each end, around which the races were run. Between the turning posts the spina was ornamented with an obelisk brought back by Augustus from Egypt as well as huge statues of the gods, which were spaced far enough apart so as not to obscure the view of the other side of the track. Above the seating areas long colonnaded walkways ran the length of the stadium in which thousands more people not lucky enough to get a seat would spend the day standing, thankful that they had got in at all. Behind the colonnades on either side could be seen the rich buildings and luxurious gardens on the Palatine and Aventine, for the Circus Maximus was set in the valley dividing the two hills.

The cheers of the crowd echoed around the stadium as

they enjoyed the antics of a group of *desultores*, acrobatic riders dressed in loincloths and strange conical hats, who, before the racing started, hurtled around the track at full gallop leaping from one horse to another in rhythm. They cracked their long whips every time they landed on a new mount to the raucous appreciation of the crowd. For their finale they stood on the backs of their horses and in unison did a backwards somersault to land astride their mounts again; the crowd was ecstatic.

'I can see my boys down there,' Gaius shouted over the roar. 'Follow me.' He led them off down the steps between two areas of seats at a pace that belied his bulk. Halfway down he turned right along a narrow walkway passing between rows of seated senators who were all enjoying the spectacle as much as the masses that surrounded them, cheering the riders as they left the arena to be replaced by a small army of slaves with brushes who began to smooth the sand in preparation for the first race.

'Well done, boys,' Gaius cried to five angelic-looking house slaves sitting in a line at the end of a row. 'Excellent seats indeed.' He gave them each a silver coin. 'Go and enjoy yourselves, my dears. I expect you back at the house after the end of the last race.'

The boys left, leaving five plump cushions and a large bag containing enough food and drink to last the party for the day.

'It was rumoured that the Emperor himself may be attending today,' Gaius said as they took their seats. 'Which is very rare, as Tiberius hates appearing in public and doesn't take any interest in racing. Perhaps he just wants to remind the public what he looks like.'

'Where will he sit?' Vespasian enquired.

'Why, there, in the imperial box,' his uncle replied, pointing to a richly decorated enclosure in line with the turning post at the wide end of the track, twenty paces to their right and slightly below them. A marble roof, supported by painted pillars, jutted out from the main body of the stadium, shading an area furnished with chairs, couches and soft rugs. 'We shall have an excellent view of him, but more to the point he will be able to see us, if he so wishes.

'Now, down to the business of placing our bets on the first race.' Gaius paused and adjusted his cushion so that it supported the entirety of his ample behind; once satisfied he continued: 'You will notice that there are lots of slaves with leather bags tied around their waists going around the crowd; they're the runners for the bookmakers stationed around the track above and below us.

'Before each race the teams are announced and paraded once around the track so the crowd can inspect them. Each of the four Colours usually enters three teams in a race, so you have no more than twelve to choose from. Now, you can bet on anything you like, the winner, first and second, on someone not finishing or even all three teams of one Colour not finishing – whatever you want. Once you've decided on your bet you attract the attention of some of these slaves and they will tell you the odds that their masters are offering; you choose the best and give him your money and in return he will give you a receipt pre-signed by his master. If you win the slave will return and give you your winnings once you've produced the receipt.'

There was a stirring in the crowd and a group of twenty men, half carrying large horns that curled around their bodies, the others long straight trumpets, marched on to the roof of the imperial box. On a signal from their leader they raised their instruments to their lips and sounded a deep sonorous fanfare that seemed to go on for an age. The crowd hushed and a man in shining military uniform came to the front of the imperial box.

'That's Sejanus, prefect of the Praetorians,' Gaius whispered, 'an adder in the long grass if ever there was one.'

Sejanus raised his arms. 'People of Rome,' he shouted. His voice was strong and carried all the way around the enormous structure. 'We are blessed today with the presence of our glorious Emperor, here to support the Consul, Marcus Asinius Agrippa, by whose generosity these games are being held. Hail Tiberius Caesar Augustus.'

A tall, broad-shouldered man with thinning grey hair, which he wore short at the front and longer at the back so it covered the nape of his neck, strode out to the front of the imperial box with the confidence of a man used to supreme power. The crowd stood as one and bellowed a series of mighty shouts of 'Hail, Tiberius'. Vespasian wholeheartedly joined in the chorus as he got his first view of the most powerful man in the world. Dressed in purple tunic and toga,

Tiberius held out his hands in acknowledgement of the ovation and then gestured to a man behind him to step forward.

'That's Asinius Agrippa,' Gaius shouted above the din, 'one of the richest men in Rome. He's sponsoring these games to ingratiate himself with the Emperor. Rumour has it that he's after the governorship of Syria when his term of office as consul finishes at the end of the year. The money he has spent on these games will seem like small change compared to what he'll cream off there, should Tiberius grant it.'

Asinius raised his arms and the large gates at each end of the arena opened. Out marched about a hundred slaves carrying buckets filled with coins of all denominations, which they hurled to all corners of the delirious crowd.

'I see what you mean, Uncle,' Vespasian shouted, catching a sestertius out of the metal rain, 'but surely this is excessive.'

'Of course it is, but it keeps the people happy and perhaps Tiberius will remember it when he comes to appointing the new governors.'

Around him Vespasian noticed that more than a few of the senators were making no attempt to pick up any of the coins that fell amongst them and had sat down with seriously disgruntled expressions on their faces. With such a lavish display of largesse Asinius had evidently managed to offend many of his peers. Asinius himself seemed oblivious of this and, basking in the reflected glory of his Emperor and the adulation of the crowd, gave another signal. The horns and trumpets rang out again and the crowd quietened and sat back down. The gates, to Vespasian's right, opened revealing the twelve four-horse chariots that would contest the first race.

The three chariots of the Red team entered first. All the horses had dyed red plumes of feathers on their heads and their tails were tied up with red ribbons. The small, light chariots, made of strong red fabric stretched over a wooden frame, had long, slightly upwardly curving poles ending in a carved ram's head. Although harnessed four abreast only the two inner horses were yoked to the pole at their withers, the outer two being attached to the chariot by traces. Two small eight-spoked wheels with iron tyres gave the vehicles a low centre of gravity making them easier to control. The charioteers all sported bright red sleeveless tunics and had a lacing of leather straps around their torsos to protect their ribs in a crash. To prevent them being dragged to their deaths they wore in their straps a curved dagger that they would use, should they fall off, to cut the reins that were wrapped around their waists. Leather wrappings around their legs, a hardened leather helmet and long four-lash whips completed their uniform.

Heralds around the stadium, struggling to make themselves heard, called out the names of the drivers and horses of each of the three teams. They were greeted with cheers from the Red factions in the crowd and hisses from the rest. Next in came the Blues.

'Driving the first Blue chariot,' the heralds bellowed, 'is

Euprepes, son of Telesphoros. It is pulled by Argutus on the outside, Diresor and Dignus in the middle and Linon on the inside.'

The Blues in the crowd cheered their approval.

Gaius leaned over to Titus. 'That's the team I fancy to win; Euprepes has won over seven hundred races, two hundred of them at least for the Blues, and three times with this team of Iberian stallions already this year; and Linon is the steadiest of inside horses on the turns.'

'In that case I shall take your advice, my friend, and have ten denarii on the Blue first team,' Titus replied, signalling to a couple of passing bookmakers' slaves.

'Father, that is a lot of money to throw away on a bet,' Vespasian said, frowning. Innately careful with money, he found it hard to enter into the spirit of the day.

'Don't be so parsimonious, little brother,' Sabinus scoffed as the heralds started to announce the White teams. 'We're here to gamble, not save. I'll have ten denarii on the Blue first team too.'

'Dear gods,' Gaius said, looking worried, 'it had better win or I shall be in big trouble. That's the last tip I'll give today, my nerves won't stand it.'

Vespasia gave a half-smile. 'I should hope so, Gaius, I'm not sure that I approve of all this gambling.' Then, turning to the bookmakers' slaves, she asked, 'What are the odds for the White third team?'

'My master will give you twelve to one on Gentius, or five for a White to win,' replied the first.

'Mine is offering fifteen, or six for a White win,' said the second.

'In which case I'll have two denarii at fifteen to one on Gentius.'

'Mother!' Vespasian exclaimed, outraged.

'Oh, don't be such a prude, it's only a bit of fun,' she said, handing over the two coins and receiving a receipt in exchange. 'Perhaps you should try placing a bet, you might find that you enjoy the race more with money resting on it.'

'I don't need to bet on a race to enjoy it,' Vespasian replied huffily.

Titus, Sabinus and Gaius managed to get three to one on Euprepes off the first bookmaker's slave, which Gaius reckoned to be reasonable odds for the favourite.

The heralds had just finished announcing the Green teams when there was a stirring in the imperial box. Tiberius got to his feet and greeted with apparent affection a tall elegant woman draped in a black palla that covered her hair and fell down in folds to below her knees. Under this could be seen a deep red stola that reached her ankles; she looked every inch a respectable and powerful Roman matron of the old school.

'That's Antonia,' Gaius said quite excitedly, 'Tiberius' sister-in-law. Tiberius made her eldest son, Germanicus, his heir as part of the deal that he struck with Augustus when he was adopted by him. Germanicus, however, died six years ago and then Drusus, Tiberius' natural son who was married to Antonia's daughter, Livilla, died four years later, so now the succession isn't clear at all,' he said, looking at Vespasian, who didn't think that it ever did seem clear. 'Anyway, Antonia's other son Claudius is such a booby the talk is that the purple will skip a generation and go to Tiberius' grandson Gemellus or one of Germanicus' children.' He looked around nervously and whispered: 'There's even talk that the old Republic might be reinstated.'

Vespasian looked over at the lady with interest as Gaius carried on his lecture. She seemed to be right at the heart of imperial politics.

'As chance would have it, I was able to perform a couple of considerable favours for her when I was Governor of Aquitania and am now very much in her favour. With luck I shall be able to introduce you boys to her.' He looked at Vespasian, expecting an enthusiastic response, only to find his nephew staring, slack-jawed, at the imperial box.

'Dear boy, whatever's the matter? You look as if you've seen a ghost.'

Sabinus, picking up on his brother's state of shock, followed his gaze and laughed. 'No, Uncle, that's not a ghost, that's a girl. There's a huge difference.'

'Well, I'm no expert on either, as you know.'

Vespasian could barely believe his eyes; in the imperial box helping Antonia to her seat was the girl in the litter who had looked at him with such intensity, only yesterday, on the Via Nomentana. She was the slave of the most powerful woman in Rome.

CHAPTER VIII

THE CHARIOTS HAD completed a circuit of the track and were now waiting to be loaded into the starting boxes either side of the gate through which they had entered. These were set on a curved line, staggered so that no one would be disadvantaged as they were funnelled into the right-hand side of the spina. The starter drew numbered balls from a revolving urn; as each team's number was called out its driver chose which of the twelve boxes to start from.

'This is the tricky bit,' Gaius said. 'Tactically it would be best for our team to have the other two Blue chariots either side of him to shield him from the opposition on the first bend. You can bet your life that the other teams will try and drive him into the spina or the outside wall.'

'Are they allowed to do that?' Vespasian asked, still staring at the girl in the hope that she would notice him.

'Of course. They can do anything they want; there are no rules. The winner is the first to complete seven laps; how you do it is up to you.'

The Red second team had already chosen the outside box and the White third team, driven by Gentius, the inside box when the Blue first team was called; Euprepes made straight for the second box on the left, next to Gentius; the knowledgeable crowd cheered.

'That's a very bold move,' Gaius said. 'He's sacrificing the chance of cover on one side for the inside track; he must be gambling that he can beat Gentius to the first corner.'

With the chariots all installed in the boxes the spring-loaded double doors were heaved closed and each secured with an iron bolt leaving the teams, unable to see out of their temporary prisons, waiting for the fanfare that would precede the start of the race.

The tension in the crowd heightened as the hortatores, again twelve in number, three of each Colour, galloped into the arena. Each of these horsemen was assigned to lead one team round the track, guiding them through the dust and confusion of the race, indicating good opportunities ahead and warning of obstacles and dangers.

'Do you know that girl, Uncle?' Vespasian had finally got up the courage to ask.

'Antonia's slave girl? Yes, I do,' Gaius replied, watching Asinius get to his feet and walk up to the front of the royal box.

'Well?'

'Well, what?'

'Well, what's her name?'

'Caenis; but take my advice and forget her. Not only is she a slave, but she is someone else's slave and a very powerful someone else at that, who wouldn't take too kindly to having their property interfered with.'

'Caenis,' Vespasian repeated, looking back over to the imperial box. As he did so the girl looked round and, for the second time in two days, their eyes met. Caenis started, knocking into her mistress, who followed her gaze to see what had disturbed her. Antonia studied Vespasian for a brief moment, and then seeing he was seated next to Gaius nodded his uncle a greeting, which he returned with a melodramatic flourish. Antonia turned back round and said something to Caenis, who smiled in response, and then engaged in a whispered conversation with Asinius. Vespasian, who could not keep his eyes off the imperial box, felt sure that the Consul's eyes flicked over Antonia's shoulder in his direction a couple of times.

Another fanfare rang out and Asinius broke off the conversation, walked to the front of the imperial box and raised a white napkin; the crowd fell silent, all eyes were on him. Vespasian could hear the snorting and whinnying of the horses in the starting boxes anxious to be released. The hortatores, who had positioned themselves in a line about fifty paces in front of their respective starting boxes, struggled to control their frisky mounts, which had been unnerved by the sudden silence.

Asinius paused for dramatic effect and then, after what seemed like an age, dropped the napkin. The starter hauled on a rope that simultaneously released the bolts that held all the doors shut. A pole behind each door, one end of which was inserted into a highly tensioned, twisted bundle of sinews, snapped forward and all twenty-four doors opened as one with a loud crash, releasing the teams who hurtled forward in a cloud of dust to the joyous roar of the crowd.

The chariots thundered in a straight line towards the right-hand side of the spina. There, 170 paces away, was a white line that ran from the turning post at the end of the spina to the outer wall; once across this they were free to take whatever line they wanted. The staggered nature of the starting boxes ensured that all twelve chariots crossed it almost simultaneously as they reached speeds of over forty miles an hour.

Euprepes' gamble had not paid off; he was still level with Gentius as they skimmed past the edge of the barrier, clearing it by no more than a hand's breadth. Instead of turning left immediately and heading up the track, Gentius pursued a straight line forcing Euprepes further away from the centre of the track and closer to the Green outside him who was now trying to cut across his path. Being in imminent danger of being crushed between the two, Euprepes leant back on the reins about his waist and, with all his might, pulled hard to the left; his team slowed dramatically. As Gentius shot past Euprepes veered left, just clearing the rear of the White chariot and headed up the track hugging the spina. The Blues in the crowd went wild at this audacious manoeuvre, punching the air and screaming themselves hoarse.

Gentius, not to be distracted from his tactics, stuck to his straight line, forcing the Green to his right to abandon his attempt to cut across and pushing him towards the next team outside who, in turn, swerved to the right causing a chain reaction down the line. On the far outside the Red second driver saw the danger that was dominoing towards him and quickly checked his speed as the White first team next to him was forced across his path, its driver desperately trying to force a passage back to the left, but prevented from so doing by the weight of the teams inside him. His outside horse hit the wall, ripping a huge chunk of flesh from its shoulder. It stumbled heavily, its head hitting the floor; the momentum of the beast's team-mates pulled the chariot forward on to its hocks and lifted its rump into the air. The terrified whinny the animal emitted as it somersaulted was cut short as the weight of its hindquarters snapped its neck. It dropped stone dead. The White chariot bumped over the body and spun on to its side, dislodging its driver, who was dragged along the arena floor by the three remaining petrified horses. He frantically reached for his knife as the traces that attached the upturned chariot to the dead weight of the lifeless horse reached straining point and, with a sharp crack, tore the flimsy vehicle in two. An instant later the hapless driver was dragged forward by three of the sets of reins tied around his waist; the fourth set, anchored by the dead animal behind him, suddenly tautened and he was jerked up into the air as the two opposite forces shattered his ribcage and yanked his pelvis from his backbone. The three stampeding horses were briefly checked but their momentum snapped the trailing rein and they sped off, hauling behind them the wreckage of the chariot and the broken, unconscious driver.

'I love the first corner,' Gaius shouted above the roar to his companions. 'Your Gentius made a smart move, Vespasia; I thought we would lose our money before the race had barely begun.'

'Yes, but he put one of his own faction out and your Blues are now two lengths ahead of the rest,' Vespasia replied as the favourite Blue team followed its hortator into the first 180-degree turn.

Euprepes slowed his team down to take the bend as close to the turning post as possible; he leant back on the reins and out to his left to prevent the chariot from tipping over. He swung the team round, cracked his whip over their withers and accelerated them down the narrower side of the spina with the ten remaining chariots in hot pursuit.

'He mustn't tire his team too soon, Gaius, there's over three miles to go,' Titus shouted.

'No, but Vespasia's Whites and the Red second team are pushing him hard and the lead Green is also picking up speed,' Gaius puffed, his flabby face red with excitement.

The Blue second and third teams came screaming out of the narrow bend just behind the Green. They cracked their whips over their horses' ears and yelled them on; the extra turn of speed pulled them almost level. Determined not to be caught between the spina and two rival teams the Green driver pulled the reins to the right, causing his team to shoulder barge the Blues next to him. Unable to pull over because of his colleague outside him, the Blue driver decided to risk himself rather than back off and, pulling his knife out ready to cut the reins, hauled his team to the left, pushing the Green chariot into the spina. Its delicate wheel shattered on impact and tipped the chariot against the wall. The driver drew his knife, cut through the reins in an instant and, without looking back, bailed out into the path of the following White team, disappearing under their hooves in a flurry of dust and blood. Deprived of his weight his chariot flew up into the air and twisted round, pulling down its team in a frenzy of thrashing legs and arching backs, before hitting the Blue driver, knocking the knife from his hand and him clean out of his vehicle. The following White team ploughed straight into the wreckage, smashing the legs of the two inner horses as they tried, but failed, to jump the stricken chariot's pole barring their way. The last four chariots managed to swerve around the crash. A gang of slaves rushed out to clear the debris before the teams came round again.

Euprepes was approaching the second 180-degree turn that would complete the first lap; he could see his hortator ahead of him signalling that there was no wreckage around the blind corner as he slowed to take it. Both Gentius and the Red team closest to him sped past, choosing to take the longer route at more speed.

'They're going to try and pass him on the outside,' Vespasia shouted, forgetting, for a moment, her decorum as the first of the seven bronze dolphins set in a row high above one end of the spina was tilted down to mark the completion of the first lap.

Despite the frenetic excitement Vespasian's gaze kept straying to the imperial box in the hope of the chance of one more glimpse of those beautiful eyes, but they were kept firmly fixed on the race; though he sensed that she was restraining herself from looking round.

He turned back to the race. The eight remaining teams had rounded the narrower corner at the far end of the arena and were now racing back down towards the senators' enclosure. Their hortatores were desperately signalling the position of the Green and White crash and the party working frantically in the dust trying to carry away a freed chariot. The slaves looked with terror at the fast-approaching chariots and sprinted for their lives to the safety of the sides, abandoning the wreck ten paces away from the spina. Two of the hortatores jumped the obstacle, earning a loud roar of approval from the crowd. Euprepes, realising that there was only room for one chariot to pass between it and the central barrier, steered straight down the middle of the gap. Half a length back to his right the Red, a brazen-haired Celt, looked nervously at Gentius just outside him, but as the wreck approached Gentius refused to give way, leaving the Celt no choice but to slow and follow Euprepes through the gap. His loss of momentum not only enabled Euprepes and Gentius to pull away but also helped the chasing Blue who had taken the outside route behind Gentius to draw level with him as they rounded the turning post at the end of the second lap.

The second dolphin was lowered and Vespasian ventured

another look towards the imperial box. She had gone. Vespasian looked closer; there was Tiberius passing some remark to Asinius on his right; beyond them sat Antonia. The only other people in the box were Sejanus and four of his Praetorians, all standing towards the back.

Gaius noticed his nephew's distraction. 'Stop looking for her, dear boy, she's probably gone on an errand for her mistress. Come on, you're missing the race. It's nearly halfway through.'

A roar from the crowd as the second Green team came to grief brought Vespasian's attention back to the track as the third dolphin was lowered. The Blue chariot of Euprepes was just holding off the White of Gentius, with the Red Celt boxed in behind by Euprepes' Blue team-mate as they raced up the far straight. Only seven chariots were still going as Euprepes rounded the bend, narrowly missing four slaves carrying the unconscious Green driver out.

With Gentius, the Red Celt and his Blue colleague in close pursuit, Euprepes cracked his whip and mercilessly exhorted his sweating team on to an even greater pace. The fourth dolphin was lowered and Vespasian glanced back across to the imperial box; the slender figure of Caenis had returned. She handed a wooden box to Antonia, glancing, as she did so, in Vespasian's direction before sitting back down behind a small table next to her mistress. He felt his heart leap again; she knew he was watching her.

'I don't think Euprepes is going to be able to hold off the challenge much longer,' Gaius bawled at Titus, barely audible over the rising wave of noise that was engulfing the circus. 'He's taken his team to their limit already, there can't be much left in them.'

Down on the track the racers rounded the narrow turn for the fifth time. Gentius, almost level with Euprepes, was keeping the pressure on. Behind him the other Blue chariot, happy that the Red was stuck safely behind the two leaders, had pulled out and was trying to draw level with Gentius in order to squeeze him out on the next corner. Seeing the threat Gentius pulled to the right, clipping the Blue's nearest horse's front leg with his wheel. The creature reared up in agony, racing along on its hind legs trying to beat away the pain, causing the rest of the team to skew around the incapacitated animal. They tumbled over each other, sending up clouds of dust and overturning their chariot, which broke free from the pole. The driver had just enough time to cut the reins before the maddened team scrambled to their feet and pelted off, hell for leather, in the opposite direction down the track straight towards the last three oncoming chariots. The crowd leapt to its feet roaring their approval at this novel turn of events. The runaway team's hortator had no chance of catching them as they surged on, driverless, to impending catastrophe.

Recognising the danger rushing towards them at a fearsome pace the three chasing drivers split formation in the hopes that the directionless tearaways would pass between them, but the loose team shied and veered to the left, straight into the path of the middle one. Eight horses met head on with a crunch of breaking bones and shattering timber. The driver catapulted over the whinnying mass of horseflesh as it floundered in a twisted heap and landed with a heavy thud on the churned-up arena sand. He lay still. Howls of appreciation rose from the transfixed spectators.

Vespasian looked over to the imperial enclosure as the fifth dolphin dipped to see Tiberius patting Asinius on the back, congratulating him on an excellent spectacle. Beyond him Antonia was dictating a letter to Caenis; how she could concentrate through such excitement amazed him but, he supposed, the affairs of state could never wait.

'That was fantastic,' Sabinus cried as yet another gang of slaves armed with knives rushed on to disentangle any of the horses worth saving and put the rest out of their misery.

'My Gentius is going to win this, you'll see.' Vespasia was looking triumphant as the two leaders rounded the narrow turn for the second to last time.

The two lead drivers, covered in dust and sweat, battled with each other down the near track. Both were tiring now and each knew it. The grim determination on their sand-spattered faces hardened into grimaces as they approached the wide bend for the last time and heaved their teams around; a mistake now and all that they had fought for in the last six circuits would be lost; there were no prizes for coming second.

The roars of the spectators echoed around the Seven Hills of Rome as the sixth dolphin tilted and the final lap began. Caenis was no longer next to her mistress and Vespasian strained to see what had become of her over the heads of the senators around him. Failing to get a clear view of the goings-on in the box he turned back to the race.

Euprepes, driving his team on with the fury of a man desperate to win, just held the lead a hundred paces from the last corner. Gentius, realising that he had no chance to overtake him on the outside and then outpace him to the finish, looked over his left shoulder. The Red Celt was almost a length directly behind the leader; it was enough of a gap to aim for. Checking his speed slightly he pulled his team to the left into the space between the two chariots, forcing the Celt to slow. The corner was fast approaching and Gentius urged his team on so that their front legs were almost on the lead chariot. Euprepes, fearful that if he braked too hard Gentius would crash into him and take them both out, was forced to take the turn faster than was prudent. His team scrambled around the bend losing cohesion as they fought to keep their footing, sending his chariot skidding out to the right. Gentius pushed his team inside the Blues, hugged the curve and accelerated away into one final dash.

Any in the crowd who had sat down were now back on their feet again yelling their teams on. With a half-length advantage Gentius rode his team for all that they were worth whilst Euprepes whipped his exhausted animals mercilessly – but to no avail. Gentius shot straight past the last turning post and the seventh dolphin fell. He punched the air in triumph and headed off for the lap of honour. The Whites had won the first race and their supporters screamed their support for the hero of the moment.

Vespasia was ecstatic. 'Thirty denarii to me, that's as much as you three men lost between you,' she gloated. Gaius and Titus took it well but Sabinus, who could never bear losing, was furious.

'That Euprepes should be strung up by his balls for losing like that, he had the race won.'

'I don't think so,' Gaius said. 'He went too fast from the start; his team were finished.'

Gentius stopped his chariot by the steps that led up to the front of the imperial box. To the rapturous ovation of the crowd he climbed up and received his palm of victory and a large purse from a very pleased Asinius; it had been a good start to the day.

The crowd settled back down to watch the jugglers and gymnasts who would fill in the time whilst the track was cleared of dead horses and broken chariots ready for the next race. Vespasian looked back over at the box but Caenis was nowhere to be seen.

'If you're looking for that girl,' Gaius whispered in his ear, 'you're looking in the wrong direction, dear boy, she's over there.'

Vespasian jerked his head around and sure enough there, coming through the same entranceway that they had used, was Caenis. She reached the bottom of the steps and Vespasian held his breath as she turned right and headed along the gangway towards where they were sitting. Unable to believe his eyes she stopped in front of his uncle and, keeping her gaze on the floor, handed him a parchment note.

Gaius took it and quickly read its contents before handing it back to the girl.

'Tell the Lady Antonia we would be delighted.'

Caenis bowed and, without raising her eyes, turned and left. All eyes were on Gaius, who had a bemused look on his face.

'Well?' Vespasia asked.

'Most extraordinary,' Gaius said. 'It would seem that the good lady has seen fit to invite myself and the boys to dinner.'

'When?' Vespasian blurted.

'Tomorrow, dear boy. A great honour; but what can she possibly want with you two?'

CHAPTER IX

VESPASIAN WAS WOKEN by the movement and murmuring of the house slaves as they lit lamps, kindled the fire and set a table ready for breakfast. The smell of freshly baked bread and the anticipation of seeing Caenis easily persuaded him out of bed.

In the atrium he found Gaius seated next to the lararium eating his breakfast whilst having his sandals put on.

'Good morning, dear boy,' Gaius boomed, rubbing a clove of garlic on to a hunk of bread. 'I trust that you slept well.' He dunked his bread into a bowl of olive oil on the table beside him and took a large bite.

'Thank you, Uncle, I did,' Vespasian replied, noticing gratefully that the young lad at Gaius' feet was wearing a loin-cloth. 'I hope that you did too.'

'Very well indeed, dear boy, very well,' his uncle replied, ruffling the hair of the slave boy kneeling at his feet, who, having finished with the sandals, smiled coyly at his master, bowed and left. 'Sit with me and have some breakfast, there's bread, olives, water, oil and some cheese. Would you like wine in your water?'

'No, thank you, Uncle, this will be fine,' Vespasian said sitting down.

'As you wish, as you wish.' Gaius took another bite of his bread and looked at Vespasian thoughtfully as he chewed on it. 'Tell me, Vespasian, which path would you wish to follow?' he asked. 'The Emperor has as much use for good administrators as he does for good generals.'

'But I thought that to climb the cursus honorum one served in both military and civilian positions in order to understand how the two are linked,' Vespasian replied, slightly confused by the question.

'Indeed you do and, as you rightly imply, they are interchangeable. However, there are various degrees of civilian and military. Look at it this way: if you were Caesar, would you send a man to be governor of a restless frontier province like Moesia when his only experience with the legions was four years as a military tribune with the Seventh Macedonica supervising road-building and latrine-digging in Dalmatia, and two years as legate of the Fourth Gallica sampling the heady joys of Antioch where, because of a recent peace treaty with the Parthians, the most martial obligation was to inspect the legion once a month on pay day? Of course you wouldn't, not unless you particularly disliked the man and were prepared to lose a province and two legions getting rid of him. Much easier just to order him to commit suicide at home in his bath, don't you think?'

'Of course, Uncle,' Vespasian replied.

'This man might however make a suitable governor of

somewhere like Aquitania where road-building is all the rage and there is no legion to inspect.

'Now, a man who served as a military tribune with the First Germanica in lower Germania fighting the Chatti or some other equally bloodthirsty tribe and then served as legate of the Fourth Scythica, curbing the raiding of the Getae and securing the northern border, is the man who gets to be Governor of Moesia and with it the chance of military glory and all the financial rewards that go with it. So, Vespasian, you see the difference. Which path do you want to follow?' Gaius asked again.

'I would choose to be the second man, Uncle. In boosting my personal standing and dignitas I would raise the prestige of my family.'

'You would also attract the attention of the Emperor and those around him, who jealously guard their power by maintaining his. Neither he nor they relish seeing any other man gain too much personal glory; so beware of serving Rome too well, Vespasian. After all, what does an Emperor do with a successful general?' Gaius paused and tore off another hunk of bread before offering the loaf to his nephew. 'The first man, however,' he continued, swirling his bread around the oil, 'does indeed go to Aquitania, a province run by the Senate, not the Emperor, and spends a very convivial year there building roads to his heart's content and quietly enriching himself off the fat of the land by taking good-sized bribes off the locals for medium-sized favours.'

'But surely that's wrong,' Vespasian interrupted.

'Why?'

'Well, he's abusing his position of authority in order to enrich himself.'

'My dear boy, where have you been?' Gaius guffawed. 'He's doing no such thing; he's using his position of authority in order to re-enrich himself. Do you know how much it costs to rise in this city with bribes, public good works, holding games, feasts and all that sort of thing, in order to buy popularity with the Senate and the people? Fortunes, dear boy, fortunes; and if you are not lucky enough to be born with fortunes, what then? You borrow, and borrowed money needs to be paid back, with interest. You won't get paid in Rome's service. Oh, no, what we do for Rome we do for love.' Gaius looked hard at Vespasian to see if this had gone in and then carried on. 'So the first man comes back to Rome covered in gold. He is hardly noticed as he settles back down in his own home with a chest full of denarii. He poses no threat to the Emperor or those around him, because he has commanded no troops.

'The second man also comes home, but he is covered in gold and glory; he receives triumphal ornaments from a grateful Emperor and the suspicion of all those who surround him. No quiet semi-retirement for him; oh, no, the Emperor wants all potential threats to his power kept close, so they can be observed, controlled.' Gaius paused and looked again at his nephew. 'Now, my boy, do you still wish to be the second man?'

'Yes, Uncle,' Vespasian replied, 'because at least he has

the satisfaction of knowing that he did everything that could possibly do to serve Rome and further his family's honour.'

'Whereas I have not?'

'What?'

'Oh, Vespasian, didn't you guess? I am the first man,' Gaius cried, clapping him on the shoulder. 'No, no, don't feel bad; I made my choice as you must make yours. I chose anonymity, which, incidentally, is the reason why I kept my provincial accent. The patrician élite look down on it and therefore don't see you as so much of a threat.' He looked his nephew in the eye. 'This evening you will meet one of the most powerful women in Rome; if you impress her she may use her considerable influence to set you off on a dangerous path. I want you to be aware of the consequences of coming to her attention and being in her debt; the powerful do not play lightly with us lesser mortals.'

The time could not pass fast enough for Vespasian as he contemplated seeing Caenis later; or slow enough, as he remembered the intimidating prospect of making conversation with Antonia. Caenis had not looked at him again during the racing, until a brief glance as she left with her mistress at midday. This had been enough to prevent him from concentrating on the spectacle for the rest of the day, which had passed in a blur of noise, speed and dust.

The allotted hour eventually came. Titus and Vespasia saw them off.

'Remember to only speak when spoken to,' she reminded

them. 'A quiet, polite guest is far more likely to be invited back than a garrulous, overbearing one.'

Gaius led the brothers down the Quirinal and up to the exclusive slopes of the Palatine. The houses here were bigger than any Vespasian had ever seen; some were two storeys high and had long marble stairways leading up to grand entrances secured by gilded doors. Each house was set in its own area of tree-lined garden, spacing them out far more than on the Quirinal and giving the area an almost park-like feel to it in the late-afternoon sun.

Gaius stopped at a huge single-storey house that, although tall and grand in style, was less ostentatious than the rest. Its windowless walls were painted a plain white, and it lacked the extravagant entrance and any extraneous decoration.

Gaius knocked. The viewing slot in the door scraped open and two dark eyes briefly surveyed them. A very healthy-looking young doorkeeper immediately opened the door to let them in without a word. They stepped into a high, wide atrium where a dark-haired, well-built, bearded man in his late twenties, dressed in a light blue Greek tunic, was waiting.

'Good day to you, masters,' he said, bowing low.

'And to you, Pallas,' Gaius replied, who was always impressed by the young steward's manners.

'You will be dining imminently; be so good as to follow me.'

He led them through the atrium; its spacious interior had

a polished pink and white marble floor and was decorated with elegant statues and busts of both painted marble and bronze. Expensive-looking items of furniture stood against the walls and by the central pool; carved wooden couches with ivory inlays were set around marble tables standing on golden lion's paws or griffin legs. Wide corridors led off the atrium on either side, leading to formal reception rooms, a library and a suite of private baths.

They passed out into a chill, cloistered garden whose carefully manicured bushes and shrubs, which had been neatly tended over the winter, waited for the spring to encourage them to blossom into a feast of colour. At the far end Pallas knocked on shiny black-lacquered panelled door.

'Enter,' a commanding female voice called from within.

Pallas opened the door and respectfully addressed his mistress: '*Domina*, the Senator Gaius Vespasius Pollo and his nephews, Titus Flavius Sabinus and Titus Flavius Vespasianus.'

'Gaius, how good of you to come.' The Lady Antonia walked forward to take his hand. Close up she was far more beautiful than Vespasian had expected for a woman of sixty. Her dark-auburn hair was dressed high on her head in intricate weaves held in place by jewelled pins. Her skin was still smooth with only a few wrinkles around her sparkling green eyes. She wore very little make-up; her high cheekbones, strong chin and full lips needed no augmentation.

'We are honoured to be invited, domina,' Gaius replied, bowing his head. Antonia turned her attention towards the two brothers; Sabinus held her gaze.

'Welcome, Sabinus; my brother-in-law the Emperor tells me that you acquitted yourself with distinction in the recent war in Africa.' She smiled at him as he visibly glowed with pride. 'You must have indeed performed well to have come to the Emperor's attention.'

'I am honoured that he even knows my name,' Sabinus replied, 'let alone that he should speak well of me.'

'Credit where it is due is one of his guiding principles. He needs to keep an eye out for outstanding young officers. How else will he know whom to promote to command the legions that keep our Empire safe?'

'Indeed, domina,' Gaius said, 'the Emperor is very assiduous in reading all despatches from the legionary legates. Sabinus does honour to our family to have been mentioned.'

Antonia turned to Vespasian. 'So this is the lad who startles my maid,' she said, looking at him with mock severity. Vespasian stared at the mosaic floor, unable to think of anything sensible to say. Antonia covered his embarrassment by gently lifting his chin with a slender hand. 'Don't worry, Vespasian, I'm not cross; I expect a good-looking young man such as you will cause quite a few young girls' hearts to flutter in his time.'

Vespasian smiled at her; he had never before been told that he was good-looking. 'Thank you, domina,' he managed to get out.

'Come and make yourselves comfortable whilst we wait for our other dinner companion to arrive.'

She ushered them into the room. It was dominated by an

enormous bay window that to Vespasian's amazement was glazed. The late-afternoon sun flooded through the near transparent glass, held in place by a lattice frame, beyond which a strangely distorted view of the gardens was visible. Three couches, upholstered in light tan leather and with gracefully curved walnut-wood headboards, stood on spindled bronze legs in the bay. The low table, around which they were set, was also made of walnut polished so brightly that it reflected the sun up on to the frescoed ceiling. At the far end of the room stood a large oak desk draped with maroon cloth and covered in scrolls of paperwork. On the floor next to it, in front of a pastoral fresco, was a strong box made of copper-decorated iron with sturdy-looking locks at each end.

Antonia clapped her hands; from behind a curtain to their left appeared three slave girls who waited as the men undraped their togas, then took them away for safe keeping.

There was another knock on the door.

'Enter,' Antonia called again.

Pallas walked in. 'Domina, the Consul, Marcus Asinius Agrippa.'

'Consul, you do me great honour,' Antonia said as the surprisingly short and balding figure of Asinius stepped into the room.

'As you do me,' Asinius replied. His quick, dark eyes flashed around the other guests; his reaction showed that everyone that he had expected was present. 'Senator, you are well, I trust?'

'Thank you, Consul, never better,' Gaius replied. 'May I present my nephews Sabinus and Vespasian?'

'I am pleased to make your acquaintances.' Asinius acknowledged the brothers with a nod of the head whilst handing his toga to a waiting slave girl.

'Gentlemen, let us recline and eat,' Antonia said, moving over to the central couch. 'Consul, you and Gaius on this side of me,' she indicated to the more prestigious right-hand couch, 'and the two young men to my left.'

Pallas pulled back the curtain and the slave girls appeared again to remove the guests' sandals and wash their feet. They replaced the sandals with the slippers that each man had brought with him and then, once the diners had settled on the couches, spread a large white napkin in front of each of them.

The girls left with the sandals, passing a group of five more slaves bearing knives, spoons, plates and drinking bowls. Vespasian felt a surge of excitement as Caenis entered last in the group to wait on her mistress. He tried not to stare as she leant down over the table and her simple dress fell away from her chest to reveal two beautifully shaped, pink-nippled breasts, swaying gently from side to side as she placed the cutlery and crockery in front of her mistress. Vespasian felt the blood rush to his groin and was forced to adjust his position on the couch before he embarrassed himself. Antonia noticed his discomfort and, guessing the cause, smiled to herself. She looked over at Asinius.

'Consul, I find myself in the awkward position of being a

hostess with no host beside me. I would be grateful if you would take the host's responsibility for the strength of the wine.'

'Of course, dear lady, it will be my pleasure.' Asinius looked at Pallas. 'We shall start with four parts water to one part wine.'

Pallas nodded and then signalled the slaves who were waiting patiently behind each diner to fetch in the first course. Vespasian made an effort not to look at Caenis as she walked away for fear of compounding an already considerable problem and cursed himself for being infatuated by a mere slave to whom he could not even talk whilst in the same room, let alone hope to possess.

The dinner progressed in a sedately formal manner; the gustatio was followed by a dish of huge lobsters garnished with asparagus, which in turn was replaced by mullet from Corsica followed by goose liver with truffles and mushrooms and finally a roast boar with a cumin and wine sauce.

Antonia led the conversation through a range of uncontentious subjects, always allowing her guests time to express their opinions and deferring to those of Asinius should there be a disagreement. Vespasian found himself relaxing and, apart from a few glances in Caenis' direction, was able to relax and enjoy the meal and contribute now and again, albeit slightly awkwardly, to the conversation. They whiled away the late afternoon in pleasant companionship, waited on constantly by the deferential slaves who padded noiselessly around them. By the time the dishes of pears, apples and figs were served the sun had set, lamps had been lit and a couple of portable braziers brought in to supplement the underfloor heating. The room, deprived of its main source of light, took on a more intimate feel and conversation grew more animated, due in part to Asinius reducing the water level in the wine.

Pallas, seeing that the diners had everything they needed, signalled the slaves to retire. He made sure there was no one listening in the serving room behind the curtain or outside the door, then he nodded to Antonia and withdrew to a darkened corner to wait, unobtrusively, on his mistress's pleasure.

Antonia picked up a pear and began to peel it with her knife. 'Well, this has been very pleasant; but, Gaius, as I'm sure you are aware, I didn't just invite you and your charming nephews here to discuss the recent campaign in Africa, racing and the hideous price of good slaves. There's a far more pressing political crisis, whose beginnings we have already seen in the rise of Sejanus in the Emperor's favour, which will, if not countered, come to a head in the coming months.' She paused, discarded the pear skin, cut a small slice off the fruit and placed it in her mouth. 'I think our esteemed Consul here could best outline the situation.'

Asinius nodded and let out a loud burp. 'Indeed; and thank you for a most delicious meal.' He took a sip of wine, savoured the delicacy of the vintage and then began. 'When the Divine Augustus created the Praetorian Guard, after the ravages of years of civil war, it was to safeguard the city from the external threat of any mutinous legions and the internal threat of the sort of rabble-rousers that we had come accustomed to in the last days of the Republic. One thing kept it in check and that was the power of the Emperor, who in his wisdom appointed two Praetorian prefects so that neither could get too powerful. Sejanus was appointed to the post in Augustus' last year and shared it with his father Lucius Seius Strabo. An honest man from all accounts, so honest in fact that one of Tiberius' first actions as Emperor was to send him to govern Egypt. Unfortunately Tiberius neglected to appoint a replacement for Strabo and so Sejanus has commanded the Guard alone now for over ten years, during which time he has managed to win Tiberius' complete trust.' He paused for another sip of wine and then continued. 'And now because of the unfortunate deaths of your beloved Germanicus, domina, and the Emperor's son Drusus, he feels that he can position himself to become Tiberius' heir.'

'Unfortunate? Pah!' Antonia spat, and Vespasian blinked in shock. All afternoon she had been the perfect hostess: mild, calm and attentive, but in that moment he saw the fire in her that made her the most formidable woman of her generation and not to be crossed. 'My son Germanicus was poisoned in Syria by the Governor Calpurnius Piso, on Sejanus' orders and possibly with the connivance of Tiberius himself, although that part I cannot prove. However, Piso's suicide before his defence had started proves to me his guilt. As for Drusus, his wife Livilla, that treacherous harpy of a daughter that I nursed at my own breast, poisoned him, I'm sure of it, though again I have no proof. She and Sejanus are lovers; he asked the Emperor's permission to marry her this year. Tiberius refused and forbade them to see each other. However, she is still Sejanus' mistress but they are too clever to let that come to Tiberius' attention.'

'That is news indeed, domina,' Gaius said, digesting the implications of the revelation. 'That would mean that he wouldn't be afraid to make an attempt on the Emperor's life.'

'No, he's too subtle for that,' Antonia replied. 'He knows that should he do so and try to take the purple for himself the Senate and half the legions would rise against him and we would be back into years of civil war.'

'He's been far more clever,' Asinius said, smiling. 'He's managed to get rid of Tiberius without killing him.'

'But he was at the Circus Maximus just yesterday,' Vespasian blurted out, completely forgetting his place.

'So he was, young man, so he was, but for the last time ever.' Asinius took another sip of wine. 'We have over the last couple of years seen a resurgence of treason trials, mostly on trumped-up charges, but nevertheless getting convictions. This has enabled Sejanus to persuade our Emperor to see conspiracies around every corner. He knows that he has never been popular; he's been nervous ever since the legions along the Rhine rose up against him on his accession. He tried to ingratiate himself with the Senate, deferring to them in foreign and domestic policy decisions, accepting votes against his wishes and even giving way to the Consuls when he met them in the street. But he now feels that this policy has backfired and that the Senate saw his conciliatory behaviour as weakness and is now trying to remove him.'

'And for Tiberius,' Antonia added, 'the proof of all this is in the successful treason trials.'

'Set up by Sejanus?' Gaius ventured, admiring the beauty of the strategy.

'Indeed, and with the two obvious heirs gone Sejanus has managed to persuade him that the Senate will try to restore the Republic – something for which Tiberius denounced his own brother, Lady Antonia's husband, to Augustus when he suggested it in a private letter many years ago. Sejanus has played him beautifully, he provided Tiberius with proof of his greatest fear whilst concealing the true source of the threat against him. He has persuaded him, for his own safety, to withdraw from Rome in the New Year, after the next Consuls are sworn in, and take up permanent residence on Capreae.'

'But with the Emperor, the one person that protects him, gone, surely Sejanus will be left vulnerable to attack from the Senate?' Gaius observed, thinking he'd seen a flaw in the plan.

'In normal circumstances yes,' Antonia said, her calm returned, 'but somehow Sejanus has managed to persuade Tiberius to appoint Gnaeus Cornelius Gaetulicus and Gaius Calvisius Sabinus to the Consulship.'

'Yes, I know. Neither of them is remarkable: Gaetulicus writes dirty poems and is popular with the army and Calvisius Sabinus is bit on the slow side.'

'Slow?' Antonia laughed. 'He makes my son Claudius seem like a quick-witted defence lawyer.'

'So who will be controlling the Senate next year, then?' Asinius asked rhetorically. 'An idiot, and a man who is popular amongst the troops, whose daughter is, coincidently, betrothed to Sejanus' elder son.'

'Ah!' Gaius exclaimed.

'Ah, indeed, my old friend,' Antonia said, 'and he's done more.'

Vespasian and Sabinus looked at each other, both wondering what other depths Sejanus had sunk to and also why they, a couple of inexperienced country boys, were being privileged with the details.

'What more does he need to do? Surely it's perfect as it is?' Gaius asked, genuinely puzzled. 'Tiberius withdrawn to an island guarded by Praetorians, hearing only the news that Sejanus wants him to hear. Meanwhile the Senate is in the hands of a fool who's too stupid to sponge clean his own arse without a diagram and someone who is practically family. It's brilliant. What more does he need to worry about?'

'The army,' Vespasian said quietly.

'Absolutely right, young man, the army,' Asinius said, looking at Vespasian with new respect and then darting an approving glance in Antonia's direction. 'The army will be his problem, but he has already started to deal with it.'

'How?' Vespasian asked.

'Who was behind Tacfarinas' revolt last year, providing him with the tens of thousands of freshly minted denarii that were found in his treasury? Whose agents encouraged the rebellion in Thracia against our client king Rhoemetalces, which is still going on at this very moment? Why did the Parthian envoys sent to Rome this year have a secret meeting with Sejanus after they had concluded their business with the Emperor and the Senate? Trouble on the frontiers keeps the army busy. The more trouble there is the busier they'll be; busy enough perhaps not to notice what's going on in Rome. You can bet on a few incursions across the Rhine and the Danubius this year, maybe Parthia will start sniffing around Armenia again; and I wouldn't be surprised if an invasion of Britain soon becomes the Emperor's policy – that would keep at least four legions occupied whilst Sejanus tightens his grip on power. Then, when Tiberius dies, the all-powerful Sejanus will be in prime position to be regent for one of the young imperial grandsons who will probably succeed to the purple.'

'And once he's regent, with the Praetorians behind him, he'll be able to get tribunician powers and become untouchable,' Gaius said smiling grimly. 'That is clever, very, very clever. You have to admire the man.'

'Oh, I do,' Asinius asserted, 'and, more importantly, I respect him. This is a man who takes the long view. He has patience to match his cunning and subtlety to match his ruthlessness. He is a formidable adversary and, for the good of Rome, he must be destroyed. The problem is that we don't yet have any hard evidence against him; we need time to collect it. This is where Antonia and I think that you could be of use.'

'Without evidence Tiberius will not listen to me, he thinks that I am just pursuing a vendetta against Sejanus because I believe that he was responsible for my son's death.'

Gaius tilted his head in acknowledgement. Asinius went to pour himself some more wine but found the mixing bowl empty. Antonia looked towards Pallas, standing quietly in the corner. 'Pallas, some more wine, if you would.'

Pallas bowed his head and disappeared through the curtain. An instant later there was a shout and the smash of a jar breaking on the floor. Vespasian and Sabinus leapt to their feet immediately and rushed through to the serving room where they found Pallas, in the half-light, wrestling with a figure on the floor. Grabbing the man from behind, Sabinus tore him off the Greek and pushed him face down onto the floor. Putting his knee into the small of the man's back, he quickly yanked his head back by his hair and slammed his face down on to the stone floor. The captive's nose and jaw shattered on impact; he let out a brief cry and lay still.

'Who is he?' Antonia demanded as she arrived in the doorway.

'I don't know,' Pallas gasped, winded, 'it's too dark.'

'Bring him in here, then.' She pulled the curtain back. Sabinus and Vespasian dragged the man by his feet, leaving behind a pool of blood peppered with broken teeth. Back in the lamplight of Antonia's room they rolled him over.

'I don't know him,' Antonia said, 'but I don't think even his mother would recognise him looking like that.'

His bloodied face was indeed a mess: his nose was flattened to one side; his swollen lips had shards of broken teeth embedded in them; and his slack jaw hung at peculiar angle.

'Pallas! Pallas, come here at once.'

'Yes, mistress, sorry,' the Greek groaned from the doorway. He hobbled into the room and looked down at his assailant.

'Well, who is he?' Asinius insisted.

'It's Eumenes, the doorkeeper.'

'One of my slaves!' Antonia was outraged. 'How long since I bought him?'

'Less than a year, mistress; he started as a house slave. He and his brother had been down on their luck so they left their native Creta and came here to sell themselves into slavery. I imagine they hoped to one day earn their freedom and citizenship. I admired his enterprise and promoted him to the door about three months ago. I am so sorry, mistress, he has probably been passing on lists of your guests to whomever he reports to.'

'Well, we won't worry about that now. How long was he listening for?'

'Not long, mistress. I checked behind the door and curtain regularly.'

'Well, let's find out what he heard and who he spies for.'

CHAPTER X

BY THE TIME he regained consciousness Eumenes had been strapped naked on to a table in the serving room. He groaned loudly but stopped abruptly as the pain from his shattered jaw magnified with any movement. He felt a hand close around his scrotum and opened his eyes in fright. Through the mist of blood he saw his owner leaning over him.

'Now, you treacherous little pile of filth,' Antonia hissed through clenched teeth, 'you are going to tell me why you were spying on me.' She squeezed his testicles with all her strength, drawing out a long shriek from her victim; it caused the five men around her to grimace in unconscious sympathy.

Vespasian watched Antonia in shocked disbelief as she continuously tightened and then eased her fist; there was no pleasure on her face, only cold determination. She was not to be crossed. She finally released her grip and the noise subsided. Blood outlined her fingernails and she reached for a cloth. She looked down at the heaving chest of her slave.

'Well, Pallas,' she said grimly, 'he doesn't want to do it the easy way, let's see if he prefers the hard way.'

Pallas nodded to his mistress and with a pair of tongs picked out a red-hot piece of charcoal from a brazier. He showed it to the terrified doorkeeper, who turned his head away. Pallas looked at his mistress.

'Do it,' she ordered.

Vespasian smelt burning flesh as the charcoal sizzled its way through the skin of the man's thigh into the muscle below. His howls echoed around the house.

'Leave it there and put another on.'

Pallas did as he was told, this time dropping it on his belly; the doorkeeper writhed and wailed but still refused to talk.

'And another,' Antonia shouted, getting more frustrated by the moment.

Vespasian remembered the crucified boy. How easy it was to inflict pain on a person with no rights. He looked around the room at the others; Sabinus had a wild grin on his face but Asinius and Gaius were intent and grim. Both realised that their lives could depend on breaking this slave.

As a coal ate through his right nipple Eumenes passed out. Silence filled the room. They stared at the twisted, smoking body and wondered in amazement what loyalty or terror beyond these walls could induce him to endure such agony.

'Brush off the coals and bring him round,' Antonia said with resolve in her voice. 'We'll see if he prefers his flesh to be cut instead of burnt.'

Pallas threw a bucket of water over him, causing steam to rise from the roasting wounds.

'We must be careful not to overdo it,' Gaius said anxiously. 'We don't want him dying on us.'

'Do you think that I've never had a slave tortured before?' Antonia snapped.

'My apologies, domina.'

Another two buckets of water brought the wretched man round. He started to moan.

'Show him the knife,' Antonia said slowly.

Pallas unsheathed a long thin blade, curved and sharp as a razor, and held it in front of Eumenes' eyes. They widened in horror as the sleek instrument reflected the glow of the brazier on to his face.

'Believe me, you will talk,' Antonia said in a quiet, menacing voice. 'It's just up to you how many ears, fingers and balls you have left when you do.'

'I can't,' he whispered.

'Why not?'

'They have my brother.'

'Who has?'

Eumenes shook his head.

'Start on his ears.'

Pallas grabbed his head with his left hand and pulled it towards him.

'No! No!' Eumenes begged.

The knife flashed and the ear fell with a light thud on to the table, which was soon covered with blood.

'The other.'

Pallas pushed Eumenes' head away exposing the other side of his face.

'About two months ago,' Eumenes cried through his broken mouth, 'a man came to the door.'

Antonia put up her hand and signalled Pallas to stop. 'Who?' she asked urgently.

'Hasdro, Sejanus' freedman. He gave me a packet and told me to open it in private. He said he would return and tell me what to do. I opened it later, as I was told, in my quarters.' Blood spilt out of his mouth and down his cheeks as he struggled to form the words.

'Well? Out with it,' Antonia urged.

'It contained a hand; on it was a ring that I recognised as my brother's,' Eumenes panted; despite his pain he blanched at the memory.

'What did he say when he came back?' Asinius pressed him, his lip curling fastidiously. He was keen to get this over with.

'He told me that I was to memorise all the visitors that you receive. I was to make no lists, not that I can write, you understand.'

'Yes, yes, go on.' Antonia was not interested in the literary abilities of a mere slave.

'Someone would call by every few days and I was to pass them on to him, that way my brother would keep his other hand.' He sobbed at the thought of it.

'But that doesn't explain why you were spying tonight, he told you just to collect names,' Asinius pointed out.

'When the man came by yesterday I gave him your name for the third time in five visits. He told me to listen in the next time you were here and to get something interesting or it would go badly for my brother.'

'Who owns your brother?' asked Antonia.

'He's a slave in the house of your daughter, Livilla.'

'That venomous little snake,' Antonia exploded. 'Spying on her own mother, prying into my private affairs and no doubt passing it all on to that monster Sejanus whilst he rams his cock up her grateful arse, literally pumping her for information. I should have strangled the little bitch at birth.'

The men in the room were silent after this outburst.

Antonia was shaking with rage; forcing herself to be calm she looked down at the sobbing Eumenes. 'We should go back next door and discuss the situation,' she said. 'Gentlemen, please.' She indicated to the curtained doorway and looked back at Pallas, giving a slight nod of the head.

Vespasian passed through the door to the sound of a sharp slice and a gurgling death rattle. He felt a little pity for Eumenes but guessed that Antonia had calculated that she could neither keep him nor sell him. If Eumenes had answered the door to Livilla's agent looking like that the man would guess that he'd talked and the brother would lose his other hand – or worse. Again, if he were sold, it would be obvious that he'd talked. His death was probably his brother's only hope, but it was a very slender one.

*

They reclined back down on the couches and Antonia looked at the Consul. 'Well, Asinius, what do you think?'

'I think that we have been lucky.' He reached for some more wine but remembered that the bowl was empty and that Pallas was otherwise engaged. 'If Sejanus is spying on you he's probably watching everyone connected to the imperial house; he has no reason to suspect you are plotting against him any more than the rest are. Had Eumenes reported any of tonight's conversation then there would have been cause for concern, but fortunately he will be unable to, nor will your other guests' presence be noted, which means we are still safe to do as we planned.'

The brothers glanced at their uncle, who tried to give them a reassuring look.

'I think you are right, Consul,' Antonia said after a brief pause. 'The only thing he knows for certain about you and me is that you've visited a few times in the last month or so. We must keep the visits going so that he thinks that we are unaware of his attentions. Meanwhile we move with care.' She turned to Gaius and smiled. 'Now, Gaius, I have a request to make of you.'

'Anything, domina.'

'I need something kept safe.'

She got up and walked over to the strong box and taking two keys from a chain around her neck inserted them into the locks at each end of the box and turned them simultaneously. With a sharp click the locks opened and she lifted the lid.

'For Sejanus to succeed he will need to eliminate all those who have the ear of the Emperor. Although I have no intention of being eliminated, if I were to be, I am sure that my papers would be gone through and certain ones removed.' She took four scrolls out from the box. 'These are two copies, one for the Senate and one for the Emperor. Should the need arise please ensure that they are read.'

Gaius took the scrolls. 'I pray that I shall never need to do as you ask. They will be kept safe in a place known only to me for as long as you wish.'

Antonia sat back down. 'Now I think that it is time to conclude our business,' she said, glancing towards Asinius as Pallas returned, still looking dishevelled.

'Indeed. Pallas, thank the gods, more wine,' Asinius cried; the steward nodded. 'Now, we have no direct way to combat Sejanus without solid evidence against him, which will take time to amass. In the meantime he needs to be frustrated in the Senate. I would ask you, Gaius, to attend as much as possible and have as many opinions as possible and speak at length on each one. You will find others, also at my request, and myself doing the same so you won't stand out as a troublemaker. We may be able to delay his long-term plans by talking out his short-term ones. Meanwhile Antonia and I, with the help of our agents, will gather the hard evidence we need to convince Tiberius of the man's duplicity. When we are successful I am sure that your long-awaited consulship will be forthcoming.'

Gaius smiled. 'I shall, of course, do as you ask, Consul,' he replied, secretly relieved that he had nothing more dangerous to do than to talk a lot. 'But what do you have in mind for my nephews? They have heard enough this evening to damn them in Sejanus' eyes should he ever find out about this meeting.'

'Yes, I was coming to them.' He paused as Pallas returned with the wine and filled his bowl, then looked over at the two expectant young men. 'It so happens that I am able to help each of you to advance your careers in a way that is beneficial to all parties. Sabinus, having completed your time as a military tribune, I imagine that you wish for one of the Vigintiviri junior magistrates' positions; I can arrange to have you placed in the imperial mint. From there you will have access to the treasury where you will be able monitor Sejanus' use of public funds.'

Sabinus saw the logic of this; he would be extremely useful to Asinius, and at the same time gain valuable experience that would stand him in good stead for when he applied to become a quaestor in four years' time after the prescribed age of twenty-four.

'Thank you, Consul, I am in your debt.'

'I know you are and I won't forget it. Neither, I hope, will you.'

Sabinus bowed his head. 'I shall not.'

'As for you, Vespasian, you need your military experience.'

Vespasian felt his stomach clench; he had not dared hope to be given his chance of serving Rome so soon after arriving.

'I shall write to my kinsman Pomponius Labeo, the legate

of the Fourth Scythica; he's serving with Gaius Poppaeus Sabinus, the Governor of Moesia, Macedonia and Achaea, who is at present putting down the rebellion in the neighbouring client kingdom of Thracia. I don't know if he is sympathetic to our cause but he owes me favours and will take you into his legion as a military tribune. We need evidence that Sejanus is giving support to the rebel tribes trying to oust our friend King Rhoemetalces. He must have an agent in the legions there, passing information and perhaps money to the tribes; unmask him and bring the evidence back to Rome.'

'I have a private interest in this matter,' Antonia interjected. 'Rhoemetalces' mother, Queen Tryphaena, is a cousin of mine and also a friend. My late father Marcus Antonius was her great-grandfather. I knew Rhoemetalces as a child; he lived here in my house for three years and I grew very fond of him. I would deem it a personal favour if you could uncover evidence that Sejanus has put my kinsfolk in danger.'

Vespasian swallowed hard. How would he, with no military experience, be able to uncover an agent of Sejanus, who, he felt sure, would be as wily and subtle as his master?

Antonia, reading his thoughts, smiled at him. 'It has to be someone like you, Vespasian. Because you are young and inexperienced the spy will see you as just another fresh-faced young tribune trying to find his feet in the legions. He won't consider you as a threat at all, in fact he may even try to manipulate you. So trust no one and keep your eyes open.'

'Yes, domina,' Vespasian said, not feeling at all reassured.

'I hope to have the appointments confirmed within the month.' Asinius took another swig of wine. 'As you know I step down as Consul in two days' time, then I have a few months before I leave for whichever province I am allotted, so we have to work fast, gentlemen: we have a snake to catch.'

CHAPTER XI

'TITUS, YOU MUST order your sons to tell us what they actually discussed at the dinner,' Vespasia demanded at breakfast the following morning. She did not believe her sons or brother for one moment that it had just been a friendly dinner, and the Consul just happened to be there as the only other guest, and he just happened to give the brothers what they wanted, without demanding anything in return other than that they become his clients. 'Preferment is never given without the promise of something in return and I want to know what they've got themselves into.'

'Calm yourself, my dear. If they are keeping something from us, which I believe they are,' Titus replied, looking shrewdly at his two sons, 'one must assume it is for our own safety. Antonia and Asinius work in a world far removed from ours and it is probably best not to know the politics of the deal they made, it would be too dangerous.'

'But that is just the point: if it is dangerous I want us to know about it! What if the boys are getting into something way out of their depths?'

'Whatever it is that they've agreed to, it's too late to go back on. You can't change your mind with someone like Antonia and expect to prosper in Rome afterwards. The deal is done. We should just be thankful that Sabinus and Vespasian have both got what we came here to arrange for them, and so quickly too. Now we should concentrate on introducing them to as many influential people as we can before Vespasian goes north. And I, my dear, shall get Vespasian kitted out with a uniform.'

With that the subject was closed, leaving Vespasian and Sabinus grateful that their father had taken their side; they would have been placed in an impossible situation had the paterfamilias ordered them to reveal the facts behind the deal. Vespasia was left to pester Gaius for information, but to no avail. Gaius himself was busy attending the Senate each day it sat, fulfilling his obligation to Asinius by talking at great length on a variety of subjects in which he had previously shown little or no interest or indeed knowledge; then giving way to other senators who showed a similar new-found zeal. In the late afternoons he organised a series of dinners, inviting this year's praetors, aediles and quaestors as well as other senators and *equites* – equestrians – whom he deemed either potentially useful to his nephews' careers or dangerous and therefore safer to cultivate than to ignore.

A couple of days after the ides of January one such dinner had just finished and the guests had taken their leave when there was a knock on the door. Gaius, thinking that it was one of his guests returning to collect a forgotten item, opened the door himself, to reveal Pallas.

'Good evening, master, I'm sorry to intrude on you so late,' the Greek steward said in his faultless Latin.

'Good evening to you, my friend. Come in. I assume that you are here on your mistress' business?'

'I am, master.' Pallas quickly looked around outside and then stepped into the atrium. 'I have taken great care not to be followed. It is a matter of the utmost urgency and highly confidential.'

'In that case we shall speak privately in my study. Follow me.'

He led the steward through the atrium to his study at the far left-hand corner. Pallas nodded his respects through the open door of the triclinium to Sabinus and Vespasian, who were still reclining at table with their parents, and then disappeared into Gaius' private domain.

'Who is that?' Vespasia asked of the two brothers. 'He obviously knows you.'

Being unable to deny it Sabinus replied: 'He's the steward of Lady Antonia; but what he's doing here I don't know,' he added, anticipating her next question.

Vespasia looked at her husband. 'I've never known anything good come of a late-night secret meeting,' she said darkly. 'I suppose it has something to do with whatever was being discussed at that dinner.'

As if to prove her point Gaius appeared at the triclinium

door. 'Vespasia, my dear, and Titus, would you excuse your sons a moment? There is something that I need to speak to them about.'

'I told you,' Vespasia said.

'Of course, Gaius, with pleasure. Go on, boys,' Titus replied graciously.

'With pleasure indeed!' Vespasian heard his mother snort as he left the room.

Gaius' study was surprisingly spacious. The far wall was shelved, from floor to ceiling. Hundreds of leather cylinders containing Gaius' books were stacked neatly between the upright partitions. In the middle of the room stood a heavy wooden desk behind which Gaius sat. In the dim light of two oil lamps and a brazier Vespasian could make out the small statuettes and artwork that he'd expected of his uncle, knowing his tastes only too well by now.

'You need to go at once with Pallas to Antonia's house,' Gaius said without asking them to sit. 'You must do whatever she asks of you, and believe me when I tell you that it is of vital importance.'

'What is, Uncle?' Sabinus asked.

'It would be best if Antonia explains it herself. I shall send for Magnus and his colleagues to escort you, it's too dangerous to travel without guards at this time of the night. How you got here unharmed, Pallas, I don't know.'

'I am but a mere slave, master, what would anyone want with me?'

'Mere, indeed!' Gaius smiled and then looked at his

nephews. 'Now go and get your cloaks and travel with the hoods up.'

Magnus arrived quicker than expected; it was almost as if he'd been expecting a summons from his patron.

'I brought six of me lads, sir,' he told Gaius as he stepped through the door, 'on the basis that if you're going somewhere at this time of night on urgent business it ain't for a convivial bit of socialising, if you take my meaning?'

'Yes, yes, very wise, though I hope it won't come to that.'

'Come to what, Gaius?' Vespasia was hovering near the door desperate to find out what was going on. 'And what's that man doing here again?'

'Good evening, madam,' Magnus said, bowing his head.

'It's all right, Vespasia; he's here to escort Pallas, Sabinus and Vespasian to Antonia's house,' Gaius said, anxious to avoid a repetition of their last encounter.

'At this time of night?'

'Yes, that's precisely why he's here, because it is this time of night.'

'But what's so important that it can't wait until morning when they won't have to go creeping around the place with a bunch of no-good ruffians?'

Magnus' face remained inscrutable; he was getting used to being insulted by 'that woman', as he now thought of her.

'Vespasia, let it rest,' Titus ordered. 'Whatever Antonia wants from our sons is her business – we should be honoured that they can be of service to such a great lady.'

Vespasian and Sabinus appeared back in the atrium in their thick woollen cloaks, each sporting a long dagger on their belts.

'Why do you need to be armed?' Vespasia asked suspiciously.

'Better safe than sorry, Mother.' Sabinus grinned. 'Good evening, Magnus, shall we go?'

'Evening, young sirs, we shall if you're ready. Where are we going?'

'To the Lady Antonia's house on the Palatine.'

'Ah! Well, if you must.' Magnus looked unsure.

'Yes, we must.'

'Take care, dear boys, I have a feeling that you have a long night ahead of you. May the gods go with you.' Gaius put a hand on each of their shoulders and gave them an affectionate squeeze.

'I don't know what you are going to be asked to do but I think that "Be careful" would be suitable advice,' Titus said, putting an arm around his wife.

'We shall, Father,' Vespasian replied. 'Mother, don't worry, Sabinus will be fine, I'll look after him.'

Sabinus gave his younger brother a sour look. 'Very funny, you little shit.'

'Sabinus!'

'Sorry, Mother. We'll see you in the morning. Goodbye.'

The two brothers stepped out of the door followed by Pallas and Magnus to the sound of Vespasia berating Gaius again for getting her sons involved in affairs that they, or more to the point she, didn't understand and could not control.

Outside Magnus' men were waiting with a couple of flaming torches. A light rain started to fall as they headed off down the hill. Their footsteps echoed around the deserted street and the torchlight reflected a deep orange off the glistening wet paving stones.

'I've taken the precaution of leaving a man hidden behind us to see if we're being followed,' Magnus told Sabinus and Vespasian. 'I told him to count to five hundred, then make his way down through the side alleys and meet us on the main road.'

'Might take some time,' Vespasian mused.

Magnus looked at him quizzically and then laughed. 'Oh, I see. Yes, you're right, he ain't the brightest of the brothers but I reckon he'll make it to five hundred in a reasonable time; had it been Sextus here I would have only told him two hundred.' He gave his mate a playful nudge and got a good-humoured laugh in response.

They reached the main road and had to wait for only a brief time before their rearguard, a huge, bald man with a stump where his left hand had been, caught up with them.

'No one behind us, Magnus,' he puffed, out of breath from his quick run through the back streets.

'Well done, Marius. How did the counting go?'

'What?' Marius looked puzzled. 'It was all right.'

The rest of his brothers burst out laughing; realising that

he must be the butt of some joke made behind his back, Marius grinned sheepishly, mumbled: 'Yeah, yeah, very amusing,' and fell in with the group as they headed off in the direction of the Palatine.

The rain was falling steadily by the time that they reached Antonia's house. Once the new doorkeeper had admitted them Pallas gave orders for Magnus and his companions to be shown to the kitchens for some refreshment and then ushered the two brothers through to Antonia's private room, where they had dined back in December.

Antonia was seated behind her desk and was alone. Any hopes that Vespasian had had of seeing Caenis were thwarted.

'Sabinus, Vespasian, thank you for coming at such a late hour.'

'Good evening, domina, how can we be of service?' Sabinus asked.

'Please sit down.' She indicated the two chairs placed in front of her. Vespasian felt a slight breeze. He looked round at the window and saw that bottom left-hand corner had been broken and was now boarded up. 'Pallas, some wine for my guests.'

Pallas bowed and left the room. Antonia studied the brothers for a moment as if assessing whether or not they had the mettle she needed. Apparently satisfied, she began to speak. 'Last night someone broke in through that window and tried to get into my strong box. Fortunately they were disturbed, but unfortunately they managed to escape, running through one of my slaves with a sword in the process. Now, the only people officially allowed to carry swords in the city are the Urban Cohort and the Praetorian Guard; the average petty thief normally contents himself with a dagger or a cudgel. But even if it was just a well-armed petty thief how did he know where exactly to find my strong box? I can't help suspecting it was a Praetorian, acting on Sejanus' instructions, who'd been given the location by my daughter Livilla. She knows the layout of the house.'

Antonia paused as Pallas re-entered and poured the wine for her guests, then retired to his place by the door. 'If the break-in was orchestrated by Sejanus it would mean that he suspects that I have documents in here that are dangerous to him, and he would be right. The two documents that I entrusted copies of to your uncle for safekeeping would make very interesting, if unpleasant, reading for Sejanus. One outlines the suspicions that Asinius and I shared with you the other night of his long-term plans to gain power and the steps that we are taking to counter it. The other details the evidence that I have so far of his role in the deaths of my son Germanicus and the Emperor's son Drusus.'

Vespasian took a sip of his wine and wondered where he would fit into all this.

'I needed to confirm one way or another whether Sejanus suspects me of conspiring against him, which led me to do something which was, with the benefit of hindsight, very stupid. I decided to invite Livilla here for dinner tomorrow, ostensibly to make peace with her, but in reality I wanted to see her reaction to the broken window, maybe that would have confirmed my suspicions. So this evening I sent my maid Caenis with an invitation to Livilla; neither she nor the slave that accompanied her have returned.'

Vespasian took a sharp intake of breath, causing Antonia to smile.

'You are right to be concerned, but it is more than Caenis' safety that should worry us, it is what she knows.'

'What information could a slave have that can be of use to Livilla and Sejanus?' Sabinus asked.

'A slave she may be, but she is also very dear to me. Her mother was my slave but died when Caenis was only three. I brought Caenis up in my household; she is almost like the daughter I wished I'd had. As such I keep her in my confidence; not only is she my body-slave she is also, as Livilla knows full well, my secretary. She knows the contents of those two documents because she made the copies.'

A look of shock passed over both Vespasian and Sabinus' faces as they realised the awful truth of the situation. Livilla, who was capable of acts of astonishing cruelty, would easily be able to torture the contents of those documents out of Caenis and pass them on to Sejanus, who would then act with ruthless efficiency to protect himself.

'So you see, gentlemen, we haven't any time to lose. We must rescue Caenis before she is broken.'

'How do we know she hasn't been already, domina?' Vespasian asked; he felt sick at the thought of that beautiful girl going through what Eumenes or his brother had suffered.

'Livilla is with the Emperor tonight for his farewell dinner; she will want to be present at the interrogation. The Emperor always dines late and never retires to bed until the early hours of the morning, so we have a little time.

'Caenis is more than likely being held in a cellar at the back of the house; it can be accessed not only from the inside of the house but also from the garden through a short tunnel, probably guarded by Praetorians. I have asked my grandson Gaius to guide you; he knows the house well and loathes Sejanus who he knows ordered the murder of his father. He's also a favourite of Tiberius', so no guard would dare execute him or his companions should you be caught, but let's hope that it doesn't come to that.'

Antonia stood up and moved towards the door. 'Pallas will bring everything that you'll need. You have to move fast, gentlemen. We have only a couple of hours before Livilla returns.'

CHAPTER XII

ANTONIA LED VESPASIAN and Sabinus back to the atrium where they found Magnus and his colleagues, looking very out of place in the palatial room, laughing and joking with each other, chewing on hunks of bread and swigging from a wineskin that they passed around. They snapped to attention as they saw Antonia.

'Domina,' Magnus said through a half-eaten lump of bread.

Antonia's eyes widened. 'I know you, don't I?'

'Magnus, domina.'

'Magnus, of course. What are you doing here?' she responded, looking not altogether pleased to see him.

'Me and me mates here are escorting the young masters, keeping an eye out for them, if you take my meaning?' he replied indistinctly, patting the dagger in his belt.

'Well, you will have your work cut out tonight: do your job well and you will receive a handsome reward.'

Magnus bowed in acknowledgement, finally managing to swallow the rest of his bread.

Vespasian heard footsteps coming down one of the

corridors that led off the atrium, and turned to see a youth of no more than fourteen enter the room. He was tall and thin with spindly legs; his brown hair fell in curls over a broad, pallid, forehead, from beneath which two bright eyes peered intelligently out of sunken sockets.

'Gaius, my sweet, this is Sabinus and Vespasian, the two young men you are to show to the tunnel,' Antonia said, kissing her grandson on the cheek.

Gaius smiled at the brothers. 'What a jolly caper this will be, eh? Rescuing slave girls at midnight from the clutches of the gruesome Livilla and the dastardly Praetorians, I can't wait.'

'Let's hope that it turns out to be just a jolly caper, as you say, Gaius,' Vespasian said, smiling back, instantly warming to Gaius' bright and friendly nature.

'Oh, please, call me Caligula, everyone does except my grandmother here who thinks that it's not a becoming nickname for a son of the great Germanicus.'

Antonia laughed and ruffled Caligula's hair with genuine affection.

'Are these our men?' Caligula asked, looking over at Magnus and his entourage.

'Magnus, at your service, sir,' Magnus said, nodding his head.

'Excellent,' Caligula cried. 'With such a fine body of men behind us, how can we fail? Let's be off. See you later, Grandmother.'

He went out into the wet night. Sabinus and Vespasian

followed with Magnus and his lads joking about being called a fine body of men; Pallas, carrying a heavy-looking sack, brought up the rear. All were buoyed up by Caligula's enthusiasm.

'I don't want to appear rude, sir, but where are we going and what are we going to do when we get there?' Magnus asked Sabinus.

'As Caligula said, we're going to Livilla's house to free a slave of Antonia's held there.'

'Livilla, eh? A nasty piece of work, from all accounts. Well, I'm sure the Lady Antonia knows best.'

'What's between you and Antonia?' Vespasian asked, intrigued by Magnus' unlikely contacts in high places. 'She knew you, but seemed embarrassed to see you.'

'I'd rather not say. I was hoping that she wouldn't recognise me,' Magnus mumbled.

'I think I can guess,' Caligula ventured. 'You're an ex-boxer judging by the look of you, aren't you?'

'I am, sir.'

'My grandmother is very fond of boxing, so fond in fact that she used to go down to their stables and watch the boxers train.' Caligula smiled mischievously. 'Now, I've heard that some wealthy widows organise boxing bouts as after-dinner entertainment and then, when the guests have gone, hang on to a boxer or two for some entertainment of another sort. Am I close?'

They could tell by Magnus' expression that Caligula had hit the mark.

'No, Magnus, surely not?' Vespasian gasped in disbelief, equally astonished at Caligula's candour in discussing his grandmother's sexual preferences, whilst resisting the temptation to ask Magnus what she was like.

'Oh, it happens all the time with upper-class ladies,' Caligula went on cheerily. 'Boxers, gladiators, charioteers, even actors. Personally I see nothing wrong with it. After all, we all have our needs, even my grandmother, and I'm sure that Magnus was well rewarded for his efforts.'

'The money was just a bonus,' Magnus said. 'She was a very beautiful woman – still is. I can't claim that it was a hardship. Well, it was, if you take my meaning?'

'I'm sure I do.' Caligula smiled at him through the rain. 'Anyway, we should concentrate on the matter in hand. Extinguish the torches; Livilla's house is about a quarter of a mile away. The tunnel entrance is in the gardens at the back, so we'll need to walk around the perimeter walls to find a suitable place to climb over; I think I can remember one.'

They carried on in silence up the hill; the wind had got up and the rain pounded down on them. Caligula stopped when they reached a narrow alley that ran off to the right off the main road between two walls, each about twelve feet high.

'This is the rear of Livilla's property, the gardens are over the left-hand wall,' Caligula whispered. 'About a hundred paces down the alley there's an overhanging tree, we can throw a rope over its branches and scale the wall there.'

'Did you bring rope, Pallas?' Sabinus asked, worried that the whole venture would come to a grinding halt.

'It's all right, sir,' Pallas reassured him, 'I have one in my bag; Master Gaius had forewarned me.'

'Oh, excellent, well done, Caligula,' Sabinus muttered, hoping that he wasn't going to be shown up by this pasty-looking youth all night. 'Magnus, leave two of your men here to secure our getaway: we don't want to be trapped in this narrow alley.'

'Right you are, sir. Marius, that had better be you, I imagine that your rope-climbing days are over.'

'Too right.' Marius grinned, looking at the stump at the end of his left arm.

'Sextus, you stay here too; when you see us coming back both of you hide over the other side of the street in the shadows. If the Praetorians are after us you follow behind them so if it comes to a fight you can take them in the rear.'

'Hide in the shadows, take them in the rear. Right you are, Magnus,' Sextus repeated, slowly digesting his orders.

'They could probably do with these.' Pallas pulled out a couple of swords from his sack.

'What else have you got in there, Pallas?' Vespasian asked, looking at the bulging sack.

'Just stuff that we may need, sir,' the Greek replied smoothly.

'Come on, we haven't got all night.' Sabinus headed off down the dark alley.

The tree was where Caligula remembered it and in a few short moments they had the rope secured around a branch ready for the ascent.

'The main house is about two hundred paces away to our right,' Caligula said, 'and the tunnel entrance is this side of it by a small round temple dedicated to Minerva.'

'Right,' Sabinus said. He was now soaked to the skin, as were all the others. 'Magnus, leave two more of your lads down here to fight off anyone coming from the other direction, and station one more on top of the wall to get the rope in place to help us back over when we return.'

Magnus gave the orders whilst Pallas dished out three more swords to the men staying behind. Sabinus led the way up the rope to the top of the wall; he peered around but could see nothing on the other side in the pitch-black rain-sodden gardens.

'Well, here goes,' he muttered to himself, and leapt down into the dark. He landed with a soft thump in some long grass growing beneath the tree.

'It's fine,' he called up softly to Caligula, who was just appearing at the top of the wall. He jumped down without hesitation. Vespasian, Pallas, Magnus and his last remaining brother, Cassandros, followed quickly.

'We're lucky with this weather,' Caligula whispered. 'If there are guards at the tunnel's entrance they'll be sheltering inside. We can approach from the side and they won't have a chance of seeing us.'

'You lead the way, Caligula,' Sabinus said, 'then when we're at the entrance Magnus and I will take the guards out. Hopefully one of them will have the key to the cellar door. If not we'll have to force it.'

'You might find that this will be of help, sir.' Pallas pulled out a heavy iron crowbar from his sack.

'Good. Anything else we may need, Pallas?'

'Just these, sir,' he replied, producing six more swords. 'Better than your short daggers, I'll warrant.'

'I was intending to knock them out, not kill them.'

'It takes quite a hit to fell a Praetorian, sir,' Magnus pointed out seriously. 'They don't go down easy. Better to help them on their way with a decent bit of sharp iron, if you take my meaning?'

Sabinus hadn't planned on killing anyone but realised that Magnus was right: better to silence them once and for all rather than risk them escaping and raising the alarm.

'All right, but we go for a quick thrust to the throat, to prevent them shouting out.'

'I know, sir,' Magnus replied.

Sabinus looked at him. 'Yes, I'm sure you do. Well, let's get on with it. Lead off, Caligula.'

They crept through the shrubs and bushes of the laid-out formal garden, taking care not to step on the gravelled paths and keeping close so that they didn't lose one another in the dense night and driving rain. After a hundred paces or so a couple of dim points of light appeared through the trees.

'There, that must be the main house,' Caligula hissed over the wind. 'We'll head towards it; the temple should be on our left quite soon.'

With the lights guiding them progress became easier;

soon they were aware of a tiny glimmer as light reflected off water running down a stone wall.

'Here's the temple; the tunnel is around the other side about twenty paces away. Follow me.'

Caligula started to lead them around the circular building. Vespasian gripped his sword handle tightly as he followed; he felt his heart accelerating and had to concentrate on breathing slowly. Once around the other side Caligula took Sabinus' shoulder and pointed. Only a few paces away a faint glow emanated from a low doorway. Sabinus nodded and signalled to Magnus to follow him.

Vespasian held his breath as he watched the barely visible silhouettes of his brother and Magnus creep slowly towards the entrance. Suddenly a loud laugh broke through the steady roar of wind gusting through trees and rain falling on leaves. Sabinus and Magnus stopped. A figure appeared in the doorway, stopped and looked up at the rain-filled sky and then out into the black night. He lifted up his tunic, eased his loincloth to one side and started to piss. It seemed to go on for an age. Sabinus and Magnus stayed stock-still, barely six paces away from the Praetorian. Eventually he finished and headed back inside saying something to his companion as he went. Sabinus and Magnus started to ease forward again. Once they were beside the entrance they stopped and looked at each other, then sprang in. Vespasian surged forward followed by the rest of the party and charged into the tunnel to find Sabinus and Magnus searching the bodies of the two guards who were lying on the floor, blood oozing from gashes in their throats and their dead eyes staring in shock at the ceiling.

'Bugger it, they haven't got the keys,' Sabinus spat. 'Look around, see if they're hidden somewhere.'

A quick search in the guttering light of the single oil lamp proved futile.

'Pass me that crowbar, Pallas; we'll do this as quickly and quietly as possible.'

'What if there's a guard in there with her?' Vespasian asked.

'Fuck knows. Bring the lamp, Caligula.' Sabinus snatched the crowbar from Pallas and headed off up the tunnel, intent on getting the thing over with as fast as possible.

The solid oak door had a thick bar across it to prevent people breaking out, not in. Sabinus slipped it out of its housings with minimal noise and eased the thin wedge of the crowbar into the crack between the door and its frame, next to the lock.

'Right,' he whispered, 'Pallas and Cassandros, guard the tunnel entrance. Caligula, you hold the lamp up. Magnus and Vespasian, put your weight against the door and follow me through.'

'What if it's bolted on the inside and we can't shift it?' Vespasian asked. He was getting increasingly nervous about this ad hoc rescue attempt; concern for Caenis' wellbeing gnawed at his belly. His brother looked at him with fire in his eyes,

'It's not, all right? It's not. Now, on the count of three push as if the harpies themselves are after you.'

Magnus and Vespasian braced themselves against the door and Sabinus took a firm grip on the crowbar.

'One, two, three.' He wrenched back on the bar with all his weight as his companions launched themselves at the door; there was a loud crack and Vespasian and Magnus went tumbling into the darkness.

Vespasian landed on the cold stone floor, grazing his knees. He could hear a suppressed whimper, as if someone was trying not to scream, coming from somewhere in the dark. Sabinus came dashing in still holding the crowbar.

'Quick, Caligula, get that lamp in here.'

Caligula did as he was told. The room was low and damp. There was another door in the wall opposite that led to the stairs up to the house. To his left Vespasian could see a small, shaking body covered completely by a blanket. He rushed over and stripped it away,

'Caenis,' he whispered, looking down at the trembling form buried in a small pile of straw on the floor; her face was covered by an arm. Vespasian gently touched her hair and the whimpering stopped.

She looked round; disbelief registered in her eyes. 'You! What are you doing here?'

'Antonia sent us to get you out. Come on, quick.'

'Have you got the key?'

'What key?'

'For this.' Caenis lifted her left arm; around the wrist was a manacle attached by a large chain to the wall.

'Shit! Sabinus, look at this.'

'Fuck!'

'What do we do?'

'Well, we'll have to get the key, or lop her hand off.'

Caenis' eyes widened in horror at the suggestion.

'Very funny, Sabinus,' Vespasian hissed.

'I'm serious, how else can we get her out?'

'There's a guard at the top of the stairs, he keeps the key,' Caenis whispered quickly.

'We can't break down that door to get him without alerting the whole house, and we need to hurry.' Sabinus was getting impatient.

'Then we'll get him to come here,' Vespasian whispered urgently. 'Magnus, close the tunnel door. Caligula, put out the lamp.'

The room descended into complete darkness.

'Caenis, I want you to start screaming and don't stop until the guard opens the door. Let's hope there's only one of them.'

Caenis had no problems screaming. Soon there was a thump on the door.

'Shut your noise, you little bitch,' a gruff voice called from the other side. Caenis went on shrieking. There were a couple more bangs and then they heard the sound of a key being inserted into the lock; the door opened quickly and a man holding a torch burst into the room straight on to the point of Vespasian's sword. Vespasian's arm tensed as he drove the point up through the guard's throat; he dropped gurgling to the floor, dead.

Vespasian snatched up the burning torch. 'Sabinus, get the key.'

'Got it!' Sabinus ripped the key off a bloody string around the dead guard's neck. He quickly undid the manacle's lock and helped Caenis up.

More footsteps came clattering down the steps and into the cell burst a bull of a man. Long, oiled black hair fell to his shoulders. His much-battered, pock-marked face was the colour of oak and adorned with a close-clipped goatee beard.

Caenis screamed again. Magnus hurled himself at the door and rammed it into the brute's face, throwing him back on to the stone steps behind, knocking him senseless.

'Magnus, Caligula, lock the stair door and pile all the straw you can find against it,' Vespasian hissed.

It was the work of moments.

'Let's go!'

No one needed a second invitation and they dashed through the tunnel door. Vespasian hurled the torch into the pile of straw and pelted after his comrades. They found Pallas and Cassandros waiting nervously. Shouts could be heard coming from the house.

'They're on to us. That was a bright idea of yours, little brother, all that screaming. Quick as you like, Caligula,' Sabinus urged.

'This way,' Caligula said, heading off into the sodden night.

Vespasian took Caenis' arm and followed. From behind him in the house he could hear the shouting intensify.

They stumbled through the moonless garden, crashing into trees and bushes that tore at their clothes and scratched their skins. The shouting was now outside; looking quickly over his shoulder in its direction Vespasian saw, in the distance, three or four torches coming around the side of the house.

'They're heading for the tunnel. Once they find the dead guards they'll be after us,' he panted as he held on to Caenis, trying to prevent her from tripping.

Caligula stopped abruptly. 'Here's the wall. The tree should be to the right, come on.'

The going was slightly easier now that they had the wall to follow, but it seemed to Vespasian that the shouting was growing nearer; he dared not look behind again for fear of tripping. Caenis was gasping for breath at his side as she struggled on, terrified for her life. The wind drove the rain into their faces making it almost impossible for them to keep their eyes open.

After a gut-wrenching length of time Caligula slowed. 'Thank the gods, we're here.'

The crossroads brother on the wall chucked the rope down.

'The girl goes first,' Sabinus hissed.

Caenis leapt at the rope and with surprising agility hauled herself up and over the wall. As Caligula took his turn Vespasian looked around; the torches were no more than a hundred paces away and closing fast. Pallas and Cassandros scaled quickly, followed by Magnus.

'Hurry, hurry,' Sabinus urged. With Magnus over he grabbed Vespasian. 'Come on, get up there.'

Vespasian clambered up the rope and got to the top of the wall; he could see the torches, now just thirty paces away, and could make out in their orange halos nearly twenty figures. He reached down to help his brother up, hauling him on to the top of the wall and then pulling the rope up behind him as Sabinus jumped down.

'There they are, get them,' came a shout from the garden. Vespasian looked up; their pursuers were almost on them, light from their torches illuminating the tree. An instant before he jumped he locked eyes with their leader; he had only seen him once before, from a distance, but recognised him immediately. Sejanus, he thought as he hit the ground.

CHAPTER XIII

VESPASIAN PICKED HIMSELF up and sprinted down the alley in his brother's wake. They found their companions waiting for them on the main street. Apart from them it was completely deserted; the increasingly atrocious weather was keeping even the Night Watch sheltering inside. Back down the alley they could see the torches appearing over the wall as the first Praetorians made it over.

'Run,' Sabinus shouted, 'run like the three-headed hound of Hades is after you.'

They hurtled round the corner and sped down the hill towards Antonia's house, less than a third of a mile away. The furious speed was too much for Caenis and she slipped on the wet stone surface, falling to the ground with a cry. Vespasian grabbed her arms, pulled her up, threw her over his shoulder and pressed on as fast as he could, aware that the Praetorians had now rounded the corner of the alley and were racing down the hill behind them.

Caligula came skidding to a halt in front of Antonia's door and thumped on it repeatedly.

'We'll carry on down the hill and try to lead them away,' Magnus called to Sabinus.

'Good luck,' he replied as the crossroads brothers disappeared shouting into the night.

The viewing slit slipped back briefly before the door was pulled open and they piled in. Vespasian looked up the hill to see the torches about three hundred paces away. They were safe. On a night as dark and rainswept as this the Praetorians would never have seen which house they'd gone into; they could only guess, but it would be an easy guess, he was sure. He stepped into the atrium and put Caenis down. The door closed behind him. Completely out of breath he leant against the wall and sucked in the air.

Caligula knelt on the floor next to him, panting also. 'That – was – brilliant – fun,' he gasped, looking up at Vespasian with a smirk on his face. 'What did I tell you? A jolly caper indeed. We should do that more often, my friend.'

Vespasian smiled back at him and held out his hand to help him up as Antonia came running into the room.

'Thank you, gentlemen,' she said, seeing Caenis and putting her arms around her. 'I trust you didn't have too many problems?'

Caligula grinned widely. 'Easy as slitting a suckling pig's throat.'

'Speak for yourself.' Sabinus puffed, his chest still heaving from the exertion. Outside they could hear the Praetorians running past following the sound of Magnus and his men down the hill.

Caenis looked round at Vespasian. 'Thank you,' she said, 'thank you all.'

Her beautiful eyes gazed at him in admiration. Her wet dress clung to the contours of her body and he felt a surge of desire for her.

Antonia must have sensed this and released Caenis from her grasp. 'You'd better go and change into something dry. Hurry along, and come and see me when you are warm.'

'Yes, mistress.' She bowed her head and left the room. Vespasian's eyes followed her retreating form hungrily.

Antonia broke the spell. 'Where's Magnus?'

'He and his mates carried on down the hill to lead the Praetorians away.'

'Good,' she said, although to Vespasian's mind there was a hint of disappointment in her eyes. 'Were any of you seen?'

'I may have been, domina,' Vespasian admitted.

Sabinus groaned.

'I recognised Sejanus as I slipped back over the wall, though I don't know if there was enough light for him to see me clearly.'

'Well, at least he doesn't know you so he can't have recognised you even if he did see you clearly,' she replied. 'But to be safe we'd better get you out of Rome as soon as possible. You, Sabinus and Gaius should stay here for the night. It won't be wise for you to try to get home now. I imagine that we shall get a visit from our esteemed prefect very shortly; I shall deny everything, of course, it will be most galling for him. He will however have my house watched so we'll have to smuggle you out tomorrow somehow.' She looked at Pallas who was standing dripping by the door. 'Give orders for the floor to be mopped dry and then change into a fresh tunic. There must be no sign of anyone having been outside when Sejanus arrives. And have these gentlemen shown to the guest rooms and provided with dry clothes.'

'Yes, domina,' he said, and clapped his hands. Four house slaves appeared from the other end of the atrium. Within moments buckets and mops had arrived and Vespasian, Sabinus and Caligula found themselves being led down a grand corridor to the guest wing.

'Get changed quickly,' Caligula said as they were shown their rooms, 'I want to see how my grandmother deals with Sejanus. She'll see him in the formal reception room; I know a place where we can listen in to everything that goes on in there.'

Vespasian and Sabinus met up with Caligula in the corridor not long after. He led them quickly down a couple of passages and stopped outside a panelled door painted crimson with black inlays.

'There's no lock on this door,' he said, opening it and stepping into a small room with a curtain on the far wall. 'The reception room is on the other side of that curtain; let's take a look.'

He pulled the curtain back a fraction and they put their eyes to the gap. Beyond was a beautiful room with a ceiling so high that it was almost in darkness, despite the efforts of the numerous oil lamps scattered around on tables and stands beneath it. Painted wooden chairs with delicately

carved backs and legs and couches with cushioned uphol-
stery of lushly coloured fabrics stood ready to receive
Antonia's official visitors.

A slave hurried into the room and looked around,
checking that everything was in order; he made a couple of
adjustments, repositioning two chairs so that they sat opposite each other either side of a low marble table, and then
scuttled away.

Footsteps approached. In came the inscrutable Pallas
leading Sejanus, dripping wet. A thin steam rose from his
damp tunic and his thick black hair hung in lank clumps
around his square-jawed face. He did not look happy.

'Please take a seat, master,' Pallas crooned, every ounce of
Greek courtesy being used to the full. 'The Lady Antonia will
be with you presently; she has been in bed these past couple
of hours.'

'I'll bet she has,' Sejanus growled.

'She told me to tell you that she will dress as fast as
possible so as not to keep your eminence waiting too long.
Would you care for some refreshment, master?'

'No! Now get out of here and leave me alone, you
smarmy little Greek cum-stain.'

Pallas bowed and beat a dignified retreat leaving Sejanus
looking around the room. He picked up and admired a
couple of bronze statuettes that were on the table and then,
placing them back down again, started a slow walk around
the room. They watched him as he inspected the furniture
and ran appreciative hands over the statues and busts. He

was directly opposite them when he noticed the curtain and started to move towards it.

'Quick, out,' Caligula hissed, leaping back. They slipped out of the door just as the curtains were ripped apart, and darted into the nearest room.

'It would have been nasty coming face to face with Sejanus in that sort of mood,' Gaius said, quickly closing the door of the unlit room. They heard footsteps out in the corridor.

'Hades! There's no lock on this one either,' he said, running his hands up and down the door in the dark. 'Quick, lean against it.'

They pressed their bodies hard against it; a few moments later they heard the door to the room they'd just vacated open and close. Purposeful footsteps approached their door and they felt the pressure of someone trying to open it from the outside. The pressure grew; they braced themselves harder against it.

'Prefect, there you are.' Antonia's voice came from the end of the corridor.

The pressure ceased suddenly and they slumped against the door.

'My dear Sejanus, what are you doing trying to get into that room?'

'Don't give me that "my dear Sejanus" rubbish. Someone was spying on me and they ran in there.'

'Impossible, that room is always kept locked.'

'How? I see no keyhole.'

'It's bolted on the inside. It can be accessed only from the library on the other side. Now, enough of this foolishness; tell me why you've had me dragged from my bed in the middle of the night?'

'You know perfectly well why, if indeed you were even in bed after what you've been plotting this evening.'

'Plotting, my dear prefect? You'll have to enlighten me. I've spent the evening with my secretary Caenis, writing letters.'

'You lying bitch, she was a prisoner at Livilla's house and you sent a rescue party there to free her.'

'If that were true how would you be able to prove it without admitting that you and Livilla kidnapped her in the first place? I am sure that the Emperor would be very interested to know why you and my daughter would want to take Caenis prisoner.'

'Three of my men are dead.'

'That, prefect, is nothing to do with me. As I have told you, I was writing letters with my secretary all evening – unless you would prefer your version of events to reach the Emperor's ears? Do you feel strong enough yet to admit to the Emperor that you are still having an affair with Livilla, an imperial princess, sister of the great Germanicus, whom Tiberius has already forbidden you to marry knowing that if you did it would make you a possible heir to him and therefore his rival? I think not, Sejanus. Now leave.'

'You've not heard the last of this. I saw one of your murderers this evening and if I ever find him I shall use all means possible to link him to you.'

'An empty threat, prefect, it would still prove nothing.'

'That may be so, but it won't stop me enjoying it.' He hit the door in his frustration, which without much weight behind it opened a fraction.

'Locked, you say? Well, it seems to be mysteriously unlocked now.'

Caligula signalled Sabinus and Vespasian to stay behind the door and walked around it. Sejanus grabbed Caligula's ear in the dim light of the doorway and pulled him roughly to his knees.

'What have we here then? A little spy?'

'Ow! Get your hands off me, you bastard.'

'That, Sejanus, as you should well know, is my grandson, Gaius Caesar Germanicus. You would do well to let him go immediately and ask him to forgive an assault on a member of the imperial household.'

Sejanus let go of Caligula's ear as if it were a red-hot iron, gave Antonia a look of utter hatred and stormed off down the corridor. Antonia smiled and then walked into the room and looked behind the door.

'I thought so,' she said, seeing Sabinus and Vespasian in the gloom. 'Out you come.'

The brothers obeyed, looking extremely sheepish.

'Well, I suppose you heard all of that?'

'Yes, Grandmother; and I thought that you dealt with him brilliantly.'

'I said that it would be a galling experience for him and I thoroughly enjoyed it. However, Vespasian, you are definitely not safe. If he were to catch you, you would be wishing for death throughout the long days of life that he would ensure remained to you.'

Vespasian blanched slightly. 'I'd better go north, then; has Asinius fixed my appointment?'

'I shall find out in the morning. Now I really am going to bed, as should you, gentlemen. Goodnight to you all.' With that she disappeared off down the corridor.

Vespasian closed the door of his room, sat down on the bed and assessed his situation. He needed to be out of Rome for a good while until Sejanus' image of him faded. Four years' military service should do it, but that would be four years with no chance of seeing Caenis; but she was a forlorn hope anyway and he would do better to forget her. Four years should be long enough to do that as well.

His mind made up, he stripped, pulled back the blanket, got into bed and closed his eyes, trying to shut out the roar of the wind outside. There was a knock on the door.

'Who is it?' he asked.

The door opened and Vespasian took a sharp intake of breath. 'Caenis, what are you doing here?' He felt his mouth go dry.

'My mistress said that I should come and thank you for what you did this evening.' She approached the bed.

'Well, that's good of you, but you already thanked us all earlier,' he replied, his heart pounding causing his voice to shake slightly.

She sat down at the end of the bed. 'I know, but my mistress said that I should come and really thank you.'

'Oh, I see,' he said in a thin voice.

He'd had women before, quite a few in fact, but they'd always been slave girls owned by either his parents or grandmother. Slave girls who could not say no for fear of punishment. Caenis was different. She was a slave girl, yes, but she was also the first person who made him feel intoxicated by just thinking of her. He wanted her more than anything but he was not going to have her against her wishes; and her mistress had ordered her to come to him.

Caenis slipped her loose tunic over her shoulders exposing the exquisite breasts that he'd caught sight of at dinner. He felt his scrotum tighten and the blood rushing to his groin.

'Caenis, you mustn't,' he whispered.

'Why not?' she asked, standing up so that the tunic fell to her ankles. In the dim light of the single oil lamp he could see the gentle roundness of her belly, the smooth curve of her hips and delicate softness of her labia, plucked clean of all hair. She stepped out of her tunic and came closer.

'Because I don't want you to do anything against your will,' he replied breathlessly.

'Who said that I'm here against my will?' She sat on the bed next to him and put a hand on his chest.

'Antonia ordered you to come.'

'My mistress did suggest that I come and thank you, but she also gave me permission to stay. I am her property; I would not give myself to you without her consent, but now I have that I want nothing more than to be with you tonight.'

She moved her hand down across his stomach and over his erection and smiled. 'Mmm, I think that you too are willing to give your consent.'

He raised a hand and gently brushed the back of it over her nipples; she shivered involuntarily and sighed with pleasure.

'I do give my consent,' he murmured, putting his hand behind her head and bringing her closer. Her fingers tightened around his penis and she looked into his eyes.

'Vespasian, you are beautiful,' she whispered.

'So are you, Caenis.'

He smiled at her and, stroking her thick, perfumed hair, pulled her into a kiss that he felt could last for ever.

CHAPTER XIV

VESPASIAN AWOKE AFTER a brief but rejuvenating sleep. The wind had died down and it had stopped raining. He felt the warmth of Caenis' body lying next to him and turned on his side to admire her beauty in the thin dawn light. He ran his hand over her back and on to her buttocks, cupping one gently, letting his fingers probe the warm crevice between them. She moaned softly and then resumed breathing quietly. Thinking that he would wake her in the lover's favourite way he nuzzled the side of her neck with his mouth and worked his fingers lower. She turned and put an arm around him and, drawing herself closer, kissed him on the mouth. Opening her eyes she looked at him with love.

'How did you sleep?' she asked gently, then she suddenly looked around the room and sat up. 'Minerva! My mistress will be furious.' She jumped out of bed and pulled on her tunic.

'What's wrong?'

'It's way past dawn, I should be attending to my mistress, laying out dresses for her to choose from for the day and getting things ready to do her hair.'

'Shall we see each other before I go?' Vespasian asked, realising that it could be four years before he saw her again.

'I don't know, but even if we do we won't be able to talk.' She gazed at him with eyes so full of love that he felt his heart stutter. 'I will wait for you, Vespasian. Who knows but in four years, if I work hard for my mistress, I may be freed; she is not ungenerous.'

'But Augustus set the minimum age limit for freeing a slave at thirty.'

She stepped into her shoes and leant over to the bed; she kissed him briefly but passionately. 'I know, but I live in hope that the law doesn't always apply to the people in power.' She stroked his cheek. 'I must leave now.'

'Wait! Before you go, last night in the cell a big man came down the stairs and you screamed. Why?'

She blanched at the memory and took a deep breath. 'He was to torture me. He took great pleasure in showing me the instruments that he would be using. He terrified me, mainly because he seemed to be looking forward to it so much.'

'Who is he?' Vespasian asked, putting his arms around her protectively.

'He's Sejanus' freedman. His name is Hasdro.'

She kissed him once more and ran out of the room. Vespasian put a hand to his face, closed his eyes and, savouring her aroma on his fingers, contemplated four years without seeing, touching, smelling or tasting her.

*

Eventually he climbed out of bed and washed his face in a bowl of cold water that had been placed on the chest the night before. There was a knock at the door and in walked Caligula, smiling as he always seemed to do.

'What a night, eh? Such fun; and I believe you rounded it off with a very grateful girl.'

'What? How did you know that?' Vespasian demanded, shocked.

'I like it when they're grateful, don't you?' Caligula carried on, ignoring the question. 'That's why I often have an ugly one. They are so grateful that they do anything you want, with anything you want, very enthusiastically.'

'I asked you a question,' Vespasian insisted.

'Oh, yes. I was on my way back from asking Pallas to fetch me this very buxom kitchen slave that I've been meaning to try for some time – she was very grateful too by the way – when I saw the delightful Caenis knock on your door and go in.'

Vespasian reddened and tried to hide it by drying his face with a cloth.

'Oh, come now.' Caligula grinned at him. 'There's no need to be embarrassed; as I said, we all have our needs and I believe that it would be a crime against the gods to ignore them; they gave them to us after all. Just imagine how dull life would be if we spent all our time suppressing our desires. You're a lucky chap, you know, my grandmother has banned me from even thinking about having Caenis and she's threatened all sorts of nasty reprisals if I try. Did you know that she's even given Caenis permission to hit me – me! Can you imagine it?'

'I'm glad to hear it.' Vespasian was relieved to learn that Antonia had taken steps to protect her favoured slave from the seemingly insatiable sexual appetite of his new young friend.

'Shall we go and find some breakfast? I'm ravenous, as you must be too.'

'Yes, gratitude does help you work up an appetite,' Vespasian observed, tying on his loincloth. He pulled his tunic over his head, fastened his belt and, slipping into his slippers, followed Caligula out of the room.

They found Sabinus already eating in the triclinium. They joined him for a leisurely breakfast of freshly baked bread, cheese and olives washed down with sweet watered wine, whilst discussing the previous night's events – which included Caligula filling Sabinus in on who he saw entering his brother's room.

'Well, well, little brother, so you've finally given up mules and moved on to slaves; well done. One day soon you may even get your cock into something that has a choice in the matter.'

Vespasian knew that it was pointless rising to his brother so contented himself by throwing a hunk of bread at him.

Antonia joined them halfway through the second hour of the day. 'Good morning, gentlemen, I hope that you all slept well.'

Vespasian couldn't help feeling that there was a hint of irony aimed at him in the remark. Antonia sat and a waiting slave poured her a cup of watered wine. She looked at the two brothers. 'It's as I feared: Sejanus has posted a group of Praetorians a little way up the hill watching the front of the house and another group down the side alley watching the stable-yard gate. So we shall have to be careful.' She gestured to the slave without looking at him. 'Fetch Pallas.'

The slave bowed and left the room.

'Is there any news from Asinius, domina?' Vespasian asked.

'I sent him a message this morning and he's promised to come here as soon as he has dealt with his clients for the day; let us hope that he brings some good news with him.'

Pallas entered the room.

'Pallas, I want you to have two covered litters prepared in the stable yard. Do not have them sent around the front until Sabinus and Vespasian have been hidden in them.'

'Yes, mistress.' The steward bowed and hurried off to give the necessary orders.

Antonia turned back to Sabinus and Vespasian. 'Once you are each in a litter they'll come out of the stable yard and round to the front of the house where Gaius and I will get in quickly, then we'll head down the hill before our watching friends have time to react.'

'That's very neat, Grandmother,' Caligula said, warming to the idea of another escapade. 'But how do we get them out of the litters? We can't just take them home; we're bound to be followed.'

'We'll go to the Forum. It's a market day; lots of people will have come into the city so it will be very crowded by midmorning; they should be able to slip out there undetected.'

'Thank you, domina,' Sabinus said.

'It is I who should thank you,' Antonia replied. 'What you all did last night not only saved Caenis' life but also bought us more time to construct a case against Sejanus strong enough to convince the Emperor.'

Pallas walked back in. 'Titus Flavius Sabinus and his wife Vespasia Polla are here requesting an interview with you, mistress; they want to know the whereabouts of their sons.'

'Bugger it!' Sabinus exclaimed. 'Why couldn't they just wait patiently at home?'

'I don't think that we can blame our father for this,' Vespasian said, looking worried. 'But I'm afraid that they've unknowingly made a big mistake coming here; the Praetorians would have seen them and if they follow them home then Sejanus will be one step closer to us.'

'I'm afraid that you may be right,' Antonia said, getting up. 'But they are here and I should see them. Come with me, all of you.'

She led them out into the atrium where an anxious Vespasia and a very embarrassed Titus were waiting.

'Domina!' Vespasia exclaimed, coming forward with her hands outstretched in supplication. 'Thank you for consenting to receive us. Where are our . . .? Oh!' Vespasia caught sight of Sabinus and Vespasian.

'Mother, you shouldn't have come,' Sabinus said firmly. 'Why didn't you stop her, Father?'

'She was threatening to come on her own, unchaperoned. I could not let myself be disgraced like that, so it was the lesser of two evils.'

Antonia looked sternly at Vespasia. 'You have done a very foolish thing in coming here. In future you should follow the example of Cornelia, mother of the Gracchi, and wait at home and spin wool whilst your sons serve Rome.'

'I – I am sorry, domina,' Vespasia said. She bowed her head in acknowledgement of Antonia's vastly superior social standing. 'We shall return immediately.'

'I'm afraid it's too late for that, you must both stay here for the time being; Pallas, show them to the formal reception room, we'll join them there presently.'

'With pleasure. Mistress, master, please follow me.'

Titus and Vespasia were led away. Antonia turned to Caligula. 'Get ready to go out. We shall leave as soon as we have spoken with Asinius.'

'Yes, Grandmother.'

'Sabinus, go and keep your parents company; Vespasian, you might want to check that you've left nothing in your room.'

'But I didn't bring anything . . . Oh, I see. Thank you, domina.'

'Don't be too long.'

'No, domina.'

Vespasian hurried to his room with a knot in his stomach; his excitement at being able to see Caenis to say goodbye was tempered by the knowledge that it would, in all probability, be a very long separation.

He opened the door; Caenis sprang up from the bed and embraced him. He held her tightly, relishing the sweet smell of her skin and hair.

'I can't stay long,' he said as they broke the embrace.

'I know. I've brought you this.' Caenis held up small silver figure on a leather thong.

'What is it?'

'My mother left it to me; it is an image of Caeneus, a warrior from Thessaly, the guardian of our tribe. He was born as a woman called Caenis. One day Caenis wandered far from her home, to the north into the wild lands before Asia, where Poseidon saw her by the sea. Struck by her beauty and unable to control himself he raped her. After he had finished she fell to her knees and begged him to turn her into a man so that she could never be raped again. So ashamed was he of what he'd done that, to atone for his crime, he did as she had asked. But not only did he turn her into a man, he also made him invulnerable to weaponry.'

'He must have lived to a great age.'

'Sadly no, there is always a catch. He fell in a battle against the Centaurs. They crushed him with logs and rocks. As he died he turned back into a woman and was buried as Caenis.

'Take it and wear it, my love, and I will pray to Poseidon that he will grant you the same invulnerability to weapons. But it's up to you to avoid Centaurs armed with logs.'

He smiled. 'I think that I can manage that.'

She reached up and slipped the thong around his neck and kissed him. 'Take good care.'

'Thank you. I shall wear it always, knowing that you are thinking of me.' He pulled her gently to his chest and he felt her sob. He held there for a moment and then she pulled back with tears in her eyes.

'Go,' she said and turned away.

Vespasian took a last look at her and quickly left the room, feeling his heart tear as he did so.

He entered the formal reception room to find Sabinus sitting in close conversation with their parents. His father looked up as he came in.

'Vespasian, my boy, your brother has told us enough of what is going on to make me feel heartily ashamed of myself. I can only apologise for our rash behaviour in coming here. Would that there was something that I could do to make amends.'

'It's all right, Father, I understand that Mother must have been very worried when we didn't return last night; we should have got Magnus to send a message to you, but things just happened too fast.'

'Worried!' Vespasia cried. 'I was up all night, not knowing where you both were or what was going on. Gaius would say nothing and—'

'Enough, woman!' Titus shouted, standing up. He had reached breaking point with his wife's wilful behaviour. 'Sometimes it is not your place to know, sometimes it is your place just to wait, and you would do well to remember that, as the Lady Antonia said. Now hold your tongue.'

He sat back down again and briskly adjusted his toga.

Neither Vespasian nor Sabinus had ever heard their father speak to their mother like that before and braced themselves for an explosion, which didn't come. Instead Vespasia folded her hands on her lap and lowered her gaze to the floor looking every inch the image of a demure and respectful Roman matron.

They heard Antonia's voice in the corridor and the men stood as she came into the room with Asinius in tow.

'Our esteemed ex-Consul has some very good news for us,' she announced smiling.

'Indeed I have,' the diminutive ex-Consul said brusquely, motioning them to sit back down. 'Sabinus, I have secured your position at the mint. You will oversee the striking of all bronze and silver coinage. It's a position open to much temptation so don't succumb – and if you do, don't get caught. I want you monitoring the treasury, not languishing on some island because you've been banished from Rome for petty theft.'

'Yes, Consul, thank you.'

'I'm not a consul any more so call me by my name.'

'My apologies, Asinius.'

Vespasian smiled inwardly at his brother's faux pas, enjoying his discomfort.

'Vespasian, Pomponius Labeo has agreed to take you into the Fourth Scythica as a *tribunus angusticlavius*. A "thin stripe" military tribune with no command is the lowest of the low, but you will serve on his staff, which is perfect for our purposes. When you get to Thracia you will first report to Gaius Poppaeus Sabinus, who is in overall command.'

'Thank you, Asinius.'

'Yes, well, do what I have asked and you will find me thanking you. Now, there is a column of new recruits for the legion assembling up north at Genua; you need to be there by the beginning of next month. That gives you fourteen days, which should be plenty.' He handed Vespasian two scrolls. 'This is your letter of introduction and a military pass, don't lose them.'

'I won't,' Vespasian said, unrolling the scrolls and reading them.

Asinius paused and looked over to Titus and Vespasia. 'Antonia informs me that you are the parents of these men. I am pleased to meet you.' He held out his arm to Titus, who took it gratefully.

'It is an honour, Asinius.'

'Indeed. I believe that there is a problem in that you were seen coming here?'

'I can only apologise, we were foolish to meddle in matters that we didn't understand.'

'Well, it's too late now, it is done. But you can't return to Senator Pollo's house; if you were seen there it would link him with us and put him and your sons in great danger.'

'Can we not just go immediately home to Aquae Cutillae?' Vespasia asked.

'I'm afraid not. You will have to stay with me for a while until I can smuggle you out of the city.'

Titus cast a sour look at his wife.

'I should go.' Asinius turned to Vespasian. 'Good luck and remember, trust no one and do not write anything down.'

'Yes, Asinius, thank you.'

'Good. I shall leave you all to say your goodbyes. Antonia, I'd like a private word with you, if I may?'

When they had gone Titus looked at his sons. 'I don't know which of you I shall be more worried for, Vespasian in the army or Sabinus under Sejanus' nose here in Rome.' He took Vespasian's arm. 'Take the Via Aurelia to Genua, not the inland route, then you can stay a few days with your grandmother. She's old and you're going to be away a long time. Give her my greetings.'

'I will, Father,' Vespasian replied, cheered by the thought.

Titus embraced each of his sons in turn. 'Farewell, my boys. I'm proud that you are serving Rome.'

Vespasia kissed both of them. 'Being unable to help you make decisions recently hasn't been easy for me. Forgive me. And take care of yourselves, my sons. May the gods go with you.'

Vespasian and Sabinus took leave of their parents and joined Pallas, who had been waiting for them in the corridor. He took them through the house and out to the stable yard. There they found the two covered litters ready with the teams of Nubian bearers waiting patiently in the shade. Six burly bodyguards, armed with cudgels and staves, talked quietly in a group.

'One of you in each if you please, masters,' Pallas said, bowing slightly and gesturing to the waiting litters, managing to be polite and formal even whilst organising an escape. 'Make sure the curtains are fully closed once you are in, and sit exactly in the middle so that your weight is evenly distributed between the front and rear teams. We want the litters to look empty when they go round to the front of the house.'

Vespasian climbed into his litter, the same one as he had seen Caenis in only a few days earlier, and sank into the sumptuous cushions and soft fabrics of the interior. With the curtains fully drawn it began to get stuffy inside fairly quickly and he was relieved when, not long later, he heard a shout and felt the litter being lifted by the bearers. Another shout and they moved off. He felt the litter turn left and heard the gates start to close behind him. The litter remained very stable so, being unable to see where he was going, Vespasian had hardly any sense of movement or speed. He was aware of another left turn, then after a short while a slight bump as the litter was grounded, Antonia got in almost immediately and sat in front of him; he felt the litter rise again.

'Our watching friends will just follow at a distance,' she said, plumping up a cushion and settling down for the ride. 'However, they wouldn't dare to try and waylay me in public.'

Vespasian hoped that she was right.

The litter felt to be at a slight angle and Vespasian guessed that they were now going down the hill. Antonia pulled the curtain back a fraction and peeped out the side looking both forward and back. She pulled away quickly.

'Another six Praetorians have appeared in front of us; they must have been waiting down the hill. We're surrounded, it will be nigh on impossible to get you out undetected.'

'Are Sabinus and Caligula behind us or in front, domina?' Vespasian asked.

'Behind. Why?'

'In that case make the litter-bearers go faster,' Vespasian replied. 'The guards in front will either have to speed up or fall behind us.'

Antonia stuck her head out of the front curtain. 'Speed up,' she shouted. There was a slight lurch as the bearers switched into a trot.

'Have a look to see if the Praetorians and the other litter are both keeping pace.'

She had another peek. 'Yes, they are.'

'Good, let's go faster still.'

Antonia gave the order and the bearers broke into a run. The litter started to sway slightly and Vespasian was finally able to feel that he was moving. He decided to risk a quick look. He pulled the curtains apart and stuck an eye to the gap. In front he could see the escorting Praetorians running, their leader occasionally looking over his shoulder. Behind,

Sabinus and Caligula's litter was keeping up, followed by six more Praetorians. On either side ran Antonia's bodyguards, brandishing staves and cudgels, ready to stop anyone from getting too close to the litters.

'Where does this street go?' he asked.

'Down to the Via Sacra about quarter of a mile away, then we'll turn left towards the Forum.'

'Is there another street parallel to this one?'

'Yes, over to our left.'

'Good, make them go faster, domina.'

She gave another shout and the litter accelerated away. It was now becoming a bumpy ride.

'That's it, we're at full speed,' Antonia said, holding on as the litter swayed and lurched, its bearers having difficulty keeping in step at the speed that they were going.

'On my order get them to turn left, domina,' Vespasian said, looking out of the left side. He could see the Praetorians in front racing to stay ahead, determined to keep them surrounded. Passersby jumped out of the way on to the crowded pavements at the sight of the small phalanx of armed guards thundering down the hill with two litters born by huge Negroes in their wake.

Vespasian saw a narrow left turn coming up; he glanced at Antonia and raised his right arm. 'Nearly there, nearly . . . nearly.'

The Praetorians went speeding past the turn; as the last one cleared it Vespasian lowered his arm.

'Turn left!' Antonia shouted.

The lead bearers reacted quickly and leaning to their left brought their comrades round behind them. Somehow the litter skidded around the corner with all the bearers keeping their footing. Vespasian and Antonia swayed around inside as the litter rocked its way around the bend. He looked out of the back in time to see Sabinus and Caligula's litter scrape around with all the Praetorians now behind it.

'Don't let them overtake us,' he called to Antonia's bodyguards beside them. They nodded and fell back to prevent the Praetorians from pulling alongside.

They raced along the narrow alley; coming to the end Antonia yelled: 'Turn right.'

The bearers had been expecting this command and the litters turned right on to the main road with comparative ease and headed the last hundred paces at full speed down to the crowded Via Sacra.

Vespasian looked behind and could see that the bodyguards were having difficulty holding the Praetorians back. If it weren't for the crowds of people on the pavements on either side they would already have been overtaken.

Vespasian looked at Antonia. 'I'll jump out of the right-hand side as you turn left on to the Via Sacra. Hopefully the litter will mask the Praetorians' view.'

'Good luck, Vespasian. Get out of Rome as soon as you can.' She turned around and looked through the curtains to judge the left turn.

Vespasian braced himself for the jump.

'Turn left,' Antonia shouted. Vespasian felt the litter-bearers respond to her command and leapt through the curtains on to the crowded pavement. He rolled head over heels along the ground as he landed, skittling over a couple of young boys.

Getting quickly to his feet he pushed through the crowd away from the road as the next litter passed by.

Vespasian breathed a sigh of relief. He watched the litters disappear towards the Forum and hoped that his brother would find an opportunity to slip out there. Concerned as he was for Sabinus he realised that there was no way of helping him. All he could do for him was to blend into the crowd, make his way quickly back to his uncle's house and ask him to send Magnus' crossroads fraternity out to search for his brother. Then he would pack; he had made up his mind he would leave Rome that night.

He nipped into a side street heading away from the Via Sacra and started to walk as quickly as possible along the busy narrow lane. He found the going easier off the pavement despite the ordure squelching between his toes.

At the far end of the street he turned left in what he hoped was the direction of the Quirinal. Suddenly a hand clamped over his mouth and the sharp point of a dagger pressed into the small of his back.

'My master is going to be so pleased to make your acquaintance,' hissed a thickly accented voice in his ear. The pungent smell of raw onion and wine hung on the man's breath.

Vespasian froze. He looked at the passersby for help but

to a man they ignored the situation, unwilling to get caught up in someone else's argument.

'Now be a good boy and you may meet him intact. Bring your hands behind your back.'

Slowly Vespasian obeyed. He felt the dagger withdraw and heard it being slipped back into its sheath. He took his chance. Thrusting his hands back between the legs of his assailant he grabbed the man's testicles and squeezed. Immediately he felt teeth bite into his shoulder and the hand on his mouth move down to his throat and clasp it. He squeezed harder. A huge roar of pain exploded behind him and he was released. Vespasian pelted forward. A quick glance behind him as he rounded the next corner told him that his attacker was doubled up on his knees, his long, oiled black hair completely covering his face.

Hasdro.

Vespasian ran.

CHAPTER XV

GAIUS WAS WAITING back at the house. 'Dear boy, how are you?' he said, waddling out of his study as Vespasian was let in slowly by the ancient door-keeper. 'Where is Sabinus? Did your parents find you? I told them not to go but I'm afraid when my sister wants something there's no stopping her. Sit down and tell me what happened.'

Gaius clapped his hands and ordered some wine from the waiting slave boy. Vespasian sat down and caught his breath. Once he had been served his wine he gave his uncle a quick rundown of the last twelve hours' events.

'As for Sabinus,' he said, finishing his story, 'I'm hoping that he'll be back here soon.'

'It sounds like you had quite a night; it was lucky that none of you were hurt. Did Hasdro see your face?'

'He couldn't have done, he was always behind me.'

'Pray to the gods that you are right.' Gaius suddenly looked puzzled. 'What I don't understand is why didn't Sejanus go straight to Antonia's house instead of following Magnus down the hill?'

'He didn't see which house we went into, it was too dark and pissing with rain.'

'Yes, but only one other person knew that Caenis was at Livilla's house and needed rescuing, and that was Antonia. As soon as the attempt was detected why didn't he go straight to her house?'

'I don't know, perhaps he's just stupid.'

'Never think that of Sejanus. But look at you, you must be tired, my boy, I'd say that you need a bath and a good rub down. I'll have them prepared.'

'Don't worry, Uncle, I must organise my packing. I'm leaving for the north tonight.'

'My steward will do that for you. Now go and relax, I must insist, dear boy; you have plenty of time, it is not even midday yet.'

Vespasian suddenly found himself too tired to argue and headed off in the direction of the baths.

An hour later, dressed in a fresh tunic and with his skin still tingling from the pummelling that it had received from the hands of one of Gaius' German boys, he walked back into the atrium to find Sabinus had just returned with Magnus.

'Your friend Caligula gave me this for you.' Sabinus threw him a heavy purse that jangled as he caught it. Vespasian opened it. Inside were thirty or so *aurei*, gold coins. 'He said that he thought you might need a war chest. So use it well, and don't go spending it on mules and slave girls or whatever it is that you get off on these days.'

'That's very good of him, thank him for me when you see him next,' Vespasian replied, ignoring his brother's insult. 'I assume that you got away unseen?'

'Only just, but just is good enough. They saw me slip out of the litter but Antonia's bodyguards prevented them from getting to me before I disappeared into the crowd. I made it to Magnus' place unseen and he brought me here by the back streets.'

'Did they get a look at you?'

'No. Caligula gave me his cloak to hide my face.'

'Sabinus, you're back, well done, my dear boy,' Gaius boomed, coming in from the courtyard garden. 'You are not hurt, I hope?'

'No, I'm fine, thank you, Uncle.'

'Good. Good. Ah, Magnus, none the worse for wear as usual, you have a charmed life, of that I'm sure.'

'I don't know about that, sir, we only just managed to outrun those Praetorians last night. Me and the lads aren't as fit as we used to be. That is when it comes to running, if you take my meaning?' he added patting his groin with a grin.

'I'm sure I do.' Gaius smiled. 'Now, what did you do to make those Praetorians follow you last night?'

'Well, nothing really, sir, we just ran as fast as we could down the hill making as much of a hullabaloo as possible to draw them bastards away from the gentlemen at Antonia's house.'

'That's my point; Sejanus knew where they were heading with the girl so why did he let himself be drawn away?'

'Ah, well, it weren't Sejanus who was following us, was it?'

'But I saw him as I jumped over the wall,' Vespasian said adamantly.

'And you may well have done, sir, but he never came over the wall, Marius and Sextus will swear to it. They watched all the bastards out of the alley and then followed them down the hill. That new tribune, who's recently transferred in from the Night Watch, he was leading them.'

'Who is he, this new tribune?' Gaius asked, intrigued.

'Another nasty piece of work, only out for himself, but aren't we all? I only know him as Macro.'

'Naevius Sutorius Macro,' Gaius said slowly, 'well, well.'

'You know him, Uncle?' Vespasian asked.

'Yes, I do, he used to be a client of mine until it became apparent that I wouldn't be able to help him to get what he wanted.'

'What was that?'

'What do you think? A transfer to the Praetorian Guard, of course; and now he's got it.'

'Well, he won't get far if he's so stupid as to go following Magnus into the night rather than just going straight to Antonia's,' Vespasian said dismissively.

'Oh, he's not stupid either, no; he will have sworn blind by now to Sejanus that he was close enough to see that no one went into Antonia's house, that's why he carried on chasing you.'

'Why would he do that?' Sabinus asked.

'Because he didn't want to catch the girl, she was an asset

to Sejanus. He's happy to have Sejanus in the dark about any conspiracies against him.'

'What for?' Sabinus was puzzled.

'Don't you see? He doesn't want to help Sejanus secure his position. He's got his sights set on becoming prefect of the Guard.' Gaius chuckled. 'Sejanus had better watch out, he's got a rat in his nest; and on the basis that your enemy's enemy is your friend we may well be able to use this rat against him.'

Vespasian was ready to leave by the second to last hour of the day. He had put on his military tribune's uniform for the first time and felt a new swagger in his step as he walked from his room into the atrium with his red cloak billowing behind him. The muscled bronze cuirass felt heavy on his chest and the protective skirt, made of strips of leather reinforced with polished iron, slapped against his thighs through his white woollen tunic as he walked. The shiny bronze greaves on his lower legs chafed slightly but he knew that in time he would cease to notice them. He brought himself to attention in front of his uncle, bronze helmet with its white horsehair plume in the crook of his left arm.

'Well, Uncle, how do I look?'

'Probably as you feel, a fine specimen of a man, but don't let it go to your head – and take your sword off, you're not allowed to carry it in the city.'

'Oh, yes, of course, I forgot.'

Feeling slightly deflated he unbuckled the short two-foot

gladius that hung at his right hip and stuffed it into a saddlebag waiting by the door next to his small kit-bag.

'I've employed Magnus and two of his friends to see you safely to Genua,' Gaius said, raising his hand and stopping Vespasian's objection before it was even voiced. 'Don't be stupid, of course you need an escort, what were you planning? Two hundred miles up the Via Aurelia on your own?'

'I'm going to stop at my grandmother's estate at Cosa for a four or five days, I don't need to be in Genua until the calends of February.'

'Oh, well, that's all right then, you'll be safe for a few nights at least. Dear boy, we don't want you running into trouble before you've even left Italia; and I'm sure your grandmother would love to meet Magnus.'

Vespasian winced at the thought, but Gaius was adamant.

'Not another word, he'll be back here shortly. Now, in the absence of your father, here's some travelling money.' He handed him over a small leather purse. 'Don't use the gold that Caligula gave you to pay at inns, you'll soon attract some unpleasant company if you do.'

'Thank you, Uncle.'

There was a loud knock and the ancient doorkeeper unfurled himself from his stool and with some difficulty opened the door. Magnus walked in with a thick, undyed woollen travelling cloak around his shoulders.

'We should go, sir, we need to cross the Aemilian Bridge and be on the road before dark; we'll be less likely to be questioned during the day.'

'Of course; where's my brother, Uncle?'

'He's here,' Sabinus said, walking into the room. He looked at Vespasian and nodded his approval. 'Well, little brother, I have to say you almost look the part, so let's hope that you've got the balls to play it.'

'I'll take that as a compliment, coming from you.'

'Do, it'll be the last one you'll ever get.'

'I hope not,' Gaius said seriously. 'Now, if that is the extent of your emotional fraternal farewell, you had best be off. Good luck, dear boy.'

He grabbed Vespasian by his shoulders and gave him a moist, rubbery kiss on each cheek. 'Write when you get there, but nothing concerning our business, only your news.'

'I will; goodbye, Uncle, and keep well. And you too, brother.' He disengaged himself from Gaius, picked up his two bags and walked out of the door to find Marius and Sextus waiting with four horses. He attached the bags to his horse whilst Gaius had a quick word with Magnus, clapping him on the shoulder as he did.

Once all were ready they led their horses down the Quirinal Hill on the same route that they'd taken to the Circus Maximus on Vespasian's first day in Rome.

Vespasian glanced back at Marius and Sextus and then leant close to Magnus. 'I don't mean to be funny, Magnus,' he said quietly, 'but what use is Marius on a horse?'

Magnus burst out laughing. 'You hear that, Marius? The young gentleman is wondering how you are going to able to fight on horseback.'

Marius and Sextus joined in the laughter.

'What's so funny?'

'Well, the very idea of it,' Magnus said through his mirth.

'Of what?'

'Of fighting on horseback like some trouser-wearing savage. No, sir, horses are for travelling on or escaping with; if there's fighting to be done we do it on our feet; we're foot soldiers, sir, and proud of it. You, sir, on the other hand, are a different class of Roman, an *eques*, an equestrian: if you do well in your first couple of years they might give you command of an auxiliary cavalry unit, and then you'll have to fight on horseback, and may the gods help you.'

Vespasian remembered the fight with the runaway slaves barely four months ago and thought it no bad thing to fight mounted.

They carried on in silence, pushing through the crowds of people making their way to whatever they called home, until they came into the Forum Boarium. The cattle market held there on market days was being cleared up. The smell of manure invaded their nostrils, and the cries of the beasts being led off to the slaughterhouses filled the air. Small boys with sticks beat the docile creatures savagely to move them off in the right direction, whilst farmers and slaughterhouse agents did last moment deals and counted their money. At a table on a dais sat a togate aedile, the magistrate overseeing the market, taking complaints from buyers and sellers alike and adjudicating on them, then and there. As the stock was moved out hundreds of wretched public slaves began shovelling the manure into sacks, dismantling the temporary pens and piling them on to carts to be taken away and stored, ready for the next market in eight days' time.

As they crossed the forum in the direction of the Tiber they passed by the small circular temple of Hercules Victor with its tiled roof supported by columns. It was almost as old as the city itself; next to it stood the massive altar to Hercules. Vespasian looked at these ancient sites and wished that he had had more time for sightseeing; he had hardly seen anything of Rome in his brief stay.

With the bridge in sight, a new, powerful smell assailed their senses. Upstream on either side of the river were many of Rome's tanneries. There they had a plentiful supply of water and an outlet into which they pumped their effluent. The stench from the process of turning dried, stiff hides into leather, firstly by soaking them in human urine, to loosen the hair enough to scrap it off with a knife, then by pounding them with a mixture of animal brains and faeces to make them supple, produced a stench of such hideous intensity that Vespasian had to pull his cloak over his face as he crossed the bridge. He looked down at the river and to his amazement saw young boys playing and swimming amongst the filth.

Halfway across a loud shout stopped them in their tracks.

'You lot there, leading the horses, stop where you are.'

Vespasian looked over in the direction of the shout. At the far end of the bridge by a guardhouse was stationed a unit of the Urban Cohort. A centurion had detached himself and was walking towards him, flanked by two soldiers.

'Don't give your real name,' Magnus hissed at his side whilst motioning Marius and Sextus to fall back slightly.

'What have you got to hide, then, covering your face like that?' the centurion asked, coming up to them.

Vespasian immediately pulled his cloak away from his face. 'Nothing, I was just trying to protect my nose from the terrible smell,' he replied honestly.

'Don't give me that, son, everyone's used to it. Can you see anyone else covering their faces like some sneaking villain? I don't think so.'

Vespasian looked at the crowds of people passing, all seemingly oblivious to the reek of the tanneries. 'I'm sorry, centurion, but I'm just not used to it.'

'Bollocks, I'd say you were acting suspiciously and I've got orders to detain anyone acting suspiciously. What's your name? And where are you going?'

'Gaius Aemilius Rufus, I'm on my way to Pannonia to serve with the Ninth Hispana.' Vespasian pulled back his cloak to reveal his uniform.

'Are you now? Well, with that Sabine accent you don't sound like one of the Aemilii to me and you're going in the wrong direction for a start. Where're your papers?'

'I'm to be issued with them at Genua, that's why I'm taking the Via Aurelia.'

'A likely story, and who are these unpleasant-looking thugs with you?'

'Tullius Priscus, sir, at your service, and these are my associates Crispus and Sallius,' Magnus said, stepping forward to the centurion. 'The young gentleman has hired us to escort him north.'

'Well, you're going nowhere until the Praetorians have had a look at you.' The centurion turned to one of his soldiers. 'Go to the guardhouse and get the tribune up here immediately.'

The soldier saluted and ran back towards his comrades. Magnus gave a quick gesture to Sextus and Marius and then, stepping forward and bending down in one swift motion, head-butted the centurion in the groin. He doubled up in pain. With a monumental effort Magnus straightened himself up with the centurion over his shoulder and hurled him over the parapet and down into the river where he sank like a stone. Sextus and Marius leapt at the remaining soldier who, before he had time to react, found himself following his superior into the brown water below.

'Mount up and ride,' Magnus shouted, leaping on to his horse and kicking it into action. Vespasian jumped into the saddle and urged his mount forward through the panicking crowd towards the rest of the Urban Cohort soldiers who, alerted to the trouble, were forming up in a line at the far side of the bridge. The crowd parted as his horse gained momentum. He could see Magnus ahead and hear the brothers behind him urging their horses on. The soldiers, shieldless and armed only with swords because they were serving within the city, took one look at the four horses only ten paces away charging towards them, and broke, scrambling over each other in their haste to avoid the trampling hooves.

'Stop!' A Praetorian tribune stepped out of the guardhouse into the road; his sword was raised, aiming at Magnus' chest. With one swift movement Magnus unsheathed his own sword and brought it crashing down, backhand, on to the tribune's blade. The force of the blow jarred the sword from the man's hand and forced him to his knees.

Reacting quickly to being disarmed the tribune whipped his *pugio*, a long dagger, from his belt and confronted Vespasian. Seeing that he had no alternative other than to charge him down, Vespasian reached into his saddlebag and pulled out his sword. He swung it wildly, sending the scabbard flying through the air, and bore down on the tribune. At the last moment before contact he pulled his horse to the left and aimed a cut at the tribune's neck. The tribune ducked and, as Vespasian sped by, thrust his dagger towards the horse's belly, hitting instead Vespasian's leg; the blade pierced the greave, embedding itself in muscle and bronze. Vespasian's momentum pulled it clean from the tribune's grasp and sent him rolling in the dirt. Pain seared up Vespasian's leg but he knew he had to keep going. He put his head down and drove his horse forward, the dagger wedged firmly in his leg as it gripped his mount's heaving flank.

Magnus looked over his shoulder and saw his three companions riding hell for leather behind him. 'Just keep going for as long as you can,' he called to Vespasian.

Vespasian gritted his teeth and concentrated on riding his horse, trying to block out the pain from his wounded calf, but every jolt caused the dagger to vibrate and seemed to force the razor-sharp point further in. He tried to reach down to extract it.

'Leave it,' Magnus shouted, slowing down to come closer to him in order to hide the dagger from the eyes of passing travellers who were looking with suspicion at the four horsemen tearing up the Via Aurelia. 'If you pull it out now you'll lose too much blood. We'll do it properly later.'

Vespasian nodded weakly and hoped later would come soon.

They passed the second milestone from Rome as the sun started to turn gold and sink towards the horizon. There was no sign of any pursuit but Magnus still urged them on. The further they got from the city the more the traffic thinned out. By the time darkness fell they were on their own.

'Right, lads, let's get off of the road and find a place to camp,' Magnus said. 'We've got to see to that leg of yours, sir.'

He slowed his horse, pulled it to the right and began climbing a gentle slope. Vespasian followed with the others; his head was light with loss of blood and his leg throbbed incessantly. He had made it out of Rome, but in this state he didn't know how much further he would be able to go.

PART III

THE VIA AURELIA

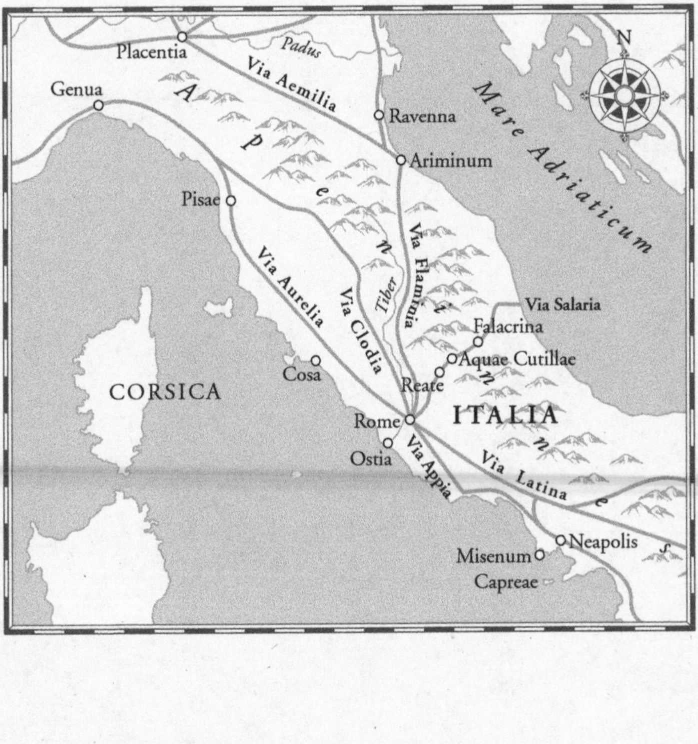

CHAPTER XVI

VESPASIAN TUMBLED FROM his horse into Magnus' arms and felt himself being laid gently down against a tree.

'You rest here, sir. The lads are getting wood for a fire; once it's burning we'll be able to remove that dagger and patch you up.' He eased Vespasian's wounded leg straight and immediately the pain lessened as the ground took up the weight of the dagger.

'Where are we?' Vespasian asked weakly.

'By a stream in a valley about a mile east of the road; there doesn't seem to be anyone else about so we'll risk the fire.' Magnus placed a blanket behind Vespasian's head and then raised a water skin to his mouth. Vespasian drank greedily; the blood loss had made him terribly thirsty. He felt the cool water flowing down inside him and his spirits lifted.

'That was so stupid of me on the bridge, covering my face like that; I just didn't think.'

Sextus and Marius returned with armfuls of wood and set to making a fire.

'It weren't the most stupid thing you did, sir, if you don't mind me saying,' Magnus said, handing him a hunk of bread and some salted pork. 'Telling the centurion that you were going to Genua, now that was stupid.'

'But he would have drowned in the river under the weight of his armour, surely?'

'He may well have done, likewise his mate, but the one he sent back to get the tribune most certainly didn't, and he heard everything you said and the accent in which you said it.'

'Oh.'

'Yes, oh, indeed; now they're going to be looking for us all the way up the Via Aurelia and keeping an eye out in Genua for a military tribune with a recent wound in his right leg who talks like a Sabine farmer.'

'We had better outrun them, then.'

'And that is particularly stupid . . . sir. Firstly you need to recuperate and secondly they're probably passing the point that we left the road as we speak.'

'How do you work that out?'

'Well, it would have taken half an hour to get a message to the Praetorian camp on the other side of the city; then another half an hour to get a cavalry detachment back to the Via Aurelia, which puts them an hour behind us. We left the road an hour ago. There you go, easy.'

'I see. Well, then, the best thing for us to do is to carry on as I planned: head to my grandmother's estate at Cosa, one day's hard ride from here. We can hole up there for a while whilst my leg heals and the fuss dies down. After that we'll have to just wait and see.'

'Well, it sounds like a plan of sorts, sir, and it's the only one we've got, so Cosa it is. But first we've got to deal with Macro's dagger.'

'Macro?'

'Yes. That was Macro you took a swipe at, then you stole his dagger and I'm sure that he'll be wanting it back.'

'I didn't steal it.'

'Well, you've got it and he hasn't, and it's probably best to keep it that way. One thing's for certain, though, he definitely got a good look at me. I won't be safe in Rome for a while so I'd best come along with you, sir, if that's all right?'

'Well, I suppose so, but how? Will you join the legion?'

'Will I fuck. No, I'll come along as your freedman, young gentlemen often take a personal slave or freedman with them on campaign; it won't look out of place.'

Vespasian was too tired to argue – not that he really wanted to; it would be a comfort having Magnus with him.

'I'll take that as a yes, then. Now make yourself comfortable, sir, this is going to hurt.'

Vespasian rested his head back on the blanket and looked up at the almost full moon. Its gentle light spilt through the leafless branches of the trees that lined the riverbank, giving them a silver outline that was filled in from below by the orange flicker of the fire that Marius and Sextus had built up.

Magnus drew his sword and thrust it into the heart of the flames, then he went back to Vespasian and knelt down to examine his right leg in the firelight. The dagger had pierced his calf by about three inches but it was the bronze greave, through which it had passed, that held it tightly in place. Magnus pulled on the handle gently to test the strength of the grip that the bronze had on the iron blade. It seemed to be stuck fast.

'Owww!' Vespasian yelled.

'Sorry, sir, just seeing what needs to be done; one thing I can tell you is that you were very lucky. If you hadn't been wearing greaves the dagger would have gone straight through your leg and gutted your horse. You would have been arrested and your walking days would have been over; not that you would have had much need for walking with what Sejanus would have had in mind for you.'

Vespasian grimaced. 'So we're looking on the bright side, then?'

'We most certainly are, sir.' Magnus looked round at Sextus and Marius. 'Now, lads, this will be a three-man job. Sextus, you hold the greave. Once I've pulled the dagger out, yank it off.'

'Hold it then yank it off – right you are, Magnus,' Sextus repeated, anxious not to get anything wrong.

'Marius, as soon as that greave is off, take the sword out of the fire and press the flat tip to the wound until I say stop.'

'Got you, Magnus,' Marius said, pleased that he had a one-handed task.

'All right, sir, we'll do this very quickly.' He handed Vespasian an inch-thick stick. 'Bite on this.'

Vespasian did as he was told and braced himself.

'It's best you don't look, sir. Ready?' Magnus asked.

Vespasian closed his eyes and nodded.

'All right, lads,' Magnus said, putting one foot on Vespasian's ankle and grasping the dagger's hilt with both hands. 'After three. One, two, three.'

Vespasian heard the rasp of metal scraping metal and felt a jolt in his leg, then a blinding flash of pain hit him; it eased slightly as the greave was yanked off, and then it escalated into red-hot agony. The smell of burning flesh hit his nostrils as he passed out.

'Wake up, sir, we need to be off.'

Vespasian felt himself being pulled out of a dreamless sleep. He opened his eyes; it was still dark. Magnus was kneeling over him shaking his shoulder.

'How're you feeling?'

'Better thank you, Magnus, but my leg is stiff as a board.' He put his hand gingerly on his wounded calf and felt a rough bandage protecting it. 'How is it?' he asked.

'Not too bad; the burning stopped the bleeding and closed it. We've been taking it in turns to piss on it. My grandmother always did that if she couldn't find any vinegar.'

Vespasian's face wrinkled. 'I'm sure that with the amount that you all drink the effect would have been the same as vinegar.'

'More than likely, sir. We should have some breakfast now and be ready to leave at first light.'

Sextus brought some bread and cheese over to them and

then started to bury all traces of the fire, whilst Marius struggled to fill the water skins in the stream.

'Which way should we go?' Vespasian asked through a mouthful of cheese.

'My guess is that the Praetorians know you are wounded and will have realised that we'd have had to stop fairly soon after dark to tend to you, which we did. So they would calculate that if they rode on for another two or three hours into the night they would most certainly pass us. Then all they need to do is block the road and maintain patrols on either side to stop us skirting round.'

'It sounds like they'll have got us trapped,' Marius said, still struggling with the water skins. 'Perhaps we should head east to the Via Aemilia Scaura; it can't be more than twenty miles away and it ends up in Genua as well.'

'I thought about that, mate, but they know where we're heading so I'm sure that they'll have that road covered too.'

'So where does that leave us, Magnus?' Sextus asked. 'Going back to Rome?'

'No way, they'll be checking everyone going into the city for days to come. No, lads, we've just got to go forward cross-country, keeping a sharp lookout, and try to slip past them.' Magnus got to his feet. The first rays of the sun had appeared over the horizon sending long shadows through the wood. 'Come on, lads, mount up. You'd best not wear that red cloak, sir, it's a bit of a giveaway, if you take my meaning? Here, take mine.'

Vespasian didn't argue and wrapped the warm woollen

cloak around his shoulders, and then packed his military one in his kit bag. He managed to get back in the saddle unaided but the exertion made his head spin and he had to hold on to his horse's neck to steady himself.

'Are you all right, sir?' Magnus asked, concerned.

'I'll be fine, thanks,' he replied as his vision steadied.

'At least we'll be going slowly, as we don't want to go carelessly blundering into any of their patrols. So you just hang on, sir, and shout if you need to stop.'

Magnus kicked his horse and moved off; Vespasian followed, praying to the gods that he would have the strength to last the day.

Keeping the Via Aurelia a mile or so to their left they picked their way across country. The undulating landscape was mainly farmland criss-crossed by small tracks and dotted with woods and olive groves. Here and there they saw a farmhouse or a country villa and skirted around it, keeping as far away from prying eyes as possible, but always maintaining a north-westerly direction. The occasional glimpses they had of the sea, a few miles to their left, helped them to keep on course, the sun now being visible only intermittently through the steadily thickening clouds. After a couple of hours, during which they'd covered over ten miles, Magnus stopped and turned to his companions.

'By my reckoning we should be nearly level with the roadblock so watch out for their patrols. From now on we'll try to keep as much as possible to the woods, olive groves and river beds.' He looked at Vespasian, who seemed to be very pale. 'Sextus, get something to eat for the young gentleman.'

A quick rummage through his pack produced some more salted pork that he gave to Vespasian, who ate it thankfully as they pressed on with caution.

By midmorning it had completely clouded over and a light drizzle of rain was falling. They were threading their way through an alder wood when a series of shouts stopped them dead.

'What was that?' Vespasian whispered, coming out of the reverie that he had fallen into and now suddenly alert.

'Fuck knows,' Magnus replied, looking around. 'But whatever it was, it was close.'

Another shout, which seemed to come from up ahead of them to the right, echoed around the wood. Suddenly, about fifty paces away to their front, three horsemen dressed in dull travel clothes crashed through the wood from right to left pursued by half a dozen red-cloaked, spear-toting Praetorian troopers.

Vespasian and his escort stayed motionless, hearts pounding, as the Praetorians raced through the wood in pursuit of their quarry. So concentrated were the troopers on navigating their way through the trees and dead undergrowth that they could neither look right nor left. They drove their horses furiously as they sped out of sight, enveloped by the wood.

'The bastards must think that was us,' Magnus said as the last red cloak disappeared.

'Then they're not very good at counting, are they?' Sextus pointed out.

Magnus looked at him with raised eyebrows. 'That's rich, coming from you. Anyway, who cares? The main thing is that they're occupied so let's take advantage of it.' He moved off quickly; the others followed. As they crossed the line of the chase more shouting came from their left, then a scream.

'It sounds like they've got us,' Marius said, smiling grimly.

'Poor buggers; still, they must have been up to no good if they ran when challenged,' Vespasian observed, feeling much revived by his racing heart.

'Even if I was as innocent as a Vestal Virgin I think I'd run from a Praetorian patrol that wanted to ask me a few questions; they're not known for their politeness, you know,' Magnus said, quickening his pace as the wood thinned out.

On reaching the last of the trees he stopped and looked ahead. In the distance, five miles off, was a line of hills, but before that was mainly rolling, open grassland used for sheep grazing. Here and there were little stone shepherd's huts that were connected by paths marked out by lines of trees and bushes.

Magnus dismounted and handed his reins to Sextus. 'Hold these, mate, I'm going for a little scout around to check whether we're clear to leave the wood.'

He darted off to the left, leaving his companions wondering how they were going to cross such a large area of open grassland unnoticed by a patrol.

Vespasian took a long slug of water and then another

bite from the strip of salt pork. He was feeling stronger than he had first thing, but he still had a long way to go before being fully fit. He wrapped his cloak tightly around his shoulders in an effort to keep out the rain and shivered slightly. He turned to Marius, who had his reins wrapped around his left forearm whilst he used his right to scratch his back.

'How did you lose your hand, Marius?'

'In the navy, sir, I was a deck—'

Magnus came dashing back, interrupting Marius. 'They killed one of the unlucky sods and three of the guards are taking the other two back towards the road. The other three are a mile off and heading back towards the wood, I assume to look for what they must believe is the missing fourth member of the party.'

'We're trapped, then,' Marius said. 'If we go forward they'll see us, and if we try to hide they'll probably find us.'

'If you can't beat them, join them,' Vespasian said.

The crossroads brothers looked at him quizzically.

'What?' Magnus asked, not understanding at all.

'We'll join them; we'll take them out and borrow their cloaks, helmets, shields and spears. That way from a distance we'll look like just another patrol and we should be able to cross that open ground unchallenged,' Vespasian explained.

'But there's only three of them,' Magnus said.

'I've got my military cloak and helmet; the plume is longer than a Praetorian's but from a distance it will do. Marius couldn't hold a spear or a shield in any case; it'll work, it's not as if we're going to try and go through a roadblock by passing ourselves off as Praetorians, is it?'

'You're right, sir,' Magnus agreed, pleased to have a plan. 'But before you pluck a chicken you have to wring its neck. So let's get further back into the wood and find a place to ambush them.'

They retraced their steps to the line of the chase, turned left along its path and followed it for a couple of hundred paces where, to their right, they saw a dell about ten feet deep and thirty paces across.

'This'll do us,' Magnus said, the beginnings of a plan formulating in his head. 'Now, sir, they'll be looking for a young military tribune, and you're the only one of us that fits that description so it has to be you that leads them here. Go back along the track and when they see you race back here, down through the dell and up the other side there.' He pointed to a gap between two large alders perched at the top of a steep bank on the far side of the dell. 'As they're following you up the bank we'll unhorse them and finish them off.'

'How?'

'I don't know, I haven't got that far yet, but we'll be on foot so let's get these horses out of the way, lads. Sextus, do the honours.' He and Marius dismounted and handed their reins to Sextus, who led the horses away.

'Good luck, sir,' Magnus said. 'We'll be ready when you get back.'

'I hope so,' Vespasian replied with a weak grin. He turned his horse and headed back towards the Praetorian troopers.

His leg was throbbing and his head ached but he felt confident that he had strength enough to stay on his horse and to ride fast through the wood for a short period of time. He was also sure that they wouldn't try to bring him down with their spears; Sejanus wanted him alive, which, in the circumstances, he found a comforting thought.

Keeping his eyes peeled he advanced cautiously, making a mental note of any obstacles that he would meet on the way back, until he caught sight of a flash of red through the trees ahead of him. He stopped and waited for them to come on, bracing himself for the dash back. He didn't have long to wait.

'There he is!' a shout came from about fifty paces away.

Vespasian turned his horse and kicked it into a gallop. As he sped back down the now familiar path, dodging trees, jumping logs and ducking under low-hanging branches, he felt an admiration for the horsemanship of the riders behind him who had earlier ridden the same route but without the benefit of a recce. He reached the edge of the dell and slowed. He looked around briefly to make sure his pursuers could see where he was going, then, satisfied, he plunged down the bank and tore across the dell in the direction of the two trees that Magnus had pointed out on the far side.

The Praetorians made it down the first bank as Vespasian's horse scrambled up the much steeper bank opposite. Its forelegs reached the top; as it tried to pull itself up on to the level ground, its hind legs scrabbled behind it to gain purchase on the loosened earth of the bank. Vespasian clung on as his horse gave an almighty heave and pulled itself clear of the bank, but the speed of its thrashing hind legs hitting the firmer ground of the woodland floor caused it to overbalance and it stumbled, sending Vespasian crashing to the ground.

'We've got him!' someone called from behind him as he rolled on to his back and drew his sword to defend himself. The first two Praetorians had almost scaled the bank when a couple of dark blurs swept across Vespasian's vision; two stout branches crunched into the troopers' faces, sending them tumbling off their mounts, who in turn reared up and toppled backwards down the slope on to the third trooper behind them. Magnus and Sextus charged down the bank from their ambush positions behind the trees, hurling their branches down at the fallen troopers. They leapt on them, swords drawn, as Marius slid down the bank behind the troopers to cut off any retreat. The horses crushed and kicked their riders as they struggled to get up, leaving the troopers as easy game on the floor. Three swords flashed almost simultaneously, blood spurted from the troopers' throats and they died beneath their terrified mounts.

'Quick, lads, try and calm those horses down, then start taking what we need,' Magnus said as he clambered back up the bank towards Vespasian. 'Are you all right, sir? That looked like a pretty nasty tumble.'

'I'm fine. Are they all dead?'

'Of course. I wouldn't be standing here chatting with you

otherwise, would I?' Magnus replied helping him up. 'Come on, let's get going.'

They hurried down the bank to where Marius was stripping the Praetorians of their cloaks and helmets, whilst Sextus struggled to control the horses.

'Take the saddles and bridles off the horses, Sextus,' Vespasian said, 'then let them go.'

With the bodies, bridles and saddles safely hidden in the long undergrowth away from the track, they donned the Praetorian cloaks and helmets, retrieved their own horses, mounted up and made their way to the edge of the wood. Looking out over the open ground they could see no sign of another patrol.

'We'll ride two by two,' Vespasian said, 'but not too fast, otherwise if another patrol sees us they may think that we're chasing someone and come to help us.'

'You're right, sir,' Magnus agreed, 'nice and easy all the way to those hills. All right lads, let's go.'

They left the wood and started to cross the grassland at a steady canter. Vespasian struggled for a while trying to control his horse with just his right hand whilst holding a spear and a heavy shield in his left, but after a mile he'd got the hang of it and he was able to offset the extra weight by leaning slightly to his right whilst still keeping his horse going in a straight line.

'Sir, look, behind us to the right,' Sextus shouted suddenly.

'Don't speed up,' Vespasian said, looking over his shoulder. Sure enough, heading for the wood that they had just left was another red-cloaked patrol.

'What do we do?' Marius asked.

'Nothing, mate,' Magnus said staring straight ahead. 'Don't look at them; just keep going. Let's hope that we're far enough away to fool them.'

Vespasian held his breath as they cantered on. He risked another quick look over his shoulder. The patrol was skirting the wood and making its way towards the Via Aurelia, seemingly taking no notice of their presumed comrades a couple of miles away out on the grassland.

'It's working. They're not interested in us, they're heading back to the road,' Vespasian shouted. 'Keep to this pace, lads, and pray to whichever god you hold dearest that we'll be out of sight soon.'

After another half an hour they had started to climb the first of the hills. The sudden shout they had feared, ordering them to stop, had not come. As the sun reached its zenith behind the rain-filled clouds they passed over the crest of the hill and down into the comparative safety of the valley below.

CHAPTER XVII

NIGHT HAD FALLEN and the rain had stopped. They had ridden fast through the hills and had now slowed to a walk as they crossed rocky scrubland. The full moon shone through the thin cloud covering giving enough light for the horses to be able to pick their way through the rough ground. Below them, to their left, the route of the Via Aurelia could intermittently be discerned, picked out by the torches of an occasional passing carriage or a group of travellers. Beyond it, high on a cliff, were the twinkling lights of a hilltop town.

'That is Cosa,' Vespasian said to Magnus. 'My grandmother's estate is just to the north of town overlooking the sea. We need to cross the Via Aurelia and find the road that climbs up to the town. About halfway up there's a track off to the right that leads to her land.'

'Well, now's as good a time as any, sir,' Magnus replied. 'It seems pretty quiet and I for one am looking forward to a hot meal and a warm bed, and I'm surprised that you're still able to sit on a horse. Dismount, lads, we'll lead them down to the road.'

They stopped in an olive grove fifty paces from the junction of the Via Aurelia and the road that wound its way up the hill to Cosa. In the distance they could hear the clatter of a large troop of cavalry coming up from the south.

'How far away are they?' Vespasian asked.

'Can't tell,' Magnus replied.

'They may not even be Praetorians.'

'I'll bet they are; if they were just army auxiliaries they would have made camp before nightfall. They'll be Praetorians all right; they must have realised a few hours ago that we had managed to get past them so I reckon they'll be heading further north to set up another road-block.'

'Do you think we should just make a run for it?' Marius whispered.

'Best not; we'll let them pass.'

The torches at the head of the fast-moving column were now in sight and they watched with bated breath as they came nearer. When the column, over a hundred strong, came to the junction their leader stopped.

'Clemens, take half the men and carry on up the road for another ten miles and block it there. Search all the inns, farms and barns on the way. I'll take the rest of the boys and search the town; if I don't find anything I'll join you in the morning. Get patrols out at first light, but only groups of more than four; I don't want a repeat of this morning's fiasco.'

'I shall do everything that is necessary, Macro.' The young decurion saluted; the torchlight glinted on his helmet as he turned to the column. 'The first two *turmae* follow me,' he ordered, and then led off up the road at a swift trot.

As the last of the sixty-man detachment passed Macro he called out to the rest of the column: 'Right, lads, we're going to turn this town inside out; anyone who's arrived today I want brought into the forum for questioning, along with all the local magistrates and tavern-owners. Don't take no for an answer from anyone – got it?' He turned to the familiar figure beside him. 'Well, Hasdro, I expect there'll be some work here for you tonight. I'm sure a few of them will appreciate a little encouragement before they talk.' He pulled his horse around and urged it up the road towards the town.

Vespasian and his companions watched the torch-lit column wind its way through the darkness up to the unsuspecting town a mile up the hill.

'Poor buggers,' Magnus whispered. 'They're not going to get much sleep tonight with Macro and his men running wild.'

'But that works in our favour,' Vespasian replied, now feeling desperately tired. 'Let's get going while the Praetorians are busy terrorising innocent provincials.'

They led their horses down to the road, mounted up and followed the column up towards the town. They found the track that led to Tertulla's estate as the first shouts and screams from the town echoed around the hills.

'We need to follow this for a mile or so to the top of the hill,' Vespasian said, struggling to see the line of the track in the dim moonlight. 'Then bear to the left towards the sea.'

Another series of screams came from the town and the group hurried on their way, not because they were in any immediate danger but in order to get away from the sounds of anguish that they felt responsible for.

The sound of distant waves crashing below them reached their ears as they came to the summit. The smell of salt water revived Vespasian and he sucked it in greedily. He had loved the sea ever since, from the age of seven, he and Sabinus had lived here with Tertulla for the five years that their parents had been in Asia.

He looked upon that time as the happiest of his life, despite his brother's constant bullying. But his grand-mother had protected him from Sabinus, inflicting severe punishments upon him every time new bruises had appeared on Vespasian's body and making sure that Attalus, her steward, kept an eye on the two boys if she wasn't around. Then one glorious day, when Vespasian was eleven, Sabinus left for Rome to seek the help of their uncle Gaius in getting a posting as a military tribune. Vespasian had then had Tertulla's undivided attention for over a year and he had basked in her love. Each day, after he had finished his lessons with his grammaticus, they would spend time together. She told him stories as they walked along the cliffs and taught him how to knot a net whilst fishing on the beach; but, most importantly, she had taught him the workings of the estate that she ran herself, her husband having died before Vespasian was born.

When his parents had returned he had not wanted to

leave Tertulla and her estate, which he had come to consider as home. It was only her accompanying him back to his parents' newly acquired estate at Aquae Cutillae, and staying for six months whilst he settled in, that enabled him to do so. She had left the day after his thirteenth birthday; he had not seen her since.

Knowing that he had less than half a mile to go before he was home he concentrated his mind on one final effort to remain conscious. The last few hundred paces were a blur to him, but eventually they arrived at the familiar wood and iron gate that he had last walked through nearly four years ago. He slumped forward on his horse, managed to kick his right leg over its back and dismounted. He felt Magnus' arm support him as he stumbled forward and knocked on the iron knocker with what little strength he had left.

'I think I'd better do that a bit harder, sir,' Magnus said, giving the knocker three huge blows.

'Who is it?' came a voice from the other side.

'Tell my grandmother that it's Vespasian and three friends.'

They waited a while and then a familiar voice came through the gate.

'If you're Vespasian tell me what name you call me by.'

Vespasian smiled to himself and looked apologetically at Magnus. 'Tute.'

The gate swung open and Tertulla, now well into her eighties, rushed forward.

'Vespasian, my darling, it is really you.' She put her arms around him and hugged him. 'Ow, you've grown a hard skin since I last saw you.'

'I'm a military tribune now, Tute, but we should talk inside; I've been hurt and need to rest. These fellows are my friends.'

'Yes, of course, come in, come in all of you.'

Vespasian lay on a couch in the triclinium drinking warmed watered wine whilst Tertulla examined his leg wound in the dim light of an oil lamp held up close by a slave.

'Not bad, Magnus, really not bad at all,' she said admiringly as she ran her wrinkled fingers over the swollen, blistered wound.

'Thank you,' Magnus replied from the other side of the room whence he and his crossroads brothers looked on anxiously.

'What did you clean it with?'

'Piss.'

'Very good, the best thing if you can't get any vinegar. The wound itself has closed, so I just need to apply a salve for the burn and then bind it tight to keep it from tearing open. Attalus!'

A tall, well-built man in his late fifties entered the room. 'There's no need to shout, I'm right here,' he said in an overly patient tone of voice.

'There you are, you great oaf. Take Magnus and his colleagues and find them something to eat, then bring some bread and ham in here. And whilst you're about it bring my cup, I don't know why Vespasian is drinking and I'm not.'

'Probably because you didn't ask for your cup before.'

'Must I think of everything?'

'Yes, you must, because you are the mistress and everyone else is your slave.'

'Well, behave like one, then.'

'I always do. Is that all?'

'That's three orders; I don't think you'll be able to remember any more.'

Attalus looked over to Vespasian and grinned. 'Welcome home, Master Vespasian, it will be so nice to have someone sensible around the house again.'

'Thank you, Attalus. I see that my grandmother and you are still getting along.'

'I tolerate her,' he said in a playful whisper.

'Why I tolerate *you* I don't know. I should have you crucified.'

'Then who would remind you what day it was and what your name is?'

'Go on, get on with it,' Tertulla said, slapping him hard on the arse and trying not to laugh.

Attalus left the room rubbing his behind and taking the bemused crossroads brothers with him.

Tertulla gently anointed the wound with a foul-smelling balm and then carefully bound it. As she was finishing Attalus came back with the food and a silver cup.

'You took your time, did you get lost again?' Tertulla said sharply, tying the linen bandage with a knot.

'I'm surprised you remembered that I'd even gone,' Attalus replied, thumping down the tray of food with a flamboyant flourish. 'Would the mistress like water in her wine or is she planning on drinking herself into oblivion again this evening?'

'I'll pour my wine and then I'll know there's no spit in it. Off you go and do something useful like fucking one of my body slaves, put her in a good mood for when she does my hair in the morning.'

'As a favour to you, mistress, I'll have all three, then you'll be surrounded by happy smiling faces when you dress tomorrow.'

'Get out of my sight, you old goat, and take your little friend with you. You'll probably need his help, considering your age.'

Tertulla dismissed the lamp slave, who knew better than to laugh at his mistress's banter with his superior.

Vespasian let out a long laugh as they left the room. 'I'd nearly forgotten how much fun it is living here, Tute. It is so good to see you.'

'He keeps my wits about me; a priceless commodity, wouldn't you say?' she said, laughing with him. She picked up the wine jug and poured a good measure of wine into her cup. Vespasian gazed at her lovingly as she caressed the plain silver cup with both hands.

'When I think of you, I always picture you holding that cup; you never drink from anything else, do you?'

'Your grandfather, Titus Flavius Petro, gave me this on our wedding day. I was thirteen years old and it was the first thing that I could ever call mine; up until then all my possessions had technically belonged to my father. I cherish this as I cherished that dear man, thirty years my senior, who gave me it all those years ago.' She smiled sadly to herself, remembering the man she'd loved, and then raised her precious cup. 'To absent friends.'

'Absent friends.'

They drank and sat in companionable silence for a while. The throbbing in his leg returned and reminded Vespasian of his wound.

'How long will it take to heal, Tute?'

'Ten to fifteen days if you rest it. Come on, you must eat,' Tertulla replied, offering him the plate of ham.

'I need to leave in seven at the most, I have to be in Genua in twelve days' time and we won't be able to take the road.'

'Why?'

Vespasian briefly related the events of the past few days. He tried to keep the details vague in order to disguise the extent of his involvement in the conspiracy against Sejanus, but it wasn't easy to pull the wool over Tertulla's eyes.

'So, you're involved with rich, powerful people and you are already choosing sides.'

'I chose the honourable side, the side that serves Rome.'

'You must be careful, Vespasian; the side that seems to serve Rome may not always be the most honourable, and even if it is it may not win.'

'So you would advise that I just choose the side that I think will win, regardless of whether it seeks to serve Rome?'

'I advise you to keep out of politics that you don't understand, and to keep away from the powerful, because in general they only have one goal and that is more power. They tend to use people of our class as dispensable tools. We're very handy for doing the dirty work but a liability once it is done because we may know too much.'

'Tute, I owe Asinius and Antonia for my commission in the Fourth Scythica; I am duty bound to do what they have asked me and that's all there is to it.'

Tertulla looked at her grandson and smiled. He was so like her husband when they had married almost seventy-five years before: the same earnestness and desire to do what he felt was right.

'Just remember what happened to your grandfather Petro; he was duty bound to Pompey Magnus, having served with him during his eastern campaigns, so he re-enlisted in his legions as a senior centurion when the civil war against Caesar flared up. He'd already served his twenty-five years with the legions, but at the age of forty-four, a year after our marriage, he found himself at Pharsalus fighting fellow citizens, whose sense of duty was as strong as his, but directed towards a different Roman cause. Pompey lost everything to Caesar at Pharsalus, but Petro managed to survive the battle and made it home to me. He appealed to Caesar in Rome and won a full pardon; he was allowed to live and became a tax-collector, though he knew he could never again expect advancement.

'Then, when Augustus came to power with the second Triumvirate after Caesar's assassination, he re-enlisted again and fought for Cassius and Brutus, Caesar's killers, against the Triumvirate at Philippi where the last hopes of the Republicans died. Augustus proscribed over two thousand equites who had stood against him or his adoptive father Caesar; your grandfather was one of them. Rather than be executed and forfeit his property he committed suicide here, in this very room, as the soldiers were banging on the gate.'

Vespasian gazed around the room and imagined his grandfather falling on his sword in a desperate attempt to save his family and property by taking the honourable way out. He looked at his grandmother; she was obviously picturing it too. 'Whenever I asked you how my grandfather died you said only that he had died for Rome.'

'And so he did. But he died for his idea of Rome, the old Rome, the Republic, not the Rome that emerged after the years of civil war, the new Rome, the Empire.'

'Do you look back at the Republic and wish that it still survived, Tute?'

'Yes, but only for my husband's sake. If it had survived I would have kept him longer. As to how Rome is governed now, I don't care, as long as I'm left alone; but I think that later tonight Rome will come knocking on my door again, so we had better get all of you hidden.'

'You think they'll come out here?' Vespasian asked. He

had been lulled into a false sense of security by the familiar surroundings.

'Of course; once they find nothing in Cosa they're bound to search the surrounding countryside on their way north. But it's all right, I've given orders to Attalus to mix your horses in with mine, and you, I'm afraid, will all have to spend the night in the loft above the slaves' quarters.'

'I didn't know there was a loft there.'

'That's because it is very well hidden; your grandfather used it to shelter Pompey sympathisers who didn't want to live in Rome under Caesar as they made their way north, out of Italia.'

'I'm learning a lot of things tonight about my grandfather that I never knew.'

'Why should you have known? You were only a child when you lived here, why should you have cared about politics? Now that you are a man, and becoming involved in politics, it's important that you understand the danger that goes with making a political choice. Your grandfather understood it but in his case the side that seemed to serve Rome most honourably lost, so choose well because to fulfil your destiny you mustn't lose.'

Vespasian looked at Tertulla eagerly. 'What do you mean: my "destiny"? I overheard my parents talk about omens at my birth that prophesied that I should go far but no one will tell me what that means. My mother swore everyone to silence.'

Tertulla smiled again. 'Then you should know that I cannot tell you either, because I too took that oath. What I can say is that the omens for you were very good, so good indeed that in these days of imperial power it was best not to make them public. However, omens from the gods will only come true if man plays his part and makes the right choices.'

Vespasian had expected a cagey answer but drew some comfort out from this. 'Thank you. You've helped me to understand something that I have never been able to put into words before; when I know that something is right I should have the strength of character to pursue it.'

Tertulla leant forward and kissed him on the cheek. 'You have grown in so many ways since I saw you last, my darling boy. But now we should find your friends and get you up into the loft; the Praetorians will soon be tiring of finding nothing in Cosa.'

'Even if they don't find us here we've still got to get past them somehow between here and Genua,' Vespasian said struggling to his feet.

'No, you don't,' Tertulla replied supporting him underneath the arm as they left the room. 'The best way to get to Genua, avoiding roadblocks and patrols and, at the same time, enabling you to spend more time here with me whilst resting your leg, is to go by sea.'

CHAPTER XVIII

'So it all comes down to who has the loyalty of the army, does it, Tute?' Vespasian asked, resisting the urge to scratch the scab that had formed over his wound. 'All these high ideals that men gave their lives for are now nothing more than a cover for the fact that power is no longer secured by constitutional right but by military might.'

They were reclining in the triclinium on the night before Vespasian was due to leave. The last eleven days had passed too quickly for Vespasian. He had spent most of the time resting his leg whilst talking with Tertulla. During the day he would lie on a couch in the courtyard garden and then in the evenings they would dine alone in the triclinium. She told him stories of his grandfather's exploits in the Republican cause. She told him of his hatred for Caesar and then for Augustus, and everything that they stood for; then of his disillusionment with the Senate and the Republican side, whose infighting and lack of decision caused their eventual defeat and the rise of autocratic power supported by Praetorian military muscle, the full extent of which, thankfully perhaps, Petro didn't live to see.

The Praetorians had come as Tertulla had expected. She had been kind and courteous to them and they had left an hour later satisfied that all that the house contained was an eccentric old woman, who could be of no harm to anyone but herself and her long-suffering slaves.

Vespasian looked at his 87-year-old grandmother, whom the Praetorians had dismissed as innocuous; she was one of the last survivors of the most turbulent period in recent history. Her memory of the time was still clear and she had been able to answer Vespasian's many questions. She had met Pompey, she had heard Caesar speak and she had seen Cleopatra when she came to Rome as Caesar's guest and lover. After Caesar's death she had hidden Marcus Brutus in this house, whilst Anthony's legions marched north along the Via Aurelia to fight his co-conspirator, Decimus Brutus. The following day she had kissed her husband goodbye as he left for Greece with Marcus Brutus to join Cassius and the Republican army. Ten years later, as a widow, she and her only child, Vespasian's father, had watched from the cliffs as the northern fleet sailed past, bound for Brundisium on the east coast, to join with Octavian before the fateful battle of Actium that finished Anthony and his lover Cleopatra and brought the Empire under the control of one man: Octavian, the Emperor Augustus.

The table had been cleared, apart from a jug of wine and some water. The oil lamps flickered in the draughts that made their way around the house, extensions, like long creeping fingers, of the howling wind outside. The sound of

Magnus and his friends' carousing could just be heard above the gale blowing in rain from the sea. The crossroads brothers had spent their time riding around the estate, ostensibly looking out for patrols but in reality hunting. In the evening they would roast and eat the day's kill, get uproariously drunk on Tertulla's wine and then retire to bed with whichever of her slave girls they fancied.

'It's more that constitutional right is secured by military might,' Tertulla replied, taking a sip from her cherished cup. 'Tiberius was Augustus' adoptive son so had the right to be Emperor although many would have preferred Germanicus. The loyalty of the army helps him maintain that right. We must hope that whoever he names as his successor can command the same loyalty.'

A knock on the door interrupted them and they looked up to see Attalus, wet and bedraggled, holding a leather scroll-case.

'You've not fallen into the impluvium again?' Tertulla asked him in mock-surprise.

'If you hadn't spent all evening exercising the well-formed muscles in your drinking arm,' Attalus replied, removing his wet cloak and throwing it at an underling, 'you would perhaps remember that you sent me down to the port to see if the ship had arrived.'

The day after the Praetorians' visit Attalus had been despatched into Cosa to find a trading ship that was prepared, with no questions asked, to take passengers to Genua. He had returned the same evening with the news that he had found one for the extortionate price of 250 denarii; they were sailing to Ostia but would be back in Cosa by today.

'And?' Vespasian asked, hoping that the weather would keep him there for another couple of days.

'It arrived mid-afternoon, before the wind got up; if it dies down by morning the captain promised to be on the beach below us by the third hour.'

Vespasian couldn't hide his disappointment.

'I know that you would have preferred earlier, master,' Attalus said, deliberately misreading him, 'but I'm afraid that you'll just have to endure an extra hour or two of her excruciatingly inaccurate memories.'

'How would you know they're inaccurate, you old satyr?' Tertulla said, grinning. 'You've never listened to a word I've said since the sorry day that I bought you.'

'What? Oh, this was at the port aedile's office,' Attalus said, handing her the leather tube. 'It's quite a modern device; if you remove the lid you'll—'

'Get out and go and join your playmates,' Tertulla laughed, swiping at her steward with the case.

Attalus departed with a conspiratorial smile to Vespasian.

'What is it, Tute?' Vespasian asked as she pulled the scroll from its container.

'A letter from your father,' she replied, unrolling it.

As his grandmother read Vespasian sipped his wine and recalled the conversations they'd had over the past few days. She had helped him to flesh out half-formed opinions and corrected many of his assumptions about the difference between the two political systems: the Republic and the Empire. She had shown him how the freedoms enjoyed by individual citizens during the Republic were slowly eradicated by the rise of Rome as a colonial power. The army could no longer be just a few legions made up of citizen farmers brought together for a season's campaigning close to home. The conquests of Greece, Asia, Hispania and Africa had meant that the men were away for years at a time whilst their crops withered and died in the fields. They returned home to find their farms overgrown and their families destitute. They were bought out at rock-bottom prices by wealthy landowners or, if they were tenants, kicked out by their landlords. This gave rise to the great estates that he could see today, farmed by the multitudes of slaves that were the by-product of Rome's Empire. The dispossessed citizen soldiers had nowhere to go other than Rome. There they became the new underclass of urban poor, scraping by in the days before the grain dole, passing their time at the free games; a degrading end to a once proud class of farmer-soldiers who had fought for the Republic because they had a stake in it.

But the legions still needed soldiers to secure the new provinces and to add to them. The tax revenue from these newly conquered lands was huge and Rome grew rich, so the idea of a professional standing army, made up of the urban poor who had no other chance of earning a living, was born. And so the grandsons of the very men who had once fought willingly for their Republic now served for twenty-five years in the legions for pay and the promise of land on discharge. Their loyalty was now not to a republic, in which they no longer had a stake, but to the generals whom they followed and to whom they looked for their promised farm and the chance to raise a family in dignity upon their discharge.

The new system had given rise to a war of wills between the Senate, who hated the idea of giving away land, and the generals, who were anxious to get their veterans settled. Once settled they kept their loyalty to their general to whom they owed everything. The balance of power shifted away from the Senate as the generals amassed huge client bases on which they could call at any time they felt their dignitas threatened or ambitions thwarted by an increasingly jealous Senate.

The civil wars soon started as the generals battled for supremacy over each other, leading to half a century of chaos. The Senate was divided and powerless to exert its authority. Order was eventually restored by the only logical means: rule by one man. The Republic had been a victim of its own success; it had created an empire but had been unable to control it. Vespasian now understood: it took an emperor to rule an empire.

'It seems that Asinius managed to get your parents out of Rome safely,' Tertulla said, putting down the letter and bringing him out of his reverie.

He felt a jab of guilt as he realised that he'd hardly thought of them in the time that he'd spent in Tertulla's company. 'I'm pleased to hear it,' he said.

'Asinius asked your father to write to you here in the hope that his warning would reach you in time: don't go to the military camp at Genua.'

'Why not? I have to get to Thracia.'

'He's heard from his source in the Guard that they're looking for a military tribune passing through Genua on his way to the Ninth Hispana in Pannonia. A Praetorian tribune by the name of Macro and a legionary from the Urban Cohort are waiting there to identify him.'

'So what should I do? Make the journey to Thracia on my own?'

'My darling boy, if you're going to command men then you're going to have to do better than that. You've just asked my advice and in the same breath made a ridiculous suggestion. The key to being a successful commander is to know immediately what to do when things go awry. A swift and correct decision will always endear you to your men; they will respect you, learn to love you even; but above all they will follow and support you. So you tell me what you should do.'

Vespasian thought for a moment. 'Wait for the relief column to leave the camp, track it for a couple of days to check that there are no Praetorians amongst it and then join it late.'

'Good. Next time something goes wrong think like a leader, not a follower.' Tertulla took a sip from her cup, placed it down on the table and looked at him intently. 'I believe that as the imperial family spends more time in its palaces and less on campaign where the soldiers can see its ability to lead it will start to lose the support of the legions. At that point the Praetorian Guard and the legions of Germania, Hispania, Syria and elsewhere would all declare for different emperors; civil war would erupt again. The Empire will eventually fall into the lap of the general with the most loyal army; let us hope that he has Rome's best interests at heart. Treat your soldiers well, Vespasian, lead them to victories, because there's no reason why you should not be that general.'

Vespasian laughed. 'Tute, you really are losing your wits; whatever the gods have decreed as my destiny it certainly is not to be Emperor. Imagine it, me?'

'Perhaps one day you will imagine it,' Tertulla said quietly, rising to her feet. 'But not today. Come, my darling, we should sleep.'

The west-facing beach was in shadow as Vespasian and his companions picked their way down the winding cliff path leading their horses and a donkey, upon which perched Tertulla riding side-saddle. A small trading ship was tying up at the jetty, which thrust out twenty paces from the shore into the now calm, slate-blue sea. Vespasian could make out six or seven crew members scurrying around with ropes making the ship fast.

The vessel was a classic flat-bottomed sailing ship that plied the shallow waters up and down the Italian coast: a sixty-foot-long, single-masted, carvel-built, high-sided, open, wooden ship. Two keel planks joined by a wooden shaft were attached either side of her raised stern; they served as a rudder as well as preventing the keelless boat from drifting too much. Between these was a six-foot-high carving of a swan's neck and head that gave the ship an illusion of grace it would have otherwise not have merited.

Attalus was already on the jetty talking with the squat, bearded ship's master as the party approached; voices were raised and the steward's worried expression was obvious to Vespasian.

'Master Vespasian, the master is now saying that he doesn't have room on board for the horses as he's taken on more olive oil than expected at Ostia,' Attalus said in a hushed voice, coming up to Vespasian as he and Magnus made their way along the jetty.

'How much have we paid him already?' Vespasian asked.

'One hundred denarii.'

'So he's willing to lose out on a hundred and fifty denarii?'

'No, he still wants that before you get on board.'

'I thought the deal was four passengers and four horses.'

'It was, but now it's changed.'

'I see. Magnus, I think we might have some explaining to do to this gentleman of the sea.'

'I think you may well be right, sir.' Magnus looked back at Sextus and Marius, who were helping Tertulla down from the donkey. 'Stand by, lads; we may have a problem that needs resolving.'

Vespasian walked up to the master. His speckled grey and

black beard almost totally covered his face, leaving only the very tops of his browned cheeks and forehead open to the elements. His eyes were barely visible from years of squinting against the sun and wind. The rough leather sleeveless tunic, which seemed to be the only garment that he was wearing, gave off an unpleasant odour, a mixture of dead fish, sweat and decomposing flesh, as if it hadn't been tanned properly.

'My steward tells me that you are going back on the deal that you made with him,' Vespasian said brusquely.

'It ain't my fault, sir, we was meant to be sailing back to Genua half empty, then the ship's owner brought an extra load of olive oil and there weren't nothing I could do about it.'

Vespasian looked down into the ship's open hold to see, at each end, two large stacks of amphorae sitting in their circular storage slots, leaving only ten feet of deck space between them.

'Surely we could fit the horses in that gap there?'

'It ain't about space, it's about weight. If you bring the horses on we'll be too low in the water and that ain't good, I can tell you, especially as it is winter when a storm can brew up without much notice.'

'But it's a lovely calm day, there's hardly a cloud in the sky.'

'Now it is, but how long will that last? I ain't going to sea in an overladen vessel, that's for sure, not for two hundred and fifty denarii.'

'Ah, so that's it, is it? So, for how much would you go to sea in an overladen vessel, then?'

'Five hundred and that's my last word.'

'And will the extra money help us to stay afloat? I think not. What if we just decide to take the road?'

'If you had wanted to take the road then you would have done, but for some reason or other you can't, so you chose to take passage on a ship in winter. My guess is you want to get to Genua unnoticed, so I think that deserves a larger fee.' The master smiled coldly in a take-it-or-leave-it sort of way. Vespasian could see that he was going to get nowhere negotiating with him.

'It would seem that you have us by the balls. I will talk with my friends.'

Back on the beach Tertulla was adamant. 'If you sail with such a dishonest rogue he'll either murder you, throw your bodies overboard and take all your money, or he'll hand you in to the port authorities in Genua and still take all your money.'

'It depends on how many of them there are,' Magnus said. 'Did you count them, sir?'

'I reckon there're six or seven plus him, maybe more.'

'Well, that ain't the sort of odds that I'd fancy in a small space like that over two days and nights; we'd best get on the horses.'

'We can't,' Vespasian answered, realising just how stuck they were. 'Even if we had the time go cross-country, which we don't any more, those bastards have seen us. When they get to Genua they'll be able to tell anyone who pays them or threatens them what we look like and where they saw us. They'll lead them straight to Tertulla's house and then it will be a simple case of deduction to lead them to me and the rest of the family.'

'You're right, Vespasian,' Tertulla sighed. 'But you need someone to sail the ship.'

'Marius, can you remember enough from your navy days to sail that thing?'

'I reckon so, sir, so long as we follow the coast.'

Tertulla smiled grimly. 'Then it looks like the master's just signed a death warrant for himself and his crew.'

'I'm afraid it does, Tute. Magnus, we'll walk back up the jetty; I'll hold out a purse to him; you take him as he reaches for it. Sextus and Marius, stay back on the beach; we don't want to make him suspicious. As soon as the master falls follow us on to the ship as fast as you can. We'll kill them quickly before they've a chance of finding their weapons. Don't throw the bodies overboard, we'll do that later, a long way from here.'

'I'll come with you, Master Vespasian,' Attalus said. 'It'll lessen the odds somewhat.'

'You'll be worse than a man short,' Tertulla scoffed. 'You'll be in everyone's way and get yourself killed.'

'Then it will be merciful release for both of us, I'm sure.' He followed Vespasian and Magnus on to the jetty.

Tertulla smiled at the bravery of her old friend, and then looked at her grandson in admiration as he walked back along the jetty. He was thinking ahead in a cold and calculating manner; he was made of the right stuff to survive in this world, she was sure of it.

The master was waiting, talking quietly on the jetty with one of the crew, as Vespasian and Magnus walked up. 'What's it to be, then?' he asked in a casual manner as if he were serving in a tavern.

'Four hundred,' Vespasian replied.

'I said five hundred was my last word.'

'I suppose we don't have any choice, then, do we?' Vespasian said, holding out the purse that contained his gold aurei.

'That's the way it seems,' the master said, his eyes fixed greedily on the heavy-looking purse. It was the last thing they ever saw.

'You were right, my sea-faring friend, we didn't have a choice,' Magnus said, pulling his sword from the master's heart. The crewman froze for an instant, not registering what had happened, as he watched his commander slump down on to the jetty. Vespasian's knee thumped into his groin, doubling him over, exposing the back of his neck to Attalus' blade, which sliced through it at the nape, into the vertebrae; he was dead before he had worked out what was going on.

Vespasian leapt on to the ship's bow, gladius drawn, and severed the sword arm of the first man he came to; the ensuing scream as he went down, clutching at the spurting stump, alerted the rest of the crew to the danger. Followed by Magnus and Attalus, he jumped over the large stack of amphorae and down into the belly of the ship, landing on the back of a grizzled old crewman who was pulling a sword from the now opened weapons box beneath the mast. He thumped his sword hilt down hard on to the back of the man's skull, cracking it open like a walnut. A shout from Attalus caused him to dodge to his left and narrowly avoid the wild slash of an axe, wielded by a tattooed monster of a man wearing only a dirty grey loincloth. The monster snarled like a wild beast as his blow missed and scythed through a line of amphorae. Olive oil gushed out over the deck. Vespasian grabbed on to the ship's side to steady himself on the treacherous surface. He heard Sextus and Marius yell as they sprinted up the jetty and jumped on board over the stern rail. To his right Magnus had gutted a ginger-haired Celt, whose writhing body he slammed with all his strength into the monster, who tried to fend it off but slipped on the oily deck and landed on his arse. The screaming Celt flipped over his shoulder, spilling hot intestines into the monster's lap as he went. For a moment the monster sat and stared, bemused by the grey innards that seemed to come from within him, before realising that he hadn't been split open; he looked up just in time to see Attalus' dagger enter his right eye. His guttural roar of pain echoed around the cliffs as Attalus twisted the blade left and right, turning the core of his brain into a jelly; it came to a sudden end as Attalus pulled the knife sharply up, slicing his brain in two.

Vespasian looked around; Sextus and Marius had secured

the stern and were leaning on the rail catching their breath; two bodies lay at their feet. Magnus walked carefully forward on the slick surface and calmly slit the gutted Celt's throat, instantly stopping his screams. The only sound now to intrude upon the gentle beat of the waves was the soft, steady moaning of the maimed man on the bow as the blood drained from his stump.

'I'll deal with him, sir,' Magnus said, trying his best to stay upright on the slippery deck as the ship rocked gently on the slight swell.

'Thank you, Magnus,' Vespasian replied, as if Magnus had just offered him a drink of water. 'Marius and Sextus, get those bodies down here then clear up this oil before someone hurts themselves on it.'

Vespasian put his hand on Attalus' shoulder. 'Thank you for that warning shout, old friend, I'm sure you'll enjoy telling your mistress this evening that she would be minus a grandson if it hadn't been for you.'

'I shall, Master Vespasian,' Attalus smiled, 'and every evening in the future; although I rather think that she will spoil it by reminding me that you wouldn't have been in danger if I'd done my job properly and got a trustworthy ship's master.'

Vespasian laughed. 'You're probably right; let's go and show her that we're still alive.'

They climbed back out of the boat to see Tertulla still standing on the beach, her hands clasped in front of her.

'Your grandfather would have been proud of you,' she

said as they walked off the jetty. 'You fight like a man who knows that he will win. That is the sign of a man of destiny, a survivor.'

'I very nearly didn't survive, though, Tute. If it hadn't been for Attalus I would be lying in two halves in the ship.'

'So you have finally proved to be of some use after all these years,' she said, smiling at her old friend.

'It would appear so, mistress, which puts me one up over you.'

Vespasian left them to their banter and went to supervise the loading of the horses. Once they had been coaxed down a makeshift ramp into the belly of the ship, and their supplies stowed in the small cabin, Marius announced that he was as ready as he'd ever be to sail.

As they said their goodbyes Tertulla drew Vespasian aside and walked with him a little way along the beach. When they were out of earshot from their companions she took both his hands and held them tight.

'I shall not be here when you return,' she said, looking lovingly into his eyes.

Vespasian opened his mouth to protest but she held a finger against his lips, silencing him.

'Nothing that you can say will make the slightest difference. I know that the days left to me are few and you will be away for years, not days.'

Vespasian knew that in all probability she was right, his father had said as much when he suggested that he should visit her; but admitting it seemed to make it inevitable. He felt tears start to creep out from the corners of his eyes. He took her in his arms.

'Shed no tears for me now,' Tertulla scolded gently. 'Leave them until after I am gone. Be grateful that we have this opportunity to say goodbye for the last time. Few people are granted that luxury.'

'I shall miss you, Tute,' Vespasian said, wiping his eyes. 'The happiest moments of my life have been spent with you here at Cosa.'

'And there's no reason why you should not have more in the future. I have left the estate solely to you. Your father will understand; he has two to run already and would not thank me for increasing his workload. And as for Sabinus, he never took any interest in the place and left as soon as he could.'

'Nevertheless he will be very jealous and will find some way to get back at me.'

'Well, that's his and your business; I am only doing what I deem to be the right thing. I have freed all my slaves in my will and have invited them to stay on the estate, and work as freed men under Attalus to keep it running until you return. When you do, Attalus will have certain documents in his possession that I wish you to have. I have also made him a substantial bequest to keep him in his old age, so that he won't be a burden to you.'

'He could never be a burden to me, Tute, because he will always remind me of you.'

Tertulla embraced her grandson and then, standing on tiptoe, kissed him on the lips. 'Remember, do what is right for you and for Rome, and you will fulfil your destiny, which is greater than you imagine.' She ran her hand through his hair, as she used to do when he was a child, and smiled at him. 'You should go now, the others are all on board. Farewell, my darling boy.'

Vespasian climbed aboard as Magnus and Sextus hauled up the sail. The little ship edged forward and Marius at the helm eased it around and out to sea. Vespasian stood at the stern as he watched Tertulla get smaller and smaller. When she was no more than a tiny dot on the beach he dropped to his knees and broke down in a series of gut-wrenching sobs, mourning his beloved grandmother who, although still living, was now dead to him.

PART IV

THRACIA, SPRING AD 26

PART IV

THRACIA, SPRING AD 26

CHAPTER XIX

'WHAT'S THAT ARSEHOLE up to now?' Magnus spat as he looked with disgust towards Gnaeus Domitius Corbulo, the commander of the reinforcement column. 'If we change direction again today I'm going to mutiny.'

'You need to be under military discipline to mutiny,' Vespasian reminded his friend as he watched Corbulo engage in another heated exchange with their local guides. 'And seeing as you're here masquerading as my freedman, and therefore a civilian, I think that anything you say or do will be ignored, especially by someone as well-born and arrogant as Corbulo.'

Magnus grunted and removed his conical felt cap, the *pileus*, the sign of a freedman, and wiped his brow. 'Pompous arsehole,' he muttered.

They had crossed the border from the Roman province of Macedonia into the client kingdom of Thracia five days earlier. For three days, following the course of the Via Egnatia, they'd marched through the budding orchards and the newly sown cornfields of the narrow coastal plain wedged between the forbidding, cloud-strewn bulk of the southern arm of Rhodope mountain range to the north, and the azure blue of the beautiful but treacherous Thracian sea, sparkling in the warm spring sun, to the south.

Corbulo had received orders, waiting for him at Philippi on the Macedonian border, to rendezvous as soon as possible with Poppaeus Sabinus' army at Bessapara, on the Hebrus River, in the northwest of the client kingdom, where the northern arm of the Rhodope range abuts the Haemus Mountains. It was here that Poppaeus had the Thracian rebels pinned down in their hilltop stronghold, having defeated their main army in battle about fourteen days before. Corbulo had cursed his luck. He had tried to find out the details of the battle, but the messenger had already departed for Rome to bring news of the victory to the Emperor and Senate.

Being a young and ambitious nobleman he was taking the request for speed very seriously, anxious to arrive before the rebellion was completely crushed and his chances of glory diminished.

They had met their guides and left the road at the eastern end of the Rhodope range, and were now heading northeast through its trackless foothills to pass around to the northern side of the mountains and follow them, northwest, to their destination. They were in the lands of the Caeletae, a tribe that had stayed loyal to Rome and its puppet, King Rhoemetalces, mainly out of hatred for their northern neighbours the Bessi and the Deii, who had revolted the previous year against conscription into the Roman army.

Vespasian grinned at Magnus as they watched Corbulo bellow at the Caeletaean guides, turn his horse and head back down the column towards where they were stationed, at the head of the first cohort of 480 legionary recruits.

'I think our esteemed leader is just about to push another tribe into rebellion,' he said, watching the red-faced military tribune approach past the vanguard of 120 auxiliary Gallic cavalry. 'If he carries on like that we'll find ourselves dangling in wooden cages over their sacred fires.'

'I thought it was just the Germans and Celts who did that,' Magnus replied, easing his travel-weary behind in his saddle.

'I expect that these barbarians have just as nasty a way of amusing themselves with their captives; let's hope that Corbulo's arrogance doesn't drive them to practise on us.'

'Tribune,' Corbulo barked, pulling up his horse next to Vespasian, 'we are stopping here for the night; those ginger-haired sons of fox bitches are refusing to go any further today. Have the men construct a camp.'

'Yes, sir.'

'And, tribune—' Corbulo peered at Vespasian over the long, pronounced nose that dominated his thin, angular face '—tell Centurion Faustus to double the guard tonight. I don't trust those bastards, they seem to do everything possible to hinder our progress.'

'I thought they were loyal to Rome.'

'The only loyalty these savages have is to their filthy tribe's rapacious gods. I wouldn't trust them with their own grandmothers.'

'We do seem to be taking a very circuitous route.'

'They're in no hurry to reach our objective. Every time I insist that we start to head northwest they find an excuse after a mile or so to turn back to the northeast. It's as if they want to lead us somewhere completely different.'

'Here, for example?' Vespasian looked up at the rocky hills to his left, and then down to the thick pine forest, which stretched as far as he could see, below them. 'This is not a place I would choose for a camp, far too enclosed.'

'My point exactly, but what to do, eh? There's little more than three hours to sundown, and without the guides we may not find anywhere better, so we're stuck here. At least there's plenty of timber, so get the men to it, I want a stockade camp tonight; we'll act as if we're in hostile territory.'

Vespasian watched his superior move off down the column. He was seven years older than Vespasian and had served on Poppaeus' staff for the past three years; before that he had been on the Rhine frontier for a year. Although he too came from a rustic background, his family had had senatorial rank for the past two generations and he behaved with the arrogance of someone born into a privileged life. Being sent back to Italia along with Centurion Faustus, the *primus pilus* or senior centurion of the Fourth Scythica, to pick up the column of recruits, and thus miss the start of the season's campaigning, had hurt his pride. His subsequent impatience with the smallest of errors or misdemeanours by any of the hapless new recruits had resulted in many a flogging and one execution over the seventy days that they had been on the march. He was, as Magnus had rightly observed, an arsehole, but even Vespasian with his limited experience could see that his military instincts were correct, and he turned to relay his orders.

'Centurion Faustus!'

'Sir!'

Centurion Faustus snapped to attention with the rattle of *phalerae*, metal disc-like decorations worn on a harness over his mail shirt, awarded to him over his twenty-two years of service. The traverse white horsehair plume on his helmet stood as rigid as its owner.

'Have the men construct a stockade camp, and set a double guard.'

'Yes, sir! *Bucinator*, sound "Prepare camp".'

The signaller raised the four-foot-long *bucina* to his lips and blew a series of high notes through the thin, bell-ended horn, used for signals within camp. The effect was immediate: the two cohorts of raw legionaries unshouldered their pack-poles and *pila* and then, guided by the vine canes of the centurions and the shouts of their *optiones*, the centurions' seconds in command, were sorted into fatigue parties; some for trench-digging, some for soil-packing and some for stake-cutting. The auxiliary Gallic cavalry turmae from the front and the rear of the column formed up in a defensive screen to protect the men as they worked. Beyond them smaller units of Thessalian light cavalry and foot archers patrolled the surrounding countryside. The camp servants and slaves offloaded the baggage, corralled the animals and levelled the ground, whilst the engineers paced out and marked up the line of the square palisade and the position of each of the two hundred *papiliones*, eight-man tents, within it.

It took only a few moments for the marching column to convert itself into a hive of industry. Every man fell into his allotted task, with the exception of the dozen Thracian guides who squatted down on their haunches and pulled their undyed woollen cloaks around their shoulders and their strange fox-skin hats over their ears against the cooling mountain air. They watched with sullen eyes, murmuring to one another in their unintelligible tongue, as the camp began to take shape.

By the time the sun had set the exhausted legionaries had started to cook their evening meal within the security of the 360-foot-square camp. Each man had either dug just over four feet of trench, five feet wide and three feet at its deepest, piling the spoil up two feet high on the inside for others to pack down, or they had cut and shaped enough five-foot stakes to cover the same length; and all this after marching sixteen miles over rough ground. They hunched in groups of eight, over smoky fires by their leather tents, complaining about the arduousness of their new military lives. The odour of their stale sweat masked the blander smell of the rough military fare that bubbled in their cooking pots. Not even their daily wine ration could produce any laughter or light-hearted banter.

Vespasian sat outside his tent listening to their grumbling as Magnus boiled up the pork and chickpea stew that was to be their supper. 'I'll wager there's more than a few of them regretting joining the Eagles at the moment,' he observed, taking a slug of wine.

'They'll get used to it,' Magnus said, chopping wild thyme into the pot. 'The first ten years are the hardest – after that it slips by.'

'Did you serve the full twenty-five?'

'I joined up when I was fifteen and did eleven years with the Legio Quinta Alaudae on the Rhine then transferred to the Urban Cohort; they only have to serve sixteen so I was lucky – I was out after a further five. I never made it to optio, though; mainly because I can't write, although regularly getting busted for fighting didn't help either. When I was discharged four years ago, it seemed sensible to make a virtue out of a vice so I became a boxer. The money's better, but it tends to hurt more.' He rubbed one of his cauliflower ears to emphasise the point. 'Anyway, these whippersnappers are only moaning because it's the first time they've had to build a full camp after a day's march; they'll get used to it after a season in the field. If they survive, that is.'

Vespasian conceded the point; since they had joined the column, late, ten miles outside Genua, they had covered twenty miles a day along proper roads within the safety of Italia, pitching camp wherever they pleased until they had reached the port of Ravenna. From there, after a long wait for the transport ships, they had crossed the Adriatic Sea and sailed down past Dalmatia to Dyrrachium, on the west coast of the province of Macedonia. Here they picked up the Via Egnatia and marched across Macedonia, only ever setting pickets around their camps. This was the first night that they could be said to be in some sort of danger. The men, many of them no older than him, would soon learn that it was better to be tired and safe in a camp than fresh and dead in an open field.

He turned his mind back to the day that he and Magnus had joined the column. Marius and Sextus had put them ashore, with their horses, just west of Genua, and then, before making their way back to Rome, had sailed the small ship into the harbour, under cover of night, to abandon it to be reclaimed some day by its rightful owner. He and Magnus had ridden across country to within a mile of the recruiting depot outside the town's walls. There they had waited for two days in the overlooking hills for the column's departure. They had shadowed it along the Via Aemelia Scauri until they were sure that there were no Praetorians travelling with it, and then had caught up with it as if they had just come from Genua. The bollocking that he had received from Corbulo for his late arrival had been excruciating. However, it didn't overshadow the relief that he had felt at being safely on his way out of Italia and, hopefully, out of the reach of Sejanus and his henchmen.

Vespasian sighed and contemplated the irony that the further he got from someone who would kill him the further he would be from someone who would love him. He fingered the good-luck charm around his neck that Caenis had given him as they had said goodbye and recalled her beautiful face and intoxicating scent. Magnus brought him out of his reverie.

'Get this down you, sir,' he said, handing him a bowl of steaming stew. It smelt delicious and, realising just how hungry he was, Vespasian started to eat with relish.

'How did you learn to cook so well?'

'If you haven't got a woman to cook for you then you need to learn, otherwise you end up living on shit.' Magnus shovelled in a mouthful with his wooden spoon. 'Most of the young lads here will be half-decent cooks by the time they finish their service. Unless of course they decide to drag a woman around with them; but that's generally a pain in the arse on campaign, as they tend to moan all the time. It's fine if you're stationed in a permanent camp where you can build her a nice little shack outside the walls, somewhere where she can have all her creature comforts and where you can go for a bit of afternoon delight, if you take my meaning?'

'I do indeed,' Vespasian replied, feeling the need for some delight himself. Any further thoughts in that direction were halted by the sound of a bucina.

'That's "All officers to the command tent", you'd better go, sir. I'll keep this warm for you.'

Vespasian handed Magnus his bowl and mumbling his thanks trudged wearily off to the commander's tent, the *praetorium*, at the centre of the camp, on the Via Principalis, the road that divided the camp into two.

*

'Good evening, gentlemen,' Corbulo said, looking around the gathering. Present, in the dim lamplight, were the Roman prefects of the two auxiliary Gallic cavalry units, twelve centurions, six from each cohort, including Centurion Faustus who, as the most senior centurion, was acting as prefect of the camp. Vespasian and Marcus Cornelius Gallus, the other newly arrived military tribune, made up the rest of the group.

'I trust that you have eaten well and feel refreshed, because we have a long night ahead of us.'

There was a small murmuring of assent, but most had, like Vespasian, been halfway through their meals when the summons had come.

'There is a high probability of an attack on the column either tonight or in the course of the next couple of days. Our Caeletaean guides have been less than helpful and we cannot afford to trust them. I have placed them under arrest with orders for their execution should an attack materialise. This means that we have to find our way to Poppaeus' camp unaided. Neither Centurion Faustus nor I travelled this way last year on our way back to Genua, as we went directly from Moesia before Poppaeus moved his legions into Thracia. I would appreciate anyone with previous experience of Thracia to make themselves known.'

'Sir!' One of the centurions from the second cohort stepped forward.

'Centurion Aetius, you may speak.'

'Sir! I served with the Fifth Macedonica under Publius Vellaeus five years ago when the Odrysae revolted, the last time we had to sort out a Thracian mess. We came in from Moesia, just as Poppaeus has done, and cut them to pieces outside the walls of Philippopolis. We passed through Bessapara on our way through. I got to know the country quite well as we stayed for nearly a year, mopping up. They're a nasty, vicious people, although Marcus Fabius, optio of the *princeps posterior* century of the second cohort, would beg to differ; he had a woman here five years ago, he even speaks the lingo.'

'Excellent, thank you, Aetius. What would you recommend we do?'

'Between twenty and thirty miles north of here we should hit the Harpessus River; it's not too wide but it's fast flowing at this time of year with snow melt from the mountains, but it's still just shallow enough to ford. Once we're across we could follow it east to the Hebrus River; we could then follow that northwest to Philippopolis and on to Bessapara. It's a longer route, but without trustworthy guides to take us directly there through the mountains it would be safer.'

Corbulo weighed up this information, trying to reconcile arriving later with the possibility of not arriving at all, and liking neither of the outcomes drew the briefing to a close.

'Thank you, gentlemen. I will make my decision in the morning. In the meantime have your men sleep in shifts, I want half the centuries to be stood to arms throughout the night. As I said, it will be a long night. Good evening.'

'Thank you, Magnus,' Vespasian said, taking his still warm bowl of stew and sitting back down.

'What did the arsehole have to say? A lot of hot air, I suppose.' Magnus laughed uproariously at his own joke.

'Well, he actually admitted to not knowing how to get—' Vespasian was cut off by the sound of weapons clashing and shouts and screams from the direction of main gate on other side of the camp. They grabbed their swords and rushed towards the commotion, weaving through the confusion of two cohorts of nervous raw recruits being formed up, in darkness, in front of their lines by the barking centurions and their optiones. Cooking pots were kicked over and men tripped on tent pegs and guy ropes as the centuries whose turn it had been to rest rushed to get their pila from the neat weapon stacks whilst simultaneously pulling on their helmets and buckling their swords and *lorica segmentata* – iron-plate armour constructed in strips – that had been discarded for the night.

Next to the gate, which was open and swinging in the wind, a wagonload of animal fodder was on fire. By its light Vespasian could make out half a dozen bodies strewn across on the ground. Corbulo was already there, screaming at a young legionary who was doing his best to stand to attention, despite the blood streaming down his face from a sword cut above his right eye.

'What the fuck were you doing just letting them through? Why didn't you block the gate, you useless sack of shit? I'll have your head for this. What's your name?'

The legionary opened his mouth and then fainted at his commanding officer's feet. Corbulo aimed a kick at the unfortunate man's stomach and instantly regretted it as his sandalled foot connected with iron-plate armour, half shearing off his big toenail.

'Tribune Vespasian,' he shouted, resisting with every fibre of his being the urge to grab his injured foot and hop around like some actor in a bad comedy. 'Secure the gate. I want a century formed up in front of it.'

'What happened, sir?'

'Those fox-fucking sons of Gorgons managed to kill their guards, steal some horses and break through the gate, that's what's happened. It's a fucking shambles and I'm going to have the balls off whoever was in charge. Now get that gate shut, and that fire put out.'

Thinking it best not to point out that it was Corbulo who was in charge, Vespasian ran off to do as he'd been ordered, with Magnus in tow, leaving his commanding officer bawling at Tribune Gallus to order the cavalry prefects have their men mount up.

The fire had been extinguished and calm had returned. Both cohorts were formed up in the sixty-foot gaps between the tent lines and the palisade on either side of the camp. Leaving the gate secured shut and a century, under

Centurion Faustus, in front of it, Vespasian turned to examine the bodies on the ground. Pulling the corpse of a fresh-faced legionary off his assailant he heard a low intake of breath.

'Sir, over here!'

'Well, what is it?' Corbulo growled. He had more or less recovered his composure.

'This Thracian is still alive.' Vespasian turned over the foul-smelling body of one of their erstwhile guides. Blood seeped from a deep wound on his left shoulder that had almost severed his arm but he was still breathing.

'Now, that is the first bit of good news I've had today.'

Tribune Marcus Gallus came puffing back to report. 'Sir, they're saddling up as fast as they can.'

'They'd better be. I want those cocksuckers caught.'

'They'll be well away by now,' Vespasian said, 'and they know the terrain, there's not a hope in Hades of catching them.'

Corbulo looked at Vespasian as if he was about to explode at the impertinence of this stocky little upstart, then pulled himself together as the truth of the statement sank in.

'I expect you're right,' he conceded bitterly. 'I'll just have them patrol around the camp, it would be pointless to put good men, or even Gauls, in harm's way now, we may well be needing them soon. Now, have this prisoner seen to; I want him well enough for questioning within the hour, and get Optio Fabius to translate.'

*

Vespasian, Gallus, Optio Fabius and the two guards snapped to attention as Corbulo entered the praetorium. The wounded Thracian lay moaning on the ground, too weak with loss of blood to warrant tying up. His wound had been sealed with pitch and roughly bound so the bleeding had stopped; it would not save his life, but it would buy them enough time to interrogate him.

'Fabius, ask him where they were running off to,' Corbulo ordered, 'and whether there are any more of them tracking us out in the hills.'

The optio knelt down next to the prisoner and said a few short sentences in the oddly singsong language of the Thracians.

The prisoner opened his eyes, seemingly in surprise, looked at Fabius for a moment as if registering who he was, and then spat directly into his face.

'Urgh! You filthy bastard!' Fabius punched the man on the mouth, splitting open both his lips.

'That's enough, optio, I'll say when he's to be hurt,' Corbulo barked. 'I want him alive for as long as possible. Now ask him again.'

This time Fabius spoke more forcefully, taking care to keep out of spitting range. The Thracian stayed quiet; a grim smile formed on this swollen, bloody mouth and he turned his head away.

Vespasian could see the futility of the exercise; the man knew he was going to die and therefore had nothing to gain by talking; in fact, the more he resisted the higher the likelihood was of his tormentors losing their patience and putting him out of his misery.

'I'm getting fed up with this,' Corbulo hissed, placing his left foot on the man's wounded shoulder. 'Now, then, you little cunt, talk to me.' He pressed down hard on the freshly sealed wound. The prisoner let out a guttural scream and blood started to seep through the dressing. 'Well, you filthy savage, where the fuck were you off to?'

The Thracian looked up at the young Roman officer standing over him, his eyes narrowed in hatred, and, lifting his head, shouted loudly and bitterly at him in his strange tongue. After a few sentences the effort proved too much for the man's heart and, with a strangled gasp, his head fell back to stare with lifeless eyes at the seething Corbulo.

'Shit! Well, Fabius, what did he say?' Corbulo growled.

'I don't rightly know, sir,' the confused-looking optio replied.

'What do you mean you don't rightly know? You speak that hideous language, do you not?'

'I do, sir, but I speak the language of the Odrysae and the Bessi and the other tribes of the north and west.'

'Well, this man is from the Caeletae. Isn't that the same?'

'That's just it, sir, it is, with just a few differences, but this man was speaking in a dialect that I have never heard before.'

'But it stated in my orders that our guides were from the Caeletae. If you're sure he isn't then where are our real guides and where does he come from?'

'My guess is that he comes from the eastern part of the country, beyond the Hebrus River.'

'Impossible, the tribes in the east are loyal to Rome,' Corbulo spluttered.

'They were when you left, sir,' Vespasian said quietly, 'but what if that is not still the case?'

Corbulo's face sank as he digested the implications of this possibility. 'That would mean that we could have one or more of the tribes across the river in rebellion, and if we move east to the Hebrus we risk marching right into them, and if we go northwest we'll have them on our heels.'

'Exactly,' Vespasian said with a grim smile, 'and to withdraw back to Macedonia would be to directly disobey our orders. I think that the decision has been made for you, sir.'

Corbulo looked at his new tribune and realised that he was right: they had no choice but to press on directly to Poppaeus' camp in the northwest, without guides; and all the while they would be looking over their shoulders hoping not to see the dust of a Thracian war band approaching their unblooded new recruits from the rear.

'Oh, shit,' he whispered.

CHAPTER XX

THOSE LEGIONARIES WHO had been lucky enough to get some sleep were woken before dawn. The men ate a frugal breakfast of dry bread, cheese and olives, before packing their kit bags and attaching them to their T-bar poles. As the sun appeared over the horizon, illuminating the high wispy clouds from underneath with a deep red glow, the *bucinatores* sounded the signal to strike camp. Two hundred tents came down almost as one and were strapped, by the camp servants, on to the mules that carried the baggage of each *contubernium*, a unit of eight men. To increase their speed Corbulo had given orders that the two larger oxen-driven carts were to be disabled and left behind. As much as possible of their cargos of replacement weapons, clothing, sacks of grain and other supplies was loaded on to the spare cavalry mounts and the smaller, mule-driven carts that carried each century's reserve rations, as well as its centurion's tent and other heavier baggage; the rest was destroyed. The oxen would be brought along as meat on the hoof; unencumbered by their heavy carts they wouldn't be a drag on the speed of the column.

The mist that had clung to the steep slopes of the Rhodope foothills above them had almost completely burnt off by the end of the first hour of the day, when the light cavalry scouts, who had been sent out in the pre-dawn half-light, returned. They reported nothing moving in the vicinity and were despatched again to spring any ambushes and to keep a constant vigil throughout the march for any enemy intent on harrying or attacking the vulnerable column.

Corbulo gave the order for the column to move out. The *cornicen* blew a deep rumbling call on his *cornu*, a G-shaped instrument made of silver and horn, which curled from his mouth under his right arm and then around to the wide bell, facing forward, above his head. The standard-bearers – *signiferi* – dipped their phalerae-strewn poles to signal 'Advance'. The day's march had begun.

Four turmae, of thirty men each, of the auxiliary Gallic cavalry led the way followed by Vespasian, with Magnus trying to be as inconspicuous as possible at his side, leading the first cohort. Next rode Tribune Gallus in front of the second cohort. Following them were the engineers and then the medical orderlies with carts on which lay those too sick or wounded to march. Then came the baggage – thirty spare cavalry mounts, two hundred pack-mules of the *contubernia*, each led by a camp servant, twenty-four carts, one for each century of infantry and each turma of cavalry plus an additional one each for the light cavalry, the foot archers, the engineers and finally one for the officers. Bringing up the rear were the last four turmae of Gallic cavalry. The column was two-thirds of a mile long.

After an hour they had covered just over two miles in a steady northwesterly direction. The forest to the south had petered out to be replaced by scraggy, mountainous grassland broken up, here and there, by ravines and small copses of mountain pine. No sign of human habitation, either in use or deserted, could be seen. The only other signs of life were two eagles that soared above the column, riding the air currents effortlessly on their outstretched wings, as if watching over the safety of the men below who marched under banners forged in their image. They drew a hearty cheer from the nervous recruits who waved their pila at them and called them their guardian spirits. Their officers encouraged it and even joined in, knowing that the men's morale would be bolstered by this good omen.

'You see that, Vespasian?' Corbulo shouted over the cheering, riding back down the column from his position at its head. 'Perhaps the gods are with us, Jupiter and Juno protecting their children from the malice of the lesser gods of the Thracians.'

Vespasian smiled; although not a superstitious man he too was encouraged by the aerial display of these two symbols of Rome.

'Let's hope that they are willing to accompany us all the way to our destination, sir. The men will march willingly with them as their guides.'

'Quite so, tribune, a lot better than a ragged band of uncouth savages, don't you think?'

'Indeed I do, sir.' As Vespasian replied the deep voluminous sound of the cornu gave the signal to halt.

'Who in the name of all the furies gave the order to halt?' Corbulo shouted, his good humour disappearing in a trice. 'Tribune, with me.'

Vespasian followed his commanding officer at a gallop up to the head of the column.

'What's the meaning of this? Who gave the order to halt?' Corbulo raged.

'I did, sir,' Sextus Mauricius, the prefect of the Gallic cavalry, replied. 'One of the scouts has reported something that I think you should see.'

'Where is he? This had better be good.'

A nervous-looking light cavalry trooper came forward.

'I thought it important, sir.' The trooper's thickly accented Latin betrayed his origins in the horse-lands of Thessaly.

'Well, where is it?'

'It's down in that ravine over there, sir,' he said, pointing to the south where, two hundred paces away, the rough grassland was split by a sharp gash, as if some Titan had cleft it with a mighty axe in the dark times before the coming of man.

'Come on, then, lead the way.'

The trooper turned his mount and galloped off; Corbulo, Vespasian and Mauricius followed.

At the edge of the ravine they dismounted and peered over the side. It was a steep drop, but not impossible to descend on foot. An unpleasant smell emanated from within it. Vespasian gazed down its length until he saw what had first attracted the trooper's attention. About sixty feet away, in amongst the boulders strewn on the floor of the ravine, lay a couple of bodies.

'Let's get down there and have a look. Prefect, you stay here. Tribune, trooper, with me.' Corbulo started to scramble down the rough bank, loosening small rocks and dry earth in a mini landslide as he went; the others followed.

They reached the first of the bodies and almost retched at the stench. Looking around they saw that there were far more than just the two visible from the top. They seemed to be all Thracians, with their unmistakable fox-skin caps and long, soft leather boots.

'What a stink,' coughed Corbulo. 'They've been dead for a good few days. How many are there?'

Vespasian walked around counting the bloated corpses, which had turned a ghastly pale green and were covered in dark grey blemishes. Further down the ravine he noticed that of the four bodies had been laid out neatly; someone had taken some effort with them.

'Sixteen, sir,' he reported.

'All Thracians?'

'Yes.'

'What do you make of it?'

'I think that we've solved a problem.'

'What makes you think that, tribune?'

'There are two different tribes here: the twelve who were just dumped here have a different style of hat from those four over there. Theirs are identical to our guides' hats. Your orders specifically stated that twelve guides from the Caeletae would meet us; I think that these are the original twelve. They must have been ambushed by a superior number of rebels, four of whom were killed, and then twelve of the rebels took the real guides' places and waited for us to march up the Via Egnatia. We never questioned whether they were genuine or not because there was the right number of them.'

Corbulo considered this for a moment before the smell became intolerable and forced them to retreat back up to their horses. 'I suppose that it proves at least the Caeletae are still loyal,' he said as they mounted.

Vespasian looked at this superior, amazed that he hadn't grasped the full implication of the ambush. 'That may well be true, sir, but how did the rebels know when our column would be arriving and exactly where it would be met and by how many guides?'

Corbulo's face dropped as he made the connection. 'Neptune's hairy sack! They must have been told. By someone in Poppaeus' camp. Someone who knew the contents of our orders. We have a traitor in our midst, Vespasian.'

'I'm afraid that it does seem that way, sir.'

*

'So there's a traitor in the army and the enemy knows our every move,' Magnus grumbled, having been informed of the grisly find in the ravine.

'Antonia and Asinius sent me here because they suspected as much, and it seems that they have been proven right.'

Magnus looked at his young friend in surprise. 'You've been sent up here after a traitor?' he snorted. 'And what are you meant to do about it?'

'I'm to find evidence that links him with Sejanus and take it back to Rome,' Vespasian replied, trying not to feel out of his depth.

'And there was me thinking that we were just going on some little jaunt to the provinces with the odd fight to keep us amused. But, no, it turns out that the young gentleman is playing high politics with the big boys, and it'll be my place to protect him when they start to play rough.'

'Well, I didn't ask you to come.' Vespasian didn't appreciate Magnus' patronising tone.

'No, you didn't, but I didn't have a lot of choice after that incident on the bridge, did I?'

'You could have gone anywhere; there was no need to come with me.'

'No need! Your uncle would never forgive me if I let anything happen to you.'

'Why? What is he to you?' Vespasian was now intrigued.

'I owe him my life.' Magnus paused.

'Go on.'

'When he was a praetor I was condemned to the arena for murder; but because I'd done him a few favours, if you take my meaning, he pulled some strings and got me reprieved. It cost him more than a few denarii in bribes and blood money, I can tell you. So to repay part of the debt I'm here, looking after your—' Magnus stopped abruptly and looked away.

'What do you mean? You were always going to come with me?'

Magnus looked sheepish. 'Well, not with you,' he muttered, 'but I was to follow you. Gaius knew that you would never let me accompany you so I was just to stay close, in case you got into any nasty scrapes.'

'For four years?'

'Well, yes, they are four years that I wouldn't have had if it hadn't been for him. I owe them to him. Mind you, he didn't tell me that you would be doing anything more than a bit of soldiering. Anyway, after Macro saw me on the bridge I had an excuse to stay with you. I knew that you wouldn't be able to refuse, so it worked out quite well in the end, didn't it?'

'If you say so.' Vespasian smiled at his friend. He was torn between feeling grateful to his uncle for cashing in a debt in order to help him and slightly humiliated because his uncle evidently thought that he couldn't manage on his own. 'Well, now we've got all that out in the open, what do you think?'

'About what?'

'About finding the traitor, that's what.'

'I would have thought that it has to be someone on Poppaeus' staff who either discussed the orders with him, or wrote them out, or conveyed them, or perhaps the person who liaised with the Caeletae to organise the guides.'

'That's as far as I've got,' Vespasian said, sounding disappointed.

'Then why ask me?'

'I was hoping for a different angle.'

'Well, don't be disappointed when you don't get one from me,' Magnus huffed; he had felt pleased with his analyses. 'I'm here as muscle, not brain.'

'I'm sorry, Magnus.'

Magnus grunted an acknowledgement and they rode on in silence. The pounding of hundreds of hoofs and hobnailed sandals on the hard ground filled the air. It was the fourth hour of the day and the sun was beginning to burn; all around men and horses were starting to sweat. Vespasian loosened the red neckerchief that he wore to stop his armour chafing. He looked up to the sky. The eagles had gone. He felt a pang of dread, but then dismissed it as superstitious nonsense; of course they weren't going to follow the column all the way to its destination, they must have far better things to do. Nevertheless he searched the cloudless sky in the hope that they were still visible. Away over his right shoulder he saw a dark blur travelling swiftly towards them. He shaded his eyes against the bright light, and tried to make out what it was. As it got closer individual shapes of large birds could be seen. Others had noticed it too and an uneasy muttering started to come from the ranks.

'What are they, Magnus?'

Magnus spat over his shoulder and clenched his thumb in his fist to avert the evil eye. 'Rooks coming from the east; not a good omen, that's going to unsettle the lads.'

Sure enough as the birds flew overhead there was much spitting and clenching of thumbs; prayers to every god imaginable were offered up and the men started to look nervously behind them.

'Keep your eyes front,' Centurion Faustus barked. 'Optio, take the name of anyone looking back.'

The column pressed on in glum silence. They were descending the last foothills on the north side of the Rhodope chain and coming down on to easier terrain. Ahead of them, about twelve miles away, could be made out the line of the valley through which flowed the Harpessus River. The column's pace seemed to quicken as the men began to think of camping near cool, cleansing water in just a few hours' time. The bad omen was soon put to the backs of their minds.

At the midday halt Vespasian and Magnus both dismounted and stretched their legs. All around men were slumped on the ground sucking gratefully at water skins or chewing on bread and dried meat. The smell of urine and faeces from over a thousand men having relieved themselves in the open was overpowering.

Suddenly shouts could be heard coming from the hills above them. Vespasian looked up. Running down the slopes, almost out of control, was a unit of their light archers, who had been scouting above them. They were making straight for Corbulo at the head if the column. Another deep cornu signal blared out: 'Senior officers to report to commander'. Vespasian hurried to the front to stand by for orders.

Corbulo stood in front of the panting infantrymen as their officer made his report.

'Over to the east, sir, a good twenty miles away, you can see it from further up the mountain.' The man paused to catch his breath, taking off his broad-rimmed leather sun hat and wiping his forehead with the back of his hand.

'What? Out with it, man!' Corbulo wasn't the most patient of men.

'A dust cloud, and smoke. We've been watching it for an hour or so, until I was certain; the dust cloud's moving but the smoke isn't, it looks like a war band on the move, burning as they go.'

'Are you sure?'

'We've been watching it; the dust cloud is definitely coming this way.' His men nodded their heads and voiced their agreement.

'Silence!' Corbulo cried, raising a hand. 'Dismissed, and thank you, you've done well.' He turned to Mauricius. 'Prefect, get hold of one of the light cavalry patrols and send them out there; I want to know just what we're up against.'

'Sir!' Mauricius saluted and rode off to carry out his orders.

Corbulo beckoned to Vespasian. 'Tribune, the midday

break is curtailed. Slaughter the oxen and get the carcases loaded on to carts. Have the men draw five days' rations before forming up; we may need to abandon the baggage. If it is a rebel war band we need to get across that river before they catch up with us.'

The marching pace had increased to quick time, a speed at which the mules of the baggage train could just keep up; it was imperative to keep the column together. Corbulo had given orders that any animals going lame or carts breaking down should be immediately abandoned with their loads. Vespasian calculated that at this rate they should reach the river in three hours, giving them just three hours of daylight to cross. It would be a close-run thing, especially if the Thracian commander sent his cavalry forward to skirmish without infantry support, forcing the column to mount a fighting withdrawal.

After an hour the foothills were behind them and they had started to cross the lush pastures of the plain that would lead them down to the river. Behind, clearly visible now from their lower altitude, they could see the dust cloud above the Thracian advance.

The fertile plain was dotted with farmsteads and small villages; horse breeding and sheep farming were the mainstays of this comparatively wealthy part of the country. Speed being essential, Corbulo steered a straight course towards the river, not bothering to avoid larger settlements; instead he sent units of his Gallic cavalry through them in advance as a precaution, hoping that his instinct was correct and the Caeletae were still loyal.

Vespasian could feel the tension of the men as he rode at the head of the first cohort. He wanted to ride up and down the centuries, encouraging them, but, lacking the innate aristocratic self-confidence of many of his rank, he felt inadequate to the task. He had done nothing as yet to win the men's trust and respect, and felt that he would seem to them to be just some callow youth, much younger than many of them. He contemplated the ludicrousness of the system that put a man as young as him, with no military experience, nominally in command of 480 men just because he came from a wealthy family. But that had been the way of Rome from the beginning, it was how the Senate kept its position in society, and the size of the Empire seemed to indicate that it was a system that worked. He decided to leave the morale-boosting to the men who were really in charge: the centurions. It was a great comfort to him that Faustus marched just behind him. He could hear him calling out to the men, praising their efforts, keeping them in formation, and reprimanding slackers. Vespasian knew that when it came to their first combat, whether it was to be here or at the river or further north, it was men like Faustus who would determine whether they lived or died.

Some anxious shouts from amongst the men caused him to look to his right.

'Silence in the ranks,' Faustus bellowed. 'Keep your heads

forward and concentrate on not tripping over the man in front.'

Across the plain, about two miles away, a small group of horsemen could be seen galloping, hell for leather, towards them.

'Looks like trouble,' Magnus muttered. 'Good news doesn't tend to travel that fast.'

The cornu sounded out once more, its deep call carrying clearly over the noise of the marching column.

'That's "Senior officers to report to commander" again,' Magnus said. 'Let's hope the arsehole keeps his cool.'

'An arsehole he may be,' Vespasian said, swinging his horse out of the column, 'but it seems to me that so far he's made all the right decisions.'

'There are still five miles to go and a river to cross; plenty of time to fuck it up.'

At the head of the column Vespasian pulled up beside Corbulo and Mauricius; Gallus and Quintus Caepio, prefect of the rearguard Gallic cavalry, were soon assembled.

'News of the Thracians' advance, I expect,' Corbulo said, grim-faced. 'Our scouts must have sighted them by now.'

They rode on in silence watching the small party of light cavalry closing in. Vespasian counted six of them and two riderless horses, and felt a chill go down his spine and start to gnaw away at him deep within his bowels: men had started to die. He steeled himself for what he knew would be the most testing day of his short life so far, more so than ambushing runaway slaves or rescuing Caenis, for this time he was on the defending side: all the initiative lay with the Thracians.

The scouts drew level and, with prodigious skill, wheeled their exhausted horses around, bringing them to the trot next to the group of officers.

'Sir!' Their leader, a powerful-looking man with a sunburnt face in his mid-thirties, saluted Corbulo. 'Alkaios, Thessalian auxiliary light cavalry.'

'Yes, yes, get on with it.' Corbulo was anxious to get to the point.

'We sighted the main body of Thracians half an hour ago about ten miles east. They're mainly infantry, about three thousand of them. They're moving quickly and with purpose; they've stopped burning as they go. We ran into one of their cavalry patrols but fought them off at the cost of two of my men, one of whom was only wounded and taken prisoner. May the gods ease his suffering.'

'Indeed.' Corbulo could guess as well as anyone else what was in store for the unfortunate man. 'You say you saw no large amount of cavalry?'

'No, sir, just patrols.'

'Minerva's tits, they must have guessed that we're heading for the river and have sent their cavalry around us to the north to hold it against us. Mauricius, take your four turmae and delay them; they must not be allowed to prevent our crossing. We should reach the river in just over an hour.'

'Yes, sir, we shall do all that is necessary.' The cavalry

prefect barked an order at his decurion and the 120 Gauls peeled away from the column and raced towards the river.

Corbulo turned to Quintus Caepio. 'Caepio, take your turmae and keep pace with us half a mile out to the east to shield us from any cavalry threatening our flank.'

Caepio saluted and raced back down the column.

'Gallus, get some horses for the engineers, I want them to get as many ropes as possible secured across that river. If they don't have enough men who can swim get volunteers from the ranks.' Gallus looked pleased with the task allotted him and galloped off to find his temporary command.

Vespasian was impressed at the calm forward thinking of his young superior; it steadied his nerves, feeling that all eventualities were being accounted for. Corbulo turned to him.

'Vespasian, get the baggage and bring it level with the head of the column fifty paces to the west. With the rear-guard gone we can't leave it unprotected. Tell the handlers to do whatever they must to speed those mules up. I don't want to abandon it unless absolutely necessary.'

Vespasian smiled inwardly as he saluted and made his way back down the column; it seemed that he was destined to always be around mules, one way or another.

There were less than two miles to go to the river. The baggage train had drawn level with the two cohorts, the mules having been beaten into more speed; very few had refused or bolted. Vespasian took his place next to Corbulo, who was now at the head of the first cohort; Magnus retreated a respectful distance to the left of the column.

'The men are getting tired, Vespasian,' Corbulo said quietly, glancing nervously at the Thracian dust cloud, now considerably closer. 'They'll be in sight soon. We won't be able to stop after we've crossed the river, we'll need to keep going and hope that the crossing delays the savages longer than it delays us. But what then? They will always move faster than us; they'll catch us in a day.'

'Perhaps we should just stand and fight, take our chances,' Vespasian replied, instantly not liking the idea.

'With two cohorts of veterans and the cavalry that we have, that would be the sensible course to take, but with this lot of rookies we wouldn't stand a chance out here in the open. We need to cross that river, and then find some way to frustrate the enemy.'

With a mile to go the ground had started to fall away gently down into the shallow river valley. Copses of beech and alder populated its sides, breaking up the smooth carpet of grass, which would normally be speckled with small flocks of sheep; but today it was empty. News of the arrival of the Roman column in this peaceful vale had gone before it and the shepherds, anxious not to have their charges requisitioned for the soldiers' cooking fires, had already hurried them to safety.

At the base of the valley flowed the swift Harpessus. Its icy water, recently released from the snowfields high in the mountains to the west, was channelled over a hard bed of shingle and bounded on either side by broken rocks. Hardy trees clung to the banks; the fast-flowing river had whittled away at the soil beneath them, forming strange archways from their exposed roots.

Ahead of them Vespasian could see the advance guard of engineers struggling chest deep in the water to secure the ropes that would aid the column across the hundred-foot width of the river. Two were already in place and a third was attached to a tree on the near bank and extended to its full length along the bank upstream. Vespasian watched as an engineer tied the loose end around his waist and then launched himself, with a strong breaststroke, against the current, keeping the rope taut. The river pushed him further away from the bank. The tension of the rope swung him across until eventually he reached the slower water near the far bank and was able to strike out for the shore, where a comrade helped him out.

As they neared the crossing point the sun sank behind the high massif of the Rhodope range, and the valley darkened as their shadow ate its way along its length.

The proximity of both the Thracian war band to their rear and a means to escape them, if only for a while, to their front caused a few of the less steady of the recruits to try to break ranks and run for the ropes. They were mercilessly beaten back into place by the vine canes of their centurions and shamed into remaining there by the reproachful glares of their comrades.

Corbulo called back to Faustus: 'Any man who tries to push himself forward will be left on this side of the river. Pass that on, centurion, and pass the word for Gallus to report to me.'

As Corbulo's warning was relayed down the column other shouts and cries could be heard coming from a wood half a mile further down the river to the east.

'Mauricius has found their cavalry,' Corbulo guessed. 'Let us hope that he can hold them for long enough.'

'How will he get across?' Vespasian asked. Corbulo didn't answer.

They were a hundred paces from the river. The third rope had now been secured and the engineers had started work on a fourth. Two hundred paces to their right Caepio had formed up his Gallic auxiliaries to cover any flank attack should the Thracians break through Mauricius' cavalry.

Gallus brought his horse to the trot next to his commanding officer and saluted. 'Sir, the river is between four and five feet deep and the current is very strong. We have lost one man swept away already.' His face betrayed a mixture of nerves and excitement at the promise of his first action.

'Thank you, tribune. Gentlemen, speed and efficiency are the keys,' Corbulo said to his two young subordinates. 'Gallus, the second cohort will cross first with the mule train and then form up on the far bank facing the enemy. Vespasian, your cohort will form up, two centuries deep, here, to cover their crossing and that of the auxiliaries, if there are any left. Have your men pile their packs by the ropes before forming up.' Corbulo looked towards the wooded area downstream whence the clash of weapons and the screams of wounded still came. 'If we are attacked we shall make a fighting withdrawal century by century; Faustus' century will be the last to cross. Call in the scouts, they're no use to us out there now, we know what's coming; then get your freedman to lead the carts into the water upstream of the ropes and keep them there, just the carts, not the pack-mules. Hopefully they'll slow the speed of the water and fewer men will be swept away.'

'Yes, sir!' They both saluted.

'And, Gallus,' Corbulo continued, 'if we are attacked and I don't make it over, cut the ropes, stay formed up on that side and oppose their crossing, that's the best chance that you'll have. If you try to run they'll catch you and cut you to pieces.'

CHAPTER XXI

M AGNUS HAD BEEN less than pleased with his role, but, grumbling, had taken the carts to their position in the river. As the mules struggled to keep their heads above the flow one of teams panicked. The animals broke their harnesses, and they, the load and their driver had been swept away in the freezing torrent, almost taking one of the ropes with them. The rest, perhaps chastened by the fate of their fellows, resigned themselves to their task and held their positions.

Vespasian sat on his horse to the rear of the second century of his cohort, at the centre of the Roman line; next to him waited the cohort's cornicen. Each century stood four men deep and twenty men across. Caepio's four turmae of Gauls covered their left flank and the Thessalian light cavalry their right. Spread out in skirmish order in front of them was the fifty-strong unit of light archers.

Behind him Corbulo and Gallus marshalled the second cohort in front of the two upstream ropes and the pack-mules by the two downstream. The crossing began. The men, eager to have the river between them and the enemy, ignored the freezing temperature of the water and, with shields slung across their backs, began to haul themselves across, one hand holding on to the ropes, a foot above the surface, the other clutching their pack-poles and pila.

The first two centuries crossed without mishap and were forming up, sodden, on the far bank, when from up the slope in front of Vespasian, audible even over the rush of the water, came a great shout. The Thracian war band appeared over the crest of the hill and stood silhouetted against the late-afternoon sky. They gave another huge roar, clashed their javelins against their oval shields, and then started to jog steadily down the slope.

A wave of fear rippled through the cohort of new legionaries.

'Steady, lads,' Faustus called from his position in the front rank next to the *signifer*, 'remember your training. Hold the line, listen for the cornu signals, release your pila when ordered and then shields together, weight on your left legs and stab through the gaps. You'll break their mothers' hearts.'

A nervous cheer went up from the ranks.

'That's not a cheer,' Faustus roared. 'That sounded to me like the squealing of a gaggle of Mesopotamian bum-boys getting it up the arse for the first time. Now give me a cheer worthy of the Fourth Scythica.'

Their confidence boosted by the redoubtable Faustus, the legionaries raised a mighty cheer and began to bang their shields rhythmically with their pila. The noise was deafening, but still the Thracians came on.

Vespasian looked back to the river; the pace of the crossing had quickened with the now-visible threat of the Thracians only a half a mile away. Four centuries were over and the last two were in the water. They would be able to start withdrawing his cohort soon, but not without first engaging the enemy. It would be, as Corbulo had said, a fighting withdrawal; he hoped that his men would have the discipline for such a manoeuvre.

Then disaster struck. The mule team nearest the far bank, unable to take the noise and the rushing water any more, bolted for dry land. Caught unawares by the sudden lurch their driver was hauled off his seat on the cart and swept downstream, the reins still around his wrists. The power of the current caused the reins to yank the terrified beasts to their right, toppling them and their wagon. The whole lot swept into the first line of legionaries, plucking eight from the rope as it crashed through them and on into the second line. The men on the second rope had time to see it coming. They dropped their packs and pila in order to hold on with both hands. The cart, the thrashing mules and their comrades cascaded into the legionaries, entangling them in a mesh of limbs, reins and wheel spokes. They held on for dear life and for a moment the whole avalanche slowed, straining the rope. The men to the front of the mess scrambled as fast as they could for the safety of the bank, whilst those behind shouted at their comrades to let go, but to no avail. With a sickening inevitability the weight on the rope wrenched the tree to which it was tied on the far bank from the ground, its roots already loosened by years of erosion. The rope with its cargo of men and debris arced out into the current towards the last of the pack-mules on the third rope. The unfortunate creatures were knocked off balance and away downstream taking those from the fourth rope with them, their handlers saving themselves by dropping their leads and clinging with both hands to the still secure ropes.

Vespasian watched as Corbulo and Gallus raced around trying to restore order to the crossing, but his attention was soon drawn away by the mounting noise of his men and their opponents. The Thracians were only two hundred paces away. With Corbulo busy down at the crossing it would now be down to him to issue the signals. He knew the theory from his lessons with Sabinus, all those months ago. He had seen them work in training on the march from Italia, but he had never seen them given for real. He knew that the timing was everything.

The archers to their front let off three quick long-range volleys bringing down nearly eighty of the tightly packed war band, but doing nothing to halt their advance.

'Open ranks!' he shouted at the cornicen. The low notes of the G-shaped instrument rumbled over the field, its deep tone audible to all over the din of battle cries. Immediately every other man of each century stepped behind his comrade to the right, creating passages for the now retreating archers to run through.

'Close ranks!' The cornicen sounded a different call and the manoeuvre was reversed.

Unencumbered by body armour the Thracians increased their speed steadily. They were a hundred paces out. Vespasian knew it would come soon.

'Shields up!' Again the cornu sounded. The rear three ranks raised their semi-cylindrical rectangular shields and stepped forward to hold them over the heads of the men in front of them. They created a patchwork roof that, if firmly supported, would keep those beneath safe from javelin, arrow or slingshot.

At forty paces from the Roman line the Thracians let out a huge roar and hurled their javelins. Hundreds of the iron-tipped missiles soared into the air and then arced down towards the three centuries and the cavalry to their flanks. With a thunderous clatter, like hail on an ox-hide drum, they rained down on to the waiting shields of the legionaries, thumping into the leather-covered two-inch-thick wood. The temporary roof held firm, with only the occasional scream indicating the inexperience of some rookie who had fatally let down his comrade to the front. The few gaps were immediately closed.

'Shields down!' Another blast from the cornu and the men lowered their shields, snapping off any javelins still embedded in them.

'Pila ready!' Shields and left legs went forward; right arms flew back with hands gripping the smooth wooden shafts of the lead-weighted pila.

On either side the cavalry commanders had both timed their charges to perfection. Giving the order on the release of the javelin volley they charged underneath it. They had smashed through and cut off the disordered flanks of the Thracians, who had not had the time to rearm themselves with their most fearsome weapon, the *rhomphaia*: a sleek three-foot-long iron blade, razor sharp and slightly curved back at the tip, attached to a two-foot, ash-wood handle.

With both flanks now isolated and fighting their own private cavalry–infantry battles, the main body came on, throwing down their shields; they would be of no use to them now for what they had in mind. Each man reached behind his head and with a sweeping movement unsheathed his rhomphaia. The Thracians broke into a reckless sprint wielding these terrifying weapons with both hands above their heads. Maddened by battle lust they screamed as they charged, bearded faces contorted with rage. Long cloaks billowed out behind them; heavy calf-length leather boots pounded down the grass.

Trying to remain calm Vespasian watched the approaching surge of hatred, counting to himself. This was the most crucial order and it had to be timed to perfection.

With twenty paces to impact he bellowed, 'Release pila!'

The cornu sounded. The Thracians had travelled another five paces by the time the legionaries responded to the signal. As one, the three centuries hurled their heavy weapons at a low trajectory towards incoming wall of unprotected flesh. At the moment of release each man drew his gladius from the sheath on his right side and then put his weight on to his left leg and crouched behind his shield. Those in the rear ranks pressed their shields on to the backs of their comrades in front. They braced for impact.

Ten paces from the Roman line more than two hundred pila slammed into the howling stampede. Men were thrown backwards as if yanked from behind by an invisible rope. The barbed points of pila passed clean through their ribs, hearts and lungs, bursting out through their backs in sprays of hot crimson blood. Faces disintegrated as the lead balls at the base of the shafts punched holes through heads, exploding grey matter over the already blood-spattered bodies of those following behind.

But still they came on, leaping over their dead or wounded comrades, heedless of their own safety. Screaming their defiance at their iron-clad adversaries, they hurtled towards the rigid wall of shields, bringing the blades of their *rhomphaiai* hissing down through the air, trying to slice through the helmets of the men behind.

At the point of impact the Roman front rank pushed their shields forward and up. The bronze-reinforced rims took the impact of the rhomphaiai, snapping handles and notching blades with clouds of sparks. Iron shield bosses thumped into the chests of the warriors as they crashed into the solid Roman line, winding some and throwing others off balance.

The line held.

Then the short pointed swords, designed to stab and gut, thrust out from between the shields at groin height and commenced their lethal work. The bellows of rage turned into shrieks of pain and anguish as the iron blades pushed up through the vitals of the now stationary Thracian front line. Bellies split open, spilling their steaming contents over the feet of both attacker and defender alike. Genitals were severed, arteries opened and blood flowed freely.

The press of their rear ranks prevented the Thracians from using their rhomphaiai to full effect. They were used to more open combat, typical of their inter-tribal battles, where there was room to swing the weapon, lopping off the heads and arms of their opponents, or sweeping the legs from under them. Here they were of little account.

The battle turned into a scrum of pushing and stabbing. A couple of the inexperienced legionaries stabbed too far and felt an icy flash of pain. They quickly withdrew their arms to find only a blood-spurting stump, and went down screaming. The men behind trampled over them knowing that to leave a gap would be fatal for them all.

And still the line held.

Unable to make headway the Thracians started to spill around the unguarded flanks of the two outermost centuries; legionaries began to fall, heads and limbs missing. From his vantage point Vespasian was aware of the danger.

'Fourth and sixth centuries advance!' he yelled.

The cornu blared and the two centuries on the flanks of the second line moved forward at a jog, increasing their speed as they closed with the enemy. Their centurions ordered their charge. In the wake of a volley of pila they hit the side of the encircling Thracians, punching those still standing off their feet with their shields and then despatching them on the ground with firm thrusts of their swords.

The Thracians started to fall back; the encircling manoeuvre having failed, they had, for the time being, lost heart. As they disengaged the severity of their casualties became apparent. More than four hundred of their dead and dying littered the bloody ground in front of the legionaries and the hillside beyond.

A massive cheer rose from the newly blooded recruits as they watched their opponents retreat. A few of the more hot-headed made to follow them only to be bawled back into line by their centurions, who knew only too well the folly of an undisciplined pursuit.

Corbulo arrived at Vespasian's side.

'We've beaten them, sir,' Vespasian said with some pride, although fully aware that his gladius remained in pristine condition in its sheath.

'You've beaten them off more like, but they'll come again. Savages like these have more bravado than sense. It's time we got out of here. Cornicen, sound "Withdraw facing enemy".'

Corbulo then turned to the centurion of the unused fifth century. 'Send out a party of men to bring in our wounded and finish off those who won't make it. We will leave none of our men behind to amuse those barbarians.'

Steadied by the shouts of the centurions in the front rank and the optiones in the rear, the centuries began to pull back, step by step, in time to the beat measured out by low blasts from the cornicen.

The cavalry disengaged from their private battles and galloped back to cover the infantry retreat. They saw off the sorties of small groups of impetuous Thracians who attempted to disrupt the retrieval of the Roman wounded with javelin volleys.

Slowly the Roman line fell back the hundred paces to the river. In front of them the Thracian warriors had retrieved their discarded shields and rearmed with javelins. Again they began to work themselves up into a frenzy.

'It won't be long before they pluck up the courage to have another go,' Corbulo said. 'Vespasian, get the rear three centuries and the wounded on to the ropes.'

The last of the archers was crossing as Vespasian ordered the fourth, fifth and sixth centuries on to the three remaining ropes. The men, having retrieved their packs, didn't need to be told the urgency of the situation and leapt into the water. Behind them the three remaining centuries formed a convex wall, shielding the ropes from the enemy.

As the last men of the rear centuries clambered into the water another great roar went up. Vespasian spun his horse round; six hundred paces away up the hill the Thracians started to move forward slowly.

Magnus appeared at his side. 'Now we're for it.'

'What are you doing here? Why aren't you with the baggage-carts?'

'Since when was I baggage?'

'Since Corbulo put you in charge of it.'

'As you said, I'm not under military discipline and I ain't going across until you do.'

Corbulo came striding up to them. 'We won't have time to get all the men over before they're on us. Tribune, get the third century across on all three ropes. I've sent the cavalry to try and delay the attack. And you,' he said, looking at Magnus, 'tell the baggage to get out of the river, then find yourself a shield and helmet. I imagine you'll disobey me if I tell you to cross with it.'

'Sir!' Magnus hastened off as Vespasian dismounted.

The first and second centuries stood grimly watching their cavalry's efforts to slow the advancing Thracians. Beaten off by volleys of javelins from the tightly packed horde, they turned and fled, back to the river.

'Caepio, get your men across,' Corbulo screamed. 'There's nothing more that you can do here.'

The thankful Gauls and Thessalians plunged their already tired horses into the river and began to wade to the far bank; a harder task now that the temporary barricade of wagons was no longer stemming the flow. The men of the third century were also struggling and the crossing had slowed to a snail's pace. Their comrades, formed up on the far bank, called out encouragement but the quicker pace of the river took its toll. As Vespasian turned to join Corbulo with the remaining men he saw two legionaries being swept away, their heavy armour dragging them under. He knew it would take a miracle for them all to cross now.

The Thracians were less than three hundred paces off and

had broken into a jog, gathering momentum for the final charge.

'Well, tribune, let's make sure that not all these men's first action is their last,' Corbulo said, turning to Vespasian. 'We'll take the impact of the charge and hold them; once we're steady the rear rank can peel off to the ropes.'

'What about the rest, sir?'

'They'll need to fight like lions. We have to make the enemy disengage, and then we run for the ropes. When the last men are on we cut the ropes and pray that we can hold on as the river swings us across.'

Magnus came puffing up the bank towards the two officers with a shield and helmet. He had a mule cart in tow.

'Looks like we need to beat them pretty decisively to stand any chance here, hopefully these will help.'

'What have you got there? I told you to get all the baggage across,' Corbulo shouted, furious that his orders had not been obeyed to the full.

'Pila, sir.' Magnus pulled the leather cover off the cart.

A spark of hope kindled in Corbulo's eyes. 'What are you waiting for, man? Get them distributed.'

Quickly they ordered the men of the rear rank to grab four pila each and pass them up the files. The men's morale was lifted by the weight of a pilum in their hands, and they started to beat them against their shields. From behind them their comrades on the far bank did the same. The noise made the Thracians pause. They had reached the long heap of mangled bodies that denoted the line of the last engagement, and were close enough now to see the new pila in their foes' hands. They had already experienced at first hand that day the destructive power of the weapon, and even at odds of nearly ten to one they needed to boost their confidence. They started another round of jeering and cheering, working themselves up into battle fever.

'We should go now, sir, whilst they've stopped. We could make it, surely?'

'No, they'll pick us off in the river with javelins; we need them to fire that volley at us whilst we're shielded. Come, tribune, it's the front rank for us. No doubt your insubordinate freedman will wish to join us?'

'That is a very kind invitation, sir,' Magnus said politely. 'I'll be a lot more use there than skulking around in the rear.'

Corbulo grunted and pushed his way between two files to the front.

Vespasian stood between Magnus and Corbulo at the centre of the Roman line, watching the Thracians getting their bloodlust up. They had found a wounded Thessalian who had been too far away for the retrieval parties to bring in. The hapless prisoner had a ropes tied around his wrists and was being stretched upright in the crucifix position by two men pulling on each arm. Around him danced a swarm of howling warriors brandishing their rhomphaiai.

'Do not look away, lads,' Corbulo bellowed. 'Watch this and remember what they do to prisoners.'

The dancing stopped and the Thracians broke into a low chant that began to rise in volume until it drowned the screamed pleas of the prisoner. Two men took up positions behind him. The chant reached a crescendo and then suddenly stopped. Two rhomphaiai scythed through the air. The Thessalian's legs dropped to the ground, but the man remained upright, screaming, stretched by the ropes, like ghastly washing on a line. Blood poured from his wounds in a pathetic imitation of the limbs he had just lost. With another sweep of flashing iron his arms were severed; they flew through the air on the end of the ropes spraying blood in macabre arcs. His limbless trunk crashed to the floor onto his severed legs. Two more warriors approached the tormented man and lifted the blood-spurting hulk in the air. Still alive but limbless, the Thessalian stared in catatonic shock at his erstwhile comrades, just a hundred paces away. Another flash and his head fell to the floor.

The Thracians charged.

'Shields up!' bellowed Corbulo.

Vespasian felt the shield of the man behind him push over his head and connect at a right angle with the top of his own, leaving a small curved viewing slit. Inside the wooden box men's breath became laboured as they fought back the rising panic induced by close confinement in stressful circumstances. The smell of sweat, fear and urine filled Vespasian's nostrils as they flared, sucking in lungful after lungful of hot air. Time seemed to slow as, in his mind, he recounted the training moves that Sabinus had put him through against the practice post at home, so far away. Calm washed through him. He was ready to fight. He was not going to die. Whatever fate awaited him it was not a death at the hands of a pack of savages. He gripped hard on his pilum. The first javelin punched into his shield. The muscles in his left forearm bulged with the strain of holding the shield firm. All around him sharp cracks filled the air as javelin after javelin thumped down on the Roman line. Men grunted through gritted teeth with the strain of supporting their shields against the barrage. Here and there a scream. Then it was over.

'Shields down!'

Vespasian quickly leant forward and broke off the four-foot-long projectile still embedded in his shield. He became aware of hissing shafts passing overhead; their archers had opened fire from the other bank.

'Pila ready!'

He gripped his pilum at the top of the shaft just behind the lead ball, and extended his arm back, putting his weight on his right foot.

'Release pila!'

Vespasian threw his right arm forward with all his strength, hurling the heavy weapon at the mass of bodies charging towards him. He had no time to look at his handi-work. He reached immediately for his gladius and swept it from its sheath. He felt the shield behind him press into his back. He braced for impact. The screams of the Thracian wounded filled the air. Men went down, tripping others behind them, who were in turn trampled in the stampede to reach the Roman line.

Crouching behind the shield wall he was aware of a blur of

metal bearing down on him. He pushed his shield up and forward. The blade of a rhomphaia ricocheted off the rim and an instant later its wielder smashed into the boss, cracking ribs and punching the air from his lungs. Vespasian's left arm jarred with the impact, but held. With most of his weight on his left leg he thrust his blade through the gap between his and Magnus' shields. He felt it penetrate soft flesh. He rolled his wrist sharply right then left, shredding the bowels of his screaming opponent, then he withdrew the blade and stabbed again as another took his place.

Next to him Magnus was punching his sword back and forth, ducking under murderous swipes of hissing iron, yelling his defiance with every swear word at his command as the bodies piled up in front of him.

To the right and left the Thracians tried to get round the flanks of the centuries but were brought down in droves by the fifty archers on the north bank.

The line was holding.

'Rear rank to the ropes!' yelled Corbulo as he felt the pressure ease on the shield wall.

Vespasian felt the weight pushing against his back lessen as the rear man of his file made his bid for safety.

'Now push, you sons of whores,' Corbulo roared. 'Push those bastards back to hell.'

With a monumental effort the legionaries shoved their shields forward and heaved the enemy back. They stepped over the first of the bodies in front of them, the second-rank men stabbing the fallen again. Many a soldier had lost his life to a wounded opponent plunging a knife up into his groin as he straddled him. As the Roman line moved forward the Thracians compacted, their rear ranks still pushing forward whilst their front ranks were pushed back. The result was chaos as the Roman blades stabbed into the tightly compressed unarmoured flesh. Some of the dead remained upright, their heads lolling bizarrely as they were piniomed between shield bosses and their comrades behind; others slipped to the ground exposing new targets for blood-covered legionary swords.

Afterwards Vespasian would remember little of the following short period of time; his mind had switched off and his instincts and body took control. He heard no distinct sounds, just a constant roaring that his brain soon blocked out as one more distraction. All he would recall was the exhil-aration he felt at the mechanical thrusting, grinding and retrieving of his sword as the Roman line, which he was an intrinsic part of, pushed forward, destroying all before it. He killed again and again with ease; he killed so that he and his comrades could remain alive.

Suddenly a shock wave swept through the Thracian line from right to left. Another threat had slammed into it from the east.

'Mauricius!' Corbulo shouted. 'The gods be praised.'

With the unlooked-for arrival of their Gallic auxiliaries the legionaries' hearts soared. These young men who had woken up in the morning as unblooded rookies now had the confidence of a unit of hardened killers. They set about their work with renewed vigour, blades flashing, shields punching, slaying everything in their path, pushing their opponents slowly back up the hill, whilst their Gallic allies rolled up the left flank, slashing down on their enemies with their long cavalry swords.

From behind them a massive cheer erupted from the second cohort. They pointed to the sky. Above, the ominous flock of rooks that had so disconcerted them that morning was heading back east, pursued by the two eagles. For a moment everyone paused and looked up as the chasing birds swooped down on their prey, plucking two out of the air with their claws. They rose back up, shrieking as they went, and released their victims in a flurry of feathers on to the mêlée below.

The Thracians turned and fled. The cavalry started to pursue them.

'Hold!' Corbulo cried. 'Let them run. Mauricius, cover our withdrawal. And don't ever turn up late again!' Corbulo smiled with relief at the cavalry prefect, who grinned in return and then started to marshal his eighty or so remaining troopers; they too had had a hard day of it.

Vespasian sucked in a deep breath and then bellowed a victory cheer with his comrades.

'That was more of a fight than we used to get in the Urban Cohort,' Magnus puffed at his side.

'That was the sort of fight that I could get to enjoy,' Vespasian replied. His round face was flushed with excitement and blood. 'If that is how a newly trained cohort fights then we may well have the gods on our side.'

'The gods be buggered, it was—'

Corbulo's shouting cut Magnus off.

'Second century's to cross next. First century's to form up to their front.'

The light was starting to fade as the men of the second century waded out into the river with Corbulo and their centurion and optio all bellowing at them to get a move on.

A grim-faced Faustus reported to Vespasian, who stood with Magnus looking up the hill. Beyond the heaps of bodies in the pale light the Thracians were still there and had again started their pre-charge ritual.

'That's all the wounded taken care of, sir, twelve in total plus seven dead outright.'

'Thank you, centurion. Have the men collect their packs.'

'Sir!'

'First century to the ropes; Vespasian, Faustus, take a rope each,' Corbulo ordered as the last of the second century struck out into the river. 'And, Mauricius, start crossing upstream of us, it will help ease the current.'

As the cavalry splashed in past the legionaries, a roar went up from the Thracians. For the third time in the day they started to tear back down the hill.

Panic spread through the legionaries; to have achieved so much in the past few hours only to be caught so close to safety seemed to be against the will of the gods. They started to push and shove to try to get on to a rope.

'Easy lads, easy!' Faustus roared at the downstream

station, cuffing a few round the ears. 'Don't lose your discipline now.'

Vespasian looked behind; the Thracians were halfway to them, and there were still at least fifteen men to get on each rope.

'When I give the order, cut the ropes,' Corbulo shouted.

The men pulled themselves out into the river; arrows flew over their heads from the archer support on the north bank. With the Thracians fifty paces away it was apparent that they would not all make it.

'Cut the ropes!'

Vespasian realised that Corbulo was right; it was more important to deny the Thracians the means of crossing than to save the last ten or so men, including himself. So much for fate; it was to be a death at the hands of these savages after all. He knew his duty was to the greater good and not to himself. He slashed down with his sword on the hemp rope; it parted, swinging its passengers out into the current. He then turned to face the enemy. They had stopped ten paces from them.

'To me, to me,' Corbulo shouted from the middle station, where he stood next to two terrified-looking young legionaries. Vespasian ran to his side with Magnus and the two men that had been left at his station. Faustus and three others joined them.

'Right, lads,' Corbulo said grimly, 'we'll sell our lives dearly.' He charged. The others followed. They swept into the Thracians slashing and stabbing, but received no counter-strikes, just blows from the wooden handles of rhomphaiai. As he went down and blackness enveloped him Vespasian realised that this time the Thracians had not come to kill. That would come later.

CHAPTER XXII

VESPASIAN CAME TO. It was dark. He felt a sticky substance in his eye and went to rub it away but found his hands firmly tied behind his back. Then he remembered the blow to his head that had felled him. Blood, he thought, blood from the wound.

His throat was dry and his head ached; in fact, his whole body ached. He groaned as his consciousness cleared and the pain started to register.

'Welcome back, sir, although I don't think that you'll be very pleased to be here. I certainly ain't.'

Vespasian turned his head. Next to him was Magnus.

'Where are we?' It was a stupid question; he already knew the answer.

'Guests of the Thracians; and after what we did to them not very welcome ones, I should imagine.'

Vespasian's eyes started to clear. All around small orange glows started to come into focus: campfires. In their light he could see huddled figures sleeping on the ground. His eyes gradually got used to the light. Closer to him, in the gloom, he saw a mesh of poles; he looked above him, the same, they were in a wooden cage. There were two others in there with them. He squinted and made out the uniforms of Corbulo and Faustus, both still out cold.

'Where are the others?' he asked, wondering about the remaining legionaries.

'I don't know. I only came to a short time before you, I haven't had time to have a wander round and suss out the accommodation arrangements.'

Vespasian smiled; Magnus had not lost his humour.

'Get some rest, sir, there's nothing we can do at the moment. The ropes are well tied; I've been trying to loosen them but have only managed to rip the skin off my wrists. We'll have to wait until our hosts untie them for us, then we'll need our wits about us.'

Vespasian knew Magnus was right – if they were untied he would need to be fresh and alert. He closed his eyes and fell into an uneasy sleep.

At dawn the camp stirred. Vespasian woke to find a Thracian in the cage giving sheep's milk to his fellow captives. He waited his turn and when it came sucked the warm liquid in gratefully, overcoming the disgust that most Romans felt for milk in its natural form. He felt it filling his stomach and realised that he hadn't eaten since the midday break the day before.

'If they're bothering to feed us they can't be planning on killing us immediately,' Corbulo observed. His hair was matted with dried blood and his right eye swollen and dark blue.

'We kill you when we ready,' the Thracian growled in broken Latin as he secured the cage's gate.

'What charming hosts,' Magnus muttered. The Thracian glared at him and then walked off, leaving three others, armed with spears, to guard them.

'Tell your man not to antagonise them, Tribune,' Corbulo hissed. 'If we're to keep our strength for an escape, we would do well to avoid a beating.'

Vespasian looked at Magnus who nodded and gave a half-smile.

'The men must be exhausted,' Faustus said, looking over Vespasian's shoulder. Vespasian swivelled round. Half a mile away, on the north bank of the river, the first and second cohorts stood formed up, with the cavalry on either flank. The baggage was corralled a little way behind them.

'Good man, Gallus, he didn't panic,' Corbulo said. 'The Thracians won't dare to cross now, they'll have to withdraw unless they want to sit here and live off roots and berries.'

'And with our archers keeping them away from the river they'll run out of water in a day or so,' Faustus pointed out.

On the slope leading down to the river parties of Thracians moved around collecting their dead, piling them up in a huge mound laced with wood. The Romans were left to rot in the sun.

'Bastards!' Faustus spat. 'Leaving our lads like that. It's bad enough them not having a coin to pay the ferryman.'

'I think we would have done the same, centurion,' Corbulo said.

'Besides, they have different gods to us,' Magnus said. 'I wouldn't like to end up in the Thracian version of Hades, would you?'

'Especially not speaking the language,' Vespasian quipped.

They all turned and looked at him; he sat straight-faced with a twinkle in his eye. Even Corbulo, for all his aristocratic seriousness, could not resist laughing.

As the morning wore on the upper slopes were cleared and the Thracians had to venture closer to the river, where a line of mangled bodies marked the position of yesterday's final battle by the ropes. The retrieval party came forward waving a branch as a sign of truce. They got to within thirty paces of the bank when a volley from the archers, on the far side, thumped into them. A dozen went down, feathered with shafts; their screams could be heard all the way up the hill. The rest scampered to safety, a couple with arrows protruding from their shoulders.

'That's going to piss them off,' Magnus said.

Corbulo looked pleased. 'Good. They can't expect to collect their dead under truce but leave ours: that is not how it works.'

'Fucking savages!' Faustus opined.

From another part of the camp, fifty paces to their right, voices were raised; a heated argument had broken out. A tall, grey-haired Thracian with a long, forked beard that came almost down to his round belly was remonstrating with a smaller, weasel-faced man with a shaven head. A young man, in his early twenties, sat between them on a folding stool. He listened with a calm air of authority to the altercation as tempers rose, never once looking at the protagonists, always keeping his eyes on the line of dead by the river. Weasel-face shrieked at the older man, dipped his hand into a bag that hung from his shoulder, pulled out a human head and brandished it in his opponent's face. This apparently settled the argument one way or another in the young man's mind; he stood up and issued a series of orders to some waiting warriors, who rushed off to do his bidding.

'What the fuck are they up to?' Magnus asked.

'I think that we've just witnessed a conflict of interests between the chief's adviser and his priest,' Corbulo said, adding with a wry smile: 'Much like Sejanus arguing with the chief Vestal, only this time the Vestal seems to have won.'

'It's not *his* priest,' Faustus said. 'Their priests wander around the country going from tribe to tribe; they belong to no one but their gods.'

More shouting came from further off in the camp and, a few moments later, the warriors returned leading five young men with ropes around their necks and hands tied behind their backs. The russet colour of their tunics identified them immediately.

'They're our lads,' Vespasian said. 'What are they going to do with them?'

'Something that I don't think will work,' Corbulo replied.

The terrified legionaries were herded down to the edge of

the camp where a line of fifty Thracians with shields had assembled. With the ropes still around their necks they were driven before the shielded line as it advanced down the slope, the burial party following close behind.

'Come on, Gallus, do what you must and really piss those bastards off,' Corbulo whispered, almost to himself.

The line reached the Thracian dead, clambered across and stopped. The captives fell to their knees; their shouts and pleas carried up the hill. The burial party started to remove some bodies. The Roman cohorts began to bang their pila against their shields. Gallus could be seen riding in front of them with his arm in the air, he stopped in the centre, turned towards the Thracians and brought his arm down. Fifty arrows sped across the river and the captives were silenced; the Romans fell quiet.

'Well done, Gallus,' Corbulo said.

'He just shot our lads, sir.' Vespasian was outraged.

'Of course he did, and if they were sensible they would have been begging him to. It may well be that any one of us would happily trade places with them in a hour or so.'

Another volley clattered into the wall of shields, then another into the burial party dragging bodies up the hill behind it, bringing down a good many. The rest dropped their loads and ran.

With their human shields dead the Thracian shield wall began to retreat, but, lacking the discipline of regular soldiers, did so piecemeal, leaving gaps which the archers brutally exploited; a little over half of them made it back up the hill.

To Vespasian's right the weasel man howled curses and shook his severed head at the Romans, whilst the chief sat impassive with his fists clenched on his knees. The fork-bearded man said something to the chief, who nodded and dismissed him. The priest wailed as he watched him make his way down the hill to the remnants of the burial party.

This time the Thracians retrieved the Roman dead left on the higher reaches of the hill, and made a separate pyre for them. Cheers rang out from the opposite bank.

Corbulo looked pleased. 'The chief seems to have an adviser with some manners; he might have a few more men alive to command if he'd listened to him in the first place, rather than to that disgusting-looking priest.'

'I don't fancy getting too close to him,' Magnus said, 'but I've got a nasty feeling we might get to meet him if we don't find a way out.'

Vespasian glared at Magnus. 'I think it would be best if you keep those thoughts to yourself.'

'He's right though, sir,' Faustus said, having another attempt at loosening his bonds.

Down the hill only the dead by the river were left untended. The burial party again approached under a branch of truce. They took the Roman dead first, including the recently shot captives, and then untangled the Thracians. No arrows disturbed their work. One body in particular was treated with more reverence than the rest, and placed on a small pyre on its own.

Eventually the field was cleared of bodies and severed

limbs; only dark red stains on the grass and the occasional pile of offal marked where men had fallen.

The Thracians lit the Roman pyre with no ceremony whatever, before turning their attentions to their own.

The weasel-faced priest stood before the massed Thracians and began a series of short chants, to which his congregation responded with ever-increasing intensity. Even the guards around the cage joined in. During this the chief made his way down to the foot of the smaller pyre that bore the solitary warrior. The chants reached a crescendo, and then abruptly stopped. The chief opened his arms in a gesture of supplication and let out a cry of profound grief.

'No wonder they were so keen to reclaim the dead by the river,' Corbulo concluded. 'Looks like their chief lost a family member down there.'

'Or lover?' Magnus suggested.

'No, they're not like the Greeks,' Faustus said. 'From my experience they're strictly women, boys and sheep; though not necessarily in that order, or separate.'

The crowd of Thracians parted, and another struggling man in a russet tunic was hauled out.

'How many more have they got?' Vespasian asked.

'If we all survived, one more after him; then us four,' Faustus replied.

The priest kept up a constant stream of prayers and ululations as the legionary was stripped, then pegged out on the ground between the two pyres; his mouth was gagged to quell his screaming. Ten men, naked to the waist, started to circle the writhing sacrifice on horses; each had a huge log or rock across his saddle. The priest drew a knife from his belt and raised it to the heavens. The first horseman lifted his log and hefted it down on to the Roman. It smashed his ribcage. A second followed, then a rock, then another log, each crushing and mangling the body part it landed on. The man was dead before the last rock landed on him.

Vespasian watched and understood what was being acted out; he could guess what would happen next. He put a hand to the pendant that Caenis had given him as the priest stepped forward brandishing his knife. He grabbed the dead man's genitals in one hand and with a flash of the blade severed them. The Thracians roared. The priest then presented the blood-dripping pile of flesh to the chief who took it in two hands and held it over the small pyre. He muttered a private prayer and laid his grisly offering on his dead kinsman's chest. A torch was plunged into the oil-soaked wood and the pyre burst into flames.

'They do weird stuff here,' Magnus said, making the sign to ward off the evil eye. 'What was all that about?'

Vespasian remained silent, thinking of the story that Caenis had told him when she had given him his pendant.

'It's like something in Publius Ovidius' *Metamorphoses*,' Corbulo said, but got no further. Whatever literary observation he was going to make was interrupted by screaming from the large pyre.

A wooden cage, similar to theirs, was being hauled up the side of the huge mound of seven hundred or more corpses.

In it was the last russet-clad legionary. He knew what fate awaited him, but was helpless to prevent it. Once the cage had reached the top the priest embarked on another set of prayers. Men with burning torches surrounded the pyre. The caged legionary screamed out pleas to the gods, his comrades, his mother, none of whom could help him. They drowned out the voice of the weasel-faced priest, who pressed on regardless.

From across the river the men of the first and second cohorts crashed their pila against their shields three times and then began to sing the Hymn of Mars. The doleful voices booming out the ancient hymn carried up the hill to their comrade and seemed to settle him. He stopped his cries, raised himself to his knees and bowed his head in silent prayer to the gods below.

On a signal from the priest the torches were thrust into the base of the pyre. The flames caught, consuming first the hair, then the tunics and cloaks of the fallen, before taking hold of the flesh itself. That in its turn blistered, then sizzled and spat, giving off the aroma of roast pork as the fat within melted and oozed flaming droplets that were consumed as they fell into the blaze below. The heat had become intense; no smoke was given off, only flames. They licked their way ever upward until the top layer of bodies caught.

The man in the cage stayed motionless, as if he'd found peace through the singing of his comrades. The flames spread towards him. His hair was singed, and then his chest started to heave with irregular jerks – but not in pain. He couldn't breathe: the fire had consumed all the oxygen. He lost consciousness as his tunic started to smoulder. His lungs collapsed. He was spared the agony of being burnt alive.

The Romans sang on.

The fire had now completely engulfed the pyre. Vespasian looked away; he exhaled and realised that he had been holding his breath for a long time. None of his comrades uttered a word. What was there to say? They were all busy with their own thoughts of death and how they would face it, and prayed that, when the time came, they would have the strength that the young legionary had shown.

The Thracians started to strike camp. It didn't take long; they had travelled light.

The four prisoners were roughly manhandled out of the cage and dumped unceremoniously on to the floor of a mule cart.

'Nothing but the best for us, it seems,' Vespasian said. 'I was expecting to have to walk; we'll be the envy of everyone.'

Corbulo nodded in acknowledgement of the attempt at humour as the four struggled to sit up with their hands and legs still bound.

'Something to eat would be nice,' Magnus said. 'I don't think much of the service. Where's a nice plump serving wench to take our order?'

The cart jolted. They were off. The column plodded its way up the hill leaving the three pyres burning and, next to them, still pegged out, the gelded legionary.

The Romans stopped their singing and began jeering.

Corbulo smiled. 'Poppaeus will be pleased when he receives those men. They've shown good character; they won't disgrace the Fourth Scythica or the Fifth Macedonica.'

'Then we shall have to make sure to be there when he does, so we can see his face,' Faustus said.

But the idea of escape seemed absurd, bound as they were hand and foot and surrounded by guards. They lapsed into silence.

The column climbed out of the valley and turned to the southeast. It plodded on for a few miles under the searing midday sun. Conditions in the cart started to deteriorate as the call of nature, so long resisted in the cage, became impossible to ignore. Although they were used to hardship, it was an affront to their dignitas to lie so close together in soiled clothes, like slaves being transported to the mines.

Vespasian, to avoid the eye of his fellows in these humiliating circumstances, spent his time staring back out of the cart. As he scanned the crest of the last hill they'd descended a lone horseman appeared. He stopped and was soon joined by a few more, and then more, until at least a hundred sat watching the disappearing column from their vantage point, three or so miles away.

'Corbulo!' Vespasian whispered so as not to attract the guards' attention. 'They're our Gallic auxiliaries, I'm sure of it. Look. Gallus must be coming to rescue us.'

Corbulo smiled ruefully. 'If he is, then he's a fool. He

doesn't even know if we're alive or not. No, I'm afraid they have just been sent out to make sure that the Thracians are really pulling back, so that Gallus knows that he is safe to move off, free from pursuit.'

As he spoke the horsemen turned and disappeared back over the crest of the hill.

'I'm afraid that that is the last we'll see of them.'

Vespasian turned his eyes back to the hill, willing the cohorts to appear. But he knew it was futile. Corbulo was right: they had seen the last of their comrades whose duty was to the north.

They were on their own.

CHAPTER XXIII

F OR TWO DAYS they bumped along in the cart. Their bonds were checked regularly; any progress that they had made in loosening them was discovered and cruelly repaired. Occasionally the inside of the cart was sluiced out with water, washing away the refuse that they were forced to lie in. They received no proper food, only sheep's milk, which temporarily sated their hunger, or the odd crust of dry bread unceremoniously stuffed into their mouths. Their joints ached and they grew weaker.

Unable to sleep for more than short periods at a time Vespasian passed the days and nights by writing letters to Caenis in his head, vowing that he would live to write them for real. He wrote of his love for her and how he first felt that love the moment he saw her outside the Porta Collina. He wrote of his fear for her when he heard that she was Livilla's captive, and his pride at being a party to her rescue. He promised her that he would win enough money to be able to buy her freedom. But most of all, he promised to love her for ever. When he ran out of things to write he composed her replies; they were full of love for him and pride at his achievements and successes, and always written on wax tablets that he imagined to be somehow imbued with her scent.

And so he passed the time in his head. The others did likewise, conversation being pointless, as it only ever led to one subject – that of escape – and the hopelessness of their situation would again be reinforced. So with an unspoken common consent they remained silent in order to preserve what morale they had.

They left the Rhodope Mountains behind and passed down into a wide valley through which ran the slow-flowing Hebrus. Although fertile, much of the valley was uncultivated and covered with forest, the inland Thracian tribes being more interested in banditry than husbandry. The burnt-out settlements that marked the course of the war band's advance, a few days earlier, attested to the fact.

Once in the valley their course changed to due east. They plunged into trackless forest. Scouts were sent out ahead through the thick undergrowth to spring any ambushes set by the tribes still loyal to Rome, wanting revenge for land that had been ravaged. But none came.

On the morning of the third day the trees thinned out and gave way to a narrow area of scrubland, beyond which flowed the Hebrus. Its slow brown water, laden with the sediment that its fast-flowing tributaries had washed down from the mountains in the spring thaw, cut a meandering path through the flat land on either side, ever eating away at the earth on its banks. Groups of small brush-covered islets ranged in gentle sweeps near the shore; the water between them was filled with reeds.

On the far bank, one hundred paces away, was a fishing village. As the Thracians appeared out of the wood a flotilla was launched. Over fifty small fishing boats and log rafts, crewed by boys, began to paddle across the river; the boys whooped as they raced with each other, all vying to be the first across.

'So that's how they crossed,' Corbulo said quietly. 'When we come back on a punishment raid we'll destroy every boat we find; not that I plan on leaving anyone alive to use them.'

Vespasian smiled to himself; he had guessed how Corbulo had spent the time in his head.

The first boats arrived and the whoops of some of the boys turned into wails of grief as they learnt of fathers or elder brothers who would not be returning.

The Thracians began to embark. Sacks were pulled over the mules' heads and the prisoners' cart was loaded on to what felt like a very unstable raft. The boys crewing it glared at the prisoners. One had tears in his eyes. Vespasian wondered if he had killed the boy's kinsman, and found himself hoping that he had.

The raft cast off and Vespasian, knowing that they would not stand a chance in the water, still bound as they were, prayed to Poseidon, who, although Greek, he felt was the most suitable god in the circumstances, to keep them afloat.

All around them the small boats bobbed in the river, heavily laden with seven or eight men in each. Some of the men were in high spirits, pleased to be going home, but the rest were quiet, mindful of the friends and kinsmen that did not share their luck.

The blindfolded mules brayed mournfully all the way across.

The flotilla made three trips before the crossing was complete; there were no accidents. Vespasian couldn't help but admire the efficiency with which it was carried out. It was a far cry from the ramshackle way in which these people fought.

Once they were all assembled on the east bank, thirty or so men, who came from the village, bade farewell to their comrades and returned home with the boys. The rest of war band moved off. The grim journey continued across the seemingly endless flat grassland of the eastern bank of the Hebrus.

At intervals, small groups of warriors split off from the column to make their way home, to the north or south, to the villages and small homesteads that could be seen scattered in the distance. By mid-afternoon there were fewer than four hundred left in the war band.

'This is more like it,' Magnus said, his spirits raised by the dwindling number of warriors that surrounded them. 'If it carries on like this it'll be just us and the guards left, then we'll see how tough they are.'

'And just how do you plan untie yourself?' Corbulo asked, coming back to the main problem.

'Ah, yes.'

They lapsed back into a silence that was disturbed, a few moments later, by the sound of horses galloping. From out of nowhere twenty or so horsemen had materialised. The column halted.

'Where the fuck did they come from?' Faustus asked, seeing no sign of close habitation.

The horsemen arrived at the head of the column where they greeted the chief; after exchanging a few words one of them rode back to the cart.

He stared at the four prisoners with piercing blue eyes. The tip of his nose was missing. A long, ill-kempt, ginger beard that completely hid his mouth covered his lower face; the rest of his head was bald. Huge gold rings hung from his ears. He picked out Corbulo as the most senior and addressed him in good Latin.

'Are you the man who is responsible for the death of my youngest son?'

Corbulo was taken aback, he had no idea who or how many he had killed in the battle.

'I am responsible for no deaths. It was not I who attacked.'

'But it was you who commanded the Roman column. It was you that led it on to Thracian soil.'

'Thracia is a client of Rome, and we have every right to be here. You would do well to remember that in your dealings with me.'

The Thracian laughed; it was not a pleasant sound. 'The arrogance of you people amazes me; even when prisoners, tied up in your own shit, you still talk down to anyone not of your kind. Well, I will tell you this, Roman, I hold you responsible and you will pay.'

He spat in Corbulo's face, turned his horse and sped off; the other horsemen followed. A couple of hundred paces from the column they disappeared down into a depression, invisible in the sea of grass. The column followed. They descended into an almost round basin about two hundred paces across and fifty deep. At the bottom was a large camp of over five hundred tents. It was so well hidden that an army could march within a quarter of a mile of it and not see it.

Night had fallen. Fires, not allowed in the camp during the day because of their smoke, had now been lit. Sheep were being roasted whole on spits; the smell of cooking mutton wafted over the camp. The drinking had started, and the Thracians' mood began to change from the sombreness of defeated men to one of intoxicated bravado. Heroic deeds were recounted and embellished, boasts were made and vows of vengeance sworn. Fights broke out, screaming slave girls and boys were brutally tupped and more rough wine drunk. The seriousness of the fights intensified and the drinking became reckless. The noise steadily escalated.

Vespasian and his companions sat at the centre of this chaos. They still wore their uniforms over their stained and filthy tunics. Their feet remained bound but their hands had been freed so that they could eat from the plate of gristle and semi-gnawed mutton bones that had been placed before them. Four guards, drinking steadily from wineskins, watched over them.

'It's like a market-day night in the Subura,' Magnus commented through a mouthful of half-chewed fat.

'Except it doesn't smell so bad,' Corbulo pointed out truthfully.

Vespasian lifted the hem of his soiled tunic. 'We'd fit in very well there wearing these, I imagine.'

'We wouldn't smell out of place at all, in fact we'd smell a lot better than most of the whores,' Faustus put in.

Magnus grinned and carried on chewing; he was determined to get that lump of fat down.

A blind-drunk Thracian tripped over one of their guards' legs and fell towards Vespasian, vomiting.

'Watch yourself, sir.' Magnus pulled his friend from out of the man's path. The Thracian crashed to the ground, convulsing as he brought up the contents of his stomach.

Vespasian recoiled from the stench; then his eyes widened slightly as he noticed the man's dagger had become unsheathed in the fall; it lay on the ground only a foot away from his thigh. The guards dropped their wineskins and rose unsteadily to their feet, casting shadows over where the dagger lay. They shouted at their comatose comrade, who, naturally, didn't respond. Magnus, who had also seen the opportunity, waved at the guards and made good-humoured drinking motions with his hands. The guards laughed. Vespasian edged his leg slowly towards the dagger. A guard stepped over him to heave the man away. He trod on the dagger but failed to notice it; as he stepped forward to lift the drunk he pushed the dagger backwards, closer to Vespasian. Magnus started pointing at himself, gesturing to the other guards to give him a drink; one of them shrugged, picked up a wineskin and lobbed it over to him. Vespasian lifted his thigh and flicked the dagger underneath.

'That is rough,' Magnus grimaced, having taken a slug of wine. He leant over and passed the skin to Corbulo, asking under his breath. 'Did you see that?'

'Yes, I did.' Corbulo took a sip. 'We'll wait a while, until they've all drunk themselves senseless – which won't take long if this is what they're drinking.' He passed the wine to Faustus who took a mouthful and almost choked.

When they had finished eating the guards retied their hands. Vespasian managed to keep his leg firmly pressed down on the dagger beneath it, even though it meant his foot rested in the pile of vomit.

They settled down to wait their chance. For the first time since their capture a sense of optimism prevailed over the group. They feigned sleep, surreptitiously watching their guards steadily drink their way through their wineskins. All around the sound of fighting, arguing and fornicating gradually abated as, one by one, the Thracians drank themselves into a stupor and collapsed next to the dying fires. Eventually the last of the guards rolled on to his back and started to snore, his wineskin resting, almost empty, on his chest.

Vespasian lay on his side and carefully worked his tied

hands down to the dagger. His fingers soon found the hilt and closed around it. Rolling over on to his other side he wormed his way closer to Magnus, holding the dagger firmly in both hands.

'You'll have to help me here; bring the binding to the blade.'

Magnus pulled his arms up until he felt the cool blade just above his wrist, then eased himself forward until it rested on the leather binding.

'There you go, sir, can you feel it?' he whispered.

'Yes. Now stay still and don't shout if I cut you.'

Magnus made a face to himself: as if.

They lay back to back while Vespasian sawed away with the dagger. Corbulo and Faustus kept a wary watch, but no one was moving in the camp. It didn't take long. As soon as his hands were freed Magnus took the dagger and cut the bonds of his comrades. Within moments they were all free.

'What now?' he asked.

Corbulo rubbed his wrists. 'Kill the guards, take their swords and cloaks then get the fuck out of here. Any better suggestions?'

'Sounds good to me.'

One of the guards stirred in his sleep. They froze. He rolled over on to his side, lifted his tunic and pissed where he lay. He fell back to sleep without bothering to adjust his dress.

'Let's get on.' Corbulo reached out his hand to Magnus. 'Give me the dagger.'

'Begging your pardon, sir, but this is my sort of work – if you want it done quietly, that is.'

Corbulo nodded; just by looking at Magnus anyone could tell that he was no stranger to administering swift and silent death.

Magnus crawled quietly to the exposed guard. Within an instant his eyes were bulging, his throat torn open and his mouth firmly clamped shut by Magnus' strong left hand. He struggled momentarily and then fell limp.

Soon the other three had gone the way of their colleague.

Wrapped in their newly acquired cloaks, and with swords at the ready, Corbulo led them stealthily through the camp. Staying low they weaved between the fires, keeping, as much as possible, to the shadows. They despatched any Thracians that they came across who had been too drunk to make it to a fire or a tent, slitting their throats where they lay. Gradually the fires thinned out and they reached the edge of the camp.

'We need horses if we're to make it back to the river before our absence is noticed,' Corbulo whispered. 'We'll skirt around the perimeter. There must be some close by.'

Outside the camp they were able to move far quicker: the moon had set and their cloaks blended in with the inky slopes of the basin. They jogged sure-footed across the even grass, keeping a wary eye out for any pickets posted in the darkness. There were none.

A quarter of the way round Vespasian stopped. 'Sir,' he hissed, 'over there.'

Twenty paces away on the fringe of the camp, silhouetted against the dim glow of the fires, were the horse-lines. The dark shapes of four or five tents could be made out just beyond. Nothing moved around them; the guards, if there were any, were sleeping.

'We don't have time to saddle them up but we do need to find some bridles,' Corbulo whispered. He peered at Vespasian through the darkness. 'Tribune, you come with me, they must be in one of those tents. Faustus and Magnus, get us four horses, we'll meet back here.'

They crept down to the horse-lines.

Leaving Magnus and Faustus untying the nervous creatures, Vespasian followed Corbulo in search of the livery tent. The snorting and stamping of the jumpy horses behind him made him very uneasy.

'How the fuck do we know which tent they're in?' he murmured.

'We'll just have to look in each one,' Corbulo replied, creeping up to the nearest tent. He took the right-hand flap and indicated to Vespasian to take the other. Very gently and with swords poised they parted them.

'Good evening.'

Two spear points pressed against their throats. They froze. Nausea flooded Vespasian's throat.

'I'd drop those swords if I were you.'

They slowly lowered their blades and let them drop. Behind them Vespasian felt the arrival of more men.

'Now step back.'

They eased backwards, the spear points biting into skin, drawing blood. The warriors holding them stepped out of the tent and behind them emerged the bearded, bald horsemen from the day before.

'Do you really think I am that stupid?' he growled, his eyes two slits of hate. 'That I, Coronus, don't know how my people behave, and don't make arrangements accordingly? Of course they were going to get drunk, of course you would try and escape, and of course you would need horses. It amused me to watch you try. So ten sober, trusted men waiting for you here, away from the temptations of the main camp, were all I needed to ensure that you would still be here tomorrow, when I have plans for you. Tie them up.'

Vespasian felt rough hands pull his wrists behind him; leather twine was wrapped tightly round them. He didn't resist; it would have been futile. Magnus and Faustus were hauled in from the horses; blood streaming from a cut on Faustus' left arm told of a less clean arrest.

'Until tomorrow, then,' Coronus crowed, 'when you will learn that the blood-money for my sons is very high indeed.'

They spent the rest of the night tied to the horse-lines. Vespasian did not sleep. Rage burned within him, rage at being toyed with. To be allowed to escape, and then to be recaptured by being second-guessed by a savage was humiliation enough; to be gloated over by him was intolerable. They would have done better staying put, but that would have been a humiliation of another sort. Coronus would have known they had not attempted to escape, and would have sneered at them for cowardice. These thoughts whirled around his head and by morning he was exhausted, but he had resolved in the future, if he had one, never to do the obvious, because if it was obvious to him it would be obvious to all.

Soon after dawn they were cut loose and hauled to their feet. Looking around he could see that the others all looked as tired as he felt; none of them had had any sleep.

They were dragged towards the centre of the camp, where a circle had been cleared of tents and fires; around it stood hundreds of cheering warriors.

Their guards pushed a way through the crowd, who aimed kicks and punches at the prisoners as they passed. The residual smell of stale alcohol, vomit and sweat from a night of debauchery hung over the Thracians, who were all eager for some diversion to help them forget their terrible hangovers.

'Looks like we're to be the entertainment,' Magnus muttered out of the corner of his mouth.

'I'm not sure that I'm in the mood,' Vespasian replied, dodging a blow from a sword hilt aimed at his temple.

They passed out into the centre of the arena where Coronus waited for them. The young warrior who had led the war band stood next to him. Vespasian could see a family resemblance and realised that he must be Coronus' elder son, and therefore brother to the man killed at the river a few days before.

Coronus raised his arms and the noise around the arena stopped immediately. He began to speak; his words were unintelligible but, from the harsh tone of his voice and the aggressive gesturing, Vespasian guessed that they were being condemned for all sorts of crimes. The speech ended with a huge roar from the crowd, and then a guttural shout that didn't need any translation. It meant death.

Coronus turned and addressed them in his fluent Latin. 'You have been condemned to death by the tribal assembly—'

'On what charge?' Corbulo shouted. 'And who defended us?'

'The charge was defiling our gods and there is no defence against that.'

Corbulo was about to argue but realised that it was pointless and held his peace.

Coronus continued. 'As their chief it is my task to choose the manner of your deaths.' He smiled a cheerless smile, and then turned back to the assembly and shouted. Their response indicated approval of his choice. Coronus switched back to Latin. 'A sword and shield each, the last man standing gets a horse and a half-hour head start before we come after him. If he is caught he will be impaled, if not then he is lucky.'

Four swords and shields were placed at even intervals around the edge of the arena. The Romans were herded into the centre, where their bonds were cut.

'Should any of you decide not to fight then you will all be

impaled. My advice is to put on a good show worthy of Rome, and one of you may get to see her again.'

Coronus took his place in the crowd. The four Romans were left standing back to back in the middle of the arena.

'What do we do?' Faustus asked.

'We fight,' Corbulo replied. 'And we fight well, so one of us has a chance of surviving.' He bent down to wipe earth on to the palms of his hands. 'The others get clean deaths. It could be worse.'

'Who fights who?' Vespasian asked; he did not want to have to fight Magnus.

'We do a free-for-all. Get your swords, we'll start back here.'

They turned and looked at each other; there were no words to say. They each knew that they had a responsibility to the group to fight and die well; there was no other way.

Vespasian grimaced at the irony of the situation as he walked to the arena's edge to pick up his sword and shield. He had never been to a gladiatorial show. He had always wanted to, but now that he had the chance it was he who was to fight. It would be his first and last show; he knew he would die. There was no way that he, a sixteen-year-old youth, would be the last man standing, but before he went he would do his best to give one of his comrades a clean death.

The noise of the crowd was growing as more and more money changed hands in bets. He wondered idly what odds were being given for him winning. He thought of Caenis and pulled out the silver amulet that she had given him. He held it tightly in his fist and prayed for Poseidon's protection.

He let go of the amulet and it swung free as he bent to pick up the sword. A Thracian near him tugged at his neighbour's sleeve and pointed. He picked up the shield. The noise around him changed to a low murmur; more people pointed. They're betting on the first man to die, he thought. He tucked the amulet back under his tunic, turned and walked back towards his comrades.

They each stopped five paces from the middle. Corbulo looked at them one by one. 'Do not ask for quarter. Deliver a clean death. It is now in the hands of the gods.'

They saluted each other and then crouched into position. The crowd had gone very quiet.

Vespasian breathed heavily, his palms started to sweat and his heart raced. He looked from Magnus to Corbulo to Faustus, their eyes just visible over shield rims. They started to circle each other, waiting for someone to make the first move.

Behind him he heard a couple of individual shouts from the crowd. Something was happening. We've not started fighting quickly enough, we'll all be impaled, he thought, and then sprang forward, crashing his shield against Corbulo's. He thrust his sword at his throat, Corbulo parried, the blades met with a clash of iron and screeched as they slid down each other to lock together at the hilt. Vespasian felt something slice through the air behind him as he pushed down on Corbulo's sword with his own. Magnus going at Faustus, he thought; but where's the noise, where's the cheering? Corbulo stepped to the left, pulling his sword away, causing Vespasian to overbalance. He fell to his left but had the presence of mind to bring his shield up to block Corbulo's back-handed cut to his neck.

He hit the ground and rolled. Corbulo pounced towards him, shield up, sword arm extended, pointing at his throat.

'Stop!'

The command was easily audible, for by now the only noises were the sound of their exertions and the clash of their weapons. The audience was completely silent.

They froze, Corbulo over Vespasian, Faustus squaring up to Magnus.

Vespasian looked round. Coronus and his elder son had pushed their way out of the crowd and were striding towards them, escorted by a dozen armed warriors.

'Drop your weapons,' Coronus shouted.

Four swords fell to the ground, followed by four shields.

He pushed Corbulo aside and leant over Vespasian. 'Show me what you wear around your neck.'

Vespasian pulled out the silver amulet.

'Where did you get that?'

'My woman gave it to me when I left Rome.'

'Where did she get it?'

'Her mother left it to her; she said it was a symbol of her tribe.'

Coronus hauled Vespasian to his feet and pulled him close. 'It *is* a symbol of a tribe,' he snarled. His eyes bored into Vespasian's. '*My* tribe, the Caenii.'

'My woman is called Caenis,' Vespasian said quickly, convinced that he was going to be killed most painfully for sacrilege. 'She told me of the story of Caeneus, but she said that he came from Thessaly, not Thracia.'

'He was from Thessaly, but it was to this land that his son, my namesake, Coronus, fled after Caeneus was killed fighting the centaurs.'

'I saw your men re-enact Caeneus' death at the river.'

'We do that when any man of our royal house dies,' Coronus said quietly. He relaxed his hold on Vespasian. 'My youngest son was also called Caeneus. My eldest here . . .' he pointed to the young leader of the war band '. . . is also called Coronus, and so it has been since the original Coronus founded our tribe and named it after his father.'

Coronus stepped back, letting go of Vespasian's tunic. 'What was the name of Caenis' mother?'

'I don't know.' Vespasian didn't take his eyes off Coronus; he knew that he was talking for his life. 'I only know that she was a slave in the household of Antonia, the sister-in-law to the Emperor Tiberius. She died when Caenis was three. Antonia brought Caenis up in her household; she is like a mother to her.'

'How old is Caenis?'

'Eighteen, I think.'

Coronus nodded slowly. 'That would mean her mother would be in her thirties, if she still lived. Skaris!'

The older man with the grey forked beard, whom they had seen arguing with the priest at the river, stepped forward.

Coronus turned to talk with him privately. His escort surrounded the Romans, spears held at the ready. Vespasian noticed for the first time that each man wore the same image around his neck, only made of wood or stone. Coronus turned back to Vespasian, apparently satisfied with what Skaris had said.

'Get up, Roman. It would seem that you speak the truth.'

Vespasian got to his feet and looked at his companions, all of whom were standing stock-still, trying to follow the course of events, not daring to believe that they might have a way out of this situation.

Coronus told his men to stand down and then addressed a few sentences to the crowd. As he spoke they murmured their assent and began to disperse. When he had finished he held out his arm to Vespasian, who took it.

'My youngest sister and her infant daughter were taken as slaves over thirty years ago. As a member of our royal house she would have been wearing a silver image of Caeneus; the one that was given to you must be it. Your woman Caenis is my sister's granddaughter, my great-niece. She gave you this amulet with love, to protect you. We will not harm you or your friends. You have the protection of the Caenii and are free to go.'

Vespasian stared at him in disbelief. 'I will not forget this, Coronus, and I will be sure to tell Caenis who her people are; she will come back to thank you one day.'

'If the gods will it, so be it. But before you go you will eat with me.'

He led them through the camp to his tent. All around people stared at the four Romans as they passed, shouting out in their strange language and making gestures of welcome and friendship.

Once they were seated with food and drink before them Coronus proposed a toast.

'May Poseidon hold his hands over his people, the Caenii, and protect them and their friends.' He drank. Vespasian, Magnus and Faustus followed, Corbulo did not. Coronus looked at him and shook his head. 'I believe you will not drink because you wish to come back and fight us, am I right?' he asked.

'You are an enemy of Rome, it would be my duty.' Corbulo put down his cup. His friends exchanged worried looks, afraid that this arrogant young aristocrat would land them back in the arena to fight again.

Coronus smiled. 'Enemy of Rome, you say? That is not so, I only do Rome's bidding and they pay me handsomely for it.'

'They paid you to attack her soldiers,' Corbulo sneered.

'They paid me to attack the Caeletae, and then to attack your column in their territory. Why? I do not know. But I will prove it to you.'

Coronus said a few words to a couple of guards who bowed and went off to do his bidding.

'Just over a month ago,' he continued, 'the priest came with four Romans and an escort of Greek cavalry. They brought me a chest, and told me that I could keep the contents if I did as Rome asked. As you know I did, and it cost me many men, including a son. It was a high price to pay, too high, but it would have been higher if I had refused. The Romans made that perfectly clear.'

'Who was this priest?' Vespasian asked, feeling sure that he wouldn't be surprised by the answer.

'His name is Rhoteces, a slippery little shit, but he has the favour of the gods and the respect of the tribes. He was with my men at the river.'

'So this priest is also Rome's agent?' Corbulo asked, unable to believe that such an outlandish-looking creature could be working for Rome.

'He's a priest, he can go anywhere in Thracia, no one will harm him or his companions. Who better to carry messages and gifts?'

'Who sent him?' Vespasian asked.

'Rome.'

'Yes, but who in Rome?'

'Does it matter? The Romans with him bore the imperial seal; that is authority enough for me.'

'What did these Romans look like?' Vespasian asked.

'Three of them were wearing fine uniforms, very ornate, the fourth was a civilian, a big man with darker skin and long black hair and a small beard; he did the talking.'

Vespasian exchanged a glance with Magnus.

The tent flaps opened and four slaves came in carrying a very heavy-looking chest. They put it down and left.

'See for yourselves, my friends; look at what Rome paid me to take your lives.'

Corbulo walked over to the chest. It was not locked; he opened it and drew his breath. Vespasian joined him and looked in. His eyes widened. It was full of silver denarii, more than he had ever seen. He dipped his hand in and brought out a handful, letting them clatter back down on to the pile. Each coin had Tiberius' head on it; each one was as clean and unmarked as the day that it had left the mint.

CHAPTER XXIV

F OR FIVE DAYS they followed the course of the Hebrus River northwest, stopping only to eat or sleep, pushing their horses as much as they dared. Coronus had given them an escort through his lands, but they had turned back once they'd reached the territory of the Odrysae. Although not in revolt, there was still a bitter resentment of Rome after its violent quelling of that tribe's rebellion four years previously. Vespasian and his three comrades kept well away from settlements, relying instead on the ample supplies that they had been given by the Caenii and water from the murky but drinkable Hebrus.

His companions took it in turns to quiz Vespasian about how he had come to be in possession of an amulet that guaranteed the protection and friendship of the Caenii, despite the fact that they had been in part responsible for the deaths of hundreds of their warriors and the chief's youngest son. But Vespasian was unable to tell them any more than he had told Coronus, forcing each man to come up with his own theory.

'Luck,' Magnus said, 'pure and simple luck.'

'The will of the gods,' Corbulo opined. 'It shows us that they have a destiny for every man and enjoy teasing us until it is fulfilled.'

'Caenis must have the power of foresight,' Faustus theorised. 'She saw where you would come into danger and gave you the amulet because she knew it would save you.'

'And by luck she just happened to have it on her.' Magnus felt that his case rested.

Vespasian smiled to himself. Each of these theories was in part correct, but there was one thing that overrode all of them: love. Whether it was the will of the gods, luck or foresight, without her love for him Caenis would never have given up her only memento of her mother.

Vespasian, however, had his own concerns. He had no doubts that the chest of denarii had come from Sejanus, using the imperial seal. And that Asinius and Antonia were right: Sejanus was financing the rebellion for his own ends. In destroying the relief column he would be able to go to the Senate, in the Emperor's name, and demand a more robust approach in Thracia, more legions to punish the Caenii, and no doubt to slyly retrieve his chest of money. This would in turn create more resentment and incite more tribes to revolt, thus escalating the problem and giving him more time and space to seize the purple while the army was looking the other way.

Corbulo would be duty bound to report the chest of denarii, where it had come from and what it had paid for, to Poppaeus. The conversation would be recorded by a secretary, and then copied by others. It would not be long before news of the discovery spread and reached the ears of Sejanus' agent, who would undoubtedly send a message to his master warning him that the conspiracy risked being uncovered. The agent would then, in all probability, lie low until he received further instructions, which could be two or three months, months in which he, Vespasian, would be unable to get any closer to discovering his identity.

Feeling sure that Corbulo wouldn't have been party to a plan that involved his own death at the hands of the Caenii, he decided to partially confide in him one evening, whilst Magnus and Faustus were away watering the horses.

'Have you given any thought as to who might have paid to see us and our men dead, Corbulo?'

Corbulo looked at him over his long thin nose, his angular face illuminated on one side by the small fire that they had set.

'Nothing troubles me more, not even how you came to have that amulet in the right place at the right time.'

'What conclusions have you come to?'

Corbulo looked around to make sure that they were still alone.

'I cannot believe that it was the Emperor, even though the messengers bore the imperial seal. What would he have to gain by killing two of his own cohorts?'

'My thoughts entirely. But if it was not the Emperor, who else has access to the imperial seal, and to that amount of newly minted money?'

Corbulo looked down and shook his head.

Vespasian decided to change tack. 'What do you propose to do once we get to Poppaeus?'

'I shall report all that we saw, of course.'

'Would that be in our best interests? After all, whoever paid the Caenii to kill us may well have someone close to Poppaeus, and then he would find out that his conspiracy has been uncovered and, more to the point, who uncovered it.'

Corbulo stared at Vespasian in the firelight as if reappraising him.

'You're right,' he said slowly. 'And I had you down as a snotty-nosed little thin-stripe tribune; I can see that there is more to you than I thought, Vespasian. So if we're to avoid the attention of . . .' He paused and looked Vespasian in the eye. 'Sejanus?'

Vespasian nodded.

'Then I should make my report to Poppaeus in private, no records and no witnesses,' Corbulo concluded.

'I think that that is a good idea of yours, Corbulo.'

Corbulo continued staring at Vespasian. He had the odd feeling that it hadn't been his idea at all.

When Magnus returned later, he sat down next to Vespasian. 'Did you have a nice little chat with the arsehole, sir?' he whispered.

'What do you mean? And he's not so much of an arsehole as I thought he was. His actions saved a lot of men back at the crossing.'

'Point taken. I mean what did you persuade the not-so-much-of-an-arsehole to do about that chest of denarii?'

'How did you know that I was going to talk to him about that?'

'Stands to reason, don't it? The more people who know that we know about it, the worse it may go for us. I hope you told him to report in discreetly, if you take my meaning?'

'I did, as a matter of fact; I got him to agree to report in private to Poppaeus.'

'Well done, sir. That was a good idea.'

Vespasian peered at Magnus through the darkness and couldn't help wondering just whose idea it really had been.

On the evening of the fifth day they arrived at the walled town of Philippopolis, the seat of the Thracian King Rhoemetalces and his mother Queen Tryphaena. Here they learnt from the commander of the small Roman garrison, a much-decorated old centurion in his last few months of service, that Poppaeus' victory had been impressive but not decisive, his field camp was another hard day's ride west, and that Gallus had brought the column of recruits through four days earlier.

They decided to spend the night with the garrison, and availed themselves of the pleasures of the small but fully functioning bath house, the first that they had seen since Philippi fourteen days before. The garrison commander provided them with a decent hot meal and some decent women, again their first since Philippi, before they retired for a decent night's sleep.

At dawn on the following morning, feeling much refreshed in body and spirit, they were about to leave with an escort of a turma of Illyrian auxiliary cavalry, commanded by an amiable round-faced young patrician cavalry prefect, Publius Junius Caesennius Paetus, when the garrison commander rushed into the stable yard.

'Tribune Vespasian, sir, there is a messenger here from the palace. Queen Tryphaena requests that you visit her before you leave.'

'Minerva's tits,' Corbulo spat. 'That could delay us all day. Lead the way, centurion.'

'The messenger was very clear, sir. Only the tribune.'

Corbulo glowered at Vespasian.

'What could she want with me?' Vespasian was intrigued.

'You watch yourself, dear chap,' Paetus chuckled. 'She's a feisty creature, and very good-looking. Partial to strong young bucks like yourself, so I'm told. Good luck.'

Vespasian decided to play along with him. 'I'll be as quick as I can.'

'In that case we'll hardly notice your absence.'

Vespasian left smiling to the sound of laughter and ribald jokes at the expense of his prowess, about which, after the previous night, he had no concerns.

The messenger led him through the narrow streets of the ancient town, older than Rome itself, to the royal palace on the top of the largest of the three hills upon which the town was built.

They were admitted without hindrance. Vespasian was

shown immediately through to the private quarters and then into a small east-facing room on the first floor. The low, early-morning sun flooded through its solitary window, illuminating the surprisingly sparse room with golden light. The walls were whitewashed and the floor was of waxed wooden boards. Under the window stood a simple wooden desk of such antiquity that Vespasian thought it would collapse if so much as a scroll was laid upon it. In the centre of the room were two chairs and a table of more recent manufacture.

Vespasian went to the window and gazed out to the east towards the rising sun.

'That is the same view that Alexander looked upon every morning he awoke here,' came a soft voice from behind him.

Vespasian spun round and stepped back from the window. In the doorway stood a tall, slender woman in her mid-thirties, dressed in a plain ivory stola that highlighted, but did not flaunt, the curve of her hips and the fullness of her breasts. Her thick black hair was dressed high upon her head. Three ringlets hung down to her shoulders on either side of her pale face, which was dominated by full lips painted with red ochre. Her clear blue eyes, delicately rimmed with kohl, sparkled in the soft sunlight.

'This was his room when he came to muster my people for the invasion of the great Persian Empire. He chose it because it looks east.'

She walked gracefully across to the ancient desk and brushed her hand lightly over it.

'He sat at this very desk each morning, dealing with his correspondence and looking out towards the lands that he would conquer.'

Vespasian looked down at the simple desk with awe and felt the closeness of history within the room. She shared his quiet reverence for a moment before moving away from the window to the chairs behind them.

'But I haven't brought you here for a history lesson, Vespasian. I am Tryphaena, nominally the queen of this country but in practice the puppet of the Emperor and Senate.'

'Domina, I am honoured to meet you,' Vespasian said, grateful for the small history lesson that she had given him.

'It is as well that through my great-grandfather, Marcus Antonius, I am firstly a Roman citizen, otherwise I might also be hiding up in the mountains with the rebels.'

Tryphaena sat down and motioned that he should do the same.

'My people have been forced into this rebellion. When Alexander came here looking for troops he brought money to pay them and asked only for volunteers. Over five thousand answered his call; most of them never came back. Now, almost three hundred years later, we have a new master: Rome.

'Up until last year Rome was content for our warriors to serve in our army, under our own commanders, keeping the peace within the borders of the kingdom. Then two things changed: firstly, recruiting officers arrived from Moesia demanding that our army be formed into auxiliary cohorts for service in Moesia; and then our priests started to rouse the tribes in rebellion against this new measure, encouraging the chiefs with money, Roman denarii, that they suddenly seemed to have in abundance.'

'Where did it come from?'

'From what my informants tell me it was distributed by Rhoteces, the leader of our priests, but from whom he received it I don't know, I can only guess.'

'Why would he encourage your people into a fight that they were bound to lose?'

'The Thracians are a proud, warlike people. They have only ever served other nations as mercenaries, never as conscripts; they see that as another form of slavery. It wasn't difficult to get them to rebel. Why Rhoteces did it is an easy question: he hates me and my son. He hates the monarchy because we rule Thracia – in Rome's name, granted, but nonetheless we rule. He thinks that if we were to disappear then power would pass to the priests, who, like us have no tribal loyalties, and Rhoteces is the chief priest.'

'But Rome would still be supreme.'

'Of course it would, and this is what that idiot doesn't understand; my son and I are all that stand between an autonomous Thracia and annexation by Rome.'

'So if the rebellion were to succeed, Rome would annex Thracia, and its people would be subject to conscription, and if it fails Rome gets its conscription anyway. Either way the legions will be busy here for some time pacifying the country.'

'Exactly, and Rhoteces has unwittingly been the architect of this disaster through his lust for power and inability to understand politics. Sejanus has played him well.'

'You are sure that he is behind this, domina?'

'Antonia is my kinswoman and friend, we correspond regularly and I am aware of her fear of Sejanus. She has told me what she believes he would gain by destabilising Thracia.

'In her last letter she asked me to look out for you on your way to Poppaeus' camp, and to give you any assistance I could.'

'She is most kind, domina.'

'Indeed she is – to her friends.' Tryphaena smiled. 'I am unable to help you in any material way but I can give you a warning: three days ago four men passed through. They stopped only briefly to change horses; they were bearing an imperial travel warrant. They were Praetorian Guardsmen – well, three of them were. The fourth could not have been as his hair was too long.'

Vespasian nodded. 'And did this fourth man also have a small beard and very brown skin?'

'I believe he did. You know him?'

'We met briefly. It wasn't the friendliest of encounters. His name is Hasdro. Should he return this way I believe Antonia would thank you for killing him. He placed a spy in her house.'

'I will see what can be arranged,' she replied, looking at

him in a different light. She admired a man who could, with good reason, so easily order another's death.

She stood and clapped her hands. A slave girl entered with a small scroll and handed it to her mistress.

'Her letter also contained this.' Tryphaena gave him the scroll. 'I will leave you to read it. When you have finished someone will escort you out. May the gods go with you, Vespasian.'

'And also with you, domina.'

She left the room, leaving Vespasian alone with his letter, the first that he had ever received. His heart pounded as he broke the seal; he looked quickly for the signature: Caenis.

Vespasian left the palace a short while later feeling as though he hadn't a care in the world. Caenis' letter had been all that he had hoped for, and more, as he had composed her replies to his imaginary letters in his head on the long, unpleasant journey in the mule cart at the hands of the Caenii.

On his return his companions mistook the look on his face.

'It would seem that your friend enjoyed the meeting with Queen Tryphaena,' Paetus laughed. 'By the looks of him I'd say that Venus was there too.'

Vespasian shrugged, said nothing and mounted his horse.

As they passed through the town gates Magnus drew level with Vespasian.

'Well?' he asked.

'Hasdro passed through here three days ago, with three Praetorians.'

'So that's why you've got that love-struck look on your face. One squeeze of his balls and you're his for ever.'

'Very funny.'

'I thought so. So the Queen was quite a looker, then?'

'She was, and she also had a letter for me from Caenis.'

'Ah, that would do it.' Magnus grinned at his friend.

Vespasian was in no mood for conversation. He kicked his horse and accelerated away.

The morning was clear and cold; a strong breeze blew down from the snow-capped Haemus Mountains to the north, forcing them to keep their cloaks wrapped tightly around their shoulders. The condensation of their horses' breath billowed from their nostrils as they made their way across the steadily rising ground, sometimes trotting, sometimes cantering to their destination. Ahead was the northern end of the Rhodope range where Poppaeus had the rebels holed up.

'Will there be another battle, Paetus?' Vespasian asked.

The cavalry prefect smiled, his bright eyes shining in the strengthening sun. 'Poppaeus has been trying to draw them out for a month now, but they won't budge. Our spies tell us that they're divided into three factions. There are those that want to throw themselves on our mercy, which may or may not be forthcoming; then there're those who want to charge out of their stronghold, after killing their women and children, and die fighting, taking as many of us with them as possible; and finally there's a completely fanatical faction that wants to kill their women and children and then commit mass suicide.' He laughed; the others joined in. 'But seriously, Poppaeus is trying to avert the last option; it's not good to create too many fanatical martyrs. He's in secret negotiations with a chap called Dinas, who is the leader of the first faction, trying to get him to talk some sense into the others. The trouble is that he can't offer complete clemency, that would send a bad message; some have got to be nailed up on crosses or lose hands or eyes, otherwise anyone with a petty grievance will rebel, thinking that if they lose they'll be free to go back to their villages, with their wife's virtue intact and all their limbs in place, to carry on as before until their next opportunity comes along.'

'Quite so,' Corbulo agreed. 'It's a tricky situation. How is he putting pressure on them? Has he dug siege lines around them?'

'He's done his best. We've constructed over four miles of trenches and ramparts around them, but their stronghold's too high, you could never completely encircle it. So we send out patrols and try and stop any supplies getting in, but they slip through at night. Water is the one thing that they're short of: they've only got one spring up there. But even so they could stay put for months, and the longer they're there the more chance there is of other tribes joining them, then we could find ourselves surrounded.'

'What about storming it?' Vespasian asked.

Paetus burst out laughing; Vespasian reddened.

'My dear chap, forgive me.' Paetus managed to get his mirth under control and reached out to touch Vespasian's arm in a conciliatory gesture. 'That's exactly what the bastards want. They've spent the winter fortifying the walls and digging ditches and traps, nasty things with sharpened stakes in. Nearly fell into one myself last time I was up there scouting. No, it's damned near impregnable, you'd lose four cohorts just to get to the gate, then two more to get through them. And behind it are sheer cliffs. Even if you could get down those, it would be with so few men that you'd be massacred once you'd got to the bottom.

'We've just got to keep them there and hope that either they see sense and come out to surrender or fight; or start fighting amongst themselves and do our job for us.'

'At least we're not too late.' Corbulo sounded relieved; the thought of arriving too late for any action had plagued him all the way from Italia.

'No, no, you're not too late; but what you've arrived in time for is anyone's guess.'

They rode on in silence for a while, eating up the miles, climbing higher and higher into the hills. After a short break at midday to eat some bread and smoked ham and allow their horses to graze on the thinning grass, they came across a series of thirty or forty large scorch marks on the ground.

'This is where we beat them,' Paetus said with pride. 'These are what are left of their pyres; we killed over half of them, losing no more than six hundred of our lads all told. There must have been thirty thousand of the bastards to start off with, all yelling and hollering and showing their arses and waving those vicious long blades of theirs.'

'Rhomphaiai,' Corbulo said unnecessarily.

'Indeed. Nasty things, one took one of my horse's legs off, would have had mine too if the poor beast hadn't fallen on the savage wielding it. Pinned him down, it did. I managed to jump clear and skewered the bastard. I was furious; it was a horse from the gods.' Paetus patted the neck of his present mount, as if to show that he meant no offence.

As they progressed across the field Vespasian spotted signs of a recent battle all around: spent arrows, discarded helmets, broken swords, javelins and shields. Here and there lay an unburnt corpse almost stripped of flesh by wolves or buzzards, strips of rotting clothing clinging to its tattered limbs. Away in the distance on either side there were countless dark mounds like large molehills. Paetus caught his gaze.

'Horses,' he said. 'We're roughly at the centre of our line; there were fierce cavalry battles on both flanks. We didn't capture enough prisoners to burn all the dead horses, so we just left them. Mine's out there somewhere, poor thing; a horse from the gods.' He shook his head mournfully and patted his mount's neck again.

They passed over the battlefield and came to an abandoned camp.

'That was our first camp, when we moved up to the present position we gave it to King Rhoemetalces for his army of loyal Thracians. Though why we didn't just send them home I don't know, they did nothing but pillage and get pissed. Fucking useless, they were.'

'Were?' Corbulo asked.

'The rebels saw them as a greater enemy than us. A few nights after the battle they launched a small attack on one of our support camps. We all ran around trying to beat them off, not realising that it was only a diversion. The main body of their army had circled around us and fell on the loyal Thracians, who of course were all too drunk on that disgusting wine of theirs to do anything about it. It was a massacre. Almost all of them were slaughtered, over ten thousand of them and their families, no prisoners taken. Still, it won't affect the course of the war. Rhoemetalces was having dinner with the general at the time so they didn't get him, which had been their primary objective. He's still lurking around in our camp, too scared to leave and make it back to Philippopolis. Mind you, I don't suppose his mother will be very pleased to see him, having lost an army.'

An hour before dusk they came finally to Poppaeus' camp. It had been built on the last piece of level ground before the Rhodope range rose from its foothills. Vespasian gawped: it was huge; one mile square, surrounded by a six-foot-deep ditch and ramparts, half turf and half wood, ten feet high. Along their length, every hundred paces, were thirty-foot-high wooden towers, housing ballistae capable of firing bolts or rounded rocks over a quarter of a mile. Barracked within it were the Fourth Scythica and the V Macedonica, plus five auxiliary cavalry alae, three auxiliary infantry cohorts, ten smaller units of light archers, slingers and javelin-men and the slaves to serve them all. Two hundred paces in front of it ran the line of the four-mile-long defensive trench and breast-work, constructed to pen the enemy in. It curved away and headed up the mountain, until soft earth gave way to hard granite and sheer cliffs, preventing it from reaching any higher. This too had towers along its length. One hundred paces to either side of the main camp were two smaller constructions, about the same size as Vespasian's column had built the night before the river battle.

'What are they, Paetus?' he asked.

'Don't you know your Caesar, my dear chap? Build smaller camps within artillery range of the main one and the enemy cannot surround you without being threatened from the rear; not that they've got enough men left to surround us, there's no more than twelve or thirteen thousand left up there.' He pointed towards the mountains; they looked up. About a thousand feet above Vespasian could see the Thracians' stronghold surrounded by a sea of tents. It looked comparatively small at a distance but he surmised that up close it must be formidable if it contained all those men and their women and children.

'That would be a tough nut to crack,' Magnus mused. 'I can see why the general is happy to sit here and wait for them to come down.'

'But for how long, eh?' Corbulo said. 'If the tribes behind us rise we could find ourselves surrounded here by enough men to besiege all three camps, hundreds of miles from the nearest legions in Illyria. That would be a nasty situation.'

'Quite so, quite so,' Paetus agreed. 'Very unpleasant indeed.'

They entered the camp by the Porta Praetoria. Paetus greeted the centurion of the watch's salute with a cheery wave.

'Good evening, Aulus. Tribune Titus Flavius Vespasianus and his freedman Magnus, Tribune Corbulo and Centurion Faustus, whom you already know, I believe.'

Aulus' eyes widened. 'Faustus, you old dog, we'd given you up for dead, captured by Thracians we heard. In fact we'd already cashed in your funeral fund and had a whip-round to send home to your people in Ostia. We'd better get our money back.'

Faustus grinned. 'I want a list of who gave what, that'll tell me who my friends really are.'

'I'll do it right now. It won't take a moment, it's not long.'

'Sheep-fucker!'

'Sailor's tart!'

'Nice as it is to stand here exchanging pleasantries with old friends,' Paetus interjected, 'we do need to report to the general. Where is he?'

'In the praetorium, sir. Good to see you back, Faustus.'

As they moved off Vespasian noticed that apart from a perfunctory salute Aulus did nothing to register his pleasure at Corbulo's return.

Inside the camp the bustle of military life was progressing on a greater scale than Vespasian had ever seen before; there were literally thousands of men. In the hundred paces between the gate and the first of the two thousand or so tents centuries were being drilled, the shouts and screams of their centurions and optiones ringing in their ears. Fatigue parties were filling in old latrines and digging new ones. The night patrols of light infantry were being assembled and briefed by their officers. Cavalry turmae, just arrived in from day patrolling, were unsaddling their mounts as slaves waited to take them to the horse-lines for grooming.

Vespasian eagerly took in all he saw whilst trying to appear as nonchalant as possible. They followed the Via Praetoria down through lines and lines of eight-man papil-iones. To their right were billeted the Fourth Scythica and on their left the V Macedonica. Outside each papilio the contubernium's slaves were busy making fires in preparation for the evening meal. Groups of legionaries, already dismissed for the evening, sat polishing armour, cleaning weapons and gear or playing dice. All around their voices could be heard arguing or jesting; the occasional fight that broke out was quickly stopped by the optiones. Vespasian saw at least two miscreants being led off, with hands tied behind their backs, to the jeers of watching soldiers.

They neared the centre of the camp and the tents became larger as they entered the realm of the staff officers and trib-unes. At the junction of the Via Praetoria and the Via

Principalis in the centre of the camp stood the praetorium, a fifteen-foot-high, fifty-foot-square red-leather tent, decorated with black and gold trimmings, where Poppaeus had his headquarters.

Paetus dismissed his turma, then he dismounted and walked up to the two legionaries guarding the entrance. Vespasian and his comrades followed. The guards saluted.

'Cavalry Prefect Paetus, Tribunes Corbulo and Vespasian and Centurion Faustus request an interview with the general,' Paetus reported.

One of the guards went inside to announce them.

'I think that means that you're not invited,' Vespasian whispered to Magnus.

'Suits me, sir, I was never too fond of generals. I'll get the horses stabled.'

Shortly, the guard came back out with a well-dressed slave.

'Good evening, sirs, I am Kratos, the general's secretary. The general will see you presently. Please follow me.'

He ushered them into a short leather-walled corridor, and then turned left through a door into a small, marble-floored ante-chamber illuminated by a dozen oil lamps. A number of chairs were laid out around the walls.

'Please take a seat, sirs.'

Kratos clapped his hands twice, sharply, and from another entrance four more slaves, of a much lowlier rank, appeared, each bearing a bowl of warm water and a towel for the visitors to wash their hands and faces. That done, two more slaves appeared with cups, wine and water. Once they had been served Kratos bowed.

'My master will not keep you waiting long,' he said, and left the room.

Vespasian sipped his wine and stared at the marble floor, resisting the urge to touch it to check its authenticity.

'The whole praetorium is floored with marble,' Corbulo said. 'Poppaeus likes his creature comforts. It breaks down into five-foot squares that are laid on a wooden frame. It takes five ox-carts to move it around, but he won't do without it. It would be beneath his dignitas to conduct business on skins or rugs.'

'It must cost a fortune,' Vespasian replied.

'Oh, I wouldn't worry about that, the general's filthy rich. New money, though,' Paetus said cheerily. 'Silver mines in Hispania. He's got nothing to worry about.'

Kratos reappeared when they were halfway through their wine. 'Follow me, sirs.'

He led them back out into the corridor, which they followed to its end, then they went through another door. They stepped into the main room of the tent, but it was as if they had stepped into a palace lit by a plethora of oil lamps. The poles that supported the roof were marble columns with beautifully finished bases. The walls were adorned with finely woven tapestries and frescoes mounted on boards. Luxurious furniture, from all over the Empire and beyond, was scattered around, forming various different-sized seating areas, but leaving the centre of the room clear. In the far left-hand corner was a low dining table surrounded by three large, plush couches and, in the right-hand corner, a solid, dark wooden desk stood at an angle, covered with scrolls.

Kratos left them standing in the middle of the room as he went and sat discreetly behind a small desk, just to the left of his master's, and began sharpening a stylus.

A door at the far end of the room opened and in walked Gaius Poppaeus Sabinus. Vespasian managed to suppress a gasp as he snapped to attention, helmet cradled under his left arm. Poppaeus was barely five feet tall. Although greying and in his mid-fifties, he looked a child in a general's uniform. It was no wonder that that he worked so hard on the external appearance of his dignitas.

'Good evening, gentlemen, this is a surprise – not you obviously, Paetus, you'll only surprise me when you stop being such verbose clot.'

'Indeed, general.' Paetus showed no sign of rising to the insult. Vespasian wondered if Kratos had noted down that remark.

'Come forward, please,' Poppaeus said, seating himself behind the desk.

They stepped forward and stood in a row in front of the diminutive general. He didn't ask them to sit down; if he always had to look up at people he obviously preferred to do it from a position of power, seated behind a big desk.

'Make your report, prefect, and make it brief.'

'We patrolled between here and Philippopolis yesterday, saw nothing unusual, came back today, saw nothing unusual, apart from four men who were supposed to be dead, sir!' Paetus managed to walk the fine line between mocking insolence and military brevity.

Poppaeus scowled. That he hated this affable young patrician was obvious; that Paetus didn't care was equally obvious. He knew that since he came from an ancient family like the Junii a New Man like Poppaeus would find it hard to touch him.

'Very good, prefect,' Poppaeus said with as much dignity as he could muster. 'Dismissed.'

'Sir! Thank you, sir!' Paetus bawled in his best centurion voice, turned on his heel and marched smartly out.

Poppaeus winced, then he gathered himself and looked slowly from Corbulo to Faustus and finally let his sharp, black eyes rest on Vespasian.

'Well, tribune? Report.'

'Tribunus Angusticlavius Titus Flavius Vespasianus, reporting for duty with the Legio Quarta Scythica, sir.'

'Ah, Marcus Asinius Agrippa's young protégé. He wrote Legate Pomponius Labeo a very insistent letter recommending you. Why do you suppose he was so keen for him to take you on to his staff?'

'I wanted a posting where there would be some fighting, sir, not just frontier duty.'

'A young fire-breather, are you? From the country, judging by your accent. Well, you'll see some action here, but you haven't answered my question. Why did Asinius help you? What are you to him?'

'My uncle Gaius Vespasius Pollo is his client,' Vespasian lied; it would be a convincing enough reason for Asinius to promote his career.

Poppaeus stared hard at him for a moment and then, apparently satisfied with this explanation, nodded. 'Very well, I am pleased to have you here, tribune. After you have been dismissed report to Pomponius Labeo, at the Fourth Scythica *principia*. He will assign you your duties, which will be minimal; you are here to learn, don't you forget that.'

'No, sir.' Vespasian saluted.

Poppaeus then turned his attention to Faustus. 'Well, centurion, I'm happy to see you, and I'm sure that Pomponius and the men and officers of the Fourth Scythica will be pleased to have their primus pilus back, apart from the acting primus pilus, of course.'

'Thank you, sir.' Faustus snapped a salute.

Poppaeus turned to Corbulo. 'Tribune, I'm intrigued to know how you all come to be still alive. Tribune Gallus was convinced that you had been taken prisoner. Begin your report, please.'

Corbulo started the story from the moment he'd left Poppaeus' headquarters in Moesia to travel to Genua, six months previously. He made it as brief as possible, including only the important details. He did however mention Vespasian's late arrival, which caused Poppaeus to raise an eyebrow and look shrewdly at Vespasian. He also commended Vespasian for his actions at the river, and detailed how Caenis' amulet had saved them, although he did not mention that Caenis was Antonia's slave. Neither did he mention the chest of denarii.

After almost half an hour he finished.

Poppaeus sat in silence for a few moments digesting the report, and then, to Vespasian's surprise, dismissed them without asking any questions about the state of the Caenii's revolt. As they turned to go Corbulo spoke.

'General, I request a private interview. Completely private.' He looked towards Kratos.

'I see,' Poppaeus said slowly. 'This is most irregular, tribune.'

'What I have to say is for your ears only.'

'Very well. Thank you, Kratos.'

Kratos put down his stylus and showed Vespasian and Faustus out.

It was dark when they emerged from the tent. Magnus was nowhere to be seen.

'We'd better report to Pomponius now, sir,' Faustus reminded him. 'The Fourth Scythica's headquarters will be this way.'

An hour later, after a long wait and a brief interview with a half-drunk and extremely disinterested Pomponius, Faustus dropped Vespasian off at the Fourth Scythica's tribunes' lines. Magnus was already there, having requisitioned him a tent, busying himself cooking the evening meal.

'I managed to get hold of some fresh pork and some lentils and onions and this.'

He threw him a skin of wine. Vespasian sat by the fire and gratefully poured himself a cup.

'How was the general?' Magnus asked, dropping cubed pork into the hot olive oil in the pot, and stirring it as it sizzled.

'He listened to Corbulo's report and then dismissed us. He wasn't interested in the Caenii's revolt at all.'

'Perhaps he got all he needed to know from Gallus.'

'Yes, perhaps, but if it had been me I would have wanted to know as many details as possible.'

'But it wasn't you, and the general's problem is here, not with the Caenii – they're miles away.'

Before he could argue Corbulo joined them. 'I need to talk to you, Vespasian.'

'Sit down, then, and have a cup of wine.'

'I mean alone.'

'Magnus is fine, he knows all our business.'

Corbulo looked at the ex-boxer and, remembering how Magnus had dealt with the Thracian guards, managed to overcome his aristocratic prejudices. He sat down on a stool and took the cup of wine that Vespasian proffered.

'I told Poppaeus about the Thracian denarii and how they got it,' he said quietly, as if anyone would overhear them in the dull roar of twenty thousand men eating their evening meals. 'I said that it was only me that saw it, the rest of you were all outside the tent, and I said nothing to you about it after.'

'That was probably a good move, sir,' Magnus said, adding the onions to the pot.

Corbulo scowled at him, unused to someone so lowly being a part of his conversations. 'Yes, well, I thought it best. Poppaeus pushed me on this point but I think that he believed me because I had insisted on telling him about it privately, and after all why should I lie?'

'So why did you?' Vespasian asked.

'I had just started to tell Poppaeus about the chest when a slave walked into the room from the sleeping quarters at the back. Poppaeus shouted at him to get out, and he ran out through the main door. As he left the room I glimpsed Kratos and another man through the door. They were eavesdropping. I recognised the other man from Rome. And then I remembered Coronus' description of the fourth Roman who came with the chest: powerfully built, dark-skinned, with long black hair and a small beard. It had to be the same man – he's Sejanus' freedman, Hasdro.'

Vespasian shot Magnus a warning look; he nodded and began to add water to his pot. 'Go on,' he said to Corbulo.

'Well, if Sejanus' freedman did deliver the money to the Caenii, to pay them to kill Poppaeus' reinforcements, why is he now here? And why did Kratos let him listen to my private conversation?'

'So you think that Kratos is in league with Hasdro?' Vespasian was intrigued.

'It's a possibility; Hasdro certainly seems to have access to enough money to buy the loyalty of a slave. If it's true, then Poppaeus and I are in danger of being murdered for what we know. So I decided that the best thing to do to protect myself and you, knowing that Kratos and Hasdro were listening, was to say nothing about its link to Sejanus, and that I didn't know who had delivered it to the Caenii, and that no one else saw it.' Corbulo drained his cup.

'That was good of you, Corbulo.' Vespasian passed him the wineskin.

'What did Poppaeus say about the chest?' Magnus asked, adding the lentils and some lovage to the bubbling pot.

Corbulo sipped his wine and thought for a moment. 'He made me swear to tell no one. He's anxious that it should be kept secret whilst he pursues his own investigation, which won't get far if Kratos has anything to do with it.' He took a slug of wine and shook his head. 'The Greek bastard,' he exclaimed vehemently. 'He is involved with Hasdro and Sejanus, I'm sure of it, and will try to cover up the attempt to have us all killed.'

CHAPTER XXV

POMPONIUS' MORNING BRIEFING of the officers of the Fourth Scythica was, true to its name, brief. Vespasian was detailed to accompany Paetus on a patrol beyond the trench and breastwork fortifications.

'I'm surprised that he even remembered you were here,' Paetus chuckled as they rode through the Porta Principalis at the head of two turmae of his Illyrian auxiliaries. 'You must have made quite an impression on the drunken old fool last night.'

'He barely looked at me,' Vespasian replied. He didn't mind; he was just pleased to be getting away from the smells and noise of the camp.

They rode the few hundred paces from the camp up to the main gate in the four-mile-long construction. Paetus gave another cheery wave to the centurion of the watch and showed his pass. The gates swung open and they rode through.

'I don't know what Pomponius thinks we can achieve here,' Paetus said, slowing his horse to a trot as the ground became rougher. 'It's not cavalry country: too steep and too many rocks. Still, it will keep the men out of trouble and exercise the horses. We'll ride up closer to the Thracians' stronghold; it's really quite impressive, worth a look.'

They continued climbing for a little over an hour, the stronghold looming larger and larger until its details could be clearly seen. The dark-brown walls, which Vespasian had assumed from a distance were wooden, were in fact stone, hewn from the mountain upon which it stood. Vespasian was impressed.

'Lysimachus, one of Alexander's generals, seized Thracia and became its king in the chaos that followed his death. He built the fort three centuries ago, to guard his northern borders from the incursions of the even more savage northern Thracian tribes, on the other side of the Haemus Mountains. They used to come over the Succi Pass, which is about ten miles to the north, to plunder the Hebrus valley. The fort stopped all that; they couldn't take it and couldn't advance without fear of being cut off by it.'

'Why didn't Lysimachus just take the Succi Pass and hold that?' Vespasian asked.

'It's too high, very difficult to keep a fortification supplied up there.'

As they were talking, movement up at the fort, now just over a mile away, caught their eyes. The gates swung open and people began to emerge.

'Now, that is strange,' Paetus commented. 'If they were mounting an attack they would have sent their cavalry out first, and we'd be running for our lives back down to our fortifications. But I can only see infantry.'

Vespasian stared hard at the ever-growing crowd swarming through the gates. 'There are women and children amongst them as well, I think.'

'You're right. It looks like they're surrendering. I'd better get a message down to the general.' Paetus turned and gave a swift order in Greek; four of his troopers peeled off and headed back down the mountain.

The last stragglers appeared through the gates, which then closed behind them. At least three thousand people were heading towards them. At their head were two men riding mules. The taller of the two, an old man with short cropped white hair and a long white beard, held an olive branch in token of surrender. Next to him rode a figure that Vespasian recognised immediately.

'What in Jupiter's name is he doing here?'

'Nothing in Jupiter's name. That's Rhoteces, one of their priests. You know him?'

'I've watched one of his ceremonies. He enjoys sacrificing Romans.'

'I'm sure he does. Nasty little bugger. He turned up about seven days ago and since then Poppaeus has been sending him back and forth to the Thracians negotiating their surrender. Looks like he's been partially successful.'

The old man stopped ten paces away from the two Romans and raised his olive branch above his head.

'I am Dinas, the chief of the Deii,' he cried, so that as

many of his followers as possible could hear him. 'I have come with as many of my people who would follow to throw ourselves at the mercy of Rome.'

'You are welcome, Dinas,' Paetus replied equally loudly. 'We shall escort you down to the camp.'

It took a couple of hours for the slow column of warriors, women, children, old and young, fit and infirm, to reach the gate in the fortifications. During that time Poppaeus, alerted to their imminent arrival, had formed up five cohorts each of the Fourth Scythica and V Macedonica on the ground between the fortifications and the main camp.

It was an impressive sight, designed to cow the suppliants as much as deter any of their number who had thought to make a break for freedom once they had passed through the gates.

The gates opened and Paetus, with Vespasian at his side, led his cavalry through and halted in front of Poppaeus. The little general sat on a pure white horse in front of the parade. He was dressed in all the finery that befitted his rank – a polished silver muscled cuirass, a long, deep-red woollen cloak spread carefully over his horse's rump, bronze greaves and a bronze helmet with silver inlays on the cheek-guards topped with a tall plume of red-dyed ostrich feathers. Behind him, dressed in equally ornate armour, sat an effete young man of twenty on another white horse. Around his head he wore a circlet of gold.

Paetus saluted. 'General, Dinas, the chief of the Deii, has offered his surrender to Rome.'

'Thank you, prefect. Take your men and form them up on our right wing, out of the way.'

Paetus showed no sign of offence at the curt response, and wheeled off to his position.

The Thracians filed slowly through the gates spreading out left and right. Some, intimidated by the show of Roman force in front of them, fell to their knees and begged for mercy; the more stout-hearted stood in grim silence to await their fate. When all were through and the gates shut Dinas, accompanied by Rhoteces, approached Poppaeus on foot and offered him the olive branch. Poppaeus refused it.

'People of the Deii,' he called in a loud, shrill voice that carried over the field. Rhoteces translated his words into the language of the Thracians, in a voice just as shrill. 'Your chief offers me your surrender. I cannot accept it unconditionally. You have rebelled against your King, Rhoemetalces, a client of Rome.' He gestured to the young man behind him. 'This act has caused the deaths of many Roman and loyal Thracian soldiers. It cannot go unpunished.'

A low moan came from the massed Thracians.

'At my order my soldiers could attack and take all your lives. But Rome is merciful. Rome does not even demand the life of any one of you. Rome demands only that you give up two hundred of your number. Half will lose their hands and half will lose their eyes. Once this is done, I will accept the olive branch. You have a half-hour to decide before I give the order to attack.'

A wail of deep anguish rose up from the crowd. Poppaeus

turned his back towards them to show that he could not be moved.

Dinas bowed his head and returned to his people. He started to address them in their own language. Meanwhile some legionaries under Aulus' command brought forward five burning braziers and five wooden blocks, and set them up on the ground in front of the Thracians.

Vespasian watched from his position on the right flank as the late-afternoon light faded. Thirty or so old men and half as many old women had stepped forward voluntarily. Dinas was now walking through the crowd blindfolded, touching people at random with his olive branch. Most of those he touched walked to join the waiting volunteers, but some had to be dragged screaming to their fate. Only children were reprieved. Eventually two groups of victims stood in front of the braziers and blocks.

Dinas came forward to join them. He called to Poppaeus.

'We have done as you have asked, general. I shall lead my people and be the first. Take my eyes.'

'As you wish.' Poppaeus looked to Aulus. 'Centurion, you may begin.'

Aulus gave the command and two legionaries held Dinas' arms firmly behind his back whilst a third pulled a red-hot poker from the fire and approached the old chief. It was over in an instant. Dinas' back arched but he made no sound. He was led away, walking with his head held high, the two blackened empty sockets in his face still smouldering. His people were silent.

Five men were then brought forward and forced to kneel in front of the blocks. Legionaries secured ropes around their wrists and pulled their arms forward so that they lay flat on the smooth surfaces, their hands gripping the edges of the blocks. Other legionaries held their shoulders, pulling them back. All five rebels turned their heads away as five more soldiers brought their swords slicing down through their wrists. Howls of pain erupted from the men as they fell back, blood spurting from their fresh stumps, leaving their hands still gripping the blocks. The women in the crowd started to scream and wail.

Pitch-soaked flaming torches were quickly thrust into the wounds to cauterise them, and then the men were dragged away.

The screaming and wailing escalated as five old men and women were brought forward to the braziers. Vespasian watched in steely silence as the red-hot pokers flashed. Five more victims were being dragged forward to the blocks when, from behind him, Vespasian heard Magnus' voice shouting over the noise.

'Sir, sir, you need to come at once.' Magnus pulled his horse to a sliding halt next to him.

'What's going on?' Vespasian asked, pleased to have his attention diverted from the grisly spectacle.

Magnus drew closer and lowered his voice.

'Asinius has just arrived in the camp; he wants to see you immediately.'

Vespasian looked at his friend astounded. 'Asinius, here? How?'

'The normal way, he rode. Now, are you coming or not?'

'Yes, of course I am.'

Vespasian turned to Paetus. 'Prefect, I have some urgent business to attend to, if I may.'

'Of course, dear fellow, I only wish that I could join you. The mutilations are always my least favourite part of the circus back in Rome. I normally take the opportunity to stretch my legs until something more to my taste comes on, like the wild beast hunt. I love that. Off you go.' Paetus waved him off.

The sun had sunk behind the Rhodope range, leaving the camp in deep shadow while simultaneously causing the gathering low clouds to burn amber and golden with its dwindling light.

Magnus led Vespasian to a large tent close to the praetorium that was always kept free to accommodate visiting dignitaries. It was guarded by two of the eleven lictors that provided Asinius' official escort as a proconsul on his way to his province. Vespasian and Magnus were admitted immediately.

Asinius was sitting on a couch with his feet immersed in a bowl of warm water and a cup of wine in his hand. A couple of travel-stained slaves hovered in the background with linen towels and jugs of steaming water.

'Vespasian, we shall talk in private.' Asinius dismissed the slaves. Magnus, taking the hint, left with them. Asinius motioned Vespasian to sit on a folding stool opposite him. 'You are no doubt surprised to see me here.'

'A pleasant surprise, sir, I have much to tell you.'

'All in good time. I will first tell you what brings me to this arsehole of the Empire.' Asinius drained his cup and refilled it from a jug on a low table next to him. 'Poppaeus' much-exaggerated report of victory over the rebel tribes prompted the Senate to vote him triumphal honours. A little prematurely, it would seem, seeing as I hear that he is only now receiving the surrender of a small portion of the rebels who are still defying Rome up in their stronghold. Nonetheless, it has been done. The Emperor was only too pleased to confirm the honours, on condition that Poppaeus returns to Rome immediately for the investiture. I believe that Tiberius is anxious, as always, to part a successful general from his victorious army and get him back to Rome where he can keep an eye on him. Pomponius Labeo will take command in his stead.

'I was due to leave Rome for my province Bithynia – I had hoped for Syria but an ally of Sejanus unsurprisingly received that particular goldmine. The Senate requested that I make a small detour and bring the good general the happy news of his award in person. They felt that an ex-Consul bringing the news would flatter his ego as well as taking the sting out of his recall.' Asinius took another slug from his cup and then, remembering that his guest was without one, gestured to Vespasian to help himself.

'In normal circumstances,' he continued, 'I would have wriggled out of such an onerous task, but your brother Sabinus brought something very interesting to my attention.

Two months ago men bearing an imperial warrant took three chests from the mint. Between them they contained fifty thousand denarii. The warrant stated that the money was to be used to pay the legions here in Thracia. Not very unusual in itself. However, Sabinus noticed from the records that it was the second such payment in as many months. He was suspicious, so he cross-checked the amount of denarii minted that month with the amount of silver bullion in the treasury. Your brother has an eye for book-keeping, it would seem; whoever taught him should be proud.'

Vespasian smiled, thinking of the long hours that he'd spent forcing his unwilling brother to master the basics of accountancy; his efforts had evidently not been in vain.

'Something amuses you?'

'No, Asinius; please carry on.'

'When Sabinus checked the bullion he found that there were exactly fifty thousand denarii too much, but the treasury's accounts balanced and there were no records to prove that the chests had been taken. In other words it was as if that money had never existed; perfect for secretly financing a rebellion. I thought therefore that bringing the Senate's message to Poppaeus would provide me with the opportunity to trace those non-existent chests.'

Asinius paused and refilled his cup.

'Someone must have replaced the silver,' Vespasian surmised.

'Indeed, but who has access to that amount? Sejanus is not yet wealthy enough to give that much away.'

Vespasian thought for a moment. 'Of course, Poppaeus!' he almost shouted. 'Paetus mentioned that Poppaeus' family have made fortunes from silver mines in Hispania. He must have used his own silver to finance that chest.'

'Poppaeus is Sejanus' agent?' Asinius exclaimed, unable to believe what he was hearing.

Vespasian then related everything that had happened since he and Magnus had arrived in Thracia, and all that Queen Tryphaena and Corbulo had told him.

'How can I have been so stupid?' Asinius mumbled as Vespasian finished. 'It all makes sense now. Sejanus and Poppaeus have managed to create a crisis that cannot be traced back to them. Poppaeus will claim that he sent the recruiting officers to Thracia because he needed more troops to defend the Moesia's northern border, and was therefore acting in the best interests of the Empire. There is no written or material evidence that links either of them to the money used to bribe the chiefs into rebelling. There is no money missing from the treasury. Poppaeus has acted quickly to contain the rebellion, while meanwhile Sejanus' agents bribe other tribes into revolt, threatening our land route to the eastern provinces. Poppaeus comes out of it as a hero and Sejanus has what he needs, another distraction from his manoeuvring in Rome, and for what price? Free silver dug out of the mountains of Hispania. Brilliant.'

'But why did they go to the trouble of converting that silver into coinage? Why not just use raw silver?'

'I don't know. Perhaps they judged that coinage would be

harder to trace than bars of silver. There are, after all, very few families with access to silver mines.'

From outside came the sound of troops marching back into the camp and being dismissed.

'There is one person who could link both of them to the money.'

'I know, Rhoteces the priest, but how could we find him? And even if we could we'd have to get him to Rome to testify before the Senate, and then it would be the word of a barbarian against those of the Praetorian prefect and a governor.'

'He's here.'

'Rhoteces here? Why?'

'He's been acting as Poppaeus' intermediary with the rebels.'

Asinius laughed. 'That priest's duplicity knows no bounds – first he gets them to rebel, then he persuades them to surrender. What can he be hoping to gain?'

'It makes no sense to me either.'

'I think we should talk to the slippery little shit. Perhaps he can tell us the whereabouts of the other chests. I'm sure you and Magnus could manage to bring him here without too much trouble. Meanwhile I'm going to let Poppaeus know that I've arrived and wait to see what he does. How he chooses to see me, whether in private or officially, will say a lot about how secure he feels.'

*

Vespasian found Magnus waiting outside, amidst the hubbub of the cohorts returning to their billets. The legionaries' brightly polished iron armour and helmets reflected the flickering flames of the torches that had been lit along the Via Principalis and the Via Praetoria. The men's mood was upbeat, having just witnessed the surrender of a quarter of their enemies. The ensuing battle, should it come, would be so much the easier.

'And so Asinius wants us to bring Rhoteces to him for questioning,' Vespasian informed his friend, having brought him up to date.

Magnus grinned. 'That will be a pleasure, and I look forward to slitting his throat after.'

'Who said anything about killing him just yet? He might prove to be useful.'

'Stands to reason, though, don't it? If Asinius leaves him alive, he'll go blabbing to Poppaeus that he knows about the chests, and then Poppaeus will have to kill Asinius to protect himself.'

'You're right. Still, it's no bad thing, I suppose. But first we've got to find him.'

'That's easy, I saw him come back with Poppaeus; they're in the praetorium. But he ain't going to be easy to grab, he seems to have got himself a bodyguard of four of the Thracians who surrendered today. We'll need a bit of help.'

'Whom can we trust?'

'Corbulo's a possibility, but he may feel that he has more to gain by staying loyal to Poppaeus than throwing his lot in with Asinius. Gallus we don't know well enough, so that leaves Faustus. I'm sure that if you told him that his general was happy to see him killed then he'll come along, and bring some trustworthy lads with him.'

'Let's hope you're right. You stay here and keep an eye out for that priest.'

A short while later Vespasian rejoined Magnus, with Faustus and two hard-looking legionaries from the first cohort.

'He hasn't come out yet, sir,' Magnus whispered. 'Evening, Faustus, come for a bit of revenge?'

'Cocksucker! Necrophiliac! Goat-tosser!' Faustus had kept up an almost constant stream of abuse under his breath since Vespasian had informed him of Poppaeus' treachery. He had been only too pleased to help deal with the priest.

A few moments later Rhoteces stepped out of the praetorium surrounded by his new bodyguard. They walked at speed along the Via Principalis towards Vespasian and his comrades, who crouched in the shadows as the priest and his retinue passed.

'We'll stay parallel with them,' Vespasian whispered, heading to the narrow path between the first and second line of tents.

After a hundred or so paces the Thracians turned left off the road; Vespasian halted and nipped into a gap between two tents; the others followed. They watched from the shadows as Rhoteces turned on to the path in front of them and stopped outside an opulent-looking tent guarded by two Thracians. A brief conversation ensued with the guards who then escorted Rhoteces and his men inside.

'That's King Rhoemetalces' tent,' Faustus whispered in Vespasian's ear.

Vespasian led his men quickly to the entrance and paused to listen. From within came Rhoteces' unmistakable high-pitched voice. Whatever he was saying sounded threatening. Another voice, Rhoemetalces' he assumed, replied in more measured terms. Suddenly the harsh grate of drawing swords rang out, followed almost immediately by muffled cries and the thuds of two bodies hitting the ground.

'With me,' Vespasian shouted, drawing his sword and leaping through the flaps.

Rhoteces had the King by his hair and a dagger pressed under his chin. He yelped, his bodyguards spun round and Vespasian forced his sword between the ribs of the nearest, grinding his wrist as it cracked through bone, sinew and muscle to pierce his lung. The man exhaled a loud groan that was curtailed by a stream of blood flooding from his mouth, and then crumpled to the floor drowning in his own blood. The three others had no time to defend themselves. They were soon lying sprawled on the floor next to their comrade and the murdered royal guards.

'If you come any closer I'll slit his throat,' Rhoteces warned. 'Move aside.'

Vespasian put his hand up, stopping his comrades in their tracks. He looked at the weasel-faced priest, who snarled, baring filed, yellow front teeth, as he pushed the terrified Rhoemetalces forward.

'If you kill him you'll die,' Vespasian said. 'But if you let him go you may live.'

'You can't touch me, I'm a priest,' Rhoteces shrieked.

Vespasian looked around at Magnus and Faustus and his lads and they simultaneously bellowed with laughter.

'You think we give a fuck about your filthy gods?' Faustus spat, enjoying the look of uncertainty that passed over Rhoteces' face. 'I'd happily slit your throat in front of all their altars and sleep easy in my bed afterwards, you hideous pile of vomit.'

Rhoteces pulled the King's head back and pressed the blade harder against his throat, cutting the skin. The young man looked at Vespasian with pleading eyes.

'Go ahead,' Vespasian said calmly. 'He's nothing to us, but he means the possibility of life to you.'

The priest's bloodshot black eyes flicked nervously around the room; five swords waited to take his life. He howled and pushed Rhoemetalces away, and fell cringing to the floor. Faustus kicked the knife from his hand and then crunched another kick into Rhoteces' solar plexus, stopping the man's whimpering as he struggled for breath.

'That's for the boys you murdered at the river, you cunt, and there'll be plenty more of that when we've finished with you.'

'Would you really have let him kill me?' Rhoemetalces asked breathlessly.

'I wouldn't have had any choice in the matter,' Vespasian replied truthfully. 'He had a knife to your throat; if he didn't kill you here then he would have done as soon as he got outside, seeing as that's what he came here to do, I assume.'

'Yes. He accused me of usurping the priests' power and defying the gods.'

'Fucking Thracians,' Magnus grunted. 'That seems to be their favourite charge. The death sentence and no defence against it, I suppose.'

'In our law there can be no defence against that charge.'

'Don't we know it?'

'Check him for any concealed weapons, then let's get this sack of shit to Asinius,' Vespasian said, aiming another kick at the still gasping priest, cracking a couple of ribs. 'You'd better come with us,' he added, nodding at Rhoemetalces.

Asinius had washed away the dust of travel, and was having his purple-bordered toga arranged by his body slave by the time Vespasian and his companions arrived in his tent. They threw the now terrified Rhoteces at his feet. The priest lay there moaning, holding his fractured ribcage.

'Well done, gentlemen,' Asinius said, dismissing the slave, who withdrew into the private sleeping area to the rear of the tent. 'I trust that none of you were hurt?'

'No, but we got him just in time,' Vespasian replied. 'He was about to assassinate his King.'

'Rhoemetalces, thank the gods that you're safe. I wouldn't have recognised you.' Asinius offered his arm to the young

Thracian. 'I have not seen you since you were a boy, in the Lady Antonia's house. How is your mother?'

'She is well, senator, thank you.'

'I am pleased to hear it. I intend to pay my respects to her on my return journey; I was in too much of a hurry to do so on my way here.'

A loud moan from the floor drew his attention back to the priest.

'Centurion, have your men stretch this creature out on his back.'

'Yes, sir!' Faustus snapped a salute and issued the orders.

Asinius drew his dagger and forced it into Rhoteces' mouth. The priest struggled fiercely, but was no match for Faustus' two lads who had him securely by his ankles and wrists.

'You have two choices, priest, either use your tongue to answer my questions or lose it.'

Rhoteces' eyes filled with terror; he had never been on the receiving end of administered pain. He nodded his head gingerly in acquiescence.

Asinius withdrew the dagger. 'Who supplied the money that you used to encourage the tribes into rebellion against your King and Rome?'

The priest answered immediately, speaking slowly. His fractured ribs were clearly making breathing difficult. 'A Roman of high standing, I don't know his name. It was done last year through intermediaries.'

'Not good enough.' Asinius forced the dagger back into

the priest's mouth and slit the corner of it a thumb's width. Blood flowed freely from the wound down Rhoteces cheek. 'Try again.'

'The intermediaries said they were acting for the Consul, Marcus Asinius Agrippa.'

Asinius hesitated, unable to believe what he'd heard.

'That's—' Vespasian started, but Asinius cut him off.

'Who were these intermediaries?' Asinius continued, regaining his composure.

'Three were Praetorian Guardsmen, but their leader was a civilian, a big man with dark skin and long hair.' Tears were now flowing down Rhoteces' cheeks, intermingling with the blood.

'Did they tell you why Asinius wanted a rebellion here?'

'They said something about destabilising the Emperor. There were going to be rebellions all over the Empire, and while the legions were busy dealing with them the Republic would be restored.' Rhoteces' words were slurred; the wound to his mouth made control of his lips erratic.

'And they assured you that your rebellion would be successful?'

'Yes, they said that there would be an uprising in Moesia, and that the two legions there would be pinned down and unable to come to Rhoemetalces' aid. We would have a free hand.'

'And you believed them?'

'Yes. Recruiting officers had come from Moesia

demanding that our men serve in the Roman army there. It sounded as if the legions were already under pressure. I saw it as an opportunity to rid ourselves of the oppressive monarchy and return to the old ways, of independent tribes united under our gods.'

'And you as their chief priest would be the King, in all but name?'

'I wanted what was best for Thracia and its gods,' Rhoteces almost shouted, despite his pain.

'So when the legions arrived, and the rebellion started to falter, you came and offered your services to Poppaeus – why?'

'After the Caenii failed to stop Poppaeus' reinforcements from getting through I realised that we could not win, so I came here to try to negotiate a surrender, before things went too far.'

'Very noble. Why did Poppaeus trust you?'

'I told him about Asinius' money. I agreed to come to Rome with him to testify in the Senate against Asinius, in return for my life.'

Asinius shook his head. 'Perfect,' he whispered, smiling, before returning his attention to the priest. 'So Poppaeus is only too pleased to have you, his new friend, negotiate with the rebels for him?'

'He makes things difficult, too many demands and conditions; I don't think he wants a surrender, he wants a victory.'

'And you still want your King dead?'

'If anything good can come out of this it would be Rhoemetalces' death,' Rhoteces hissed, glaring at the King, his bloodied weasel face contorted with the hatred of a fanatic.

Asinius stepped back and looked at Magnus and the two legionaries.

'Knock him cold, then tie him up in my sleeping quarters and stay with him.'

They did as they were asked with relish.

'It would seem that Sejanus and Poppaeus have been too subtle even for me,' Asinius said to Vespasian. 'To have set me up as the instigator of all this is a masterstroke that I did not foresee. It's obvious now why they used coinage; it's much easier to link to me than silver bullion.'

Vespasian stared at him, unable to decide what to think.

'Oh, come now, you don't believe him, do you?' Asinius demanded.

'No, I suppose not,' Vespasian replied, remembering that Coronus had said that Rhoteces had been accompanied by Hasdro and some Praetorians on his visit to the Caenii.

'Good,' Asinius huffed, 'because I don't have the time to defend myself against spurious charges to lowly tribunes.'

'What about to kings, Asinius?' Rhoemetalces asked.

'Or kings. I shall defend myself in the Senate, but if you want some proof, ask yourself why I didn't have Magnus kill that little shit, eh? He's going to testify against me if he gets a chance, and what's more, as far as he's concerned his testimony will be the truth, so if he's tortured, as I expect he will be, it will be the same story. So what do I gain by keeping him alive?'

Rhoemetalces looked at Asinius and shrugged.

Asinius gave a look of despair and slumped down on the couch. 'In order to back up the priest's story Sejanus will have forged documents, proving that I authorised money to be taken from the treasury. If the priest is dead those documents could still be enough to convict me. If I take him before the Senate they will see that I am not afraid of his accusations. I will be in control of the situation, and will be able to get him to identify the intermediaries as Praetorians and Sejanus' freedman Hasdro, people over whom I have no control, as every senator well knows. Sejanus' star witness will be turned against him. So I need to take him to Rome, alive.'

Rhoemetalces looked chastened. 'I will accompany you and speak on your behalf.'

'That won't be necessary; a letter will suffice. You should return to Philippopolis and start to heal—' Asinius stopped abruptly. There was a commotion outside the tent, and then the flaps flew open. In walked Poppaeus, brushing off the lictors' attempts to stop him.

'Good evening, Asinius,' Poppaeus crooned. 'This is a surprise. To what do I owe the pleasure of your company here?'

'Poppaeus,' Asinius replied, rising to his feet and signalling to the lictors to return outside. 'I am here at the request of the Senate and the Emperor.'

'Messages for the King and this young tribune, no doubt?'

'King Rhoemetalces and Tribune Vespasian are, as you know, personal friends of mine.' Asinius paused; faint shouts and cries were coming from the direction of the fortifications. 'They are here to pay their respects.'

Vespasian saluted the general, who ignored him and the distant shouting.

'And Centurion Faustus is also an old acquaintance?' Poppaeus asked, eyeing Faustus suspiciously.

'Don't be absurd, general.' Asinius was indignant. 'The centurion is providing a guard for the King, whose bodyguards seem to have gone missing.'

The explanation seemed to satisfy Poppaeus. 'What news have you brought me from Rome that's so important that an ex-Consul, no less, is the bearer?'

'I had hoped for a formal interview, general.'

'I will have my secretary make an appointment for the morning; in the meantime I would appreciate a verbal summery.'

Asinius looked in the direction of the noise that was now unmistakably the sound of battle.

'I shouldn't worry about that, Asinius,' Poppaeus assured him. 'It's just another raid by the few rebels that are left up in the hills, nothing serious.'

'Very well. In recognition of your glorious recent defeat of the Thracian rebels, the Senate has voted you triumphal honours, which the Emperor has been pleased to confirm.' Asinius paused as a Poppaeus gave him a self-satisfied smile.

'The Emperor has requested that you return to Rome immediately to receive the honours.'

'Return to Rome immediately?' Poppaeus exploded. 'Why?'

'Your report stated that the rebellion was crushed. A little premature, I would say,' Asinius said, indicating the ever-growing noise from beyond the camp. 'The Emperor felt that there was evidently nothing left for you to do here, so he has ordered you return to Rome. Pomponius Labeo is to take over your command, with immediate effect.'

'Pomponius Labeo replaces me! You have done this,' Poppaeus spat, pointing an accusatory finger at Asinius.

'Me? I am only the messenger, delivering the good news on my way to my province.' It was Asinius' turn to look smug. 'I have no power over the Emperor's or the Senate's wishes. I rather think that it was your exaggerated report that has caused your good fortune.'

Poppaeus clenched his fists and looked for a moment as if he would strike Asinius.

Corbulo's sudden arrival broke the tension.

'Sir!' he said breathlessly. 'Thank the gods that I've found you. Our defensive wall is under attack in four or five places, and has been breached in at least one. It seems that the Thracians have thrown all their remaining troops at us in a final bid to break out.'

Poppaeus looked aghast. 'Have the men fall in. Senior officers to the praetorium immediately.'

Corbulo snapped a salute and ran out.

'Tribune, centurion, return to your legion,' Poppaeus barked, turning towards the exit.

'It's too late to really earn those honours, general,' Asinius purred. 'You have been relieved of command.'

Poppaeus stopped in the doorway and gave him a black look. 'Bollocks to your orders! We'll resume this conversation later.'

He swept out as the bucinae sounded the call to arms throughout the camp.

Asinius shrugged. 'Disobeying a direct order from the Emperor and the Senate – I do hope he knows what he's doing. It will be an interesting meeting later.'

He quickly dismissed Faustus and his two men, and then summoned the rest of his lictors. They were not long in arriving.

'However, this attack is an extraordinary piece of luck,' Asinius said, beaming at Vespasian. 'Get Magnus in here.'

Magnus appeared from the sleeping area, having been relieved of his guard duty by two burly lictors.

'Are we off now, sir? It sounds like we've got a bit of a fight on our hands.'

'You're staying with me, Magnus,' Asinius ordered. 'I have an errand that will suit your skills admirably.'

Vespasian cut off Magnus' protest. 'I'll be fine, my friend; I don't need you to always nursemaid me around the battlefield. Do as he asks.'

'If you say so,' Magnus replied gruffly.

'I do.'

'What do you want done, sir?' Magnus asked grudgingly.

'I want any letters that link Poppaeus to Sejanus. With the camp almost empty, apart from the slaves, now is the perfect time to break into the praetorium.'

435

'What do you want done, sir,' Magnus asked indignantly
want any letters that link Corbulo to Sejanus. With the
camp almost emptied and from the slaves, now is the period
time to break into the praetorium.

CHAPTER XXVI

VESPASIAN AND MAGNUS stepped out into the night. It
had started to rain. The bellowed orders of the centurions and optiones forming up their men echoed around the
camp. The Via Principalis and Via Praetoria were full of
legionaries, standing in centuries, buckling on armour and
securing helmets, some still chewing on the last mouthfuls of
their interrupted dinner. Most of the men knew their places,
having been through the drill many times before; it was only
the new arrivals who suffered the beatings from the centurions' vine sticks as they struggled to find their stations in the
torch-washed shadows of the camp.

'Break into the fucking praetorium,' Magnus grumbled.
'It's easy for him to say, but how the fuck am I meant to do
that?'

'His personal correspondence will be locked in a chest in
his sleeping area at the back, so cut a hole in the rear of the
tent and you should be right there,' Vespasian suggested.

'Then I've got to break open the chest.'

'Take a crowbar.'

'You're as bad as Asinius, but there's one problem that

neither of you have thought about: how will I know which letters are from Sejanus? I can't read.'

Vespasian stopped still. 'You're joking?'

'I'm not.'

'Why didn't you say?'

'I told you ages ago. Anyway it didn't occur to me that it would be a problem until just now.'

The senior officers had started to file out of the praetorium. Vespasian shook his head. 'I've got to go and report to Pomponius. Just take anything that has the imperial seal on it or is signed with a name beginning with the letter "S". That's the squiggly one that looks a bit like a snake.'

'That's a great help, that is. This is going to be a fuck-up.'

On the opposite side of the Via Principalis a tent flap flew open. Four figures emerged into the torchlight; three wore the uniform of the Praetorian Guard. The fourth was in civilian clothes; his hair fell to his shoulders.

'Hasdro,' Vespasian muttered under his breath.

The four men crossed to the praetorium and entered without even acknowledging the sentries.

'Fucking great, now the place is crawling with Praetorians. What do I do now?'

'I don't know, just do your best. I'll see you later. Good luck.'

'Yeah, and you.' Magnus slapped Vespasian on the shoulder.

Vespasian crossed the road, weaving through the centuries that were by now formed up ready to move out. He pushed through the Fourth Scythica's public horses, waiting outside the legion's command tent to be issued to those officers requiring them, and slipped into the briefing just before Pomponius returned from the praetorium.

The assembled officers snapped to attention as their legate entered the tent.

'At ease, gentlemen,' Pomponius said, passing through the group. At the far end of the tent he turned to address them, resting his ample behind on the edge of his desk. 'The bastards have finally plucked up the courage to fight.' His red, jowly face broke into an excited, piggy-eyed grin. 'We are to hold the wall to the right-hand side of the gate; the Fifth Macedonica will be on the left. The auxiliary cohorts will cover our flanks. No special orders; just react to circumstances and kill the lot of them. We need to move fast, so return to your units. Dismissed! Tribune Vespasian, get a horse and stay with me, you will act as my runner.'

Vespasian sat waiting on his public horse as Pomponius was helped up on to his mount. The rain had increased to a steady downpour, inveigling its way under armour, soaking tunics next to warm skin; steam from thousands of wet, sweating men replaced the smoke in the air from the cooking fires that the rain had doused. A steady series of grating screeches, twangs and thumps indicated that, despite the wet conditions, the artillery in the towers facing the attack had opened up. They fired iron bolts and rounded rocks blindly over the fortifications in the general direction of the enemy, knowing that only in the morning light would they be able to gauge just how successful they had been.

Poppaeus and Corbulo appeared out of the praetorium and swiftly mounted their waiting horses. Poppaeus raised his arm dramatically and threw it forward. A cornu blasted out the six deep, sonorous notes of 'Advance'. Around the camp the call was repeated by each cohort's cornicen. The gates on three sides of the camp swung open, the signiferi dipped their standards twice and the lead cohorts began to move forward at the double.

'Pomponius, follow me,' Poppaeus ordered, kicking his horse forward and accelerating past the columns of waiting legionaries. Vespasian raced after the command group, out of the camp and towards the defensive wall.

The Thracian attack was concentrated on a mile-wide front, centred on the gates. Despite the rain the wooden ramparts were on fire in several places, silhouetting tiny figures in life-and-death struggles in the sputtering light. In two places, to the right of the gate, there were bulges in the line where the Thracians had breached the wall and the two hard-pressed defending cohorts had been forced to use a couple of precious centuries to contain the breakthrough.

Poppaeus galloped up to the gate, dismounted and clambered up the steps up to the parapet. The wooden walls resounded with the thwack, thwack, thwack of repeated slingshot and arrow hits. The centurion commanding met him with a salute. Behind him his over-stretched men were running to and fro desperately pushing ladders away from the wall, hacking at ropes slung over the breastwork and hefting pila into the massed ranks below.

'Report, centurion,' Poppaeus ordered brusquely, shouting to make himself heard over the combined din of battle and rain.

'Sir! They came out of nowhere about a half-hour ago. They must have ambushed our forward patrols as we received no warning.' He flinched slightly as a slingshot fizzed past his ear. 'They've filled in the trench with brush-wood and corpses in six places and managed to get to the wall. They've torn down a couple of sections of it with grappling irons, and set a few more on fire with oil. We've been too thinly stretched to be able to do much more than contain them.'

Sheet lightning flashed across the sky, illuminating for an instant the damage done to the defences.

'Well done,' Poppaeus shouted, realising that they had mobilised just in time. 'Get back to it; relief is on its way.' He called down to Pomponius, who waited below him at the foot of the steps: 'Legate, order four of your cohorts to reinforce the two on the wall to the right of the gate; then form two up here behind the gate, ready for a sortie under my command...'

A double crack of thunder burst above them, forcing him to pause as it reverberated around the mountains, its many echoes returning with diminishing vigour until he was able to continue.

'The final two cohorts I want stationed behind the wall, just beyond the main attack. Have them issued with planks to get over the trench, and then loosen the stakes on an area of wall wide enough for twenty men to get through. Wait until we charge out of the gates on our sortie and then pull down the wall, cross the trench and take the fuckers in the flank. I'll have the Fifth do the same on the other flank. We'll crush them between us.'

'My men will do everything necessary, they will be ready,' Pomponius yelled, yanking his horse round. 'Tribune Vespasian, ride back to the legion; tell Primus Pilus Faustus the third and fourth cohorts are to form up in column at the gate; fifth, sixth, eighth and tenth are to join the seventh and ninth on the wall, I shall see to their deployment personally. You and Faustus are to take the first and second cohorts, and any auxiliary cavalry you can muster, and to start preparing the flank attack. Report to me when it is ready.'

Vespasian galloped through the driving rain to convey the orders to Faustus. Within moments they were issued to each cohort by a system of cornu calls and hand signals. Watching the swift deployment of the legion, Vespasian realised that he had a lot to learn about the secret world of the centurions. Away to his left, just visible through the rain and the dim night, then lit up for an instant by a searing blaze of lightning, he could see the V Macedonica deploying to their section of the wall, the urgency to reinforce it growing with every new section torn down.

Vespasian rode at the head of the first cohort, which was the regulation double strength, nearly a thousand men. Faustus puffed along on foot at his side as they quick-marched along the rear of the wall. Behind them followed the second cohort and Paetus with a full *ala* or wing of 480 auxiliary cavalry. Legionaries from the other cohorts swarmed up the many sets of steps onto the ramparts. A quick succession of lightning flashes seemed to slow their ascent into a series of jerky movements. Another peal of thunder snapped over their heads, forcing some to duck involuntarily, as if there was more to be feared from the imagined wrath of Jupiter than the immediate danger of the enemy's relentless missile barrage.

Eventually the cries and screams of conflict lessened; they had reached the limit of the Thracian attack. Vespasian leapt from his horse and beckoned Faustus to follow him. They scrambled up some deserted steps to the walkway that ran behind the wall. Behind them the two cohorts halted. The sodden legionaries waited for orders, no doubt wondering what they were doing so far from the main action.

Vespasian removed his helmet and inched his head over the parapet. The sight took his breath away; it was his first view of massed battle. Thousands upon thousands of Thracian warriors were hurling themselves towards the towering Roman defences across the wood and corpses piled in the trench. They flung ladders up the wall and scaled them, with the bravado of men who consider themselves already dead and therefore have nothing to lose. Archers and slingers concentrated their fire along the parapet at the apex of each ladder, forcing the defenders to stay down until the warriors reached the top, then the covering fire would stop for fear of hitting their own men. Bitter hand-to-hand struggles ensued, generally resulting in the attackers being hurled backwards off their ladders to disappear, screaming, into their comrades twenty feet below. As they fell volleys of missiles slammed into those defenders not quick enough to duck back down, cracking open skulls, piercing eyes, throats and arms and throwing men back to fall as lifeless dolls at the feet of their comrades, whose turn it would now be to replace them in the line.

Most of the breaches in the wall had been plugged by the timely arrival of the main Roman force. Those attackers who had made it through were now either lying dead in the churned mud or fighting to the last man, in ever-decreasing pockets of defiance. Surrender was not an option, they had come here to kill and be killed.

In a few places, closer to the gates, fires still burned, fed by skins of oil hurled into their midst. Their flames lit up a large tent-like construction, pushed by hundreds of tiny figures, which was slowly moving forward towards the gates.

'They've got a battering ram,' Faustus said, joining Vespasian. 'We'd better get a move on.'

Vespasian ducked back down. 'This will do,' he said to Faustus as he slipped his helmet back on. 'The nearest fighting's a good hundred and fifty paces away. Get ropes secured over the top of each stake and start digging around the bases to loosen them. Once that's done get the men dismantling the walkway; they can use the planks to cross the trench.'

'Yes, sir.' Faustus turned to go.

'Faustus, tell the men to keep their heads down. We don't want the enemy to know we're here.'

'Of course not. We wouldn't want to spoil their surprise, would we?' Faustus grinned and hurried back to his men.

The legionaries of the first and second cohorts set about their work with enthusiasm, relishing the prospect of a surprise flank attack that would roll up the Thracian line. Within a quarter of an hour, ropes were in place around the tops of the stakes along a sixty-foot length of wall, and the walkway behind it lay in ruins.

Vespasian raced off to report to Pomponius, whom he found with a couple of centuries of the eighth cohort, sealing up the last breach of the defences with a human wall. Thracian missiles were taking their toll on the defenders, who were finding it hard to keep a solid testudo formation on the uneven muddy ground. The numerous Roman dead and wounded littered around the breach bore witness to the close-range accuracy of the Thracian archers and slingers, only thirty paces away.

'The flank attack is set, sir!' Vespasian yelled at his commanding officer.

'About fucking time too.' Pomponius looked relieved. 'These bastards aren't going to give up until they're all dead, so let's oblige them before they kill too many more of our lads. Report to Poppaeus at the gates and then join me on the flank.'

'Sir!' Vespasian saluted as he kicked his horse on.

The gates now trembled from the repeated blows of the iron-headed ram. Four cohorts stood behind them ready for the sortie. Poppaeus was pouring all his auxiliary archers up onto the walkways on either side in an effort to dislodge the warriors manning the ram and the scores of men waiting behind it, ready to burst through once it had done its work. Vespasian shoved his way past the lines of archers towards the diminutive general who, despite his size, was easily recognisable in his high plumed helmet. The archers were sending volley after volley into the massed ranks of enemy below, who had begun to waver under the onslaught. The ram, though, was covered with a tent of thick hide that completely protected the men toiling inside. It continued beating relentlessly at the gates, each resounding knell weakening the structure and making the walkway shake beneath Vespasian's feet.

'That bastard priest must have known they had a ram up in their fort when he came in this afternoon.' Poppaeus spat as Vespasian approached him on the walkway. 'The little cunt said nothing; I'll have his tongue out when I find him. This had better be good news, tribune.'

'Yes, sir, we're ready on the right flank.' Vespasian stepped back as an archer crumpled at his feet, gurgling blood, with an arrow protruding from his throat. Poppaeus kicked him off the walkway.

'Good. Get back to your position and tell Pomponius that as soon as our archers force the bastards to withdraw far enough away we'll open the gates and deal to them what they planned to give us. It'll be the last thing they expect, us opening the gates when they're trying to batter them down.' He rubbed his hands together and then turned to exhort the archers into more rapid fire, seemingly impervious to the hail of missiles being returned. Despite all Poppaeus' treachery Vespasian couldn't help but respect his composure under fire. Cowering in the rear and issuing orders that would get men killed was not for him: he led from the front, as should any Roman general who expected his men to fight and die for him.

Vespasian gave an unnoticed salute, turned and walked steadily back along the walkway, emulating, he hoped, Poppaeus' example of sang-froid amidst the chaos of battle all around him.

The men of the first and second cohorts stood ready. Another flash of lightning ripped from the sky, turning their highly polished iron armour momentarily golden and causing a myriad of reflections to sparkle through the ranks. Rain poured off the legionaries' helmets and down their necks, chilling them as they waited motionless for the order to attack. Despite the unpleasant conditions their morale was high. They replied with good humour to the encouragement of their centurions as they walked up and down the files inspecting equipment, praising their courage and reminding them of previous battles and exploits in which they had all shared.

Just behind the wall a century waited, with ropes in hand, for the order to pull it down. Behind them another century, with the planks ripped from the walkway, stood ready to span the trench beyond the wall. A lone sentry stationed up on the parapet peered across the battlefield, watching for the main gates, clearly visible in the fires surrounding them, to be opened and for Poppaeus' sortie to storm out.

Vespasian stood next to Pomponius in the front rank of the leading century. Over to his right he could just make out Paetus' cavalry. Adrenalin pumped through his body as he mentally prepared himself to kill without hesitation or pity. He flexed the muscles in his shield arm to prevent them from stiffening and checked, yet again, that his gladius was loose in its sheath.

'When we go through it must be quick,' Pomponius told him for the third or fourth time. 'But not so quick that we trip on any stakes left lying around.'

Vespasian glanced at his commander, who was thirty years his senior, and felt reassured by the look of tension on his jowly face; the waiting was evidently playing on Poppaeus' nerves as much as on his own.

A sudden shout came from the sentry above them. 'They're through, sir.'

Pomponius glanced at Faustus. 'Give the order, centurion,' he shouted.

'Make ready, lads,' Faustus bellowed.

The ropes went taut.

'On the count of three pull like you'd pull a Nubian off your mother. One, two, three!'

With a massive simultaneous heave sixty feet of wall stakes crashed to the ground as one. The men carried on pulling on the ropes, dragging most of the stakes clear from the path of the waiting legionaries. As the century with the planks rushed through the opening Pomponius gave the order to advance. The cornu blared out the deep notes of command and the cohorts broke into a slow jog, up and over the rough ground disturbed by the uprooted stakes and down across the newly laid, wooden bridge over the trench.

Before the majority of Thracians had registered the new threat away in the darkness on their flank, the first cohort had covered two hundred paces and the second had cleared the wall. Behind them the ala of auxiliary cavalry streamed past to form up on their extreme right.

Pomponius gave the orders to halt and then to form up two centuries deep to the left. Fifteen hundred men turned as one to face the enemy.

A wave of panic swept through the Thracian masses. They were already aware of the sortie at the gates; now this new threat meant that they would be fighting on two fronts, as well as having to endure the barrage of missiles from the wall. Then, from further up the hill, came the prolonged shrill cry of hundreds of female voices. A flash of lightning lit up the hillside and, for a couple of moments, the source of that cry was plainly visible. The Thracians' women had come, bringing their children with them, to live or die with their men.

The sight breathed fire into the hearts of the warriors. They abandoned their efforts to scale the wall and with a swirling, chaotic manoeuvre turned and faced the new foe.

'Forward!' Pomponius cried, excitement causing his voice to rise an octave.

The rumbling cornu notes resonated over the Roman line, the standards dipped and, with a crash of pila against shields, it moved forward.

A hundred paces away, just visible as darker shadows against the lighter fire-flecked background, the Thracians let out a soul-shivering howl and stampeded towards the Romans. A new series of lightning flashes revealed them brandishing rhomphaiai, spears and javelins wildly above their heads, splashing through the pools of water and mud that caused many of their number to lose their footing and disappear beneath the tide of trampling boots surging after them.

All around him Vespasian could hear the cries of the centurions exhorting their men to hold the line, and keep the steady advance under control. The first arrows and javelins had started to fall amongst them, bringing down an unlucky few. There was no order to raise shields, there was no time, the two sides were closing far too quickly. The next order would be 'Release pila at the charge'. When it sounded the legionaries of the front three double-centuries of the first cohort and the front three standard centuries of the second pulled their right arms back, counted three paces, hurled their heavy pila skywards and immediately drew their swords without breaking step. Over seven hundred pila rained down into the oncoming mass of howling, hate-filled warriors, cracking through bronze or iron helmets as if they were no more than eggshells, slamming men to the ground in a welter of blood, throwing others backwards with the weight of impact, long razor-sharp pilum heads protruding out behind them and skewering the man following, leaving them obscenely coupled by shafts of iron, thrashing in the mud in the last throes of life.

Vespasian felt the cold air scrape down his throat as he pushed himself forward the last few paces. His shield was raised so that he could just see over the rim. Next to him, on his left, Pomponius was wheezing with the exertion of the charge, and, for a brief moment, he wondered how a man of Pomponius' bulk could still find it within himself to fight in the front rank. That thought was pounded out of his mind by the shock of impact that shuddered through his body as the two sides collided. Though less numerous, the heavier and more densely packed Roman line punched the Thracians back, knocking their leading warriors off their feet, pushing on a couple of paces before coming to a grinding halt, their rigid wall of shields still intact.

Then the close-quarters killing began. The lethal stabbing blades of the Roman war machine began their mechanical work, flashing out from between the rectangular shields, blazoned with the crossed lightning bolts and goat's head insignia of the Fourth Scythica. Vespasian's first sword thrust was a firm jab to the throat of a stunned Thracian at his feet, opening it in with a surge of blood that sprayed up his legs. He quickly turned his attention to the screaming horde in the darkness in front of him. Rhomphaia blades hissed through the night air, spear points thrust out of the gloom; it was almost impossible to know whom you were fighting. He held his shield firmly in line with those on either side and stabbed again and again, sometimes feeling the jolting rigidity of a wooden shield, sometimes the soft give of pierced flesh and sometimes no contact at all. A close-by scream to his right suddenly distracted him: the legionary next in line collapsed, almost knocking Vespasian off balance; blood from a deep rhomphaia wound to the man's neck sprayed over his sword arm and the side of his face. Vespasian just had the presence of mind to crouch low behind his shield and aim a wild stab into the belly of a Thracian pushing into the resulting gap. The man doubled up; his head was immediately punched back by the shield boss of a second-rank legionary, stepping over his fallen comrade to plug the breach in the line. Vespasian felt the replacement's shoulder close to his and continued stabbing forward.

He kept at it as the Roman line inched forward, aware of nothing more than the need to survive. He parried blows coming out of the darkness with his shield, thrusting and grinding his sword, his whole being given over to the exhilarating terror of hand-to-hand conflict. Rain poured down, mixing with the blood on his face, clouding his eyes; he blinked incessantly as he worked his blade. Gradually he began to make fewer and fewer contacts; the Thracians were pulling back.

Pomponius took the opportunity to order 'Relieve the line'. Every other file stepped to the right, integrating with the file next to it, creating gaps through which charged the relieving second-rank centuries of each cohort. Once they were clear of their tired comrades the fresh centuries formed up into another solid line of shields. The cornu boomed a new attack. They surged forward towards the retreating enemy, releasing their pila at the charge, ten paces from the disordered mob. Another hail of seven hundred and more lead-weighted iron spikes pummelled down on to the Thracians. It was too much for them. Those that could turned to flee; the rest lay sprawled on the gore-soaked mud of the field, pierced and bleeding. Those with any life still left within them moaned pitifully as it ebbed away into the earth of their homeland, whose freedom, like their lives, was now lost for ever.

Vespasian wiped the blood from his face and sucked in the cold wet air, steadying himself after the elation and fear of battle. Pomponius had ordered the halt of the second charge and had recalled Paetus' cavalry before it became isolated. He had also brought the tenth cohort, whose length of wall had been cleared of enemy, around, through the gap in the wall, to join them. He was now issuing orders to his centurions and Paetus for the final decisive blow.

'Primus Pilus Faustus, take the first, second and tenth cohorts and advance steadily. Push the enemy back towards Poppaeus' men at the gates. Kill all their wounded as you go. As each section of wall is cleared order the defending cohort to double round to join you. I shall take Paetus' cavalry and cut off any retreat back up to the fortress. Any questions, centurion?'

'No, sir.' Faustus saluted and disappeared off into the wet night, issuing a string of orders to his subordinate centurions.

'Paetus, get a couple of spare mounts for the tribune and me; let's get at them again before they regroup.'

'My pleasure, sir.' The cavalry prefect grinned, flashing his white teeth in the gloom.

By the time they were mounted and had swapped their infantry shields for oval cavalry ones, Faustus' three cohorts, rearmed with pila brought up from the camp in mule carts by teams of slaves, had begun to press forward. They sang the victory anthem of the Fourth Scythica and beat their newly acquired weapons on their shields in time to the pace of their advance. Audible over the driving rain, and occasionally visible in the bursts of sheet lightning, they drove the Thracians back until they were pressed up against their comrades, who were being pushed from the other direction by Poppaeus' men.

Vespasian stuck close to Pomponius and Paetus as the auxiliary cavalry shadowed the infantry's advance, blocking any endeavour to outflank them, and ready to take any attempted retreat in the flank.

'They know that there'll be no mercy if they surrender,' Vespasian said, 'so why don't they just get it over with and attack?'

'They will,' Pomponius assured him. 'Now that they're grouped together they'll use a small force to try to hold Poppaeus' cohorts, whilst they throw as many men as possible at our lads in an effort to break through.'

The mêlée had now reached the burning sections of the wall, which still raged with enough intensity to evaporate the heavy rain into clouds of steam. The light of the fires lit up the still substantial Thracian horde as they formed up for their final, desperate charge. Vespasian guessed that there must still be at least three thousand of them left on this side of the gates; he couldn't see how the V Macedonica was faring on the other side.

With a huge roar that drowned out the singing and beating of the Fourth Scythica, they charged. As Pomponius had predicted, a small portion went at the cohorts coming from the gates, the rest, more than two thousand of them, flung themselves on to the Fourth Scythica.

Vespasian watched as the Thracian mass launched an enormous volley of javelins and arrows. They disappeared as they rose above the light of the flames, only to reappear again as they descended on to the Roman line. This time, however, the Romans took the charge standing and were able to raise shields, taking the sting out of the volley. But many gaps still materialised along the ranks as more than a few of the lethal missiles found their mark. The Roman shields came crashing down and, an instant later, a return volley of pila ripped through the air, illuminated all the way to their target owing to their lower trajectory. The volley lashed through the oncoming Thracians, felling many, but deterring none. They fell on the Roman line howling like furies, slashing, stabbing, gouging and hacking, giving and expecting no quarter, in a fight so violent and bestial that, even from a distance of a couple of hundred paces, Vespasian could almost feel every blow.

'Now we take them in the flank,' Pomponius shouted. 'Paetus, order the attack.'

Paetus nodded at the *liticen*, who raised his five-foot-long bronze *lituus* with an upturned bell-like end, the cavalry equivalent to the cornu, and put his lips to the ox-horn mouthpiece. The horn sounded a shrill, high-pitched call and the 480 men of the auxiliary ala, in a line four deep, broke into a walk. Another blast after twenty paces and they were at a trot. With fifty paces to the nearest enemy a final blast of the lituus took them to a canter. With a volley of javelins they smashed into the unprotected flank of the Thracian line. Vespasian drove his horse forward through the mass of bodies, riding down everyone in his path, slashing and cutting at those who remained upright, feeling again the exhilaration – bordering on joy – of conflict, until a prolonged, shrill howl came from behind. He glanced over his shoulder in time to see a new force crash into the cavalry's rear.

The Thracian women had charged.

Dismissed as bystanders and forgotten since their first appearance on the field, they had left their children in the care of the elderly and advanced unnoticed, down from their position up the hill, through the darkness as the auxiliary ala charged. Armed only with knives, pointed fire-hardened sticks and their bare hands, the women, hundreds of them, fell upon the unsuspecting cavalry. They swept between the files of troopers like ghostly harpies, uncaring of their own safety, intent only on causing as much havoc as possible, hamstringing horses, jabbing at their rumps or bellies to make them rear up and dislodge their riders, and pulling others from their saddles. The grounded men disappeared beneath a wave of teeth, nails and improvised weapons, shrieking in agony from innumerable wounds as they were gouged, clawed, bitten and ripped to death.

Vespasian turned his horse, just in time, as the first of the women reached the front rank. With a swift downward cut he severed a knife-wielding arm aimed at his thigh, then brought his sword quickly forward to pierce the eye of its erstwhile owner. All around him troopers disengaged from the Thracian warriors to their front and spun their mounts around to face the unforeseen danger in their midst, hacking and stabbing at the strange, wild, long-haired foe. But it was too late. The unit had been almost completely infiltrated; outnumbered two or three to one and their cohesion gone, most of the men were fighting off attacks from all directions.

A few paces away to his right, a knot of fifty or so troopers under Paetus' command still held firm. Vespasian glimpsed Pomponius tumble from his shying horse as he attempted to force his way to the relative safety of the steady unit through a sea of blood-drenched women. Vespasian called to the troopers closest to follow him, and struck out towards his fallen commander. He forced his horse to rear up so that its flailing front hooves cracked the skulls and collar-bones of those in his path, then he urged it forward to trample its victims. Supported by half a dozen men, he hacked a path to where Pomponius now knelt, surrounded by baying women. As Vespasian approached they pounced upon the legate, throwing him to the ground under a hail of thrashing arms and clawing nails. Vespasian leapt from his horse on to the writhing pile of bodies and stabbed indiscriminately and repeatedly into the unprotected backs of his commander's assailants, puncturing lungs, piercing kidneys and ripping open arteries in a rapid, murderous assault. His men formed a protective cordon around him as he pulled at the pile of limp corpses to reveal Pomponius, shocked but alive.

'Can you stand, sir?' Vespasian asked urgently.

'Yes, I'm fine, tribune,' Pomponius replied, hauling himself up, gasping for breath. 'I owe you more than my life, I owe you my honour; to have been killed by women in these circumstances – what shame.'

At that moment Paetus' men began a concerted drive forward. In close order, knee to knee, they advanced, riding down any women who stood against them. The other small pockets of surviving troopers took heart and fought with a ferocity that outmatched their desperate opponents. Gradually the small groups linked together, forcing the women back, killing as many as possible, until all the survivors of the auxiliary ala had regrouped. Of the original 480 men there remained only 160 still mounted, and a further 90, including Vespasian and Pomponius, on foot. Nearly half their number lay butchered on the rain-sodden ground. They were now to be avenged.

With the main battle still raging behind them, and the flank of the Fourth Scythica now secured by the recent arrival of two more cohorts freed up from the wall, the auxiliaries began to corral the women into a tightly packed herd. A few score managed to escape the net and raced back up to their children, but eventually the main body was surrounded. They stood, now silent, as they awaited their fate. Not one fell to her knees to beg for mercy; they knew to expect none after what they had done. They would die as their men were dying, in full view of their children, defiant to the last.

The troopers dismounted and, with sharp grating of metal against metal, drew their weapons. The order came to advance. Vespasian gripped his sword hilt, raised his oval cavalry shield and moved towards the motionless women. Not even as his sword thrust into the throat of the young girl before him did any of the women move or make a sound. They just stood, defenceless, and defied the Romans to kill them in cold blood. And kill them they did, systematically, vengefully, thinking of their fallen mess-mates.

Vespasian butchered his way forward, without pity,

killing young, old, beautiful and haggard; it made no difference to him. He was full of hatred and cold fury. This was not the frenzied elation of battle. This was the awakening of the deep desire that men keep within themselves to see people not of their tribe or creed die, knowing that only through their deaths would they, the killers, feel cleansed and secure.

As the last of the women fell beneath the blows of gore-dripping swords the auxiliaries turned away, their thirst for vengeance sated. There was no victory cheer, no embracing of comrades in relief and joy at remaining alive. They just remounted their horses and waited in silence for orders, scarcely able to look each other in the eye. The wound to their pride ran deep.

CHAPTER XXVII

VESPASIAN HAD RETRIEVED his horse and sat next to Pomponius, watching the last stage of the battle below them in the pre-dawn gloom. The main body of the Fourth Scythica had fought its way almost to the gates, which were now securely held by the cohorts of Poppaeus' sortie. The remaining Thracians were being crushed between the two bodies of Roman heavy infantry, their resistance dwindling as more and more fell to the relentless, disciplined swordwork of the legionaries. On the far side of the gates the V Macedonica was playing out the mirror image of the struggle. There was nothing left for the cavalry to do; the Thracian rebellion was finally crushed by the generalship of the man who had been, in part, responsible for its instigation.

'We should report to Poppaeus,' Pomponius said quietly, 'and congratulate him on his victory.' He raised his arm and ordered the cavalry forward at a trot towards the gates.

'It should have been your victory, sir,' Vespasian replied.

'What do you mean?' Pomponius asked, kicking his horse forward.

Knowing that Asinius would need a formidable ally in the coming confrontation with Poppaeus, Vespasian told Pomponius of the general's refusal to obey the Emperor's and Senate's order and return to Rome. He told him of his and Sejanus' treachery and Rhoteces' and Hasdro's involvement in it. As they crossed the corpse-strewn field, which now resounded to the clamour and cheers of the victorious legionaries, Pomponius' anger grew; it was not aimed so much at Poppaeus' duplicity, but more at the damage done to his personal dignitas. The troops now cheering their victorious general should instead be hailing him. He had been robbed of the glory that was by rights his, and in its place he had had the humiliation of almost being torn to death by a pack of female savages. By the time they reached the gates Pomponius was fuming with indignation. The sight of Poppaeus riding through the throngs of cheering soldiers, helmet raised in the air, accepting their acclaim, was almost too much for him.

'The treacherous little shit,' he fumed. 'Look at him basking in the praise of the men. They wouldn't be cheering so loud if they knew that he helped to fund this revolt, and that their mates have died solely to further his ambition.'

At the gates a rostrum had been hurriedly set up in front of the smouldering remains of the battering ram. Poppaeus pushed his horse towards it, through the crush of jubilant legionaries. His progress was slow as each man wanted to touch him, or make eye contact, or receive a word of praise from his general. Eventually he reached the rostrum and managed to jump on to it directly from his horse. He raised his arms in the air and, in a dramatic gesture, thrust them forward and apart, to include every man present in his victory. The men of the Fourth Scythica and V Macedonica roared their acknowledgement. The noise was deafening. It started as a huge unending wall of sound and then, gradually, it developed into a chant. At first the words were indiscernible, coming only from a small section of the crowd, but they quickly grew in volume as more and more of the delirious legionaries took up the chant. Before long it was clear.

'Imperator! Imperator! Imperator!'

Thousands of men now chanted in unison, punching their swords in the air in time to the beat. Poppaeus stood alone on his raised dais amidst a sea of faces lit by the first rays of the sun. With his head tilted back and his arms open wide he slowly revolved, taking in the praise that was coming at him from all angles.

Pomponius turned to Vespasian and raised his eyebrows. 'It's a brave general,' he shouted above the din, 'who allows an army to hail him as "Imperator" in this day and age.'

'It would be a shame for him if the Emperor found out,' Vespasian shouted back.

'A great shame,' Pomponius mused, noticing a disturbance close to the platform. Four of Asinius' lictors had pushed their way from the gates, through the mob, to the rostrum and were now helping him on to the platform. Dressed in the purple-bordered toga of a proconsul, he approached Poppaeus and embraced him. From where Vespasian sat he could see that Poppaeus' face had set into a fixed smile as he was forced to return the embrace of his enemy. Asinius released himself from the embrace and lifted Poppaeus' right hand. The chanting broke into a mighty cheer. He then stepped forward, his palms facing the crowd in a gesture that demanded silence. The noise died down. He drew himself up to speak.

'Soldiers of Rome.' His voice rang out through the cool dawn air. 'Some of you know me, but for those who don't, I am Marcus Asinius Agrippa.' A few ragged cheers greeted him. 'I come here with a message from your Emperor and Senate for you and your glorious general. A message so important that it was deemed that only a man of consular rank should bear it.'

This was greeted by more enthusiastic cheers. Poppaeus' expression hardened as he realised that he had been outmanoeuvred. Asinius waited for silence before continuing.

'Your general's efforts have been justly recognised. The Senate has voted him triumphal honours and the Emperor has been pleased to confirm this award to his remarkable and trusted servant.' His voice betrayed no hint of the irony in his words.

The roars of approval for this echoed around the field. Asinius caught Pomponius' eye and motioned him forward. Vespasian followed, forcing his mount through the heaving mass of legionaries to the base of the rostrum.

Asinius gestured for silence again.

'General Poppaeus is required to leave for Rome at once

to receive his just reward for his faithful service.' Asinius turned and smiled at Poppaeus, who stood transfixed with anger but impotent as Asinius worked the crowd. 'But the Emperor has replaced him with a good man, a brave man, a man many of you know. Soldiers of Rome: the Emperor gives you Pomponius Labeo.'

Pomponius was lifted from his horse by the men of his legion and helped, with some difficulty, on to the rostrum. He embraced Poppaeus, who remained helplessly rooted to the spot as his moment of glory was hijacked. Pomponius turned to the crowd, which once again fell silent.

'Poppaeus has today won a great victory and his reward is indeed just. I shall do my utmost to lead you as well as he has done. He can return to Rome in the knowledge that his men are in good hands. I shall make sure that your cries of "Imperator" will follow him. They will echo around the Senate in tribute to his deeds here today. No one in Rome will be unaware of how you, brave soldiers of Rome, have honoured him. This I swear by Mars Victorious.'

As the cheering broke out again Vespasian could see a shadow pass over Poppaeus' face as he realised that he had gone too far in accepting the accolade that was now reserved only for members of the imperial family.

Asinius joined Pomponius at the front of the rostrum and again asked for silence.

'Soldiers of Rome, your parts in this victory have not gone unnoticed, neither will they be unrewarded.'

As he spoke, Magnus and the other seven lictors pushed

their way to the rostrum and lifted on to it two heavy chests. Vespasian recognised them as being larger than, but otherwise very similar to, the one he had seen at the Caenii's camp.

With a dramatic flourish Asinius threw the lids open, to reveal them full to the brim with silver coins. The colour drained from Poppaeus' face and his mouth opened and closed in a vain effort to say something that would stop the nightmare.

'The Emperor and Senate have decreed,' Asinius continued smoothly, enjoying his enemy's mortification, 'that, in recognition of your valour in defeating the Thracian revolt, a bounty should be paid from the imperial treasury to every legionary and auxiliary.'

At this news the cheers of the men erupted into a cacophony that outdid all their previous efforts. Vespasian kicked his horse through the crowd until he reached Magnus.

'Is that what I think it is?' he asked, dismounting.

Magnus grinned. 'If you think that it's my life's savings, then you'd be wrong, but if you think that it's Poppaeus' other two chests, then you'd be right.'

'Where did you find them?'

'They were just sitting there, in Poppaeus' quarters, when I broke in to get the letters. It seemed such a waste leaving them, so I nipped back to Asinius who kindly lent me a few of his lictors to help liberate them – though not before I helped myself to a couple of bagfuls to cover our travelling expenses, if you take my meaning?'

'I think I do.' Vespasian laughed, clapping his friend on the shoulder.

Asinius had started to speak again. 'My duty here is done and I shall now resume my journey to my province. It has been an honour to bring you your Emperor's reward. I am sure that General Poppaeus will wish to distribute it immediately, before he returns to Rome. Centurions, fall your men in here, on this field of victory, and they will all return to camp richer. Hail Caesar.'

As he moved to the edge of the rostrum, where Vespasian and Magnus waited to help him down, Poppaeus caught him by the arm and looked at him with an expression of unbridled hatred.

'You will pay dearly for this,' he hissed.

'My dear Poppaeus,' Asinius replied smugly, 'whatever do you mean? I have the distinct impression that you are the one who is paying dearly.'

Walking back to the camp Asinius was in a fine mood. His lictors cleared the way through the thousands of troops hurrying to form up as fast as was possible on the corpse-strewn field into their centuries and cohorts, in order to receive the promised largesse. They cheered him as he passed and he waved back, all the while talking animatedly with Vespasian and Magnus.

'Your man did a commendable job last night, Vespasian,' he said, slapping Magnus on the back. 'Not only getting the letters, but also stealing Poppaeus' war chests; that was a coup that I hadn't dreamt of. It made Poppaeus' rout complete. I trust that he is not distributing the full contents of the chests?'

'No, sir,' Magnus replied. 'A small percentage was deducted for expenses.'

'Very good, you deserve it; I have to admit to helping myself to a few handfuls to distribute to my lictors.'

'What of the letters, Asinius?' Vespasian asked.

'Magnus managed to get a half a dozen letters that implicate Poppaeus and Sejanus in this Thracian affair. I despatched Rhoemetalces with three of them before dawn, he should be well on his way to Philippopolis by now. From there Queen Tryphaena will send them to Antonia, who will add them to the growing collection of evidence that we shall lay before Tiberius when the time is right. I think that, in the meantime, the other three will prove to be enough of a deterrent to prevent Poppaeus and Sejanus from hauling me up in front of the Senate on treason charges.' He patted a leather pouch that hung around neck.

'What are you going to do with that priest, then?'

'Oh, I think that I'm going to give him back to Poppaeus as a little going-away present,' Asinius chuckled. 'I reckon they deserve each other, don't you?'

'I think Poppaeus will judge that he's too dangerous to keep alive.'

'I do hope that you're right.'

They had reached Asinius' tent and he stopped to bid them goodbye.

'I shall be leaving immediately. I have no wish to be here when Poppaeus returns and finds that his letters are missing, and much less to find myself as his travelling companion when he leaves later on today. If you take my advice, Vespasian, you should make yourself scarce until he's gone and Pomponius is fully in command.'

'I will, Asinius. May the gods go with you.'

'If I believed in them I'm sure they would. Good luck and I'll see you in Rome in four years or so.' He gripped Vespasian's forearms with both hands and then turned to Magnus.

'Thank you, my friend, I owe you a debt that I shall not forget.'

'I'll come and see you in Rome when I need a favour.'

'It will be my pleasure; until then, farewell.'

Keeping four of his lictors to guard his person, and leaving two to guard the entrance, Asinius dismissed the remaining five to prepare for their return journey, and went into his tent.

'Well, you heard him,' Vespasian said, heading off to his quarters. 'Let's get out of here for a day or two.'

'Suits me fine.'

They had not gone ten paces when the clash of weapons and a scream stopped them in their tracks. They turned just in time to see the two guards rush into Asinius' tent.

'Fuck!' Vespasian gasped, drawing his sword as the unmistakable sound of two bodies slumping to the ground came from within the tent. The other lictors had heard the commotion and were running back, swords drawn. With no thought of tactics Vespasian, Magnus and the five lictors crashed through the entrance of the tent.

'Stop right there or he gets hurt, nastily,' Hasdro shouted. He had his sword across Asinius' throat and, with his left hand pressing hard down on his head with a vice-like grip, forced the proconsul to his knees. His three Praetorian companions stood in front of him, amongst the bodies of the lictors, warily pointing their swords at Vespasian and his comrades, two paces away. Behind him was Poppaeus' secretary, Kratos, holding three letters. Slumped in the corner was the semi-conscious Rhoemetalces.

'This is an interesting situation,' Vespasian said, breathing hard. 'We outnumber you, so how do you imagine you'll get out alive?'

'I'd say that it's quite straightforward.' Hasdro's black eyes gleamed malevolently and a smile played on the corner of his mouth. 'The proconsul gives us what we want, then, in return for his life, you let us go.'

'Don't let them—' A fist to the side of his face silenced Asinius.

'One more word and I'll have your nose off,' Hasdro spat, shaking his bruised hand. He tugged at the leather bag around Asinius' neck, snapping the strap, and threw it at Kratos. 'Check them,' he growled.

Kratos quickly pulled the letters out of the sack and flicked through them. 'They're all here,' he confirmed, adding them to the three that he had already retrieved from Rhoemetalces.

'Burn them all, so that idiot master of yours doesn't lose them again.'

Kratos threw the letters on to the brazier.

'Save them,' Asinius shouted as they burst into flames. He thrust his throat forward on to the edge of Hasdro's sword and forced it along its length. Blood sprayed across the room as the blade sliced through the soft flesh. Hasdro looked with horror at the quivering body of his now useless hostage as it fell, gurgling, at his blood-drenched feet.

'Now!' Vespasian cried lurching forward. He crashed into the nearest Praetorian, grabbed his right wrist and forced his sword into the air. With a lightning thrust he pushed his blade up into the vitals of the startled man and, feeling hot blood squirt down his arm, twisted it through his bowels. The Praetorian doubled up, pushing Vespasian on to his back. The shriek of pain, so close to his ear, almost deafened Vespasian as he fought to withdraw his entangled sword. Magnus flew past him and hurled himself on to Hasdro, who slipped in Asinius' blood. The pair crashed to the ground, grappling and wrestling with each other, their swords useless at such close quarters. Behind them the lictors descended on to the last two Praetorians, who went down under a welter of stabs and thrusts that continued even after their lives had been expunged.

Vespasian managed to kick himself out from under his howling victim, leaving his sword lodged in his lacerated abdomen. In the corner of his eye he caught the blur of Kratos darting for the exit.

'Get him alive!' he barked at the lictors as he retrieved a discarded sword. He stepped up behind Hasdro, who now sat astride Magnus closing his huge hands around the struggling boxer's throat. Vespasian drew his sword arm back. Magnus' eyes focused briefly on the movement. Hasdro turned, the look on his face showing that he knew what to expect. With a powerful, clean sweep Vespasian cleaved his head from his shoulders, sending it spinning through the air in a spray of blood. His severed long black hair slithered down his back. His torso fell on to Magnus, disgorging its contents from its open neck onto his face.

'Was that necessary?' Magnus spluttered, heaving the corpse aside. 'I was just about to turn him.'

'Better safe than sorry, I thought,' Vespasian replied, amazed at what he had just done. 'It seemed from where I was standing that you were having a little difficulty.' He held out his hand to help up his friend, who looked like he had been the victim of a particularly grisly sacrifice.

Vespasian looked down at Asinius, who lay motionless, his eyes staring lifelessly at the brazier in which the precious letters were now no more than charred fragments.

'Shit!' he exclaimed as he realised how devastating their loss was. He looked over to Rhoemetalces who was sitting bolt upright in the corner, staring at Hasdro's severed head.

'What happened? I thought that Asinius sent you off hours ago?'

The young King pulled his gaze away from the macabre object and replied, with difficulty, through his swollen mouth. 'He did, but they came after me and caught me. They killed my escort and brought me back here to wait for Asinius. They knew about the letters. Kratos got here to verify them just before Asinius came back. Then you arrived, that's all I know.'

Vespasian turned to Kratos, who was cowering in the firm grip of two lictors. He placed the tip of his sword under his chin.

'Well?' he asked.

'I saw that my master's quarters had been broken into, there was a slash in the tent and the chests of silver were gone, so I checked his correspondence and some was missing. I suspected Asinius immediately so I informed Hasdro.' Kratos spoke quickly in his anxiety to give as much information as possible, knowing that his life was at stake. 'We came here to Asinius' tent and found Rhoteces, the priest, tied up in the sleeping area. He had overheard Asinius send Rhoemetalces off to Philippopolis.'

'But Rhoteces didn't mention the letters.'

'No, we just assumed that he had gone with all the letters. It was the logical thing for Asinius to have done.'

'Where is the priest now?'

'Gone.'

'Where?'

'He went with Hasdro and his men to catch Rhoemetalces.'

'Where is he now?'

'I don't know.'

Vespasian jabbed his sword forcing the terrified secretary's head further back.

'I swear I don't know! When I came back to check the letters that were found on Rhoemetalces he wasn't here any more.'

'He ran off after they caught me,' Rhoemetalces croaked from the corner. 'He wanted to kill me, but when Hasdro refused he galloped off. Hasdro didn't have the time to chase him; when he found that I only had half of the letters he wanted to get back here and find Asinius, to retrieve the rest.'

A glimmer of hope came into Vespasian's eyes; the situation was perhaps retrievable if they acted quickly. He smiled as he looked at the cringing Kratos. 'So apart from us you are the only person that could tell Poppaeus when he discovers that his letters are missing that they've been destroyed, aren't you?'

Kratos gulped. 'Yes, but I won't, I swear on my life.'

'I don't believe you.' Vespasian thrust his sword up through Kratos' chin and into his brain. His eyes popped wide open in surprise and then his body went limp.

'Let's get out of here before the army and Poppaeus get back,' Vespasian said, wiping the blood off his sword on the secretary's tunic. He looked at the lictors. 'Take your master's body and ride as fast as you can to Philippopolis. You can cremate him there, but do it quietly. Then, when you get back to Rome, go and see the Lady Antonia; I shall make arrangements for your loyalty to be repaid. Rhoemetalces, you go with them to help; we need to make sure that Asinius' death is kept secret for as long as possible.'

'Why?' the King asked, getting painfully to his feet.

'Because when Poppaeus finds that the letters are missing, he'll come straight here, where he will find six of Asinius' lictors, his secretary Kratos, Hasdro and his mates all dead. But he won't find Asinius or the letters. He'll assume the worst and will have two choices: suicide; or go back to Rome and hope for the best. Neither of them will be very attractive to him. You must get your mother to write to Antonia and tell her everything. If Antonia can make Poppaeus believe that she has the letters, she may be able blackmail him into feeding her information about Sejanus, and Asinius' sacrifice won't have been in vain.'

'But what happens when Poppaeus finds out that Asinius is dead?'

'It won't matter, as long as he doesn't find out he died here, which he will if he comes back to find us still talking about it. Now go!'

The lictors quickly picked up Asinius' body and covered it with a blanket. Vespasian led them hurriedly through the deserted camp to the horse-lines where they strapped the corpse onto the back of a horse. In the distance the hubbub of the army receiving its bounty could be clearly heard.

As he watched Rhoemetalces and the lictors race out of the camp, taking with them the evidence that could put Poppaeus' mind at ease, Vespasian felt an overwhelming sense of relief; he was in a game of very high stakes and, although the victory was not complete, he was still alive. He remembered the words he had overheard his mother saying:

'He will have the Goddess Fortuna holding her hands over him to ensure that the prophecy is fulfilled.' He would make a sacrifice of thanks to Fortuna to ensure her continued protection. He looked at Magnus and smiled. 'Quick, my friend, let's go,' he said, jumping onto a horse.

'Where to sir?'

'Firstly to find some water to clean you up and then, like Asinius said, we make ourselves scarce for a couple of days until Poppaeus is well gone.'

'Suits me fine, but what then?'

Vespasian shrugged and kicked his horse forward. 'Who knows? Whatever the army wants, I suppose.'

THE EPIC SAGA CONTINUES IN...

VESPASIAN
ROME'S EXECUTIONER

AUTHOR'S NOTE

This is a work of fiction based upon the histories of Suetonius, Tacitus and Cassius Dio. Most of the characters are real; of the principal ones the exceptions are: Magnus and his mates, Rhoteces, Hasdro, Faustus, Atallus, Coronus, Kratos and Pallo. As this is historical fiction and not history I have taken some liberties with a few of the characters. There is no evidence, to my knowledge, that either Corbulo or Paetus served in Thrace whilst Vespasian was there; however, as theirs and the Flavian brothers' offspring intermarry I thought that it would be a good time to introduce them into the story. I must offer my apologies to the descendants of Poppaeus; his intrigue with Sejanus is purely the work of my imagination and there is no reason to suspect that he was ever more than the reliable but unremarkable man that Tacitus describes him as; indeed, had he been more than that it would have been most unlikely that Tiberius would have kept him in position for so long or awarded him triumphal ornaments in AD26 for the defeat of the Thracian rebellion.

The details of the Thracian revolt are taken from Tacitus and it happened pretty much as described in the book with the glaring exception of the attack by the Thracian women. Tacitus mentions their presence that night on the field as bystanders, cheering their men along. They were too much of a temptation to have just standing idly by and I couldn't resist having them charge.

The Roman army system of signalling that I have used I extrapolated from two excellent books: John Peddie's *The Roman War Machine* and Adrian Goldsworthy's *The Complete Roman Army*. Any mistakes are my own. In order to keep it reasonably simple I have ignored the tuba – mainly because the word conjures a different image in the modern mind than what it really looked like – and used the bucina for signals within camp and the cornu for signals on the march or in battle; the lituus I have left in its rightful place with the cavalry. This will, I hope, not annoy the purists too much.

I have taken the dating of Vespasian's career, throughout the series, from Barbara Levick's biography of him entitled simply *Vespasian*. She points out rightly that Vespasian probably arrived in Thrace soon after the rebellion was over and would have spent three or four years on boring garrison duty; but where's the fun in that? So I brought his arrival forward by a few months to ensure that he was a part of the action.

The omens surrounding Vespasian's birth are all taken from Suetonius who was very keen – as were most Romans – on that sort of thing and took it very seriously. Suetonius provides Tertulla's remark to Titus concerning him going senile before her when he claims that the omens show that Vespasian is destined for greatness; as well as Vespasia's remark to Vespasian about always living in his brother's shadow when he refuses to embark upon a career in Rome. He also mentions Tertulla's silver cup and states that Vespasian kept it after her death and always drank from it on feast days.

For brevity's sake I have used just one name of each of the real characters once they have been introduced and for clarity's sake I have felt free to use whichever one I fancied so as not to end up with too many people called Titus or Sabinus. The only name that I've left in its anglicised form is Vespasian, who should of course be Vespasianus.

Caenis and Pallas were both in Antonia's household and Caenis was her secretary so would have known the contents of those scrolls had they really existed – and who's to say they didn't? Whether she was descended from the Caenii – or Kaenii as it is spelt on some old maps – is debatable, but to my mind it seems likely.

When I claim that Antonia was the most powerful woman in Rome it is not strictly true; Augustus' widow, Tiberius' mother, Livia was still very much alive and involved in politics but she died in AD29 before Vespasian returned from Thrace so I decided to leave her out. It was through Antonia that Vespasian received preferment due, in part, to his relationship with Caenis, which lasted until her death in AD75.

Antonia's assertion that Gnaeus Calpurnius Piso was responsible – perhaps with Tiberius', Livia's or Sejanus' connivance – for the poisoning of her son, Gemanicus, was accepted by most historians in the Roman world, his suicide before the end of his trial proving his guilt. Robert Graves puts forward another theory in *I, Claudius*; if you want to read an interesting conspiracy theory I recommend Stephen Dando-Collins' *Blood of the Caesars*.

Exactly when and how Vespasian met Caligula is not recorded; however, due to his ties with Antonia, Vespasian would almost certainly have come into contact with him.

Asinius was consul in AD25 and did die the following year but how and where we don't know; however, the fact was very convenient for the plot. His being in league with Antonia against Sejanus is my invention but is not unlikely.

Sejanus' request to marry Livilla was denied by Tiberius in AD25 but their relationship did carry on in combination with his quest for ultimate power.

Gaius' lifestyle is totally made up but, as there is no record of him ever having had children, completely within the realms of possibility and an enjoyable excursion into perceived Roman decadence.

My thanks go many people. First, to my agent, Ian Drury at Sheil Land Associates, for taking me on and always being so positive; and to Gaia Banks and Emily Dyson in the agency's international rights department for all their hard work on my behalf. Second, to Nic Cheetham at Corvus Books for publishing my book and also for getting Richenda Todd to edit it; working with her was a great experience. Thanks also to Emma Gibson at Corvus for guiding me through the publishing process, of which I have no previous experience.

No education is complete without memories of special teachers. I would like to thank three masters at Christ's Hospital School, Horsham: Richard Palmer for introducing me to Shakespeare and Donne and the joys of the English language; Andrew Husband for giving me – though it may not have been obvious to him at the time – a lifelong love of history; and Duncan Noel-Paton who showed me that imagination has no boundaries.

Heartfelt thanks to my aunt, Elisabeth Woodthorpe, and my sister, Tanya Potter, for their support and enthusiasm whilst I was writing this.

Finally my deepest thanks to my girlfriend, Anja Muller, who, when I first mentioned this idea to her six years ago, went and got me a notebook with Vespasian's picture on the front, printed off everything that she could find about him on the internet – beware! – and then told me in the kindest possible way to stop talking about it and get on and write it. Once I did eventually take her advice she sat and patiently listened to what I had written every evening; thank you, my love.

Vespasian will carry on his rise to power in *Rome's Executioner*.

Keep reading for an exclusive preview of

VESPASIAN
ROME'S EXECUTIONER

Available in all good bookshops from May 2012

CHAPTER I

VESPASIAN EASED HIS weight cautiously onto his left foot, trying not to rustle the dead leaves or crack any of the twigs that carpeted the snow-patched forest floor. He had covered the last few dozen paces with hardly a sound, his breath steaming in front of him as he tried to lower his heart beat after a long chase. He was alone having left his companions, two hunting slaves borrowed from the Royal stables, a couple of miles back to follow on slowly with the horses as he stalked his wounded prey on foot. His quarry, a young stag, was close now; the trail of blood from the arrow wound to its neck that he had inflicted earlier seemed fresher, a sign that he was gaining on the slowing animal, weakened by loss of blood. He pulled back the string of his hunting bow and brought the fletched end of the arrow to his cheek, ready to release. Hardly daring to breathe he took another couple of steps forward and peered around, looking through gaps between the crowded trees for any sign of dun coloured fur in amongst the umber and russet hues of a forest in winter.

A slight movement in the corner of his eye, off to the right, caused him to freeze momentarily. He held his breath as he slowly turned his stocky frame to face the source of the distraction. About twenty paces away, half hidden in the tangled undergrowth, stood the stag, motionless, with blood-matted withers, staring dolefully at him. As Vespasian took aim it collapsed to the ground making the shot unnecessary. Vespasian cursed, furious at being denied the excitement of the kill after such a long chase. It seemed to him to be a metaphor for the past three and a half years that he had spent in Thracia on garrison duty, since the quashing of the rebellion. Any promise of action would always fizzle out to nothing and he would return to camp, frustrated, with an un-bloodied sword and sore feet from chasing a few brigands around the country-side. The harsh truth of the matter was that the Roman client kingdom of Thracia was at peace and he was bored.

He had not always been so; the first year had been reason-ably interesting and fulfilling. After mopping up the remnants the Thracian rebels, Pomponius Labeo had marched the V Macedonica, most of the IIII Scythica, the cavalry alae and the auxiliary cohorts back to their bases on the river Danuvius in Moesia, leaving Publius Junius Caesennius Paetus, the prefect of the one remaining auxiliary Illyrian cavalry ala in command of the garrison. Vespasian had been left in nominal command of the two remaining legionary cohorts, the second and fifth, of the IIII Scythica; although in practice he deferred to the senior centurion Lucius Caelus, the acting Prefect of the camp, who tolerated him but made it plain what he thought of young upstarts placed in positions of command solely because of their social rank.

However, Vespasian had learnt a lot from Caelus and his brother centurions as they kept their men busy with field manoeuvres, road and bridge building and maintenance of equipment and the camp; but these were peacetime duties and after a while he had grown weary of them and yearned for the excitement of war that he had experienced, only too briefly, in his first couple of months in Thracia.

But war never came; instead he'd been subjected to endless parades and drills and more dinners at the palace with Queen Tryphaena and various visiting Roman dignitaries than was good for his waist-line. He had become fluent in Greek, the lingua-franca of the east, and had mastered the local Thracian tongue well enough, but that had been a necessity rather than a pleasure. Hunting had been the only activity that had provided any satisfaction, exercise or excitement; but this morning that too had been an anti-climax.

Vespasian shot at the prone form of the stag in irritation, the arrow passed through its neck and skewered it to the forest floor; he immediately chided himself for acting out of pique and failing to show due respect for the creature that had so bravely tried to evade him for the last hour. He pushed his way through the undergrowth and after muttering a perfunctory prayer of thanks to Diana, goddess of hunting, over the dead animal he took out his knife and began to eviscerate the still warm body. He consoled himself with the thought that his four years in the army were over; March was coming to an end and the sea-lanes were reopening after winter, his replacement would arrive soon. Soon he would be going back to Rome with the prospect of advancement, a junior magistrate's post, one of the Vigintivirarii and also, as importantly, the prospect of seeing Caenis. She flickered before his eyes as he worked his blade in and out of the stag's belly; her delicate, moist lips, her sparkling blue eyes so full of love and grief as she had said goodbye to him; her lithe body, naked before him in the dim light of a single oil lamp on the one and only night that they had slept together. He wanted to hold her again, to smell and taste her, to have her for his own; but how could that be? She was still a slave and, according to the law, could not be manumitted until she was at least thirty. He worked his blade harder and faster as he contemplated the futility of the situation. Even if she were freed he could never marry her as he had dreamed of doing with the naivety of a sixteen year-old; someone of his position, with his ambition, could never take a freedwoman as a wife. He could, however, keep her as his mistress, but then how would that be for the woman who he would take as his wife? *She would just have to live with it* he decided as he pulled the last scrapings of offal from the carcass.

'I could have put a dozen arrows in you in the time that I've been sitting here.'

Vespasian started and spun round, cutting his thumb on the knife in the process. Magnus sat on a horse, twenty paces away, grinning as he levelled his hunting bow at him.

'Hades, you gave me a fright,' Vespasian exclaimed, shaking his injured hand.

'You'd have had more of a fright if I'd been a Thracian and shot this arrow up your arse, sir.'

'Yes, well you're not and you didn't,' Vespasian said calming down slightly and sucking the mixture of his and the stag's blood from his thumb. 'Why were you creeping up on me anyway?'

'I weren't creeping sir, I rode and I was making as much noise as a century of new recruits saying goodbye to their mothers.' Magnus replied lowering the bow. 'You were just too lost in your own world to notice, and, if I may point out the obvious sir, that's how you get to be dead.'

'Yes I know, it was stupid of me, but I've got a lot on my mind Magnus,' Vespasian admitted, rising to his feet.

'Well you're going to have a lot more on your mind very soon.'

'How so?'

'You've got a visitor; your brother arrived at the garrison late this morning.'

'What?'

'You heard.'

'What's Sabinus doing here?'

'Now how would I know that? But I would hazard a guess that he ain't come all this way just for a nice brotherly chat. He just told me to come and find you as quickly as possible so let's get going. Where's your horse?'

By the time they had found Vespasian's hunting slaves and strapped his kill onto his horse it was well into the afternoon. The thickly overcast sky had brought an early dusk to the forest floor and they were forced to lead their horses for fear of them stumbling in the fading light. Vespasian walked next to Magnus contemplating what could have brought his brother hundreds of miles to talk to him, and started to assume the worst. His father had written to him two years earlier with the expected news of his beloved grandmother, Tertulla's, death, and he still felt a pang of grief every time he thought of her drinking from her cherished silver cup.

'One of our parents must have died,' he mused, trying not to hope that it was not his father. 'Did he seem upset to you Magnus?'

'Quite the opposite sir, he was anxious to see you as soon as possible; if he had bad news he wouldn't have been in such a rush to talk to you, in fact he seemed very disappointed when I told him that you weren't there.'

'Well that's a first.' Vespasian smiled wryly; he and Sabinus had never got on as children and he had been subjected to years of brutality by his brother that had only stopped when Vespasian was eleven years old and Sabinus had joined the legions. Although the tension between them had eased since Sabinus' return from the army, Vespasian could never imagine his brother being disappointed not to see him.

'I'll know what it is soon enough I suppose,' Vespasian said, looking around and adjusting the hunting bow slung over his shoulder to ease the chafing of the string. 'Come on, let's ride, the trees have thinned out.' He moved to mount up. 'There's enough light for...' A brief hiss and a heavy thwack cut him off; two arrows appeared simultaneously in his horse's jaw, just where his head had been an instant earlier. The animal reared up, whinnying piercingly, knocking Vespasian to the ground; another shaft slammed into its shoulder quickly followed by one into its exposed chest, felling it.

'Juno's crack, what the...' Magnus flung himself on top of Vespasian as his own mount bolted. 'Quick,' he shouted, 'the other side of your horse, jump.' They leapt over the prostrate animal and crouched behind its back as two more arrows thumped into its belly; it raised its head and screeched, its hooves thrashing at the air as it tried but failed to get up. The two hunting slaves sprinted to join them behind the nearest available cover; with a sharp cry one spun like a top, his billowing cloak wrapping itself around his body as he twisted to the ground with an arrow protruding from a blood-spurting eye socket. His companion flung himself through the air and landed next to Vespasian and Magnus as another shot punched into the still writhing horse causing it to spasm violently then lie still.

'What the fuck do we do now?' Magnus hissed as two more shafts fizzed just over their cover to land quivering in the ground five paces behind them. No more came.

'It appears to be me that they're interested in,' Vespasian whispered, 'all the shots were aimed at me until I got behind cover; then they went for the slaves.' He looked at his two companions, pulled out his knife and began sawing on the leather straps that secured his stag to his dead mount. 'There only seems to be two of them, I suggest that I make a run for it in one direction and you two go the other way; with luck they'll go for me and you'll be able to get round behind them. What's your name?' he asked the hunting slave, a middle-aged man with curly jet-black hair and a Greek sigma branded on his forehead.

'Artebudz, master,' the slave replied.

'Well Artebudz, have you ever killed a man?' The straps parted and the stag slithered to the ground, another two arrows thumped into the horse.

'In my youth master; before I was enslaved.'

'Kill one of the bastards out there today and you'll be a slave no more, I'll see to that.'

The slave nodded; a look of hope and determination crossed his face as he eased his hunting bow from its holder hanging from his belt. Vespasian patted him on the arm then, grabbing the stag's forelegs, slid the creature over his back.

'On the count of three I'll lift the stag; as soon as they hit it run whilst they reload, alright?' His companions agreed. Vespasian tucked his right knee under his stomach ready to push off. 'Let's do it then; one, two, three!'

He raised the stag so that it emerged over the withers of the dead horse, immediately he felt the violent impact of two arrows striking the carcass almost simultaneously; he pushed down on his right leg heaving himself and the dead weight of the stag up and forward and with a monumental effort accelerated into a sprint towards a thick-trunked oak tree twenty paces away. Two fierce blows from behind made him stumble, but he kept his footing and felt no pain; the arrows had hit the stag that shielded his back. With cold air rasping at his throat from the intense exertion, he reached the tree and dodged behind it to the vibrating report of two more shots burying themselves in its trunk.

Vespasian leaned his head back against the soft moss growing on the bark and sucked in lung-fulls of winter air; the stags head lolled on his shoulder like a new-found, drunken acquaintance expressing eternal friendship. He cautiously peered round towards the dead horse and the trees beyond; there was no sign of Magnus or Artebudz. He held his breath and listened; nothing moved. Realising that he had to keep the attackers occupied as his two comrades worked their way around into a favourable position he eased the stag down, unslung his bow and notched an arrow. He dropped to his knees whilst working out, from the trajectory of shots already fired, the direction in which to aim. Satisfied with his estimation he took a deep breath and swung his bow around the trunk releasing his shot a moment before a single arrow passed a hand's breadth above his head. Vespasian smiled; they had split up, that would make matters a lot easier. Ten paces to his left was a fallen hulk of an oak, high enough to provide adequate cover. He notched another arrow, then, holding it securely across the bow grip with his left hand and lifting the stag with the right, he rose slowly to his feet keeping his back pressed against the tree.

A sharply curtailed cry came from the direction in which he had been aiming; then a shout.

'One left!'

It was Magnus. He knew that he could not now risk another wild shot for fear of hitting his friend. As their positions were known he had nothing to lose by shouting. 'Are they Romans or Thracians?' he called.

'Neither, I've never seen one of these savages before; he's wearing fucking trousers,' Magnus replied.

'Let's hope they don't speak Latin then. Can you see the dead horse?'

'Just, it's about fifty paces ahead of me; you sound like you're to the left of it.'

'Careful then, you must be close to the other one. I'll make a move, he might show himself, keep down I'll shoot at head height. Artebudz, don't reply if you can hear me, just watch out for any movement.'

Vespasian steeled himself for another quick burst of energy. He pushed the stag to his right, heard the sharp hiss and thud of another hit to the carcass, then leapt left towards the fallen tree, drawing and releasing his shot in one swift movement. He rolled head over heels through the under-growth and made cover as an arrow embedded itself, juddering, in the trunk. An instant later came the faint, but unmistakeable, sound of sudden and violent exhalation; someone had been shot.

'I got him masters,' Artebudz shouted, his voice raised an octave in his excitement.

'Is he dead?' Magnus called. There was a slight pause.

'He is now.'

'Thank fuck for that.'

Vespasian found Magnus and Artebudz standing over one of the bowmen's corpses.

Magnus wrinkled his nose as he approached. 'I can't believe we didn't smell them before they saw us, I've never smelt a savage as strong; they must have kept down-wind of us.'

It was indeed a pungent aroma: a heady cocktail of all the major human male excretions, secretions and discharges that had been allowed to fester for years within clothes of semi-cured animal hide, which had probably never been removed since they were first donned; it was crowned with the acid stench of very old and ingrained horse sweat.

'What is he?' Vespasian asked recoiling, unable to believe his nose.

'No idea. Artebudz, have you ever seen one of these?'

'No master; but his beard's ginger and his cap seems to be Thracian in style.'

Vespasian studied the man's clothing; his cap was definitely Thracian in appearance, a leather skull-cap with long cheek flaps and neck protection, similar to those of the northern tribes in Moesia, as opposed the fox-fur hats of the southern tribes in Thracia itself. But this had crude depictions of horses embroidered in it with dyed twine and the cheek straps were tied under the chin. Apart from knee-length boots, the rest of his attire was definitely not Thracian: hide trousers, well worn on the inside thighs, suggesting a long time spent in the saddle, and a thigh-length leather top-coat worn over an un-dyed woollen tunic.

'Scythian perhaps,' Magnus ventured, picking up and examining the dead man's composite horn and wood bow.

'No, we've got one of them at home, they're darker and they've got strange eyes; this man looks normal. Well, we can't worry about it now, I need to get back to see my brother; we'll send Artebudz back with some slaves to pick them up tomorrow.'

Artebudz grinned, enjoying the implication that he would soon be freed.

Vespasian turned away. 'Come on, let's find the horses.'

It was dark by the time they reached the permanent garrison camp just outside the gates of Philippopolis. Vespasian dismissed Artebudz back to the Royal stables with a warning to say nothing of the day's events until he had spoken to the Queen, whose property he was. Returning the centurion of the watch's salute at the Praetorian gate he and Magnus rode as quickly as possible, without causing alarm, down the Via Praetoria, between the low brick-built barrack huts towards his more comfortable residence on the junction with Via Principalis. Such was his anxiety that he barely noticed the ill-feeling and restlessness with which over a thousand soldiers were taking their evening meal washed down with the generous garrison wine ration that was supplemented with stronger stuff that they had bought locally. His thoughts were alternating between the reason for his brother's journey, how he would react to seeing him again after four years and why two outlandish-looking men had tried to kill him that afternoon.

'The lads seem tense this evening.' Magnus broke into his train of thought.

'What?'

'I've seen it before sir, it can happen quite quickly; after a long time farting about doing a lot of bugger all on a regular basis with nothing to show for it, the men start to get edgy, and wonder what the fuck they're doing here and how much longer they're going to be stuck in this arsehole of a place. They're legionaries and they haven't had a decent fight for over three years, whereas the lads that went back to Moesia are getting plenty of action if half the rumours are true.'

Vespasian glanced around at the men sitting around braziers and saw more than a few of them glaring at him with resentful, sullen eyes over the top of their wine-filled cups.

One or two of them even held his look, a minor act of insubordination that he would normally have dealt with then and there had he not been so preoccupied.

'I'll speak to centurion Caelus in the morning and find out what's going on,' he said wearily, knowing full-well that it was Caelus' duty to come to him and report any bad feeling amongst the two cohorts that he commanded. It was just another example of how Caelus sort to subtly undermine his authority.

Vespasian dismounted outside his quarters; it was the same construction as that of the men's but slightly larger and he was not obliged to share the two rooms inside with seven others.

'I'll get the horses stabled,' Magnus offered, taking the reins from him.

'Thank you, I'll see you later.' Vespasian took a deep breath and walked through the door.

'So little brother, you're back from skulking about in the woods,' drawled the familiar voice with no trace of affection or even friendship. Sabinus was sprawled out on the dining couch; he had evidently made use of the officers' bath-house as there was no sign of the dust and grime of travel about his appearance, and he was wearing a crisp, white, Equestrian toga over a clean tunic.

'I may be your younger brother but I ceased to be little when I joined the Eagles,' Vespasian snapped. 'And, furthermore, I do not, and never did, skulk.'

Sabinus raised himself to his feet; his dark eyes glinted in the dim light of a couple of oil lamps as they glared mockingly at his brother. 'Playing the big soldier are we? Next you'll be telling me that you don't fuck mules anymore.'

'Look Sabinus, if you've come all this way to have a fight let's have it right now and then you can piss off back home again, otherwise try to remain civil and tell me what you've got to say.' Vespasian squared up to his brother, his fists clenched by his side. Sabinus smiled thinly at him. Vespasian noticed that he had put on a bit of weight; four years out of the army and living the good life in Rome had left its mark.

'Fair enough, little brother,' Sabinus said sitting down on a camp stool, 'but old habits die hard. I'm not here to fight; I'm here on the Lady Antonia's business. Aren't you going to offer me a drink?'

'If you've finished insulting me, then yes.' Vespasian crossed to the far end of the room and took a pitcher from a cheaply constructed wooden chest standing next to the door leading through to the bedroom. He mixed a couple of cups of the rough local wine with water and handed one to his brother. 'How are our parents?'

'They're both well, I have letters for you from them.'

'Letters?' Vespasian's eyes lit up.

'Yes, I've got one from Caenis too, you can read it later; but first you should clean up and get changed, we have to deliver a letter from Antonia to Queen Tryphaena. We've got a job to do and we need her help.'

'What sort of job?'

'One that will make rescuing Caenis seem like a pleasant stroll through the Gardens of Lucullus. Do you know a Thracian tribe called the Getae?'

'Never heard of them.'

'Well I don't know much about them either except that they live outside the Empire across the Danuvius. They generally keep themselves busy fighting the tribes to their north but recently they've taken to crossing the river and raiding Moesia. The raids have been getting larger and more frequent in the last year or so and the V Macedonica and the IIII Scythica have been struggling to repel them; the Emperor has become concerned enough about the situation to reinstate Poppaeus Sabinus as Governor.'

'What are we supposed to do about it?' Vespasian asked, not liking the idea of going anywhere near Poppaeus again.

'Antonia doesn't want us to do anything about the raids, they're no concern of hers; but what does interest her is a piece of intelligence that one of her agents in Moesia sent a couple of months back.'

'She's got agents in Moesia?'

'She's got agents everywhere. Anyway, this one reported the presence in the last three or four of the raids of someone with whom the good lady is keen to have a nice little chat with back in Rome.'

'And we've been asked to go and fetch him for her.'

Sabinus grinned. 'How did you guess?'

Vespasian had a sinking feeling in the pit of his belly. 'Who?' He asked already suspecting the answer.

'Sejanus' go-between; the Thracian chief-priest, Rhoteces.'